I0739086

[DEEP JYZE]

Annals of The Jyze Age

Jyzeburst

Jyzemelt

Jyze and Jyze Alone

Jyze in Love

Deep Jyze

The Jyze Millennium

Jyze of the Heavenly Year

Scat Jyze

Deep Jyze

G.P. Sandefjord

Annal Five of The Jyze Age

Copyright 2024 G.P. Sandefjord

Draft printings 2020, 2022, 2023

This book is a work of jyze fiction. Names, places, characters, and incidents either are products of the author's imagination or are used fictively. Any resemblance to actual events or locales or persons, living or dead, is entirely fortuitous.

Cover art by GPS
Published by House of Jyze
ISBN 978-0-9964173-6-5
Library of Congress CIP pending
www.HouseOfJyze.com

For Ticiang

    The true life, life at last, discovered
and illuminated, the only life really lived,
is that of the jyzer.
                -- Marcel Proust
                [but he said "artist"
                for "jyzer"]

    The aim of jyze is not to resolve a
question irrefutably, but to compel one
to love life in all its manifestations.
                -- Leo Tolstoy
                [but he said "art" for
                "jyze"]

    I am led to the proposition that there
is no fiction or nonfiction as we commonly
understand the distinction: there is only
jyze.
                -- E. L. Doctorow
                [but he said "narrative"
                for "jyze"]

BOOK I

[Can This Be Jyze?]

1

The fifth year of jyze starts randomly and -- by a coin flip -- on the 4th of January. A Sunday, last day of a long New Year's weekend. At the hideaway, because this is just how it is. Back home would be inconvenient anyway if not exactly awkward, with boxes piled to the ceiling as they await unpacking. It's not as stuffed as it was up there, though, because today we finally did make some headway on settling in.

An overload of heavy boxes down here too, most of which will eventually go into storage. The fan's spinning and the door to the foyer's wide open; I haven't come in for a week and the air's bad. Or was. Now it's fresh, relatively, but also much cooler. The building heat's probably been running at minimal weekend level since New Year's Eve -- last Wednesday -- and a cold front roared into the area yesterday.

Earlier tonight I flipped an old dollar coin maybe two hundred times (a number of which went awry in the tight quarters here on my desk). Now the jyze schedule for the entire year is set. It's divided into forty-five jyzeweeks, forty of them the standard eight days long, five with one extra day. Each J-week will feature one J-day chosen at random just like today. Therefore the intervals between J-days will vary greatly, some being as small as a day or two, others as large as eleven or twelve; the average, of course, will still be close to the traditional eight. And I've left room for up to three "wild card" J-days to use during the visit Z and I hope to make to our old stomping grounds in late summer or early fall.

"Z," Zoelie. Zoelie B. The saga continueth.

Six minutes to ten now on J-day No. 1. Building dead quiet. I'll be taking the bus home later, my first solo bus trip to the hilltop. After ten p.m. this route runs every half hour on the quarter hour, with the last coach at one-fifteen a.m. (exactly the same schedule as that for the route which until last week I was taking in the opposite direction out to Z's place, or now former place). Whenever possible I'll be riding on Z's pass, which she receives free as a perk of her job. She'll use it during the day and then hand it over to me when she arrives home at five-thirty or so. Some nights -- maybe even most -- this won't work, but the sharing should still save us five or ten bucks a month. Or rather not us; me. But then I'm giving up my close-in apartment in order to live with her; if I were still domiciled there I'd have no work-related transportation expenses at all. Which isn't to say I'd want to be living alone rather than with Zoelie B. Nope. No way.

I'm ecstatic about the new life. Love the apartment, love the location, love the hill itself, and love -- am crazy in love with -- the new "domestic partner," or DP (pronounced "Deep"). Sheer luck brought us together and now (after our nine-month "gestation" or get-acquainted period) nothing short of death could tear us apart. Or so sez I. And likewise she! True, on last year's J-day No. 1 I was still thinking I'd be living alone the rest of my life -- doubting anything could ever separate me from old unit B-2 -- but both of these notions turned out to be much more a matter of will than of heart. And not long after that, not even a matter of will.

No attempt here tonight to describe the new digs. I'll save that for a time when I can do the jyze thing up there. And that, as decreed by the coin flips, should come as soon as this Friday.

How will the new life differ from the old? If "the old" refers to the pre-Z life in B-2, I expect I'll be canoodling and socializing a whole lot more and reading and muttering aloud to myself a whole lot less. I won't

be anywhere near so self-engrossed ("artyrish") nor will
I be aching with loneliness. I'll be more politically
engaged. I'll be at least an auxiliary member of a gang
of friends and I'll be a quasi father or uncle surrogate
to a gang of kids whose final number is yet to be
determined but will certainly be at least one (and that
one a gang all by herself). And barring some calamity I
expect to be wildly happy with this life.

Some lesser differences. For one, I'll be doing
most of my provisioning by car (Z's) rather than on
foot. I'll be hitting the sack somewhat earlier, say
two or three a.m. rather than four or five. I'll be
doing dishes in a dishwasher and laundry in a washer/
dryer combo located right there, inside the apartment.
I'll be seeing a lot more movies for sure and maybe even
an occasional live play.

On the other hand I may not be pushing out as much
of my own work. And if so, this could pose a worrisome
problem. But as of now I'm thinking the gain in social/
emotional stability will more than make up for the time
lost on personal projects, and the overall result could
well be a net boost in productivity. And what's better
than that? (Damn right I'm serious!)

-- Without doubt some difficulties and
embarrassments lie ahead. For one, I'll need to seek a
"fail-safe divorce" from Lady S (as I've promised Z I
would) and I fear that doing so will stir up new
troubles with Lady S. For another I'll need to address
the issue of medical care (again, a promise) and this
could cost me horribly, in pride, in time, in pain,
maybe even in money (though my new status as a Deep
sharing Z's city medical coverage should take care of a
healthy portion, or perhaps more accurately an unhealthy
portion, of the money part).

And then for a third major concern, or better just
to come right out and say it's the single true major
concern at this time, there's the matter of sexual
consummation. Will we or won't we be able to coax the
sputtering old genital apparatus -- mine -- into proper
operating order? The signs are good, I'd say, but it

still hasn't happened and we've been working on it for
roughly eight months now. -- The best of the good signs
being this: Z seems to be accepting the status quo. No
more meltdowns over the J-slinger's deeply bizarre
priapic foozles. She appears to be doing better at
accepting that these malfunctions aren't her "fault" in
any important way and in the same sense aren't really my
fault either. -- Though in truth I still think the
cause is more psychological than physiological.

In fact I'll turn right around and say our loving
the past few days, just as for the entire eight months,
has been spectacular even if, again, startlingly strange
and incomplete. First time in the new place, four or
five hours of it. In bed. On the couch in the living
room in front of the view windows with stacked boxes
teetering overhead. Morning noon and night, and early
night, middle night, late night, early morning, late
morning. We've both been flabbergasted again and again.
We've also been downright alarmed. (Though it's mostly
been her, I swear, with her fear of "sexual addiction"
and of running me off with her "insatiability." But
nope, it'll never happen; I've been dreaming pretty much
since adolescent sexual-awakening days of finding a
lover like this. But sure, could be I'm unconsciously
intimidated too, as I've acknowledged from the start. I
mean this astounding woman's burned through a lot of
sexual partners. But hell no, I'm not saying that's bad
or all that different from my own history. And so on.
And yes, the whole matter's still just as complex and
flat-out discombobulating as it's been all along.)

Any other big concerns I should mention? Or are
the three already brought forward, or just the one truly
major one, enough all by themselves, or itself? But
then what if Jyzer Ink (its renewed annual business
license newly aflutter as of an hour ago on the wall
here above the fan) -- what if J. Ink loses its one and
only client? What if one of my writing projects, say
for instance this one going down in these pages right
here at this very moment, veers disastrously off course?
-- But really now, what's the point in thinking about

such things? Deal with them when they occur, if they
occur -- and beseech the jyze gods that they don't.
     And then marriage. If all goes well it could
happen this year. Z's let me know she'd like it to take
place before a judge, and preferably one she knows
personally, Edna F. She continues to worry over whom to
invite to the ceremony itself and about the site for the
reception afterwards and who will handle what for that.
The father of her best friend Aida hopes to "present"
her, Z, at the altar, and she, Z, doesn't know how to
tell him there won't be an altar (he's very religious).
Personally I'm not too concerned about any of these
details one way or the other. I do want this marriage,
yes, but mainly because she wants it; I'd be just as
happy going on as Deeps forever. For me, if it does
occur (and I assume it will at some point), it'll be,
as I like to say, my first truly serious real marriage.
For her it'll be the first real marriage, period. (And
so I'm nervous about it. -- But ach ach ach, never mind
nervous.)
     Last night after returning home from dinner with
Z's grad-school chum Lee M. and his new flame (we think)
and two of their kids (one for each), Z and I sat on the
couch batting around the idea of making joint New Year's
resolutions. She wanted to write down secret ones and
then reveal them at the end of the year to see how we'd
done, but this struck me as curious: how can resolutions
be "joint" if you don't know what the other's
resolutions are? My counterproposal -- admittedly about
as corny and sappy as they get -- was that we do a few
minutes of close but nonsexual "deep breathing" together
every day. (I reminded her that the very first poem she
wrote for me spoke of wanting to "breathe deep.") But
how to determine, she wondered, when a day's session
would stop? And then answered herself this way: it
should go on "as long as a song." I liked that. And
she decided she liked the proposal as a whole. So
that's the one we'll go with; and though I'm not sure
how we'll know exactly when the daily song has come to
an end, I trust we'll somehow be able to figure it out.

[Deep Jyze]

     Tonight we tried it for the first time. She sat
on my lap. At first I had trouble keeping my hands
still, but then I hit on the simple notion of using
this time with her each day to appreciate the fabulous
good fortune of our having found each other. Is it even
slightly odd that after that it went well? I say no.

     The final day of moving -- and also the final day
of the year -- was a blast and a nightmare. Another old
friend of Z's arrived in town unexpectedly, Z lost track
of our carefully worked-out plans, adverse coincidences
occurred (my phone was disconnected a day earlier than
scheduled, I had to sit around waiting for Z for hours
and lost crucial cleaning time -- eventually found her
lying in bed at the new place reading a whodunit while
anxiously awaiting my arrival, as she'd been doing for
hours) -- and we had it out in the car at a fast-food
joint on New Year's Eve. And somehow managed to emerge
from all this with no apparent damage done.

     Then we worked together cleaning B-2 until five
a.m., pausing at midnight for no more than five minutes
to welcome in the new year with swigs from a bottle of
blush wine set atop a packing crate. She took great
pride in scouring the kitchen and bathroom and also in
the fact that she was doing it for "a MAN," something
she swore she'd never done before (meanwhile she'd paid
to have her own place tidied up by a cleaning service);
and at her friend Adele's New Year's party the next
evening she couldn't stop cackling about all this, and
neither of us could hide our excitement about moving in
together and didn't really want to or try to. Hauling
loads crosstown at three and five a.m. through streets
aswarm with drunken revelers -- wotta trip it was, wotta
series of trips. And staggering up to bed and then
"fucking" away for hours (and we both continue to call
it "fucking" just because we like using the term, among
others, and would hate to give it up merely because it's
technically inaccurate -- and besides, what term could
be less technical than "fuck"?).

     Once we were fully moved in, Z just wanted to kick
back for a couple of days. And that's pretty much what

we've done, together for the most part, attending the
parties and seeing a movie (bad) at the bargain theater
up north and scoping out our new hilltop hood by car and
on foot. We've also picked up Kat and Betty at the
airport, dropped off another load of wood at Jess and
Gwen's house (these being smaller pieces from my
dismantled loft and destined, Jess says, to become
birdhouses), attempted without luck so far to arrange
home newspaper delivery, puzzled over the exact location
in the stacked boxes of a seemingly endless list of
crucial items needed immediately such as shower-curtain
rings and shaving cream. And all along we've been
conducting running "negotiations" over what should go
where. And laughing a lot too. (And what wasn't funny
at all, Z retweaked an old sacroiliac injury and for a
while could scarcely bend over without crying out in
pain. -- And how impressed I was with the way she
soldiered on regardless!)

  So now I find myself happily enmeshed in my new
"extended family." This afternoon Betty called to ask
if I could pick her up at the hospital tomorrow morning
and drive her home (she's having a lump removed from a
finger -- hopefully nothing too serious, especially
since her lump looks a lot like a slightly bigger one on
my own left pinkie). As a night worker I'm the only
person she knows who's "free" during the day. True,
I'll have to get up a few hours early to do this and I
can't let her -- or anyone -- make such requests a
regular practice, but I'm still flattered to be asked.

  We've already met the occupants of six of the other
eight apartments in the building. We both think it's
terrific that only one of these folks is, by appearance
anyway, a full-fledged Cawk. And new issues are
arising. Why is our part of the hilltop so short on
street mailboxes? Why does the nearest bus stop lack a
trash can? Why are more hookers strutting their stuff
on our block than on any other we've seen? Z is
swinging into action. Min, the building owner, even
though he's a passing acquaintance of hers from work,
isn't responding well thus far to her pleas to jack up

the joint's safety and cleanliness standards (also known
as, to be sure, gentrification level).

   Yipe: I look up and see it's almost midnight. No
longer do I have the luxury of staying down here as late
as I want to. By deeply ingrained habit I tend not to
be as aware of the clock as I'll now have to be. (And
as Z reminded me, I should be careful tonight not to
start walking home the old way on autopilot. Head
south, me laddie, not north! And if it's nighttime,
head to the bus stop by the post office! -- which is
just across the street from the stop I haunted for a
while almost a decade back in a whole other era. To
which era, by the way, for reasons both politic and
romantic, I'm scarcely referring at all anymore, at
least not out loud, and may never mention again, in
these J-pages or elsewhere.)

   No doubt jyze will be forgetful in lots of ways
this year, and probably more so than ever before. It'll
be rushed, incomplete, and, if I don't keep my wits
about me, massively incoherent. It'll offer abundant
random glimpses but seldom anything more. Under the
demanding conditions it's facing I'm just hoping to have
fun with it. -- Well, no, I'm always hoping for more
than just to have fun. But just having fun I'm willing
to settle for when necessary, if necessary, or even if
unnecessary so long as the damage won't be too bad.
-- And so...let the fun begin!

2

   Sheez, bad planning. Or maybe just raw self-
subversion, unconscious reluctance to start this up
again so soon or something like that. This notion in

turn possibly inspired by the profile of a well-known
female performance artist I was just reading, she of the
sexual-empowerment rap so impressive to Z -- and to me
too, though with reservations to be sure, for example,
how about a little heartfulness, eh, O performance-
artist person? Maybe even every now and then at least a
faint spirit of reciprocity?

In any event: No. 203, the new apartment. I'm
here. Jyze is here. Z's old black armchair is here in
the living room and I'm sitting in it. To my left a
snazzy eastward picture-window view of snowcapped, gray-
cloud-swaddled mountains. Every ten or fifteen minutes
the topmost portions of twin power poles underscore this
view, sort of like a two-pronged lecturer's pointer, as
a trolley bus rolls by on the street three stories below
(though we're officially second story, the garage is
street level and above it there's another level of
apartments and then ours and then one more) (and the
garage is covered and gated, the gate operated remotely
with a device you keep in your car; and this is one of
the features of the place Z likes best, even though she
agrees it lends living here a "faint but unmistakable
odor of gated community").

So this is the place, no question. Furniture
crammed into the view corner of the main room here; the
rest of the room -- and the two bedrooms as well --
stacked high with trunks and boxes, most still unpacked
and most, in fact, Z's (I have a lot less stuff to start
with -- because most of mine's in storage -- and also a
lot more free time for unpacking). One of the two big
bookcases salvaged from the B-2 loft stands proudly in
its new spot at my back along the north wall of the main
room -- living room, or "great room" in the lingo of Min
the landlord -- as does its mate in the hall opposite
the front door, both bookcases fully stabilized as of
yesterday, their shelves mostly filled (though not in
any organized way). Otherwise I've accomplished nothing
but basic necessities: setting up a place for us to
sleep, clearing a kitchen counter for preparing meals,
locating some blankets and utensils. And the first

dishwasher and laundry loads have been successfully run.

Meanwhile a time squeeze. It's Friday afternoon and I have to drive to the nearest large supermarket (several miles distant to the southeast, down in the valley hidden beneath that mountain panorama and an in-city ridge) -- drive down there to pick up my usual essentials: bread, milk, bananas and so forth. I'm just beginning an unusually heavy work weekend and tonight must hit the scope office by seven at the latest. And it's already half past three. Yet I got up at ten. Where did those five and a half hours go?

(Answer: mostly to the usual stuff. Reading a couple of newspapers, doing a few exercises, talking with Z on the phone. Not even a shower in there. But everything takes longer when things are so chaotic. And I did break down some empty boxes. And I've been pausing often to think, seemingly with just about every step. What should go here? Is there a better way to do this? What will the first dinner guests think of that over there? Or more important: what will Z think they'll think? And I'm losing minutes in big bundles as I impulsively move things about: by all means let's at least cluster all the unattached lamp shades in one conspicuous and easily accessible spot.)

I don't want to be contending with rush-hour traffic on the main drag down in the valley. Don't want to put the shopping trip off until tomorrow either; supermarkets are too crowded on Saturdays. And the current very good coupon sale at this particular one ends this weekend. Oh well. Just go, don't sweat the traffic.

For intimacy I'll say the past four days have been not so good. We've tentatively agreed to do dinner together at home Tuesdays and Thursdays, but first Z had to break the Tuesday engagement and then scoping demands forced me to break the ones for both Wednesday (at first we reset Tuesday for then) and Thursday. Also we failed on all three of those days to abide by our "breathe deep" New Year's resolution. If we don't talk much or at all during the day Z tends to, as she says, "go

chatty-Cathy" when I get home late at night; and since
she doesn't much like to nuzzle or fondle or be fondled
or to do anything else at all distracting while so
chatting, our sex life can suffer as a result. She's
also been in a self-proclaimed (but I'll proclaim it
too) bad mood, in part because, in her words, "I'm tired
of being good for so long while we were packing and
moving" -- but also because, although this may seem
contradictory, we're seeing so little of each other.
     Are things working out poorly? Is it the old
living-together hex that's derailed the Z-woman several
times in the past (and in all but one case before the
move-in was even attempted)? She's worrying aloud about
such things in talks with Olwen and other friends,
though perhaps not yet too seriously. During today's
call to me from work she said she was experiencing "the
old high-school dependency thing" of not being able to
see her boyfriend; when I reminded her she'd told me she
wasn't allowed to have boyfriends in high school she
switched the time period to college when she had plenty,
as she reminded me, which she didn't really need to do:
I already had a firm grasp on that important chunk of
her history. And in bed late last night and again this
morning a meltdown often seemed imminent. At one point
she even said she really wanted to let it happen and
asked me to explain once more why I think meltdowns are
not so good for us. The preplanned a.m. "horsing
around" session which she herself had insisted on
setting up went nowhere; instead she rattled on and on
about the effects of certain nasty neurotoxins on liver
and, more to the point, penile functions (she's been
attending another toxins conference the past two days).
     But we're hanging in there. Presumably these
glitches can all be written off as a normal part of the
settling-in process. Like me she's unusually busy at
work this week, trying to squeeze in the conference
while also tending to matters neglected or postponed at
the office during the two weeks she took off for moving
over the holidays. Tomorrow night she'll be delivering
her eagerly awaited Christmas present, the jazz recital

to be personally performed for this jyzer right here --
for me alone! -- and she's anxious about that because,
as she says, she's afraid I'll hold her to overly high
standards (which is absurd; that's the very last thing
I'd do and she should know that). Saturday afternoon
we'll be picking up Aida at the airport (she's been
visiting family in S.E. Asia for almost a month) and
Z's worried, as I am also, about whether last year's
frictions with her will be starting up again. And
Sunday she'll be prepping for her upcoming promotion
interview and I'll be standing in for the notoriously
tough interviewer she'll be facing next week.

I'd like to be describing the apartment in more
detail but -- no time now. So be it. Jyze is gonna be
what it's gonna be. No regrets. (But lots of rushed
platitudes regardless. And I admit it: these I regret.
But my hands are tied. "My hands are tied" -- yeek!
Talk about platitudes! -- And that wasn't a setup.)

Whole new life, not really. But enough newness in
it to cause lots of disruptions. I can't stick around
the scope office until three or four a.m. if I have an
extra-tough job; the last bus for the hill leaves at
quarter past one and I must be on it. I've promised: no
more walking home at night. It's too dangerous. I'd
never have made such a promise if I didn't believe this
myself. But even so I may have to rethink the promise.
Might even have to break it surreptitiously on occasion
(but how could I, since my arrival time at home is
obvious and Z knows the bus schedule).

As a result I have to go to the scope office as
early as possible in the evening to check on the size of
my workload for the night, and I hate to do that because
if no work's awaiting me I've wasted the time and effort
of walking all the way up there and then all the way
back to the hideaway, close to a two-mile round trip.
And if a big job does await me I might not be able to
finish it before the last bus and thus will have to come
in a second night, where before I could just stay on
until everything was done and take the next night off.

Also by arriving so early I risk running into the

day crew if they stick around a little late, as happened
last night, and this can have unfortunate consequences.
For one, I, as a lowly independent contractor, might not
be able to work at all because they're using the space
or the machines and their needs come first. For
another, I don't want to be reminding them that I'll be
down there all alone when everyone's gone, because from
a whole lot of bad experience I know they'll start
worrying I'm getting away with something shady and then
they'll want the bosses to impose new conditions on the
Jyzer Ink contract.

    Work, blah. A livelihood, that's all it is. And
what's more just enough of one that I can barely scrape
by on it. For the past eighteen months I at least had
everything tightly integrated for maximum time-
effectiveness; but now under the new regime that's all
threatening to come unraveled too. Panic, though, is
not yet called for. Keep your cool, Jyze Guy.

    (Time passing. I'm thinking the supermarket
jaunt is out for today. Maybe a quick run to the local
hilltop market instead. It's only about a mile and a
half round trip. But: higher prices, fewer choices,
unfamiliar store brands, more anemic coupon sales. So:
just take care of crucial needs there today -- milk,
bread, bananas and that's it -- and keep scraping by on
peanut-butter sandwiches until I can get down to the
supermarket.)

    -- But I love the hood, yes I do. Love the walk
downhill from here into the city core. Wotta
spectacular panorama as you cross the high bridge over
the freeway! Not just the sweep of the downtown skyline
but also the bay, the sound, the jagged mountains
jutting up along the entire western horizon (and the
eastern too if you can tear your eyes away from the
western). And then the hike through the old Asian
quarter, that's fine as well. Living on south hill:
it's a longtime fantasy come true. I'm a vanilla north-
ender no more. It's a whole different city down here,
seems like, and it's one I'm a whole lot happier with
despite the admittedly plentiful drawbacks.

[Deep Jyze]

     And loving Zoelie B. It won't do to be forgetting
for even a moment that what's difficult about living
with her is just the flip side of what's marvelous about
living with her. The good far outweighs the bad and --
let's gird up and admit this too -- couldn't exist
without it. I'm taking on the entire package. "No
regrets." (But of course some. This is real life!
We're talking trade-offs here! The mere fact that it's
one hundred percent bona-fide all-out crazy lub -- a
typical Z-ism right there -- doesn't change that.)
     Okay, hilltop market here I come. If I'm swift
about it maybe I can still finish up this entry later
tonight. This year I'll be doing my best to confine all
jyze sessions to their appointed J-days, with kwikjyzes
to cover shortfalls being my one concession. At all
costs hang on to the randomness. (After J-day No. 2, by
the decree of the dice, a ten-day gap until No. 3.)
     Ideally, hit some downtown fast-food chain eatery
by six p.m. and finish up the jyze there. For logistic
reasons the one across from the scope building would be
best -- although this would be my third straight night
for that sorry joint. Shame! But for all the others
I'd have to walk six or eight blocks farther. And for
an eatery that's not fast-food or chain but still
affordable I'd have to walk a helluva lot farther than
that, and of course I'd also have to be all cleaned up
and have time to burn and basically when it comes down
to it be living a whole different kind of life, and that
I'd definitely not want to be doing. -- So no shame,
no. Pride! (In-my-own-face kind if it comes to that.)
                    *   *
     Nope. Change. Scratched the hilltop market too.
A downhill hike at dusk (seems a lot farther than the
1.81 miles I think I remember from our odometer
measurement) and here's the hideaway for an unscheduled
warm-up stop, seven minutes to six, my nose and cheeks
still thawing with audible cracks (seems like). The
first real Arctic Express of the season has rolled in,
the mercury plunging into -- brrrr -- the low teens.
     On the way: scores of century-old brick buildings,

spaghetti bowl of the freeway intersection (as viewed
from a hundred feet up on the high bridge), tangled
industrial district and working port with huge orange
cranes to the southwest, domed stadium, steaming
manholes, jangling streetcars, roaring trucks, a freight
train rumbling along below street level and disappearing
into the ancient smoke-darkened arched entrance of the
tunnel that runs beneath the heart of downtown. The
knockoff (but still quite handsome) Venetian clock tower
of the train station. Rows of "ethnic" restaurants,
mostly Asian, and lots of "ethnic" faces too. Fine,
fine walk. Also very easy because almost every step is
downhill. Yet going back up isn't too bad either, or at
least it didn't seem so to me the one time I've done it.
But probably it'll steepen with time and familiarity.

   Today something new: my first batch of forwarded
mail arrived at 1511 (our street address). Three mags,
a lit quarterly, a couple of bills. Now I have proof of
occupancy to offer when I go in to sign up at Z's
fitness club. Fortunately for me, its sharply
discounted family membership also applies to domestic
partners; you just have to perform a domestic sex act in
the membership office to prove you're not faking the
partners bit. (Naw, just kidding.) -- And a new set
of the city's DP papers is laid out on the end table at
home, awaiting interpretation of certain puzzling
clauses by my thoroughly city-jargon-savvy DP, or better
Deep, yes, before I try to fill in my portion.

   -- Mock-heroic jyze. Sure enough. And this week
the jyzer pulled off another mock-heroic act. One
morning when the shower malfunctioned and Z couldn't
shut it off he sprang buck-naked from bed and labored
over the glitch for some twenty minutes while sloshing
about in ankle-deep water until it finally yielded to
his magic wrench. This inspired Z to write a poem
declaring that viewing this bare-ass manly feat was just
as sexy as being "fixed" by her M'bao in bed. ("Fixed"?
Surely not intending to evoke the veterinary sense of
the term.) ("M'bao"? My beloved & adored one: another
Z-ist acronym from last year.)

Ritual moments too. The official changeover of keys, in which the ones for the old place are wrestled off the key-chain ring and the new ones wrestled on. (My key chain, by the way, is a piece of punched steel, size of a movie ticket, with half its original coat of black paint worn off. In turn it's been wearing holes in my pants pockets for roughly a decade now.)

Somewhat shockingly, most of the Christmas cards that came in for me last month remain unopened. But in the next week I'll try not only to open but to answer them, or rather those from people I didn't already send cards to, this time using reconfigured versions of the cards I made up in December which are now obsolete. Therefore I'll convert them into New Year cards, and since Chinese New Year falls later this month I'll seize on that as the occasion for celebration marked by the cards and apologize for their earliness and maybe paint in some "Year of the Tiger" stripes to make them look authentically lunar.

Now half past six and I must be moving on. Eat something real quick. Plunge into grand-jury scoping. This week's two sessions will go over 550 pages combined and one might hit 325 all by itself, with both numbers close to and maybe even at or beyond Jyzer Ink's all-time highs. History in the making! (And next to this what's the Asian financial crisis, massacres in southern Mexico, starvation in North Korea, the worsening AIDS pandemic in Africa and elsewhere, swelling homelessness right here in Jyze City even during boom times -- just to note what makes the front page of today's paper. -- And as per usual the ongoing USAn economic/military stranglehold on much of the known world's not even in there, front or any other page. Nor is global broiling for which we're also, to be sure, the chief culprit. "Old news," don't you know.)

*   *

-- Okay, kwikjyze. I did pick up Betty at the hospital on Monday. Then "kept an eye on her" at her house for an hour, as per doctor's orders, except I nodded out on the couch and she wound up keeping an eye on me as the dogs and cats burrowed in close and the hamsters thundered on their treadmills -- all of this barely retrievable now, as in a distant freaky dream (Kat was at school, sorry to say).

And I failed to mention Z's bout of gum pain and how it reminded her of the fiasco with ex-fiance Arvin, the one other man she's lived with. The stress from that turbulent six-month cohabitation caused so much damage she needed major mouth surgery. But this new bout a week into living with me was mercifully brief. (And her recipe for relieving the stress, presumably the same as back in Arvin days: "lots of sex.")

And this: the pleasure we get, Z and I both, from listening to the train whistles, which are quite audible on the hilltop, especially late at night as we lie in bed. (And they're doubly haunting if the night is rainy.) -- They remind her of riding the elevated trains as a young girl, which in turn recalls -- for her, and now for me also in imagination -- the marks left on the back of her thighs by the carved borders of the seats on those same trains in later years when she was wearing microminis as she loved so much to do.

And all week we were trying to unravel snags over delivery of "that snarky far-coast newspaper," and still to no avail. And Z's antitoxins postcard, mailed by the utility to twenty thousand homes in the south end of the city, contained a typo in the printed address message ("To the people who lives [sic] at") over which she hit the roof. And she asked me regarding the Deep forms: "Is it the best information you have that you're not married?" (To which I answered in the affirmative. And it is. But my hunch, which surely wouldn't go over well in court and so I probably should be keeping it to myself -- but I told her anyway -- is I still am.) And Z gave her explanation of why, if things are good between us, she tends not to be too effusive about it: when she was a kid and something good happened to her, her mother always warned her to keep quiet so her older half-sister Camilla wouldn't be envious.

[Deep Jyze]

3

    What should jyze be? What can it be? Four years
on (or almost) and I'm still wondering. And also I'm
still thinking I'll likely always be wondering. The one
thing I know is this: I do want to keep it going no
matter what. -- And therefore, let's get on with it.
    A ten-day gap since the last entry. Marvelous days
too. All kinds of stuff happening: heavy snowfall, jazz
serenade, political demo, Z's big job interview and
much, much more. And the usual kinds of ongoing stuff
as well, of course. Here I'm thinking of the post-move-
in getting-settled process, the spicy and dicey and,
yes, truly deeply (and Deeply) bizarre sex life, the
exploration of the new hood, the failed New Year's
resolution, the adjustment to all sorts of puzzling new
parameters regarding the quotidian. And at the same
time our social life continues to perk away, for me at
least at a far higher level than any social life of mine
has perked away in years, if not ever.
    But this jyze. What about it?
    For one thing, ten days is a very long period. It
stretches to and maybe beyond the limit of jyze's
ability to report on the doings of the interim, that is,
the J-gap. It's not just a matter of inadequate memory,
though this too plays a part (and of course as the years
go by the part will only grow). Too damn much stuff to
keep track of! And in addition to this, a crisis of the
form itself arises. What comes first, the temporal
account of what's gone down since the prior J-day or the
free-form scribbler's splurge which is jyze's very soul?
You can't be jyzin' if you gotta be thinkin' and

rememberin' all the time! Filling up the pages with a dutiful historical account -- no no no no no.

First principles first: keep it lively and have a good time doing it. If it starts to feel mostly like work, it can't be jyze. I don't want to stop looking forward to these sessions. If memory serves -- and if it knows how to get into the swing of things -- fine. If not, ignore it. Suppress it. Jyze what the J-lobe is lit up with -- period!

Presumably this means focusing more on immediate surroundings and contemporaneous happenings. It might also mean resorting to more abstractions and conundrums and whatnot, which in turn might be less informative -- yet more delicious to jyze about, around, from, or into. And if so, so be it. And also it be SO, not just so-so.

Ulk. Yes. So where am I? The scope-office conference room on a dark and stormy night out there, a well-lit and quiet one in here. And actually not so stormy out there now, although earlier it was. Meanwhile all office lights are blazing because the janitor's already been through on his trash run but hasn't returned yet with his huge snarling industrial hoover.

It's the semi-holiday for Martin Luther King. This year, by the morning newspaper's count, about a quarter of all workers in the city got the day off. My muscles aren't sore but Z and I did march with a streetwide line of folks three or four blocks long from the city's most racially diverse high school to the heart of downtown. "Hey hey, ho ho, I-200's got to go." The political right is trying to bust affirmative action by initiative, here just as they did successfully last year in the megastate to the south. Our multirace, -class, -culture action group the Friends & Deep of Zoelie B. is of course fiercely agin I-200.

It felt good to be marching again. Didn't even seem particularly futile. It may be futile, but the socializing aspects ease the frustration a whole lot. (Next year after this initiative passes, as it almost certainly will, the protests relating to racial

issues might take a slightly more militant turn.) -- And
then I'm hanging with some movers and shakers. Several
of Z's friends were among the rally organizers. Z
herself has helped organize plenty of rallies and
marched in many, many protests. Today she went up to the
ex-gov and said, "You can always count on seeing Matt O.
here," and he said the same thing right back about her
and they high-fived. So maybe this is a power trip or
something and I should be wary. For myself, I mean.
(But then again I have no power to trip with -- other
than Z -- and no prospect of gaining any otherwise and
for that matter no desire to. I'm just a fringe
character in this scene, a foot soldier, a fascinated
onlooker, a groupie with the hots for a certain
charismatic movement leader who miraculously
reciprocates the fascination -- to which I say: right on!
More power to you, Z-bird! Show your G-bird the way!)

Some odd week it's been. Beautiful snow atop our
hill, slanting down like showers of relatively slow-
moving feathery meteorites in the glowing cones beneath
streetlights visible outside our east living-room
windows. A thick white frosting for our gritty grimy
grungy -- yet still gorgeous -- hood. Then a slew of
days nastily dark and wet. But today, luck. For just
the right few hours, good marching weather: dry, not too
cold, with sun breaks. Yay!

Because of the move, meanwhile, many of my habits
remain out of whack, most only a little disjunct but
some a lot. Dinners are suffering most. Almost every
day it's been one more stop for double-stacks at the
same sorry burger joint katty korner from this building
right here. Each new visit involves a reluctant
override of the previous visit's vow that it would be
the last for a while. (Tonight's too, dang it anyway.)

Finest moment of the week, Z serenades me at the
apartment of her accompanist, Ted I., up in the Scandi
quarter. The first three tunes, all revered standards,
she set in advance -- she and Ted rehearsed them a few
times -- and then a fourth I got to choose from Ted's
fakebook and they winged it, sight-reading. We recorded

the whole session but haven't listened to the tape yet
for fear of tarnishing the memories. "Night and Day,"
"You Do Something to Me," "I Get a Kick Out of You"
were the three set in advance; "Under My Skin" was my
choice. Z looking so jazzy-lovely in tight black jeans
and black platform-like heels and lacey black camisole
top, the way she spun around from the piano to face me
with arms spread wide show-biz style and burst into
song. I marveled. I melted into a large puddle of
double-stack grease. How'd she do it? Didn't seem at
all nervous! Her wonderful voice which I've loved from
the very first phone call, and which played a big role
in my falling hard for her before I'd even seen her --
that voice was in top form. And so was the rest of her!
I was mesmerized. For the whole gig and for hours and
days afterward and right up to the present moment I was
-- and obviously I am again right now -- gulping with
wholehearted blubbering supergooey lub-lub-lub (forgive
me, O jyze gods, for stealing this lub lingo from the Z-
warbler again and even enhancing it twice over this
time).

One drawback to having an active social life in
which you're spending time with lots of different people
serially is that you're called upon to tell the same
stories over and over (but you do get to hear many new
ones as well and add some of those to the list of
stories to be told over and over in future rounds). Z's
"one-woman concert for her Deep" has been at the top of
our hot-story list this week for sure, followed
distantly by the move-in stuff, the mountains of boxes,
and the one about Z's boss, Dale, telling her she's
"seemed so much mellower" ever since she started seeing
this new guy, that is, yr. faithful jyzer (she expresses
mock indignation over this, and then whoever's hearing
the story usually offers something like, "But you know,
your boss is right!" and she sputters a little more and
I beam triumphantly before saying something along the
lines of, "Her boss just likes to have her on") (and she
probably says, "Have her on what?")

Other prime tales of the week: the malfunctioning
shower (ongoing), the Aida airport pickup (she kindly

brought me a tiny tin toy jeepney from the Philippines,
having learned from Z that Jeep was one of my childhood
nicknames). Also our first policing of the 1511
hallways and garage and grounds. And now I'm reminded:
Z's apparently come around to my view that it's best
not to ask too much of our landlord, Min, whom she's
begun calling a slumlord: it would only give him
another excuse to raise our rent. Instead we'll do all
we can to come up with solutions on our own.

    -- Time for a break here. Why? To work out! This
would be hard for any longtime acquaintance of mine to
believe but it's become a regular part of my life now,
all day long, whenever I take a break: do some dips,
push-ups, jumps, whatever. And I haven't even joined
"the WOC" yet! (That's still what we call Z's fitness
club, as in her acronymic daytimer reminders, standing
for "Work Out - Club.") But I will join it, because I'm
not fooling myself. I realize I've hit the divide:
reached that point in life where it's either be
extremely exercise-conscious or decay fast or maybe just
drop dead any day now. -- Yes yes, I'm aware I could
croak before the end of this sentence no matter what I
do -- of course! -- and that I'll no doubt keep on
decaying whether I work out or not. But I'm hoping I
can goose up my longevity odds a bit and maybe slow down
the decay for a while. In a few areas I might
temporarily halt it, and in fewer still I might even
reverse it. Temporarily for that too, of course. ("And
not all things?" -- Buddha.) ("Yes, right, Mr. Buddha,
but all things at vastly varying rates of deterioration,
as you well know, sir, but tend to play down, thereby
making such impermanence look boringly absolute rather
than intriguingly relative." -- Jyzer G.)

*   *

    -- Back fifty minutes later. No doubt red-faced
but no longer panting. Or only shallowly.

    So anyway: yes, I'm still trying to get my personal
act together. So far I've gone at this task mostly
piecemeal and half-assedly because I've been focusing on
wrestling the apartment into half-decent shape. That

26

must come first. And since Z's usually not around
during the week and is often too busy with other things
when she is (prepping for her interview last week, for
instance) I've been doing most of the setup work, to the
extent I can. And I don't mind it either: in fact I'm
pleased to be able to put in something extra since she
carries a larger share of the financial load (mainly by
paying for upkeep and most other expenses on the car,
which of course is hers anyway). So I've made a big
bookcase and the promised "soundproof" headboard for the
bed, I've gradually cleared various areas, unloaded my
boxes, so on and so forth. And as I do all this I'm
finding I like the place even more than I already did.

What have I set aside to do later? Answering the
Christmas cards with Chinese New Year cards. Filling
out the Deep papers (Z can't fathom why I'm taking so
long: she wonders if I'm stalling). Resuming the typing
up of last year's jyze. And lots of other stuff.

And then there's sex. Sex, sex, sex. Sex. This
very morning my G-tab visited her Z-slot for a fairly
long spell, she taking matters into her own hands and
climbing aboard, shoving it in, riding, sending up a
love-sounds hullabaloo, climaxing -- but not me. And
then afterwards she worried. How she loves to worry!
How very skilled at it she is! One theme of the week,
raised by her, making me wince: is she not seductive
enough? Is that why I don't come when I'm inside her?
(I wish it were -- because then I could hope for an easy
change -- or at least I'd know what was causing the
foozles.) But really now -- the most sexually gifted
woman I've ever known not "seductive" enough? Am I
perhaps confused about the meaning of the word?

However -- no Z meltdowns. And the hours and hours
of good stuff far outweighed the effects of the foozles,
which in any case have the dubious virtue of being quite
familiar to both of us. (I did manage half a dozen
ejacs over the ten days -- must've been the impact of
those many fast-food burgers. All by hand, and each and
every time the hand was hers. At handjobs she's doing
much better than back in our early days, when her excuse

27

was that not since freshman year in college had she
found it necessary to undertake in the sexual realm
anything so primitively manual. For this limited kind
of activity anyway she's now willing to accept
"suggestions" without going into a funk because they
seem like "implied criticism.") (Ah yes, what weird
mammals we all are, and myself weirdest of the entire
zoological class right now. And perhaps at a few other
times too, sure. Of course! I'm not in denial here!)

     She says things like this: "You're my best lover
ever and also my biggest challenge ever." Without being
falsely modest at all I can say I'm not so sure about
the first part of that but have no doubt whatsoever
about the second. (Or to put it differently: I'm sure
her previous good lovers came a lot closer to being able
to do whatever good things I can do for her than any of
her previous challenges came to causing the woes I can
and do cause her. So far, that is. Because damn it, I
still think all this will change. I can do it for her
with my joystick too, I know I can. -- Though maybe
I'll never be able to do what the fabled Bradley did.
That's true too. Because more and more it sounds like
old Bradley was one helluva joysticker with one helluva
joystick.) (Is it knowing about her ecstasies with
Bradley that makes me such a foozlin' flop? Not likely.
I was doing no better -- worse even -- before she'd said
a single word about him.)

     But sexy sexy sexy. Yesterday all day she wore no
underwear. Lately she's taken to whispering bawdily in
my ear in the midst of crowds or in the backseat of cars
or on buses. "Baby, I want you to swyve me so bad" is
my current favorite -- half spoof, half real -- sort of
burlesquey -- and we're making a signifying/dozens game
of it, with twists and surprise reciprocations. We're
even harmonizing to it, as in barbershop duets.

     -- And such a heavy social weekend this was.
Scrabble with Olwen and her son Trent Sunday afternoon,
dinner and a movie with Gerry and Leola Saturday night
and the same with Jess and Gwen Sunday night. Also some
shopping at a corporate big-box home center and a new

grocery co-op (new for me) on the next hill to the
north, also known in jyze as east hill (where, in the
parking lot, Z suddenly burst into tears and wailed,
"When we go on our trip this fall you won't find
anything glamorous or exotic in the hood where I grew
up!" -- this in reaction to my observation that her
friend Jody's mother, whom we'd been talking about
earlier with Jody herself during the march, grew up on
the same tropical island as Lady U's mother and they
probably knew each other) (I hadn't said anything about
this to Jody, but I miscalculated in thinking I should
mention it to Z as an example of how I can restrain
myself with her many Asian friends just because I know Z
bridles to hear me talking with others about Lady U or
Lady S or things too closely related to them or their
Asianness) (and later I went further and ventured a new
approach -- is she trying to drive me away with all
these boggling overreactions? -- but at least did manage
to put it in variant form, saying I bet all her friends
could see how crazy I am about her and maybe one or more
would soon be asking her, "What are you doing, this
guy's so crazy about you and you're trying to drive him
away?" -- And she saw through this immediately, but I
wasn't sorry I'd said it, because I truly would like her
to clamp down a bit on the overreacting: I mean, I'm
committed to her, I'm in it for the long haul, I want
her to start feeling and acting more secure so we can
stabilize the relationship and avoid some of the
squabbles -- and maybe that'll help with the fribbles
and foozles too).

So this too is jyze, the above. Yes. The less
sense it makes, the better the odds it's crossed over
into the real thing.

The trouble is, Z is not accustomed to living with
anyone. She's adjusting, she's generally good-humored
about it, but the evidence mounts that it's tough for
her at times. (And of course she resents the fact, and
even has the gall to say so, that it's not as hard for
me -- just as I suppose I must resent her because she
can come thirty or forty times or more -- sometimes lots

more -- in the time I come once, or less than once. But
then again that's just one of probably hundreds of ways
I must resent her, because this woman has got chops to
burn of so many kinds and knows how to do diva and also
how to do "virtual only child," as she calls it.)

It's all summed up for me in the way she habitually
throws her coat over the top of the coatrack, blocking
access to every one of the pegs on it. It's her
coatrack; she's the only one who's ever used it -- for
fifteen years! (Or however many. She hasn't specified.
It might be even longer than that.) -- So what I did,
finally, I mounted some coat hooks for me on the side of
the adjacent six-foot-high bookcase. And in general
this is how we've solved or dissolved most of our
conflicts. Each of us gets half the fridge, half the
sink, half the countertop space, half the bedroom, half
the bed, half the whatever. But many conflicts, of
course, fail to lend themselves to this easy half-and-
half (or half-ass, could say) type of solution. For
instance, she doesn't like to have to wait for me.
She's used to leaving when she's ready to leave. And
she likes to leave early. Sometimes very early. And I
like to make use of spare moments and leave "just in
time." I JIT, she ABEs (that's "always be early") (and
she used both of these acronyms in a note yesterday --
she loves acronyms so much!) (and also loves her cute
little red kitchen garbage pail which is nowhere near
big enough for two people's garbage even from a single
takeout meal but occupies just enough room that we can't
fit a real garbage bin in the kitchen without banishing
the red one and that ain't gonna happen).

None of this is terribly worrisome, no. And lots
of it provides prime material for our ongoing live home
sitcom. Neither of us has too much trouble dealing with
such blatantly minor irritations. And when trouble does
arise it's often because of stress induced from some
outside source (her job interview, my extremely heavy
workweek) and has nothing to do with our largely
peaceful, even if quite often sparky, domestic life.

Knock on wood! But no, I'm not even bothering.

I'm ecstatic. (As is she. Sometimes anyway. And she used the word first, at least for this round. I asked her how come she wasn't happier -- wasn't showing it -- when things were seemingly going so well, especially compared with what she'd feared and predicted back in December: a variation on the Arvin fiasco. And she said: "I'm quietly ecstatic." Wrote it. Wrote me a poem too, one of several this week. It was about riding the bus home. -- And several times she's been offered a seat on that bus, and she hardly ever was offered one on the previous route she rode in the supposedly more civilized north end. "Why is that? Am I aging fast or what?" Granny Zoelie, ha! But if that, then it must be Grampaw Glen too, so I can't accept it. Won't. In its own good time I will, sure, but we're not there yet. Not quite. And I wouldn't want to get out ahead of myself here and I'm sure she wouldn't want that either.)

I've scratched and I've scratched. I've forgotten too, and plenty, and furthermore what I've forgotten will almost certainly stay forgotten as far as jyze is concerned. Or in other words: this is more like it. Fun. Don't hardly know what I've said here and look forward to the surprise of finding out maybe a year or two down the road when I type it up. (And I've got one more round of exercises to go for tonight. Decay is accelerating by the minute! Gotta quit here!)

4

An unusual night. One-thirty a.m. and Z's not here. A Friday night too. But there's a reason, and a sad one: Leola's father and Gerry's mother died within two days of each other (both having been diagnosed with terminal illnesses in the past year or so) and the funerals are back in their home state, and Z's over house-sitting for them while they're away.

Why is it Z is everyone's indispensable friend? We've discussed this more than once. I'd say it's her big heart. Her strong sense of responsibility. Her loyalty. And not least, her childlessness. But those other qualities, they're a major part of why she's become my indispensable friend too. Pal supreme as well as lover supreme. And this even though I've been a whole lot less than a lover supreme to her myself.

So for three nights in a row, with tonight included as the third, I have, or will have, slept here alone. We're getting together at other hours, but this is probably the longest we've gone without sleeping together since late last spring. I'm often reminded of the lonely days in unit B-2 before the Z-woman came into my life. I wouldn't want to go back to those. No way. Not a chance!

In the eyes of city government she and I are now official domestic partners. We're DPS, we're Deeps, we're D'eeps! (her preferred wording of the acronym). I'm covered by the city's health plan, including dental and optical and various other specialties. Soon I'll have to start grappling with the question of what, if any, body parts to let the docs and the dentists and the rest of the health-care posse get their grody hands on, not to mention all those nasty instruments and machines and drugs. Tough decisions ahead. But in the event of an emergency I'm grateful my ass will be covered. And all other meat cuts too, yeah.

Materially I'm gaining more from this relationship than Z is, no question. She of course is well aware of this. We discussed it briefly while working out at "the WOC" on Tuesday (my first day as a member, which I get to be at a hugely reduced rate as her Deep). We josh about it. She usually seems pretty sure I'm not out to exploit her (except when the ghost of Arvin surfaces to bend her ear). Nor do I want to be feeling obligated or guilty. Yet...I might feel just that way if she were ever to press too hard on this issue. It's one of our prime possible danger areas, that's for sure.

(Jazz. Deep night. Scarves of hillside lights twinkling to the east. The damnably distracting view. And now my bedtime is also edging into the picture.)

During this long jyze gap we rutted twice, intromissive style, including one that was by far the longest-lasting up to now (she lying on her back, I on my side, my body almost perpendicular to hers), but still no vaginal ejac for me (with "gnarly whatzis" engorged therein, I mean). Also, a fight and a meltdown, two separate incidents. Both were quickly contained but they took us into two other major danger zones. One, her tendency to be controlling (and mine to be touchy about lack of respect for my promises; once I've said I'll do something I dislike being hounded about it). The other, the sexual conundrum, which no doubt could be analyzed in imposing psychological terms but I'm not planning to try to do that anytime soon.

This most recent coin-flip-determined gap in jyze entries was even longer than the previous one. That one was ten days, this one eleven. Too long. I'm about ready to bail on the whole experiment. In theory the random variation in time between entries is fine but in practice I find (again) that toward the end of such large gaps I start to dread jyzing. The strain on my memory becomes too heavy. I'd like to be able to ignore this but it seems I can't. So...maybe a change is called for. I'm thinking on it.

Z didn't get the management job she applied for. But she took the defeat well -- even seemed relieved to dodge the complex technical duties associated with the position -- and it already appears Dale will be offering her a promotion to analyst for the conservation unit. It's bigger bucks. Right now she earns between five and six times what I do on average and the new gig would raise the multiplier to seven or more. But I don't think it'll make for any meaningful difference in our relationship. She'll be the one with the money and so I'll be the exemplar of frugality and "live light"

ecological correctness -- and all the better since I
strongly believe in, and like to practice, both.

Chinese New Year fell night before last. We were
scheduled to celebrate with June (who happens to be a
descendant of the most renowned Axial Age Chinese sage
of them all) but Z's house-sitting for Leola and Gerry
complicated that too much logistically. It was
surprisingly quiet around here that night, given that
the hill is close to half Asian. As a small celebration
of my own I bought two sheets of the nifty new "Year of
the Tiger" stamps and used them on my delayed Christmas
cards, which I did finally manage to get out yesterday,
which is to say: on Chinese New Year's Day itself.

In eleven days a lot can happen when you're living
with Zoelie B. We heard a mordantly funny Afrusan
comedian of national repute speak about the never-ending
war on Afrusan businesses. Lee M. stayed a night with
us. Kat came over for the afternoon last Sunday and
helped us police the grounds using Adopt-a-Street gear,
including three pairs of fabuloso mechanical litter-
pickers. (Afterwards she fell asleep in my arms on the
couch and Z told me the sight almost made her heart
burst. She loves the way I am with Kat -- and I was
aglow to hear her say so. Kat's become the very model
of the daughter I would've wanted for myself back in the
pre-Z era if a few things had turned out a bit
differently.)

And then there's the mercurial Aida. She and Z
have already quarreled twice since her return, yet with
a peaceful and very touching evening in between: a
preview of a video about Filipino immigration featuring,
among others, Aida's family, "the D's," who arrived
almost thirty years ago in what was then not yet known
as Jyze City. The showing took place at the small
museum located in the Asian quarter just a mile or so
down the hill from here -- and the curator of this
museum is none other than Doug T. who lives directly
above us in 303, the very apartment we might've been
living in ourselves if not for Aida's exasperating flip-
flop on it last fall when Doug thought he and his family

would soon be moving out -- and the aftershocks from
that incident are still rumbling to this day.

Then, even more oddly, Aida tried to call Z at home
yesterday when she was out, I answered, and we had a
fairly good talk. She insisted we're friends -- "But
remember, if you and Zoelie break up, I was her friend
first" -- and she also proposed we double-date this
weekend. Her date for the occasion, she let me know,
would be none other than Colin K., the smooth-talking
Japusan we met at Adele's New Year's party, where he
appeared to be with Adele herself, although he later
left with Emiko. It seems Aida met him way back in
early December and has now proclaimed first dibs over
the other two. "He's a little old for me, but...since
he's just broken up with his wife after being with her
even longer than you were with yours, it'll just be for
fun." Fun? Hey, nothing wrong with that! Go for it!
-- But no, I really do hope it works out for her.
However, on the phone today Z scotched the double-dating
idea, at least for now, and didn't seem at all taken
with it for the future either. And to me this further
confirms that jealousy has played a significant role in
Z's difficulties with Aida since we met. Betty also
thought so when I talked with her -- very cautiously --
about it. (And just so the record's clear I'll note
this: my "wife" whom Aida referred to -- Lady U -- was
never an official wife. And I didn't think it was
really necessary for Aida to bring her up at all. On
the other hand it remains true that Aida reminds me of
Lady U at times -- her drama-department persona in
particular -- just as I'm said, by Z, to remind Aida of
her ex-husband Tom in my highly objectionable views on
frugality and social status, among many other matters.)
And -- what. One real good news item: the far-
coast paper is now being delivered to us at 1511 seven
days a week (or nights actually, so I'll probably go
back to calling it "the night paper"). After all the
wrangles with the distributor I can still scarcely
believe they'll suddenly do this on the hilltop. Yet it
arrives about the same time as it did at B-2 and it

flops down outside the lobby door with a THWACK that's
usefully audible up here. Z and I are splitting the
cost, along with that for the two local dailies. Since
she likes to read the morning local daily on the bus
going in, I rarely see it until the following evening
(or the early a.m. hours after that if I've already left
for work in the evening before she gets home) -- that's
the one drawback for me in our present scheme. As a
newspaper junkie from way back I have to say it hurts.
But I can live with it, I guess. Though sometimes, I
admit, it's a stretch. Yes. But then stretching's
supposed to be good for you, is it not? (Z's often
telling me exactly that regarding our workouts at "the
WOC." "M'bao," she says, "you should stretch more!"
Whereas I think I stretch plenty already, there and
elsewhere, and not just in the physiological sense.)
     The big mound of boxes in the "great room" looks
about the same as it did eleven days ago. Nonetheless
life is shaking out into some dependable routines, and
they're just the kind I like to have. Oddly enough (or
not), they're turning out to be much like what they were
when Z and I lived apart. In ordinary times we sleep
together all five weeknights instead of just three as in
pre-Deep days (and as a rule we get it on at least once
most of those nights, usually when I slip into bed at
two a.m. -- the middle of her sleep time -- and
sometimes again when her alarm goes off at six). The
sleep problems are much the same too, and this week she
came up with a new gimmick, a circular hand-drawn
"Perkiness Scale" with an adjustable arrow which she
sets each evening at her bedtime. She leaves the scale
outside the closed bedroom door to let me know how alert
and energetic -- "perky" -- she needs to be for work the
next day. And this seems to be doing the job quite
nicely. But we can have dinner together only twice on
weekdays: Tuesdays and Thursdays. Weekends we're
together much more, but again this is how it was before.
     For me the two biggest changes so far have to do
with "the WOC" and my need to take a bus home. I'm only
getting started on devising a workout protocol but I

plan to put in two hours at the WOC three afternoons a
week (with Z present for the first hour each day). Not
only will this reduce the time I'll have free for
writing projects, but I suspect it'll make me, at least
for a while, an even worse copulator than I've been up
to now.

Details, details. I think I'll be able to adjust
to the changes and I think my various parts and
appendages will too. In general I'm delighted with my
new life. And now I can work out any time I like
between five a.m. and eleven p.m. and the club is just
two blocks from my office (and one from Z's).

*   *

-- And so to bed. It's late, half past three, but
when will I get another chance to jyze here in the
bedroom at this hour? I hope not for a good long time.
And if I did, it would probably mean things were going
badly between us. Jyzing is different when all's well.

(All's well for us, I'm saying. And even that's
relative, of course. For Leola and Gerry all's nowhere
near well right now, as an example of the relativities.
And for the top dog back in D.C. it's a bad time too:
week of the outbreak of a big presidential sex scandal.)

Our combined futons, one (hers) atop the other.
They amplify each other's flaws, it turns out, and
thus the new center trough is far deeper than either
futon's trough by itself. And is this how it is for
our lives as a whole? I say no! The opposite! We
fill out each other's troughs! Even our lumps are
complementary! -- But I digress, and with far too many
exclamation points deployed along the way. Must keep
calm here. So...I was about to mention the new
headboard. The lamps. The shelves. Jerry-built, all
of them, by me, and I'm damn proud. Big new bookcase
made from bare two-by-tens salvaged from the
disassembled loft. Back behind my feet, prettified by
a patchwork "throw" of Z's, squats my infamous funky
green armchair but with not a trace of its greenness or
funkiness in view. At least it made the cut for
apartmental inclusion. For a while I was all but

certain it wouldn't.

      (And the Zoelie Trope? Her friend Manny's terrific
gift to Z that used to ride a similar shelf above the
head of Z's bed at her old place, flashing out images
of, among others, Z and Aida eternally chasing each
other on their papier-mache hogs, which is to say huge
fake motorcycles? It's set up in Z's room now -- the
extra bedroom here, that is, for which she's paying an
extra $47.50 a month in rent to make her own, while I'm
paying $47.50 less. As she likes to say, "You have your
hideaway and now I have mine." And I say: fine! All
the better for both of us!)

      -- And on the equivalent shelf here, in the Z-
trope's former place more or less, is the lady's latest
reading matter: "Sex Tips for Straight Women from a Gay
Man." She says she's discovering much she didn't know.
As we long ago established, but this week she's
reconceding, "I was just coasting for all this time."
It's true: she never had to work to get a guy up and in
and spurting because on those rare occasions when her
looks and shape didn't do the trick, her extreme sexual
hotness did without fail. -- And also on that same
shelf, my own latest reading matter, an "Operating
Manual" for the male body, from which I too am learning
much. For one thing, just to keep this foozly fleshy
groinal -- or crotchety -- appendage and all its
associated plumbing in working order I ought to be
ejacking at least three times a week. And even at my
advanced age (almost three months into Stage III now by
the Glennarian calendar) I should usually be ready to
hump again after twenty-four hours at the longest.
-- So go to it, you slacker N'dow! (To revive Z's most
amusing penile sobriquet of them all.) Do as the specs
say you should! And if it's too much for you, at least
show some proper shame!

      Tick of Mother's little faux antique clock (the one
that stood for years on her bedside table and had to be
unplugged to make way for an oxygen machine shortly
before her death). Also blinking up there is the
digital clock on the small black dual-alarm radio from

my peninsula days with Lady U. And, on Z's side of the
bed, glaring blankly from its perch atop one of my
wooden folding chairs, her small black-and-white TV.
I've never seen it turned on. But a TV in our bedroom,
even a bona-fide antique, I'm not ecstatic. To accept
this uncomplainingly, what greater love hath a Deep?

It's odd how Z's sex meltdowns usually seem to
occur shortly after we've made new progress. This most
recent one fit the pattern: it hit just a few days
after what she called "our first real fuck" (because I
guess this was, after all, the first time she's come
with my wanger inside her, or anyway come powerfully,
or at least memorably -- since she has no memories at
all of those several other times she told me it
happened -- perhaps because extreme pleasure blanked
them out?). But if such a triumph doesn't quickly
repeat itself she's doubly disappointed and starts
working up "timetables" along the lines of if we're not
shagging regularly by such and such a date she wants
me to promise I'll go see Karen, her mainstream
doctor. (Fat chance. I will not be seeing Karen about
this, not now and not ever. Period. Her or any other
doc, mainstream or woo-woo (the latter, for Z, would be
Lorraine). Not unless utter desperation sets in. And
for that to happen old N'dow would just about have to
fall off.)

-- Yes, I cause Z lots of pain by being unable to
perform conjugally at anything even remotely approaching
her standard, or for that matter anyone else's standard,
including, according to the "Operating Manual," those of
legions of randy centurions. But I do try. And I do
all I can to compensate for my foozles. And by and
large she's patient and loving and accepting. But
regardless these occasional meltdowns still threaten to
mess up everything. However. So what. Just keep
plugging away, polebearer dude. (Ha.)

So, lamp shadows, intricate ones. Sperm towels, a
whole stack (there's positive thinking for you). And
Z's due back sometime before noon and it's already past
four a.m. so I'd better stop so I can be ready should
tomorrow prove to be a day when I truly need to be.

[Deep Jyze]

5

So now a new jyze plan. Random is out. Toss the
whole blinkin' yearlong schedule. Draw up another one
based on J-weeks of standard length, but change the
standard, at least for this first volume of the annal,
from the traditional eight days to six days to make up
for pages and time already lost. "On the sixth day he
jyzed." See how it works.

And drop the idea of trying to do even the
sketchiest direct description of this first year of
living with Zoelie B. "The Jyze of Living with Z" now
becomes backstory. Hopefully it'll be backstory with,
as the rapper sez, "a whole lotta back." -- And
besides, and anyway, backstory paradoxically set in the
present is the only kind of story that truly jyzes.

What I'm saying is I'll try not to be looking at
"the big picture" so directly all the time. See, it's
stupefying, the head-on take. So gaze instead at the
little things. Peripheral stuff. Inchoate stuff.
Details for a story that doesn't yet exist. (How could
it exist in advance? And even if it did, how could
anyone, myself most certainly included, or indeed any
jyzer, know what it was?) -- And hope at least a few of
these items will open new angles on life as a whole as
it spins out -- meaning unspools, not veers wildly.

Ach, it's all a crapshoot anyway. Whatever it
takes to get the ol' J-stick moving, glom onto that.
And as noted from J-day 1 of J-annal 1, the J-stick
doesn't want to move at all if a heavy sense of duty is
weighing it down. The paralysis induced by overloaded
memory. I'm not sure but I think I can handle six days.

40

                    [Can This Be Jyze?]

"Sixers."
     The negative trade-off: less space to stretch out
in on any particular J-day. And more disruption of the
regular non-J part of the jyzer's life; now J-day will
roll around again two days sooner than he's -- I'm --
accustomed to. But, again, the two hours (cumulative)
needed for each session shouldn't be all that
disruptive. Two hours, ten handwritten pages (if jyze
is zipping along). Can fit them in.
     Saturdays will be toughest. A bit of what Z calls
"parallel play" could be the ticket. It's true I don't
like to ask her to indulge my jyzing. Why is this? If
it's some sort of hang-up, maybe I can at least find a
way to plug into it for a booster jolt of daemonic
energy. -- As if I'm not trying to do this already, and
in numerous realms, including the biggest of all: the
love hookup. Plenty of hang-up energy in that.
     So today's a Friday. I'd like to be leaping out of
bed at nine-thirty a.m. on weekdays but as usual today I
didn't make it. This time I was an hour and a half
late. No big deal, but it means my jyze hole shrinks
and these lines take on a rushed air. Nothing new here
either. And yet: can't I do better?
     Under the new regime I'm planning to leave the
house between two and three p.m. on M/W/F so I can
squeeze in a midafternoon workout at the WOC. If I can
finish breakfast before noon I'll be fine. For Tuesdays
and Thursdays, the days when Z and I are slated to do
dinner together in unit 203, I'll bring my personal work
home with me the night before so I can stick around the
house all afternoon. On days when we don't eat here
I'll make myself a box meal to take downtown.
     All this, however, is a plan and only a plan.
Faced with the new reality who knows what might happen.
     The black armchair. Z's. Almost three o'clock
now. Intriguing clouds hanging over the mountains
today, I notice, including a big black anvil-shaped one
good perhaps for forging the nibs of celestial J-sticks.
I do love this setting, I do, I do. But today I'll be
leaving it soon and with, again, scarcely any jyzic

justice done to it or for that matter to anything else.
This is it, the J-book of record. Without it most
everything happening in my life would be lost forever.
Thus the week just past: much has already vanished and
all but a sliver of the rest will soon follow. Same for
the coming week. All weeks, to be sure, but these two
especially. I'm regearing, that's why. -- But
regardless I want to hit a few highlights.

Last weekend, a fine night reading and loving and
sleeping in Leola and Gerry's king-size bed. (A real
bed I could stretch out in undiagonally. The most
recent previous one for this kind of stretching was my
mother's deathbed some twenty-six months ago, and that
too was for a single night -- or no, two.) And dinner
with Z and June at a Chinese restaurant with a delayed
New Year's Lion Dance kicking up just outside, about
two feet away, the lion at one point pressing its nose
flat against the window as if hungering for our grub,
its nostrils flaring truly dragonian vapor plumes on the
glass. (All this out in the burbs. The usual reentry
culture shock hit me out there and a surge of relief
followed on our return here.)

And also here, a fight. My fault, I guess,
because I bridled at Z's indifference to my sage advice
about how to handle the uproar at her office over
selection of three males for the three open management
positions. As a result, in less than twenty-four hours
we came up with a new acronym, SLOF, and a slogan to go
with it: "Just SLOF off." The S refers to cutting the
other some slack at times of stress (both of us); the L
refers to offering critiques of the other lovingly as
opposed to nastily (Z) or "avuncularly" (me, supposedly,
though I deny it); the O refers to saying "ouch" when
something said by the other hurts (as opposed to going
stoic, as I admittedly sometimes do and Z almost never
does); and the F is for "fourth dimension" and waiting
calmly while the other goes off to that dimension for
simmering or fuming, as we both agree can occasionally
be necessary even at merely mildly uproarious times.

So anyway we're trying. Still not seeing much of

each other during the week. With major meetings looming
at the office she warned me she'd have to be "Balzacian,"
meaning hoard all her erotic energy for those work needs.
For two nights in a row no fucking. (My vow to myself
is never to let more than a single night go by without
sex unless she applies for a pass.) -- And I'm sorry to
acknowledge this "fucking" is, as before, not true ejaco-
fucking. At the moment I'm not even trying for that.
I'm still recovering from her latest meltdown over this
hugely frustrating issue. Supposedly she's now seen the
light again -- this time it was kindled by the
realization that "it not only takes two to fuck, it
takes two not to fuck" and thus she needn't blame
herself alone for my member's inexplicable funks and
foozles. And so she assures me the meltdowns won't be
happening ever again, EVER, I can take it to the bank.
    3:22 p.m. Rush rush. I'm sore all over, by the
way, so today I think I'll settle for an abbreviated WOC
workout. Thus far I haven't missed a single day. But I
can't expect to be able to go anything close to full
tilt right at the start. I'm resigned to working into
things with a gradualism commensurate with the long
period of neglect. Sometimes I forget what a big deal
this return to in-shapeness is (physiologically, I mean;
but I don't doubt it's just as true psychologically).
    And unexpectedly I'm in the midst of yet another
humongous scoping week, the third in a row. Again over
five hundred pages of grand jury. Somebody at the
D.A.'s office must've noticed this jury was languishing.
A lucky thing for me moneywise, and just in the nick of
time. But also this avalanche is hitting at the point
where I can't be as flexible about working late.
Therefore I must push hard while in harness. Stress.
And Z, through no fault of her own, doesn't fully grok
this yet. (She's only just beginning to realize my
eccentric nightscoper hours may pose some intractable
problems for us.)
    As for this week's increment of progress on
settling into the apartment, I've finally wrestled my
part of the bedroom into pretty good shape. Even my

closet is somewhat orderly. And I began setting up a
working surface for the art table in the living room (by
sheer serendipity my old butcherblock desktop,
originally bought for my first writing shed, fits almost
perfectly into the alcove on the south side of the room,
except the butcherblock itself is four inches too narrow
when placed atop the old redwood worktable; so I'm
filling in these four inches at the back with quasi-
matching quality pine strips glued atop a ratty nail-
hole-riddled two-by-four). And I bought more quality
wood to make shelving for Z's tea boxes and spices.
That's the next big fixer-upper project.
        -- Or no. Valentine's Day is. Heart fixer-upper.
And I'm remembering (as Z is too, I know) that it was
the emptiness of this same day a year ago that triggered
my effort to stir up some romantic action in my life
which by amazing good fortune wound up being this very
Z. (And in this week's poems she wrote about, first,
the pain of confronting her own "vintaging" when a sleek
high-school girl sat next to her on the bus, and second,
about her putatively "unmediagenic" moles; and also she
showed me a big binder containing poems she's written
over the past decade, many of them about the fading hope
of finding "true love." Touching stuff. Masterfully
written. But also I have to say: way too self-critical.
This is a woman who's ogled everywhere she goes! -- And
often she wakes up at two a.m. "by instinct" and comes
wandering naked out into the hall on her way to the half
bathroom in her room, possibly just to remind me how
sleek she still is herself. I mean, otherwise why
wouldn't she use the big bathroom, which is much closer
to our bedroom? -- And ooh do I love to go over and
nuzzle her when she wanders in like that.)
        (But she's again itching to call Min, the landlord.
Agrees we shouldn't be complaining too much right at the
start of our residence here but says she just can't help
herself. Wants the toilet in her bathroom to be made
fully functional -- something about the flushing
mechanism is messed up and I can't fix it. Also wants
the recycling area downstairs to be arranged just so.

wants the entrance lobby door to close and lock more easily. -- And one of the grand-jury cases this week focuses on a nasty pan-Asiusan gang most of whose members live on our hilltop. So I don't mean to be either exaggerating or playing down the dangers. And as she reminded me this week, she'd never risk living up here if she were still on her own. Nonetheless we're both delighted with the place -- a thought that still rings in my head, for one, quite regularly, almost like quarter-hourly chimes -- even at times minutely.)

    3:54. Okay, move 'em on out. Again hit the usual fast-food joint for takeout double-stacks. Cut back the WOC workout even more than previously planned. 340 pages to scope, so if I start in by six I'll have a fighting chance to finish before the last bus rolls.

6

    Arrrgh. Thirteen days later, not six. In the middle of a fight with Z -- one after another they're suddenly roaring in just like this year's El Nino winter storms.

    Up until last night I didn't think these wrangles were all that bad. Now I'm wondering. (Ten minutes ago the phone rang while I was in the bathroom and I wasn't able to pick up until midway through the fourth ring, just in time to hear the hang-up click. Z probably. Now she's even more likely to have it in for me when she arrives home tonight.)

    Whose fault is all this? Who knows.

    (Phone again.)

       *

Same deal. Almost. Start of the fourth ring and

silence on the other end, then a click and a dial tone.
Maybe four or five seconds of silence before the click.
     Well anyway. A Thursday afternoon this time.
Didn't peel myself out of bed until noon today because
last night's squabbling kept me up until close to six.
(And it's even harder on Z, as indeed she doesn't fail
to remind me and quite often. Yet she's the one who
keeps wanting to thrash things out immediately. Oddly
enough I'm the peacemaker around here. So far, though,
I haven't been able to figure out what it is she's so
worked up about, so how can I conjure any peace?)
     Gives me a bad case of the desponds, all this. The
megrims.
     Years ago I would've busted my brain trying to
analyze such "problems." Wouldn't've been able to rest
until I could point a finger at this or that. Blame
this, blame that. Must resolve this, must resolve that.
But no more. And it's not because I don't care. It's
because I do care. (Yes, I insist on this.)
     Almost exactly a year ago this Z-woman and I first
came into contact via the printed word. Valentine's
week. This year we spent much of the three-day
Valentine's/Presidents Day weekend quarreling via the
shouted (sometimes) word. And even so I was still under
the impression it was all minor stuff and we were fine.
     Friday night I stayed up late making her a giant
Valentine, two feet by three, from a torn-up cardboard
box, spiffy paints and markers and glue, lacy napkins
featuring red and purple and white hearts of various
sizes -- the works. "Da Troth & Nuttin But" says the
cover, with a big goofy loving message inside affirming
I can't help but go for her in the biggest way possible
forever and ever, amen. Also gave her, in increments
over several days, an array of personalized cheapo
jewelry and an "erotic meditation toy" (another hippo,
to match the Christmas one, this time the squeeze kind)
with lusty/mushy messages scribbled all over it.
     None of this made her happy for long. And she has
her reasons, I'm sure of it. But what are they? -- And
what if they're loony? What if they're truly weird

neurotic or schizo or psycho stuff? -- Won't really
matter, I say. The real question is how do I make the
woman happy for longer periods. I'm not saying for
eternity. Incrementally longer, that's all.

Yes, she's difficult. She can be a load and a
half. "High maintenance." Everyone knows it, including
the woman herself. She takes great pride in it! Yet
she's extremely good-hearted too, and everyone, herself
again included, knows this as well. These are the
givens, the poles, with our conflicts strung on a high-
tension line between them like big smoking transformers.

Idiosyncratic sex continues. No recent meltdowns
over it, at least not of the direct kind. Now she
simply refers to it with some equanimity as "our freaky
sex life." We're still stoned on each other erotically
for hours at a time, lost in the miracle (seriously!).
In a single thirty-hour period last week I came four
times. Again my joystick was inside her for a lengthy
but "ejacoless" period during which she O'd at least
half a dozen times. And so forth. For once I don't
think it's really the sexual weirdness that's disturbing
her. Must be something else. But what?

She talks with her friends about these fights. I
don't like this -- not when I'm being asked to accept
the friends as my friends too -- and she stews over my
not liking it. She tells me she's the "highly
emotional, dramatic" type -- as if I didn't know! -- and
tries to cast me in the role of the overly rational or
reasonable one. "I have lots of melt-ups too," she
points out (nifty turns of phrase like this one being
yet another bonus of life with Zoelie B.). She asserts
grimly she'll keep hanging in there; "I'm in this for
the duration." Weeps and moans like to break my heart.
Whence this misery? I tell her I'm shocked to see how
extensive it is. And I am.

She informs Leola (back in town after the double
funeral back on the high plains) we've been fighting a
lot. Leola asks her if it means the honeymoon's over.
Z repeats this to me as if she thinks it's indeed over.
Does she? I ask her. "I think we're doing our same

minuet as before," she says, "but at a higher, scarier
level." I ask for specifics, just what it is that's
troubling her so much, but she resists offering any. In
fact she seems not to have any to offer. But I can't
believe they're not there.

She did yield "a clue." When her father withdrew
from stormy emotional scenes with her at home, she
either confronted him or withdrew herself. (Is that
what she said? It was all rather unclear.) For me a
more revealing part of the "clue" was her sharp reaction
when I told her I think it's not so much a matter of
where our emotional patterns come from, it's what we do
now to live with them or even once in a while in some
sense surmount or transcend them. (Yesterday she
attended a full-day psychobabble conference. No doubt
this had something to do with her surly mood last night,
as did my sullen reaction to it. I'm sorry, I just
can't blithely turn the other ear when she starts
spouting some of this stuff. I have to tell her I see
this as part of the problem -- one of our areas of
strongest "Yenom" or YNM -- "Yer Not Me" -- friction.)
(Even under the gnarliest of conditions she can still
pump out the acronyms. "Yenom" is another of her
originals, although it's a retread from last year.)

Tonight we'll be doing dinner together as usual on
Thursdays, but this week is yet another heavy one work-
wise for me and so we won't be able to dig into this
latest rift (or whatever it is) until the weekend. More
skirmishing ahead, no doubt.

Is it her self-destruct component? Can't accept
anything that's going too well? Her hot temper? High
expectations from being a "virtual only child"?
Hangovers from serious psych problems, including suicide
attempts, in her late teens and early twenties?
Historic inability to keep a love relationship going or
to live with a man? Strong controlling tendencies?
Critical mind? Radical spirit? Fiery feminism?
Traditional Catholic atavisms? Class suspicion?
Longtime habits of living alone? Deep attachments to
friends who now feel cut off from her just as she does

from them? Mixed-race hybridity pains? Colonial or
neocolonial resentments? Fear of aging? -- Oh, all
kinds of demons here. But I'm still believing my own
demons can dance with hers. Do better at it, I mean.
Keep hers happier. It's her misery that's hardest for
me to take. (But I don't like her attempts to order me
around. And she hates thinking I'm thinking she hounds
too much or worse bitch-hounds too much -- and I'll just
say she used that nasty "bitch-hound" term first and I
haven't even managed to repeat it out loud yet.)
     Meanwhile lots of jyzeworthy things have been
happening. We took Kat to Jess and Gwen's lezzie party
and Kat painted everyone's faces, captivating all the
women and the one man (me) in the room. With Paz and
Tobey we saw, as part of Z's Valentine present to me, a
local production of Byron J.'s "Red Light on Behind."
(This is the same Byron J. who has a hideaway office
across the building from mine and two floors up -- we
nod on the staircase sometimes. And I liked the play a
lot better than I thought I would from the reviews.)
(Paz, by the way, wants me to do the captions for a book
of her photos -- and I'm nervously equivocating.) We
also saw "The Last Chrysanthemum," a longtime favorite
of mine, and Z strongly disliked it because of its old-
timey Asian slowness (the contradictions in this
woman!). June broke down and wept bitterly, as Z
snoozed nearby on our couch, during our long talk about
raising her two boys all alone. Z, one of three reps
from the Filipino city workers group, met with the new
mayor, a gung-ho developer who attended Mezzu (and
played football there, though he's supposedly big on the
arts now). We helped Aida throw a "No on 200" disco
fundraiser at her house and I found I'm not much good as
a money-grubber, the one who goes around begging people
to cough up the twenty-dollar "entry donation." I
rassled hilariously with Kat. Z and I, with Kat's help,
cleaned up the entire length of our block, both sides,
as part of our Adopt-a-Street duties. I took a full
load over to the storage unit and again checked out the
old backwoods digs en route (evoking the same feelings

as back in December; and no new info about Lady U).

Z devoted a whole day to sifting through her boxes. The mound is finally starting to shrink. As a result, though, another big load's ready for storage. (We're now aiming to finish the settling-in process by the end of June and to throw some sort of housewarming party in July -- and to travel back to Mentoka/Centropolis in late September so I can meet her mother and we, Z and I, can explore each other's complicated family roots.)

-- About jyze, well, best not to worry too much. I'm still hoping to stick to the every-six-days schedule. My new thought, however, is that this year just might turn out to be jyze's playtime and nothing more. I've pretty much abandoned the notion of doing even a backstory "Living with Z." Better to build up the reservoirs for next year's "special edition." Do this edition here, No. 5, just to stay loose. It'll be what it'll be, but the "Deep version" thereof. "Deep" is really the only peg now. (And maybe that's been true all along and I've just failed to see it.)

Other little incidents.

One, Z weeping over a "naked encounter" (literally) with Jess P. in the gym locker room. Jess's "Miss Universe body" and her shock at the large scar on Z's lower belly from her fibroid operation. Z, recovering: "I'm just mourning my lost 'climax period' again." (I came across a photo of a model who looks a lot like Z in those marvelous pix of her from her late teens. When I showed it to her she seemed displeased, though, as if I'm not supposed to be aware other beautiful women exist in the world -- including even her own younger self!)

Two, Z mentioned, when we were talking about our "origins myth" as a couple, that prior to our meeting she'd had a certain guy at work in mind as the kind of person she hoped to hook up with. What was he like? I asked. Long hippie hair, a tailored suit, shiny Italian shoes, she said. Oh my god no! But then she assured me that the guy no longer interests her in the least. Snickered about the massive differences between me and him. And she keeps bringing up Gordon F., the grad-

school teacher whose boffo studliness first sparked her
into thinking she was in serious need of hormonal
distraction, thus setting the wheels in motion for our
meeting via the personals. Now she's saying she thinks
he was attracted to her too. (Could well be -- hard to
see how it could be otherwise -- but my impression is
she's dangling this more as another flashy little move
in the jealousy-provoking phase of "the minuet.")

Three, she's again saying she's ready to talk about
my love history -- except anything involving Lady U.
(And she did manage to withhold comment -- though her
silence was bristling -- when I mentioned that Lady U
also, like Z herself, took a strong interest in causes
involving social and/or environmental justice.) -- Now
she's saying the time has finally come when she's ready
to delve into my photo box and albums from the pre-Lady
U era. I'm wondering which ones I should yank from the
mix (just as Z disappeared most photos of previous
lovers before letting me paw through her own box last
fall -- or at least most of the ones that still existed.
Many she had long ago, she informed me, ripped up into
tiny pieces or burned or both).

Four, she continues to leave me lots of primo notes
and poems and drawings, all of her own creation. The
best of the lot this week was a sketch of herself naked
as "Our Lady of the Tender Nipples" one morning after an
exceptionally lusty breast-focused night in bed. She's
also upset, and doesn't hesitate to say so and make me
suffer for it, if I don't leave her an equivalent stash
of notes and drawings (no poems required, thank god).
One of her poems, "A Kiss for Possum" -- "Possum" being
her latest moniker for my refractory appendage -- led me
to leave her a note about "ol' Possum always wanting to
play even when he's playing possum." Two nights ago she
told me she thought a certain henley made me look "buff"
and that night when I got home a note greeted me,
"Mmmmm, gimme buff." (But then she coolly shrugged off
my attempt to do so. And then yesterday she apologized
for this rejection, saying she realized in retrospect --
this in yet another note -- her "gimme buff" note could

be seen as an instance of prickteasing given her failure
to follow through on it. And my note in reply to this
second note didn't satisfy her (and I thought it should,
but I can't remember exactly why anymore).) (Why so
many notes between us? Because during the workweek we
see each other mostly in the dark in bed -- "the Deep
dark" -- except for Tuesdays and Thursdays if she has no
other engagement, which she often does (and no doubt
will continue to). She feels a strong need to be able
to talk regularly about the latest gossip and news and
hot-button and often even cold-button issues. Usually
doesn't like to get it on until that sort of stuff's all
been aired. Finds it too distracting, as noted before.
-- So, a little conflict there.)
        -- And by the way, last week she lobbied for
another change in our nookie routine. Before then we
were trying to alternate (provisionally, to be sure):
first the middle of her night, then the middle of mine.
But she said the morning rounds were leaving her too
"postcoitally languorous" at work and so she asked me to
"collaboratively agree" to limit loveplay to the middle
of her night (that is, when I come to bed after arriving
home from work at half past one) and not to keep her
awake after three. (And this boosted last night's
tension: I didn't even make it to bed before three. And
at ten to three she stumbled out naked in pursuit of a
snack and suddenly lit into me for "ignoring" her, which
she viewed as retaliation for her "gimme buff" rejection
of the previous night. -- Some truth to this, I
suppose. Mostly I thought I was just trying to dodge
another wrangle. Instead I provoked a worse one.)
        -- All this from the black armchair in the living
room. Five p.m. now. And I need a shower bad. Must
gird up for the scope battles ahead. -- And by the way,
I'm still trying to adjust to the non-Z parts of the new
life. All's not yet sufficiently "in train." My
eating, working out, bill-paying, letter-writing, tax-
figuring, walking, writing, revising, reading, jyzing --
all still a mishmash. Build outward from the daily
breakfast at home, that's the new strategy. And

meanwhile continue with all the little settling-in
tasks. The art worktable over there is now stabilized,
the surface installed, the shelves up, the white
banker boxes all unpacked -- but the table's still
groaning under massive unorganized piles of stuff of
all sorts and kinds, some still mostly unknown to me.

Did I say? Looks like my two favorite plants from
B-2 days, the hardy fuchsias, are done for. However my
hair's getting fairly long again and that's good. And Z
has reversed herself and said she likes my short green
hooded canvas jacket after all. ("I don't always stay
in the same place, you know. What looks good one week
might be unbearable the next.")

Five Valentine's cards she sent me in the mail. An
amusing poem titled "Ol' Possum, Meet Ol' N'dow." She's
still saying I'm "prettiest and funniest" when I've just
awakened. We're in a down cycle, relatively speaking,
it's true, but reasons for hope still abound.

7

Funky black armchair again. Finally toggling back
into jyze (but looking forward to it the whole gap
period, with some deepening anxiety toward the end until
I remembered once again it's all just trippin' anyway).

Got up late, by about an hour or so. Not bad,
though this week I'd intended to be tougher on myself on
wake-up times. The usual extended breakfast, slow and
easy, and for once with the bulk of the newspapers
already read (by virtue of Z's impulsively staying home
sick yesterday, though she wasn't very sick, if at all,
and said as much herself). So I focused instead on my
stack of unread periodicals, which has mounted

alarmingly high during this transitional settling-in
period. And cleaned up the kitchen. And hatched a plan
for nudging jyze back on track in the next few weeks.
(The test will be: do I find myself going at it the day
before Z's birthday, that is, eve of the Caesarian ides?
-- But how unrealistic, to expect such a thing when
surely I'll be immersed in frantic last-minute gift-
conjuring. However, we'll see.)

Prickly heat on forehead and scalp, under arms, in
crotch and behind knees. It's just hitting now. I'm
wearing two heavy long-sleeve henleys, so off with one
and let's see what that does for me (it's the blue one
that goes, a traditional winter favorite, now fraying at
the cuffs). -- The sun's popped out a few times this
afternoon, and the days have mostly been warmer than
usual in this second straight exceptional El Nino winter
(as the globe heats up like a shut-in with a fever and
everyone argues ridiculously about whether it's really
happening). And despite all this it's surprising how
rarely unit 203 here gets chilly, not to say cold, even
though we hardly ever turn on the heat. Presumably our
location in the building has a lot to do with this, as
does the fact that Thuy and the kids in 303 directly
above are almost always home. It also could be that
Aboula and his wife, directly below in 103, like to keep
their place tropically hot (from their accents we're
guessing they're recent immigrants from East Africa).

In any event our heating bill should be very low.
And that's good because I'm living on the edge again
financially. And tax time is coming up. Word has it
the forms will be quite complex this year for do-it-
yourselfers like me, and especially for those of us who
report capital gains (as I do, though I'd much prefer
not to, and one of these days I might even close out the
deep-reserves account because of this).

Well what the hey, life on the home front is good.
It's going along quite well. Could it be better? Not
much, I'd say. Basically for the past year I've been on
a rapture float. I've been a drooling idiot of delight.
(It was just about a year ago today that Z's first

postcard came in from a certain remote mountain resort, "and on that day the world changed forever.")

So we fight a bit every now and then. As Z says herself, she just can't stand too much happiness. She needs to be able, at times anyway, to see herself as the Wicked Witch of South Hill. Wotta drag -- but you gotta take the frictional with the smooth. Not even in outer space can things be totally drag-free. And wouldn't you know she insists our fighting is all "systemic" and it's not just her fault, the G-man has something to do with it too. (Well yeah, I suppose. I guess if I were playing my appointed role I'd find some way to distract her from her own witchy/bitchy tendencies -- is that it? Could be, sure. I think so. But it's too deep and complicated for us to be able to reach anything beyond shakily provisional understanding just yet.) (Gives us something to grapple with on the slow days.)

The series of Valentine's quarrels came to a head when I staggered in from work last Friday night. She talked extreme talk and even did one of her Hollywood-class flaming stomp-outs. "Will you please let me know if it's over for good!" -- and SLAM!! goes the door to her room. (I'd insist from here to Doomsday nothing I said or did suggested I wanted it to be over for even one second.) Then when I reminded her -- through the closed door -- of her vow to abstain from high-drama stomp-outs, she surprised me by stomping right back into the living room. And after a couple of grindingly intense hours of struggle there in the streetlight-lit, sharply shadowed predawn, she in her chair and me in mine, we made up and she even sidled grudgingly over to sit on my lap and we got into some consolatory nuzzling.

At least she's now more aware that I dislike her running to her friends when we're fighting to wail about what a monster I am. And supposedly we've installed a tough new fail-safe mechanism. If the fighting escalates beyond the bearable (including my withdrawals-in-place) either of us can utter the term "moskstraumen" (Norwegian for a giant maelstrom: her idea, of course, after coming across the term in the news) and the other

will pull back, sheathe all weapons, and extend a kind
of life support, to the extent possible.

(In truth I think all's fine between us. So we
fight a little, big deal. -- But didn't I just say
that? So this time I must be saying it for emphasis.
Nail it! Nail that ukase! -- But I do wish she'd let
herself be a bit happier with what we've got going. For
some reason she can't see how astoundingly good it is
despite our many flaws and especially my sexual one.)

-- Quarter to four now. Tonight we'll be heading
over to Jess and Gwen's to put in a long weekend of
house-sitting while they go snowboarding. Meanwhile
June will be staying here, just because she feels lonely
in her big empty house in the northern burbs with her
boys off at school, and therefore Z and I will need to
be cleaning up a little before we leave. But only a
little. We're still just about where we were last week
as far as the settling-in goes and can do only so much
in an hour or two. The mounds of boxes, less
spectacular than they were two or three weeks ago but
still impressive, will stay pretty much as they are
until next week at the earliest. But it's fine in here
once you slide past them, very comfortable. And June's
visited us enough to know how to slide past them.

One of the reasons Z likes to house-sit for Jess
and Gwen, she says, is that their house is freestanding,
"a real house," and therefore she feels she can let go
vocally during sex. (And boy, does she ever do just
that. Even here sometimes. Even if we can hear Aboula
and/or his wife moving around directly below and/or Thuy
playing bouncy-ball with the kids directly above.)
-- And this will be the perfect time for Z to break
loose like that because we're on a tear right now, just
can't get enough. In the past week we've launched into
three long sessions, each several hours or more, plus
numerous shorter ones. Her hookey-playing day,
yesterday, what an afternoon. Hoo the whiff! And the
makeup session after the fights ended, that was even
better. Did she have pop! (Even I did: four times in
twenty-four hours, though then I needed forty-eight

hours plus to recover.)

Quite often these days she's wondering aloud if anyone else as far beyond their first teenage hormonal surge as we are is so heavily into rutting. We both doubt it -- though neither would we want to claim we're anything special. But oh how she can O. O after O after O -- and never an O OD! Can anyone else in the world O as Z can? Probably, sure -- but I do wonder.

-- And she gave me a postcard: a copy of the cover from a schlocky old private-eye mystery, "Finger Man." Hmm. True, I'm still not ejaco-shagging her (and I didn't mean to imply otherwise in writing "rutting"), even though at times I've felt it was on the verge. Something about our dynamics has been bollixing it up. I'm mystified just what it is. But I'm still willing to go with the flow (or lack of it, yes). I've asked her to tell me, if I'm stiffened up, just when she wants ol' Possum to push on in. But she doesn't do it. Not yet. Even so I continue to believe the ejaco-shag impasse will soon give way. Then again I think both of us would be plenty happy to stick with what we have right now. I mean, reproduction is not in the cards for us (for sure!), so why should a shag require an ejac?

Meanwhile this is the Katgrrrl's birthday week. Saturday she was over here most of the day and we took her to a movie that evening as an early birthday present. This was "The Borrowers," my first kids' movie since "The Bad News Bears" half a lifetime back with Lady V and Danny. Kat and I also did some rasslin' on the bed and played various kinds of high-energy games in the garage -- I spin her around, we kick a ball, we nerf it up. Can't deny I'm crazy about the grrrl. (Z said she might've given up on me last week had it not been for the "Kat factor," how hurt Kat would be to lose me, "her one and only subuncle." No way do I believe Z would've really sent me packing, but neither would I want to say the "Kat factor" is anything less than crucial for both of us.)

Tuesday the grrrl turned eight. Z and I went over to her and Betty's place for a home-cooked dinner of

barbecued ribs, just the four of us. We came bearing
stacks of gifts -- da kid is spoiled, and how! From me
a J-book, a necklace kit, a sticker book, and a black
felt detective's fedora (and I wondered if unconsciously
I'd picked out this hat because it reminded me of photos
I'd seen of Central and South American indigenous women
wearing similar ones). A picturesque double row of
"luminary" bagged candles greeted us along the outside
walk. Kat was so excited -- in sparkling form. After
dinner she and I played hide-and-seek upstairs and then
she invited me into her room and gave me a present of my
own: a little green rubber frog on which she'd written
"I love you Glen! -- Kat." -- And Saturday we'll be
chaperoning twenty kids at her birthday roller-skating
party. Oooeee, this is all a monkeybarrelful of fun....
     And it's all Z's doing that suddenly I have such a
full and lively and lovely life. And it's just one way
of a thousand she's so damn good for me.
     -- For ongoing stuff, start with Z's concern that
cigarette smoke is sneaking into our main bathroom via
the vent system. This is kicking up all sorts of queasy
paranoia about pollutants and chemical sensitivities
(like her friend Olwen's). Z wants to buy an automatic
closer for that bathroom door because, despite her
frequent reminders, I sometimes forget to shut it before
leaving 203 in the afternoon. (And this paranoia of
hers, which is of course at least partly justified,
deepens when she's feeling poorly, since she suspects
the chemicals are making her ill. And being ill itself
brings on childhood memories of how she hated to be
taken off to the hospital for foot operations and how
her father coddled her and this gives her the notion I
ought to be doing the same -- with chicken soup and at
least symbolic "gam cackers" (since their high sugar
content now causes her to shun the real things) and lots
of fawning solicitude, which indeed I'd be happy to
provide if only she'd give me a chance. But before I
can start in on it she's gone off in another direction.
Ooh ooh ooh she can be a pouter and a whiner when sick.
And at other times too, but at least then with a less

wrenching intensity. -- But "in sickness and health,"
wasn't that part of the Deep deal? I acknowledge it
was. Tacitly part of it, true, but still real enough.)
     What else? She's been taking down the recycling
handbills she posted at various spots around the
building and also the signs she hung near the mailbox
cluster asking residents to help with trash removal.
All for "retooling": newer, bigger, better versions will
soon be going up. In our ongoing morality play it seems
I'm destined to be the one who's forever advising her to
tone it down, not to harangue people too much, not to
take strong measures too quickly. (I mention seeing a
hooker working the busy corner half a block south of our
house and Z's immediately on the phone to the cops.)
     Things don't stand still. She's reading a new pop-
psych book supposedly based on chaos theory. This was
recommended by a woman whose seminar she attended
Valentine's week (a woman whose nostrums, it turns out,
also helped spark Z's sudden displeasure with our life
together that week). "The Tao of Chaos" or something
like that. Now I'll probably have to read it myself
just to have some idea what Z's talking about. -- And I
overheard her advising her friend Irene on the phone to
try an exercise promulgated at this same seminar,
starting with "Tap your knees twice and imagine you're
in a theater with your problem on the screen" and then
it became doubly and triply reflexive ("Imagine your
highest and best self watching you walk out of the
theater...."). But at least she has a sense of humor
about all this stuff, Z does. Now she's starting out
her nightly notes to me with "Tap your knees twice...."
     (During the fights she came within a whisker of
seeing a "counselor" about our conflicts. That's what
she told me afterwards. And I replied she oughta be
proud she didn't give in to the urge. To her our
differing views on the usefulness of psych "counseling"
derive from our Catholic/Protestant split: I like to be
self-sufficient, she likes to seek authoritative help.
This is another ongoing theme for us and also an ongoing
source of disgruntlement for me. I think she makes way

too big a deal of our differences as a cause of trouble
rather than as a source of inspiration and fascination.
She thinks this view of mine itself is a manifestation
of our Catholic/Protestant split. And she just might
be right or at least partly right. -- But I still think
our chances are good for dodging a Deep version of a
Hundred Years War. Nor do I hesitate to tell her so.)
      And then her office life. The developments there
are steeped in irony as she and the other champions of
diversity grump and grumble about Roy, their newly
selected boss -- a black man. The makings of a raw TV
drama are here: "The Trash Team." Jess threatening to
sue because she, an out white lesbian, was passed over
for the same position and now Roy's allies are accusing
her of having it in for black hetero males. Leola,
black and hetero herself, was also passed over and sees
an antiwoman conspiracy at work (possibly an ageist one
too, but she decided to drop that angle) -- and she's
refusing to attend unit meetings. Roy, poor guy, has
not one minute of management experience. White hetero
Dale, who picked him (probably, in Z's view, under
orders from higher-ups), is now sending out bathetic
bulletins raving about the slave-mutiny movie "Amistad."
-- Every day Z regales me with the latest twists and
turns in the tale. And I'm glad she does. Only trouble
is I have nothing a tenth so good to offer in return.
      -- Well, not nothing. An occasional morsel. For
one, a small crisis arose at the scope office this week
when some important mail disappeared and I became the
default suspect. Since I work alone at night and rarely
interact with the day crew they automatically finger me
when they discover something's missing or out of place.
A flurry of calls followed. Turned out the latest new-
hire janitor, another recent African immigrant and
totally confused about what's expected of him, thought
the mail (splashed on the carpet next to the entrance-
door mail slot after a Saturday delivery) was trash and
tossed it when he found it still there during his
Sunday-night round. He fessed up. So far, I'm happy to
say, but also surprised to say, he hasn't been fired.

[Can This Be Jyze?]

     -- But should I go for a more involved life?
Dabble in political stuff again? I'm thinking about it.
At times it becomes a little embarrassing to be such a
do-nothing "white-boy artist type" among all these gung-
ho activists of color and/or nonvanilla gender identity.
How long can I hold out? Well, it's something to
explore. No hasty new commitments. Not when I've
already sold my soul to the exalted high deities of jyze
just so I can be churning out these pages right here.

                        8

     Okay, I'm back. See what I can do. This time
starting out at the hideaway, half past ten on a
nondescript Monday evening exactly 364 days after the
Monday evening Z and I first talked on the phone.
Tomorrow night we'll be celebrating the anniversary in
the way we celebrate best (except Z's in the midst of
her first herpes outbreak in several months so ol'
Possum's playmate ol' Peaches will be under quarantine).
     Door open a crack, fan blowing air out. Nobody
around. I'm feeling a little sad, I don't know why.
Probably because I still don't know how to cope with
this stunning new life. Maybe it's just too rich for
me. It gets away from me sometimes, perhaps because I'm
adjusting too slowly, and generates some chaos. But if
I were to adjust more quickly I couldn't savor the
richness. -- Oh well. This is not a complaint; it's
just a blurt of dumbfoundedness. Yet another!
     (Muscles creaking sorely as I shift about in the
venerable brown armchair. Today I worked out at the WOC
-- for a while with Z and Leola -- and pushed up one
more notch toward all-out physical engagement. I'm just

about there now. It's another phased transition which
has taken much longer than anticipated. Too many
transitions going on at once in my life -- obviously.
But so be it. No big deal really. S'all right.)
     -- Alas, we're still fighting more than I'd like, Z
and I. This J-week we mixed it up twice, once minorly
and once majorly (so majorly we both forgot to invoke
"mokstraumen"). Now Z's vowing to tone down the
feistiness for a while and promising our domain will be
much more peaceable. "Unconditional cherishment" is the
new watchphrase. I like it! But then today's note she
left for me gives some pause. It says she wants to
"balance support and leveling." Ulp. At this point I'd
like at least five parts of support for each one of
leveling. To me leveling means saying something cruel
that nonetheless must be said because things have gotten
dangerously out of whack -- and damn the consequences.
     We do give pretty damn good note, I'll say, both of
us. Dozens in a week -- way too many for me to post
more than a few samples in these pages. And once in a
while, inevitably, we miscommunicate. A note of hers
taped on the bathroom door, "T-ZIN NO MORE," as I read
it, helped provoke the big fight. I thought it was
referring to our botched erotic signals of the previous
night and was saying she'd henceforth dispense with the
prickteasing (which is what she herself had called it).
But the pun she'd intended was a different one -- not
"TEASIN' NO MORE" but "J -- ZIN NO MORE" -- reminding
the jyzer ("J") not to leave the bathroom door open.
What I thought was a T and a hyphen was, she insisted,
an artifact of hasty writing which to her was "hardly
even unclear" and should've been legible to me in any
case "because you've seen enough of my sloppy J's by
now." (And I should also be well aware she likes to
convert "S" to "Z" to make things sound more personal,
as when she calls me her "Zole Mate." So then when I
did indeed leave the bathroom door open right after
reading the note (probably because the note distracted
me!) and she discovered this, she flew into a rage. To
her it was obvious: either I didn't believe her or I

didn't care, and therefore I was a "hopeless case." And it escalated from there, Friday night into Saturday afternoon. (I was furious that she would attack me like this over an innocent misreading.)

Ancient history now. We're even experimenting with keeping the offending bathroom door open at night after having vacuumed around the ceiling fan which Z suspects is venting toxic gases (possibly Aboula's or Felicia's smoking -- he in 103, she in 202 -- is the source by some sort of backdraft action). Maybe we'll install an air cleaner in the bedroom. And I'll be trying again to do better at saying "ouch" when something she says really hurts. (This time she did most of the giving -- she knew very well she'd gone way over the top -- but I wanted to give some too. -- And she doesn't fail to let me know her sudden attack-dog outbursts are mild by the standards of the tough inner-city hood where she grew up. And reminds me she was brainwashed by her mother to believe no one would ever love her -- that she was a kind of freak, as symbolized by the extra toes which the surgeons lopped off, and therefore undeserving of love. Also, her mother, a blond, truly believed that gents love only blonds.)

This was a bad fight. Yet next to all the good stuff that happened as a result of it, it now looks even more minor than the other fight, the one I previously dubbed minor (that one hinged on my stupidly answering in the affirmative her smart-ass question about whether any of my previous girlfriends had ever commented about the ass-seam on my jeans not being straight). Sunday morning -- aiiieee. No woman's ever made love to me like this. Nor even come close. And then there were the two new poems she wrote (one about the ass-seam incident). The mash notes stashed everywhere. The crazed humping at Jess and Gwen's, Z's lovesounds so wild they set all the dogs to howling, first the ones in the house and then the ones in the hood and finally what seemed like every goddamn dog north of the ship canal (and she vowed not to do that again).

And: the goofy/mushy telephone calls during the

day. The "ratification" affection in public at the co-
op and the supermarket (the south-end branches of both).
The sparky conversations about numerous matters, and
best of all about James H.'s alternative-psych books
(which she's suddenly focusing on after my yearlong
sporadic attempts to steer her to them as an antidote to
the leadership institute's combative family-psych
rugged-individualist "assertiveness" stuff).

(Notes secreted where? Hers in my coffee cup or
coffee-filter holder, in the microwave, in my bathroom
drinking cup; mine under her pillow, tethered to her
toothbrush, inside a book she's reading.)

-- And we're still grappling with the sleep issue.
A magazine article convinced her our brains will be
fricasseed if we sleep fewer than eight and a half
hours a night. Worse, we'll stop being creative. And
those eight and a half hours must come in a solid block.
Therefore, the middle of the night is pretty much ruled
out for loving. But the early morning has already been
ruled out because loving at that hour leaves her
fending off the postcoital blahs all day while trying
to deal with those unending "Trash Team" crises. So
we're now joking ruefully about our sex life grinding
to a halt except on weekends. (And even then we should
be racking up the zees.) Related to all this, I found
a very funny hand-drawn movielike poster for "Z & G's
8-1/2" tacked to the bedroom door when I arrived home
one night, the theme line warning "Nookie delayed is
nookie denied." One of Z's finer creations. (This is
another area where she leaves anyone I've been with
before sprawled in the dust.)

-- And so, to skip over lots of juicy details, I'm
now thinking what I should do is tamp down on the eros
for a while. What the hell. Weekends and Tuesday and
Thursday evenings when she gets home and any other late
nights/early mornings when either of us just gotta have
it -- that should be enough.

I've also abandoned my experiment with rising at
nine-thirty every day. It was leaving me too tired to
work out. And why strain to hit the sack before three

a.m. if we'd just be sleeping? True, a new crunch would
appear when I arose at noon if I wanted to be out of the
house by two, so I decided to cut back breakfast reading
to no more than an hour. The other hour I'll try to
hold steady, devoting it mainly, as now, to household
chores, with any leftover minutes going to catching up
on periodicals and the occasional book chapter. (But
these days most of my book-reading takes place on either
the homeward-bound bus or at one of the two downtown
stops where I wait for that bus's arrival at 1:15 a.m.)

     This too an experiment. And I'll continue taking
some of my own work home for editing/revising on Tuesday
and Thursday afternoons (since on those days at least in
theory Z and I meet at home for dinner and nookie).

     Nookie nookie. Yeeee-ha! Last week, though, Z
bummed me out a bit by griping about the struggles she's
had to undergo in adjusting to being (not to mince words
here) finger-fucked so much after "a whole adult
lifetime of clamping on penises whenever I wanted to."
Sheez. Admittedly I have no right to complain given ol'
Possum's continuing waywardness (though by hand she can
now make the beast come alive almost at will -- not just
roll over and play but stand up and spurt). And she
proclaimed her pleasure with the strengthening effect
which the wild-yam applications (three times daily, I
think it is) have had on her tender vaginal membranes.
-- But then, POW, a couple of nasty-looking clusters of
small white blisters riding atop dime-size red welts
appeared on the sides of her pretty little ass cleft
about an inch behind her "bahookie" (anus). At first
she thought they were something else because her herpes
outbreaks have always been more like canker sores
located on or near the perineum. Then in the herpes
literature she found some photos of outbreaks that
closely resembled these new ones. (All this was back on
Friday or Saturday. Today the blisters are gone and the
welts are fading rapidly.)

     (And I suppose it's fortunate we weren't nookie-
making during the most infectious period. I'm still not
sure, though: wouldn't it be easier for both of us if I

too had this annoying disease? She dislikes the notion,
however, so I'll keep trying to stay herpes-free. But I
won't go so far as using condoms. And this means I'll
almost certainly fall victim to the malady sooner or
later -- and knowing now that her case of it is becoming
more active, probably sooner.)

       -- Today, by the way, a big story on the spread of
STDs in the U.S. hit the news, with herpes ranking, as
it happens, among the most common but also the least
harmful. But this doesn't prevent Z from feeling she's
part of the epidemic and she's being punished for her
"zin" (as we know she likes to spell it) of having been
so sexually active in earlier years. "Promiscuous." I
tell her I don't see it that way -- and I don't, since
in those years the oncoming explosion of STDs looked so
unlikely -- and this does seem to make her feel better.
What I'm really trying to do, though, is counteract the
Catholic guilt thing she has -- and she calls it that
herself -- about God punishing her for being too happy.)
                              *

       Midnight now, straight up. I'm just back from the
men's room. It's still true, I'm holding the fort all
by myself, this whole building. Or at least I can
detect no sign of any other human presence (as, through
an abundance of dangling and thickly leaved philodendron
tendrils, some at least twenty feet long, I gaze up past
four floors of balconies to the darkened north skylight).
It's amusing to think I'm almost an old-timer here now
in my tiny J. Ink office as other tenants move in and
out on all sides. If I'm not wrong, only two occupants
of the dozen or so offices closest to mine are the same
as on the day I first set up shop here a little over two
years ago. And since it's a good bet Z and I will make
Jyze City our permanent home and I doubt I'll give up
this space so long as I'm physically capable of getting
to it, someday -- maybe not all that far off -- I really
will be a building old-timer.

       I'm still not coming down here anywhere near as
often as I did before meeting Z. And when I do drop by,
I'm staying nowhere near as long. Happily, I'd say, now

that I have someone at home I might in theory want to
get away from, to hide out from, I find I don't need to
do so and the hideaway's existence becomes almost
superfluous. But only almost -- not completely. Having
it is still very good psychologically. It's always
here if I need it, and knowing that, I don't need it, or
need it much less than I otherwise might. Also its
existence is useful for boosting my own belief in the
proposition that I'm a serious writer, when by most
standard definitions I think I'd have to concede I'm
not. (Which doesn't mean I'm buying the standard
definitions. On the contrary, I'd contend I'm as
serious as they come. But once in a while when
nothing's going well I start to waver.) -- And the fact
that this office is located just a single diagonal
block southwest of Z's office at the utility lends the
"work world" aspect of our relationship an aura of
closeness and balance which we both like a lot.

     And so, and so? Less than an hour now until the
last bus home. What to squeeze in?

     At least mention my frustration with the shortage
of time, how ironic it is and how acutely aware of its
ironic nature I am. -- What, me stressed out because I
can't find enough hours in the day to scan the
newspapers and flip through a magazine or two?

     -- Okay, okay, drop that line. Go to Kat's
birthday party at the roller-skating rink. Out in the
sticks. Kat the cutest kid I ever did see, including
even the previously untoppable tykes of Japan and Korea.
Oh that dazzling deep-dimpled Mayan smile! Kat in jeans
darting about on her white-and-pink roller blades, long
jet-black hair flying. Z looking mighty fine herself in
a black fedora identical to the one I'd bought earlier
for Kat (Z fell for it when I had her try it on at home
and secretly bought another one at the same shop the
next day to surprise me with at Kat's party).

     Then, alas, Z suddenly felt sick as we were leaving
the rink. Bad stomach. Bad sick too -- wailing in the
car. An emergency antacid stop at a nearby drugstore.
At first she begged me to take her home but I managed to

persuade her we'd be better off going to Betty and Kat's
place as planned, since it was much closer and Betty's
a nurse by profession. And once there she, Z, quickly
recovered after maybe twenty minutes of intensive
nursing by the Deep himself in the garret bedroom (Betty
and Kat hadn't returned yet but Z has a key for their
back door). The Deep did his very best to minister to
her just as her daddy used to do. (As she pointed out,
for eight years she's fallen ill alone and grumpily
retreated into solitude, so now she scarcely knows any
other way. -- And she does bring up this eight-year
business way too often for my taste, and especially
during fights. "Glen, I've lived alone for eight years.
I'm not used to trying to get along with someone." All
I can do is point out it hasn't been eight, it's been
fifteen, since she never did officially live with Jerry
II. But then a few days later she's back with the eight
years again. My conclusion is that in her own mind she
really did live with Jerry II. -- But then shouldn't
this mean she'd have an easier time living with me?
It's not really all that new to her after all?)
     Meanwhile a new reason for her to feel insecure
(and me too): our next-door neighbors were robbed in
broad daylight. This was Friday before last and I
happened to be home at the time. I heard a big boom but
thought it came from upstairs, where Doug and Thuy's
kids had been jumping around noisily as they frequently
do. This boom was so loud I wondered idly if D&T had
finally found a new house and begun to move out -- maybe
a mover had dropped a heavy box or one end of a couch.
Instead, as I soon learned, someone had kicked in the
door of unit 202 just a few feet from our front door.
Most likely the culprits were acquaintances of Felicia
and Derrick, the Afrusan couple living there, or
otherwise why that particular apartment (they had hosted
a big party a week ago)? Poor Derrick. When he arrived
home from work he knocked on our door in hopes we'd seen
something -- he was in shock, his hands visibly shaking.
Their door was splintered, the frame gone. TV, VCR,
laptop, jewelry, various other items missing.

[Can This Be Jyze?]

(When Z learned about this she immediately swung
into action with a letter to Min, the landlord,
demanding the ground-floor lobby door be repaired.
Actually I was able to fix it myself the next day --
spurred on by guilt for having dissuaded Z earlier from
writing Min about it. But I still think her complaints
about shortcomings in the building will wind up causing
us more grief than having them repaired would clear up.)
      -- And this reminds me: Flora C., the locally well-
known radical activist at the utility, seventy-four
years old and retired for several years, died this week.
Z knew her well but didn't care for her all that much --
because, ironically (what, me overuse the term?), she
found her too pushy and controlling -- but from what
little I know of her she was quite a lot like Z (though
no way such a fox). Some say Z's reputation as a loose
cannon/boat rocker/"conscience of the utility" has been
second only to Flora's. Now she may rise to No. 1.
      And another friend of Z's died this week. Another
funeral. In retrospect Z thought this death -- and its
reminder of Manny's, Ruth's, Julie K.'s -- was what
caused her low mood leading to our big fight.
      The feisty one. I've known it from the start
(which now that we're past midnight was one year ago
today). No doubt she'll never lack for grounds for new
feistiness episodes. I still think I can handle them.
I'm also still hopeful they'll detensify somewhat over
time, at least as they apply to the two of us. I'm a
believer! This week I chained her love rock to the
small erotic meditation hippo after she'd complained
that Possum's erratic behavior was putting her into a
double bind, maybe even a quadruple bind (invite him in
or not was one of them). "Bound for bliss," said the
label on the chain. My attached note pointed out that a
true admirer of "The Story of O" would be calling for
Possum to double and redouble the binds (every now and
then she reminds me how disturbingly erotic "O" was for
her -- and still is, I don't doubt -- but then she tries
to play it down again, possibly for fear I'll think
she's too much like Lady V). And I left her a couple of

[Deep Jyze]

"POSS/PUSS Forever!" notes.   -- And the point of citing
all these things now? They worked! She loved them!
     Doesn't mean the fights will go extinct, no. Does
mean, however, I think we can "go deep" and undermine
them. Cut off some of their fuel. (For her, "go deep"
has a more meditative meaning, connoting not movement
toward greater understanding, whether conscious or
otherwise, but movement into a noncognitive realm where
understanding is superfluous -- as suggested, for
instance, by that "breathe deep" line in the very first
poem she ever gave me. But I'm guessing this will turn
out to be a distinction without a whole lot of
difference. And even if not, I still believe we can "go
deep" in both ways at once. And others as well, sure!
Both capped and not: deep or Deep (or D'eep, fine).
-- I mean, who's going to stop us except ourselves?)

9

     Beneath a ceiling-clinging cluster of birthday
balloons. The black armchair (where Z prefers to sit
when I'm not around, she's admitted, because it's
farther away from those microwave-emitting electrical
wires attached to the side of the building). Somehow
I've frittered away most of the afternoon, leaving
myself only about an hour for what I'd thought would be
a big jyze carnival. True, I'm a day late already, and
in fact the entry intended for yesterday had already
been postponed two days. Obviously I didn't make it
here before Z's birthday and so I flunked the test I
set for myself an entry or two back.
     Today is St. Patrick's Day. This is the month of
anniversaries. One more big one still to go, our Meet

Day on the 29th. After that I hope to do better at
thinking about other things, including my own personal
projects. (Or maybe I'll have to wait until after
April 15, Tax Day, for those. -- Most likely, yeah.)

But the big one, Z's birthday, is now out of the
way. Not that it wasn't a fine occasion, because it
was. Exciting, touching, fun. Revealing too. But the
stress of coming up with something -- or rather lots of
things -- to make her feel feverishly fussed over --
original stuff, at the very least on a par with the
stuff of our earlier celebrations -- yes, I can breathe
a lot easier now. Meet Day anniversary, momentous
though it is, won't call for nearly so elaborate an
effort. Or at least that's how I look at it right now.

A six-foot-long "Happy Birthday" banner (with
scores of custom annotations) still hangs a few feet to
my right, suspended on a clothesline above the high
counter between the kitchen and dining area. A similar
banner, even bigger, and much more X-rated in its
annotations, hangs on the wall above our bed.

She couldn't recall how she celebrated her birthday
last year. But I don't think she'll soon forget this
year's. It included a stroll through the quad at the U
which might be called the Early Taste of Global Broiling
Birthday Ramble, because this year's monster El Nino
caused the cherry trees there to blossom more than a
month early. The festivities also featured a brief
quarrel over one of her "ice-overs" which led to a
lengthy intimate talk in bed. In the end she proclaimed
herself to be both deeply happy and deeply in love --
and also fell into a daze because, as she said,
sometimes she still can't believe this love is for real
and fears she'll lose it. She told me again I'm not
only her dream lover (and of course "biggest challenge")
but also, again, and more fervently than ever, her
"zole mate," "like a best girlfriend too."

It keeps getting better. We're fighting at times,
yes, but the cycles appear to be slowly spiraling down,
not up. And she sees it this way just as much as I do.

More birthday details. She'd announced beforehand

a desire to stay home all weekend, lounge around, "read mysteries and drink wine and fuck-fuck-fuck." That's pretty much how it went down too, except her lingering herpes outbreak put a damper on the F-F-F part (even though reading the book "Spending" kept her on a high sexual sizzle). In her words: "It wasn't just a birthday, it was a birthweekend!" Friday evening she and "the grrrls" went out for dinner and "to get drunk" at a fancy wine bar, with D'Arcy also celebrating ---

*   *

-- Right there she arrived home a little early. Nookie city! (Tuesday and Thursday evenings, the only times during the workweek we see each other at home when neither of us is at least putatively in a sleep period.) -- And now it's a Thursday, two days later, pretty much the same time and station. One other difference, though: tonight we'll be making a shopping run and on the way back she'll drop me off downtown. No nookie this round. -- But nookie is especially good these days, and also intriguing. On the phone today she said she wants to start writing about it. "It keeps changing! It's never the same!"

But are we sexually consummated yet? Not at all. If we were, the nookie probably wouldn't be changing nearly as much. And besides, we're still constrained by the herp. She's wearing intentionally unsexy "H-rag unners" to bed just so I'll be reminded of her status. We're at a stage now where finger-fucking is okay again, but afterwards I hold my hand limply aloft (goofing) to keep it from touching anything until I can wash up. Another day or two of this, though, and we'll be back to the consummation chase.

Oh the humiliations and embarrassments of aging. And so run-of-the-mill they are! -- But is that what's happening here? Even in retrospect I may never know. Only if we do manage to consummate and then get into a regular consummatory rutting routine of some sort will I know for sure aging wasn't the culprit.

Regardless I'm a happy camper these days. In so many ways life is so good right now. Obviously this

can't last forever (and just today -- though scarcely
for the first time -- Z announced that in her view we're
no longer in "limerence/loverence") but I'm still hoping
for a good long blissed-out run. And I'm ready to work
my glutes off doing whatever it takes to make it happen.
I'm dedicated. I'm sold. I'm pumped. (Though alas
only metaphorically pumped and not so much physically --
not when and where it counts most. Though in a sense
this makes the metaphorical part all the better.)

Goofball note exchanges the past few days saluting
our "Merxx Day anniversary." Puns. In honor of my
comment a year ago in the messenger-service note -- jyze
rules exception on "Merxx," the name of the service --
about getting my nose inside the tent, two nights ago
she threw a sheet over the bedroom door and called it
the entrance to our camels' tent. In return I entwined
a couple of kiri ribbons, including the one I sent her
in the box last year, into a DNA double helix and said
that's how we're twisting in the wind now. "Luv U --
the original Mr. Twister" (another exception). And the
birthday balloons remain clustered overhead -- somewhat
shrunken, true, but still buoyant enough to stay aloft
-- and the big banners are also still hanging around.

Flowers profusely abloom everywhere in Jyze City
these days. Camellia, rhodies, hydrangea, azalea, many
others. Wotta extraordinary winter this has been!

No more time here today. Likely I'll be doing
another installment or two for this entry, stretching it
out into the weekend. Work late tonight and tomorrow
night, hit the WOC tomorrow afternoon, take care of Kat
Saturday afternoon while Z and Betty catch the Hollywood
blockbuster of the year, so maybe Sunday for jyze? Or
possibly I could try a late-night entry, because I'm
starting to stay up later again (trying to respect Z's
need for uninterrupted "power sleep," as she's calling
it nowadays, perhaps not entirely in jest -- but also I
enjoy having an hour or two for reading late at night
and I sleep better because I have more time to wind down
before hitting the sack).

A fine romance -- so the other parts of our lives

must become dull and ordinary? We've been talking about
this. I say they don't have to, but Z's resisting --
suspects I'm trying to repeat the way it was with some
other woman I lived with and she wants no part of that.
Where else, she observes, would my "wisdom" come from?
From the heart, sez I. Simple. But she still needs
persuading. (However: in the long run I don't think
we'll have much trouble keeping things fresh.) ---
                      *   *
    -- And right there she arrived home even a little
earlier than on Tuesday. So now it's Sunday evening,
three more days on. I in my newly hand-decorated "Katz"
shirt (the main decorations the little scamp put on it
being flowers, long-whiskered cats' faces, and a winged
heart) holding forth amid funky flapping flags of airing
gym gear in the hideaway. I'm nibbling at my self-made
and -packed lunch (Z saw me slapping it together -- a
first for her -- and seemed touched; just guessing, it
was probably because her father also made and packed his
own lunch). It's nine p.m. It's one of those nights
where I have little Jyzer Ink work to do and so should
be able to sling a fair amount of the jyzey good stuff
right here (and also type up more of last year's same
kind of good stuff at the scope office).
    (Pausing now to peel a banana.)
    Have to say it's not been a good weekend for Possum
the Penis. Over the entire three days, one measly ejac.
I sensed a Z meltdown coming on as a result, but today
she went off for an arboretum walk with her friend Olwen
and upon return reinvoked "unconditional cherishment."
But she also said, even while reassuring me our sex life
is "great," she's troubled because it doesn't fit her
longstanding mental picture of how a great sex life
oughta be. But then again she wonders why this should
make any difference if it's great anyway.
    I just keep trying to convince her I'm as pleased
as can be with that same sex life. Of course in a sense
it's not true, but this is not owing to any fault of
hers. And I'm plenty pleased enough with it regardless
of what's missing -- almost preposterously so, I'd say.

who could believe things would be this good? Not the
pre-Z me, that's for sure. (At one point this week she
stung me a little by quipping that we ball like a couple
of aliens. I tried to mask the sting by joking about my
middle and index fingers being a "dual reproductive
organ" just like those wielded by all other aliens from
my home galaxy. That odd-looking fleshy protuberance
dangling between my legs is of course an alien liver.)

     Also today we discovered our smoke alarm isn't
hooked up (apparently the previous occupants snipped the
wires). We presented Doug and Thuy, the folks upstairs,
with the remaining third of the huge apple pie Betty
baked for Z's birthday (and we learned that their smoke
alarm is properly hooked up). I installed Z's special
screen on the bedroom window, lining its one loose edge
with a piece of foam she hustled up for free from a
futon shop. And I -- for shame -- had a bad stomach
from (among other possible causes) eating too much apple
pie as well as a big bowl of shredded wheat topped by a
cup of mixed berries and literally had to shit into my
own hand as I made a mad dash for the toilet. Not a
pretty scene at all. Sure am glad no one was around to
witness it. But still, better a shit in the hand than
even a tenth of a handful of shit on Z's beloved
Nepalese dragon rug.

     Yesterday Kat. A grand time. Too short though.
And bizarre, because either I heard wrong or the box
office at the movie theater provided us with some bad
info and we arrived an hour and a half early to pick up
Z and Betty, and it was raining and Kat and I were
cooped up in the car for much of that time. Played a
whole lot of slap-hand games. Also did horsie rides in
the rain and checked out all the aisles of two nearby
grocery stores. -- Then to a late dinner at a sit-down
"south pole" restaurant with Z and Betty. Kat feeding
her electronic pet (a beeper going off) and becoming
absorbed in her hand-held electronic game gizmo while
sipping a huge fancy drink named for a child movie star
not half as cute and funny, all agree, as Kat herself.
(The waiter somehow misheard my order and brought the

wrong order of bourbon, but I was having such a good
time I didn't even notice until the bill appeared and I
saw what he'd written down. In retrospect I realized
the drink had tasted rather odd, but I had dimly assumed
that was just a matter of bad ice cubes or stale water.)
    -- I should go back. Z's birthday. The minifight.
Z's description of how her mother held her underwater in
the bathtub as a way of teaching her how dependent she
was: it scared Z "like nothing else ever" because she
thought she might really drown. The sexual abuse, her
mother would draw her to her naked breast in bed (they
slept together most nights until Z was eleven), saying,
"You used to suck here; don't you want to now?" or put
Z's hand on her genitals, Mama E's, saying, "You came
out of here. Don't you want to see how it feels now?"
We didn't go into how often these things happened or how
much pleasure, if any, her mother might've gotten from
them (Z herself got none as far as she remembers).
    It's not at all easy talking with her about such
matters. My natural inclination, given how little I
know about the real facts, is to try to play down the
"abusive" aspect of it -- try to see things in the best
possible light. To me there's a big gray area between
innocent playing around and true "bad" abuse. For Z
it's not so easy to see things this way, though she does
appear to have forgiven her mother.
    -- Meanwhile: the six-day experiment is over. I'm
going back to eight-day jyze. "Sixers" out, "eighters"
back in. Just have to be tougher with myself about
suspending some of my routine when J-day rolls around.
But rather than try to (A) catch up on all the pages I'm
behind or (B) give up on filling in the volume by its
May 1 deadline, I'll simply start over where I am. This
coming week, I'm saying. It's at least possible the
upheavals over moving in at 1511 and starting up our new
life together have subsided to the point where they'll
no longer overwhelm jyze protocol.
    Incoherent, yeah. Am I ever. It takes everything
I've got just to be able to work out at the WOC three
times a week. Scan the newspapers. Flip quickly

through the mags, reviews, journals. Snatch a few extra
winks now and then on the scope-office or hideaway
carpet. Keep my sweetie as happy as possible. (And
next Sunday, whooee, it's Meet Day anniverary. Maybe
that'll be the time to start up the new jyze regime.)

10

    Here's some tandem anniversary jyze. First time
ever! It's our meet cafe exactly one year after the day
that so hugely changed our lives (another such day,
yes). The very same seats. And, if we remember right,
the same refreshments: tea, cherry cider, oatmeal-raisin
cookie. And Zoelie. (She be jyzin' away too, her
notebook propped on her thigh, her knee propped on the
bench seat -- and she's wearing the same black tights;
and the back of my left hand -- here's a change for sure
-- is pressing against her right shin.)
    I'm dressed the same too, with a couple of close
substitutions (brown soccer shoes for the black chucks,
which are now part of my WOC gear; gray canvas shirt for
the green one, which has been banished to the repair bag
since it lost a button a few months ago). And I'm
decked out in different jewelry: the five-buck stars-
and-crescents "engagement ring" (but it really is that!)
which I've been wearing since last August and the
stainless-steel photo locket she gave me for Christmas.
    Sentimental fools, both of us. But me especially.
(For instance, she disliked "Wings of the Dove," which
we saw earlier this afternoon, because it's "one of
those twisted tragic love stories," whereas I liked it a
lot.) But our own personal sappy stuff works her up at
least as much as it does me; she just lets it show less.

(For instance, moments ago I gave her a little shrink-
plastic pendant I made for her to commemorate Meet Day;
she reacted to it just as she did to the "Comet Zoelie"
card I painted up for her a year ago, which is to say:
scarcely at all. But now I know how to read her a whole
lot better and I'm sure she likes it.)

Any doubt at all we'll be together forevermore?
None. Not on my side. And she reluctantly admits to
having none on hers either but says she's superstitious
about coming out and proclaiming it.

-- So will this love ever be consummated? Well,
here we have a much tougher question. (Hi Zoelie! She
flicks a scathing eyebrow at the two young women at the
next table talking loudly and pretentiously about their
Eurasiusan backgrounds -- taking what I call the hybrid-
vigor view of their own superior energy levels. "My,
my, my," confides Zoelie.) This morning we worked
diligently on consummating but didn't quite get there.
Twice we were carnally conjoined but neither time could
I come up with the jizz. She says she's now convinced
it's physiological. I say it's almost certainly not. I
say it's just gotta be a head case messing us up here
and of course mine's the head I'm talking about.

In any event, we've decided to try something new to
inaugurate our second year together. Or rather two new
things. First, strictly as an experiment, I'll be
touching her sexual parts only with my own sexual parts
(not with hands, lips, biceps, etc.); thus if she 'gasms
it'll be genitally induced. I proposed this with some
trepidation but she immediately agreed. She thinks it
might make things "more balanced between us." Oddly, I
too think it could work. It almost did today.

Second, no more talking about the foozle thing for
a whole year. Whatever ol' Possum does is right and
good and accepted, period, by both of us. And the same
goes for ol' Peaches.

Can we possibly abide by either of these vows? I
dunno. But might as well give them a try.

Speaking of one whole year, that's how long we've
already made it as a linked pair. We're there right

now. Today. This hour. Foozles or no. Mondo
conflicts or no. Or -- yes! All tangled up together!

     -- We hit most of the major anniversary spots,
starting with the magazine shop around the corner. I
learned something new: on that fateful first day she
drove her car down and parked it near the co-op. We
disagree about whether her red liner was or was not
zipped into her jacket. (She'd been intending to wear a
skirt today and do without underwear, then changed her
mind, I don't know why. Sentimental reasons maybe. She
was definitely wearing underwear a year ago: she's quite
clear on that.)

     (Has my jyze lost half a step since last year? Has
mutual entanglement slowed me down? Contentment?
Success? Love's labor found?)

     (Now she starts "playfully" punching my non-jyzing
arm because I'm ribbing her about the way she pressed me
to leave last year before I finished my cider -- then
did the same thing again a week later at the ORB cafe.)

     The day itself looks much like last year's Meet
Day. Sun's out and shadows are falling at an angle that
seems just right. Even the clouds look about the same:
impressively stratocumulo and abundant to the east above
the mountains (great cliche galleon fleets riding great
cliche stormy seas in ultra-slow and stately motion).

     "Okay," she announces, "I'm done. Let's go!"
-- With a big yuk. (Ooh how she hates to wait.
Patience is not her strong suit, nor is it her weak
suit; it's simply not in the cards. -- Now offers to
read aloud the part of her entry she thinks I'll like.
-- But no, she's started writing again. For her J-stick
today she's using Manny's ancient fountain pen, which
Betty gave her as a birthday gift two weeks ago.)

     -- Well, I knew I'd be unable to jyze up anything
worthy of the occasion. Not that it matters all that
much. -- So it's time to check out the part she thinks
I'll like.

*   *

     A day later. Live music playing downstairs, very
unusual for a Monday night. And the bass is as loud as

any I've heard up here. Everything in sight is
vibrating, my leg propped on the hassock included. The
leafy philodendron cascading down the side of the large
bookcase appears to have caught a severe case of
delirium tremens -- and an unusually rhythmic one too.

The hideaway. Now workout clothes are always
hanging everywhere. And something else new: I removed
those album pages of photos, the ones taken at home in
Gatewood with the whole family on my thirtieth birthday,
from the wooden display frame atop the glassed-in
bookcase. I put them up there roughly a year and three
days ago to be sure Z would see them on her very first
visit, and I took them down last week to be sure Z would
see their long-hidden backsides while she was looking at
my photo albums for the first time since then.

Yes, she's finally done it: begun checking out my
photo bona-fides. Last Friday night (after a late
workout at the WOC) we dined right here on takeout from
the Chinese place on the corner as she flipped through
the albums and pawed through the box. For the first
time she saw photos of Ladies S, K, and C, as well as of
Cindy L. and Karen A. -- and didn't seem bothered by any
of them. Maybe they didn't live up to her imaginings of
them? (Yes, she later confessed having feared they'd
"out-beauty" her.)

Afterwards I was the one feeling awkward and
insecure. Was she now seeing me, I wondered, as having
been just some typical burb-bred Cawkazoid of that era,
as some of the photos may have made me appear to be?
(Falsely, of course.) It seemed so, though she denied
it. Several times she commented that my love life had
been a lot more "complicated" than hers. But on the
whole I doubt it was. The main difference is mine has
three kinds of subthemes hers lacks: having to do with
marriage, with having a kid, and with relationship
longevity exceeding two and a half years (her limit).
-- Oh, and also with abortion (she never had one).
Otherwise her love life seems to have been every bit as
tangled and tortuous and heated as mine. (Also at least
as active. She offered no objection to my "assumption"

she'd had a couple of hundred lovers. But she did say
three or four hundred was "probably too many." So
let's say somewhere in between and let it go at that.)
     After leaving the meet cafe last night we stopped
by Jess and Gwen's. While there I showed off the
anniversary pendant. Today (at our usual three p.m.
Monday workout) Z told me Jess had said to her, "Glen is
one in a billion." Z's reply was, "Well, what about me?
I'm one in a billion too!" Jess: "Yeah, but he
appreciates you. I don't think you appreciate him
enough." -- It's not really true, though; Z shows me
plenty of appreciation. Nonetheless I like to tease her
about not showing more, and so I pounced on Jess's
words. "See! See!" -- Now in Z's latest show of
appreciation she's taken to calling me her "Adonis man,"
with just the right gently mocking tone. And after I've
told her she's beautiful a million times in a thousand
different ways she's used that same word for me -- once.
Just yesterday. It was the way I looked while lying
naked on my back in bed, not even a sheet covering me,
when she came in to say goodbye yesterday morning.
Later she lightly let it drop, however -- the punch line
-- that there was one place I was covered: a pillow was
pulled over most of my head. -- And those lines she
read me yesterday from her J-book at the cafe came from
a memory of earlier that morning: something about
Possum's redness "seeping" into her. (Did she perhaps
mean "thrusting" or "pistoning"? And red's not really
right. Slightly rosy tan maybe at its most colorful.
Her inner vulva is several rosy shades closer to red.)
     -- Also on the topic of beauty, she told me two
lines of Jerry II's she especially remembers (this is
her last serious lover before me). Jerry was highly
critical and rarely gave compliments, so the few he did
bestow made a strong impression. One night he said he'd
caught a glimpse of her from a certain angle and she was
"so beautiful it took my breath away." (When I've told
her the same kind of thing -- in a hundred different
ways! -- it's seemed to make no impression at all. So
maybe I too should be more sparing with the

compliments.) The other, she and Jerry II entered a
room where an older Afrusan woman was holding court,
splendidly handsome and strong and proud-looking, and he
said, "when you're her age you'll look even better than
that."
     Well. So what? I mean, I wasn't there but I don't
doubt he was right. Okay, Z-duck? This be okay? Eh?
     This afternoon she told me she couldn't get back to
sleep last night after I came to bed at four a.m.
That's why maybe ten minutes later she started caressing
my back and asked, "Are you asleep?" According to her I
said "Yes," though I have no memory of it. And she let
me sleep on. But I told her today I always like it when
she awakens me for loving and I don't want her to hold
back ever again when it appears (or even if I say) I'm
asleep, not a single time, and she promised she wouldn't.
(And in the past she rarely has. Usually the way it
happens is we're sleeping spoon fashion on our sides,
she behind me, and her hand starts wandering down from
its usual resting place on my chest and she winds up
lightly stroking my gen set and/or nearby areas until I
awaken. I love surfacing that way. Even more I love
her getting me off that way. -- And most of all I love
having such a lusty lover who climaxes so frequently and
powerfully and almost always wants more.)
     Even if I don't ejac inside her (and I still
haven't) just being in there leaves me very horny
afterwards, as if her juices have soaked in and
precipitated massive new hormonal production. Yesterday
I was in that lusting state all day, ol' Possum seeming
overly confined and itchy inside my jeans, swollen and
tingly and twitchy at times and just sort of glowing at
others. When we arrived home last night we hit the bed
again right away (it was only a little after seven) and
this time she succeeded in getting me off by hand. And
was it ever explosive: jizz shooting all over the place.
Afterwards I glanced down and was startled by the sight
of a long, thick streak slung across my upper belly with
a little gob further up, sort of like -- as I said at
the time, making her roar with laughter -- a vanilla

exclamation point squirted out by a cake decorator.
-- And after that first powerful spurt a series of deep
glug-glug-glug spasms going on and on. -- Strange too,
the way the hard-on appeared suddenly after a period of,
as she said, "Possum playing possum again."
     (She'd had a similarly exceptional morning a few
days earlier when the pleasure was so intense and sweet,
deep and long lasting, she couldn't stop talking about
it even as it went on and on. "Oh Jesus, baby, it's so
good, I'm coming so good right now, it just keeps going,
oh Jesus Jesus....")
     -- And how do I transition out of this?
     Just do it, my man! This is the time of our time!
No need to be artful about anything to be true to this
extraordinary time!

*

     -- So this surprising news. One evening I dropped
by the old "north pole" bookstore and heard a seemingly
familiar voice. It was coming from the next aisle and
as I eavesdropped I realized it was indeed brother Rob
and he was helping a customer -- he was working there!
And it turns out he's been doing so since mid January.
He finally got out from under that horrible new manager
at the store in the Yuke and transferred over. And he's
infinitely happier. True, he can only rarely listen to
classical music on the PA at the new place, but then
it'd been years since he could do it at the old one.
-- He apologized for not getting in touch but clearly
the fault was just as much mine. Still, it's no big
deal to either of us, though it's shocking to Z and to
some of her friends, and especially those with a more
traditional Filipino notion of family. (In fact I wish
Rob and I could be a little closer myself. And Mother
would certainly want that for us, and probably with just
as much family-togetherness spirit as any traditional
Filipino mother or for that matter any mother anywhere.
And I'm still hoping it'll happen.)
     Rob's starting to show his years a bit. His hair's
still long -- in a ponytail -- and only very lightly
threaded with gray, but his face is wrinkling noticeably

83

here and there, mostly, he thinks, owing to his years of
smoking a pipe. From my own decades of working at night
-- and giving up smoking for good after Dad's death
twenty-two years ago -- I might look younger than Rob
does now. -- But I'll still acknowledge I'm old and
only getting older. And I'll also say that except for
being unable to perform to the norm or even to the
minimum sexually and knowing death is closing in I don't
mind the aging at all -- so far. This is the good time,
yes, I'll say it again: in many ways it's the best time
of my life. My weed-whacker elbow even seems to be
healing. And my ruptured left Achilles tendon is back
to, maybe even beyond, the adequately functioning state
it reached in my peninsula bicycling years -- before it
unraveled again.

    -- And another major news item: I'm about to hit
the deep reserves for five grand. This will underwrite
the "roots road trip" in the fall, pay off my debt to Z
(stemming from the move), cover my extra-high taxes for
last year (owing mostly to the growth of the fund
itself), finance my divorce and my wedding clothes (or
better to say some new clothes which I expect to use for
the wedding among other things), take care of various
small debts and needs I've put off dealing with (new
shoes, for instance, and also last year's Christmas gift
for Rob), and set up a cushion for next year. (As of
now I'm not planning to use any of it for medical or
health purposes, but Z might have some different ideas
on this. She's chomping at the bit while awaiting, in
just two more months, the end of our one-year moratorium
on the topic.) -- And after paying out the five grand
the fund will still have something like eight grand more
in it than when it began at the time of Mother's death.
The stock market continues to boom. Irony of ironies,
I'm profiting from the very expansion of USAn economic
power -- heavily enforced militarily, to be sure --
which I've inveighed against my entire adult life.

    And this: the scope office is moving, or rather
just has. My first knowledge of it came only hours
beforehand. It's not much of a move -- from one end of

the hall to the other, to the old law-firm suite
(they've taken over the entire floor below us) -- but
it's the end of an era for me. Nine years I've labored
in that setting. Or maybe eight, or maybe seven. (I
sound just like Z when she's trying to remember how long
it's been since she and Jerry II parted ways.)

Meanwhile the ballyhooed new "erectile dysfunction"
drug is finally hitting the market. It was front-page
news, above the fold (where else?), in all three papers
one day last week. Sounds like it works best for men in
exactly my predicament. Apparently we number in the
millions, with more and more coming along as the baby
boom ages. Just pop one of these pills and roughly an
hour later, if all the hype is true, you'll stiffen up
to the max like a randy teenager. The side effects
include headache, nausea, and a "blue visual haze," but
the studies say these strike only about one user in
eight. And what's the cost of this miracle? Assuming
all the pills in a bottle work, about nine bucks a pop.
Which is to say: same as the three-piece halibut and
chips at my favorite fish house.

I'm not ready to go for it. Not yet. And
hopefully not ever. I'm still counting on the same kind
of healing that's mended my frayed Achilles and the
weed-whacker's elbow. "Ol' Possum" is just a little bit
slower to heal, I'm hoping, than those other body parts.
And before I'd go for this new sex pill I'd try some of
the herbal remedies Z favors -- saw palmetto and all
that, the pyramids of dubious virility potions on
display at health-food stores -- but again I'm not there
yet. I'd just feel so much better if I could beat this
thing myself and not depend on some expensive pill or
remedy or course of treatment. ("Course of treatment"
-- I should add that anything "psychotherapeutic" would
be absolutely the last resort; they'd have to be
lowering me into my grave. Or poor Z be weeping and
carrying on, almost literally dying for a real fuck for
a change: maybe that would do it.)

Other items.

We saw a terrible movie, "Afterglow." Z said

something remarkable for her, at least as I know her:
"My love is resilient." She also repeated in slightly
different form her observation that we ball like a
couple of aliens: "I alienmate you, you alienmate me."
(It's true, kind of, but her saying it over and over
sure doesn't help make it any less true.) Also, she's
reached the limit on print absorption: wants me to
recommend no more books or articles for a while.
(Trouble is she devotes huge chunks of time to plowing
through female-oriented detective stories. And that's
not about to change. If she falls short on her quota of
these her soul freezes up; she's told me so herself.)

   And then there's this (since I'm in vamp mode
anyway): I bought a bottle of cheapo blackberry wine,
and such a fine Marcelian effect it had, bringing back
swigging in the bathtub -- this a quarter century ago --
with the bottle silhouetted on the ledge of the open
window against the lights of uphill houses and the
starry night sky in my old "city No. 2/7" (reviving the
"Jyzemelt" lingo). And also I vaguely recall going
blotto on the stuff a few times in the months after my
return from overseas (at the time of Dad's death)
roughly five years after the bathtub tootling.

   And: so delighted was Z to hear me repeat the story
about her image jumping out at me from the contributors
photo in "12-P/AQ" (published three years after Dad's
funeral) that all day at work, or so she said, she was
looking for people she could pass it along to. And this
even though she'd probably told it to everyone last year
(but not so, she said, or at least the others didn't
remember it; "This was like a whole new story!").

   And: she told me Aida thinks I'm "sorta pretty,"
especially in my old pictures (kind of a backhanded
compliment, innit?). (True, I can't deny it: I don't
like Aida anywhere near as much as I once did. Why is
it even when she's sworn to be "really good" she's still
always finding some sneaky new way to stick it to me?)

   And: we attended a neighborhood planning confab at
the rec center at the far southern end of the hilltop.
Z didn't take me seriously when I guessed it would be

the kind of affair where you don't have to show up at
any particular time. I foolishly let her pry me out of
bed three hours early, at nine a.m., so we could be
there for the opening. And my guess was right: the
event was a kind of open house. But it was still worth
attending, and for me this was mainly because it took
me back to newspaper days and the endless planning
meetings I had to attend in that era; and thus it
brought out the contrast between the way I thought in
those days and my current views as well as the vastly
different political climate then and now. Back then I
was primarily concerned (as this exhibition was and as Z
is now) to find ways to make life in the city more
livable, more exciting, more just. Of course I'm still
concerned about these things, but now I see much more
clearly how the "livability piece" (to deploy another Z-
ism) in many ways works against the "justice piece."
The more livable our hilltop hood becomes, for example,
the more it'll cost to live there. Rent increases will
drive away many of the current low-income residents.
Every scrap of litter we pick up makes it a tiny bit
more likely we'll be forced out ourselves, and we're
more like median income. And that's with or without my
paltry earnings included.

11

An unexpected hole for jyze. "It's the wrong day,
and the wrong place, though the space is thrilling it's
the wrong space." (Okay, that's strange. But is it
complete nonsense? I say no.)
So how it is, the scope-office move from one end of
the hall to the other is taking forever. And it's going

down piecemeal, and other than that I have no idea
what's happening or why. I just show up after
everyone's gone home and I try to figure out where
things stand and where things are stashed (temporarily?)
and whether, given all this, I can do my contracted
Jyzer Ink work or not. If I can't, it's sure as hell
not my fault.

Tonight none of the machines are hooked up. The
safe's still standing where it was in the old office,
the computer I ordinarily use is ignominiously riding
the carpet in an otherwise completely empty room in the
new office, the printers are set up on tables in a
different room with connecting cords detached and strewn
about like downed tree limbs after a storm. I've got a
new scoping job to tackle and GJ finals to correct and
print, but I can do nothing. So I leave a message for
Naomi -- no one's answering at her place -- and then
grab a miniature chocolate bar from the candy bowl and
take off. -- Then decide I'd better not leave my laptop
in the safe, for fear it might be damaged in the move.
I grab it too and roll on down to the hideaway.

(Do the rolling in the Z-mobile because this is
Tuesday night and I now regularly drive in on this one
night of the week so I can stay home a bit longer with,
yes, Z. -- And it so happens that tonight I arrived
down here in the historic quarter just as a baseball
game was letting out and huge crowds were surging
through the triangle and along all the nearby roads and
alleys. As of a few days ago the major league season
is underway and our guys are opening with a two-week
homestand. Z and I must pay attention to this sort of
thing because traffic in the area and up into the Asian
quarter becomes a nightmare before and after the game
and buses tend to run late and in bunches.)

So here I am, brown chair. My fingers still
sniffing faintly of Z-juice. Yeah yeah, thass the way I
like it. Ooh ooh, wotta sexy funky early evening at
home. And, surprise, no music going down at the club
below, even though it's a game night. (And last Monday
night wasn't! -- Must've been a private party, maybe?)

[Can This Be Jyze?]

    I'm doing just fine. April is here. April Fool's
Day, I let it slip by -- tricked Z and everyone by doing
nothing (you sly jyzer you). And the clocks jumped
forward an hour. Suddenly the birds are twittering
outside our windows well before I go to bed at four a.m.
And they're loud: Z wears earplugs to combat them (as
well as to block out the roar of the jetliners surging
overhead, which are a big annoyance to hilltop
residents, especially those living farther south and
thus closer to the airport where the planes are flying
lower -- in fact closer to two airports -- but I swear
the birds are louder, at least up at our end).
    Birds, planes, trains -- it's Gatewood Road all
over again. I'm Kat's age or a little older. A few
times the flashbacks have nearly moved me to tears.
Yup, true -- as I lie on my side and Z spoons in from
behind, her hand surprisingly warm against my chest
(especially the left nipple, which even in male
vestigial form is, I'm ready to testify -- and I swear I
wasn't really aware of this until Z came into my life --
far more sensitive than the surrounding skin to both
heat and touch). And her left leg resting atop my hip
so her muff can press against my ass because we both
like the way that feels. And her lips pressing against
my upper back, damp, warm -- her steady breathing. Her
heart beating on both sides of mine, not just in her
chest but, in pulse form of course, in her wrist as
well, and tactually noticeable in both places.
    Life is so damn good right now. It's so good I'm
starting to join Z in feeling superstitious about it.
Will the good times keep on rolling a while longer if I
declare to the appropriate deity that I don't deserve
them? It's true, I feel I don't deserve them. It's
also true I feel I do deserve them at least somewhat
after all the bad times I've been through -- will it
perhaps help to be candid and admit this to the deity?
Especially I feel Z deserves them. I love Z. I want
the best for her. I do I do I do. (Babbling idiot.)
    Aw shoot no, we still haven't consummated. But the
experiment remains in effect, when we don't forget or

don't say to hell with it and focus on her pleasure
(because she obviously needs to come so badly and I
obviously won't be getting there myself anytime soon).
Four or five times I've been inside her this week, I can
at least say that. Once was from behind as she lay on
her side, nearly contorting herself off the bed trying
to find a position in which it felt right. -- But now
she's more likely to be the one reminding me we're not
supposed to be talking about it, just doing it. When I
deflate I'm assailed by a nearly irresistible impulse to
say something droll and/or regretful and/or self-
reproachful. (Today she came across some sort of
sexual-frequency survey on which I supposedly did fairly
well for a man of my vintage. -- Great. She can get me
off by hand two or three or four times in a week. And
she does. And she's less bothered now by those times
when she can't quite do it. -- But I want to be fucking
for at least an hour every day! Pumping it into my
honey! I can't stand being so sexually lame!)

But no, that's not true. I can live with it. As I
frequently remind myself, it even has advantages. It
inspires me to do everything possible to keep her
feeling erotically hot and orgasmically fulfilled. It
leads both of us to appreciate much more the noncoital
aspects of sexual loving and to keep searching for new
ones. In a way we reap extra pleasure precisely because
we're working at overcoming this damnable obstacle.

Okay okay, enough of that. (Jyze is reluctantly
taking on a therapeutic role here. Other than Z
herself, I have no one to talk with about our sexual
matters, and in fact now I'm not supposed to be talking
with her about them either. Not that I'd want to be
talking with anyone but her about them anyway. But
evidently I need to be, and at this point in my life
jyze is the only listening post available. So I grump
and grouse in here, twist and squirm. Don't know if it
helps or not. Just have to do it, it seems.)

Oh but tonight was a beauty. On the phone she said
she'd like it better if she could meditate a bit before
we hit the sack on early Tuesday evenings after she

returns home from work. Okay, fine, I said, sounds
good, let's see what happens. So we try it. She
arrives, we kiss, into her room she scoots, closes the
door. (I love awaiting her arrival home on Tuesdays and
Thursdays when she's not otherwise occupied. In its own
way it's every bit as erotic as the sexual loving
itself.) Then after twenty minutes or so out she sails,
changed into more casual clothes, a white "Polapinas
Rule" T and soft clingy blue shorts with slits up the
sides. Looking fabulous, as if the cameras are about to
roll. Pours us some wine. We sit in facing armchairs
and she tells me about her day. We both sneak glances
at the newspapers she's brought home. Wine drained, Z
all chatted out, we head for the bedroom. (And this
morning in bed she'd been unable to resist -- "Just one
little come" -- and then one more. Fourth time it's
happened in the past week alone. As she reminds me
often, she likes it best in the a.m. just after waking
up. She also likes me best then -- oohs and aahs about
how "pretty" and sexy I look to her -- and does this
often enough I can't help but pout about her failing to
tell me such things at any other time of day.)
    So what is it about my morning self that makes me
so much more appealing to her then? I asked her this
very question. Her reply: "Maybe it's just me -- I'm in
the mood then." But she went on to say she finds me
"more relaxed." I said maybe she's more relaxed too,
for example about my alleged bad hair, which according
to her looks at all times as if I've just slept on it.
-- But for her the morning sex this past week has been
exceptionally good. "Fabulous." Why she thinks so or
how it's different from other times, I don't know and
she can't or won't say. "Just is."
    So a couple of hours in bed. Clothes on at first,
removed only slowly. "Talking comes" (that is, caused
solely or mainly by words alone). One in which she
squeezes ol' Possum between her thighs, pressed against
her vulva, coming in from behind -- but it's not stiff
enough that I want to risk venturing inside and foozling
(as I can tell is likely) and meanwhile scuttle her

pleasure. A two-finger finger-fuck come follows. And half a dozen others, one clitoral and one vulval and the rest nipporal. And talk of how I like to awaken in a state of high arousal induced by her gentle fingers -- and she's vowing to climb aboard more, shove it in if I've got that good morning wood or she can conjure it.

Then dinner. She reheats leftovers from lunch, I nuke soy "bacon" strips. We sit in facing armchairs. The telephone keeps ringing. We laugh a lot at each other's jokes -- wotta pair of comedians! And she, no doubt about it, laughs louder, more heartily, and more often. (Why the hell does she think I'm so funny? It's a miracle, maybe almost compensating for the malfunctioning wanger. Supposedly I'm a mix of her two favorite comedians, with bits and pieces of several of my own favorites added in (I keep naming names, she keeps saying, "Him too"). Me, I'm just goofing around -- and maybe she thinks I overdo it a little sometimes. Yet I can still reduce her to tears and even cause her to wet her pants from laughing so hard.) (She laughs hard for other people too. And in theaters she's a classic guffawer, one of the loudest and most frequent I've ever come across, and it's not at all unusual that she's the only one laughing. In short, as she comes, she laughs. It might even make a good first-date rule of thumb: hearty laughs, hearty comes.)

-- Then at nine I should be leaving but she sits on my lap and notices "sump'n gettin' sorta hulky down there" and soon we're stumbling bedward again. (Unusual moment, I'm straddling her torso, cockhead in her mouth as her hands work on the shaft -- boy did I want to gush then. And I was ready! On the brink, I swear! But couldn't.) Finally at ten I manage to break away (but only after feigning it and then dragging her back into the bedroom for one last ultra-quickie).

(I guess I'm starting to think my "e-dys" -- that's "erectile dysfunction," need I say? -- may be more a matter of physiology than psychology. It's certainly not unheard of that men my age and even younger suffer from it. It's just that in some ways I'm young for my

age and in most I'm probably about normal, so maybe I'm
slow to accept this one very conspicuous way in which I
seem to have turned prematurely ancient. In one of the
many e-dys-related articles appearing in newspapers and
magazines these days a doctor is quoted as saying
problems like mine in men under sixty are "almost always
a form of vascular disease." So maybe my arteries are
clogged. Maybe I'm desperately sick and don't know it
yet. -- But shouldn't my heart then be pounding when I
walk up hills? It doesn't. -- Could be a bad prostate
though. Seems to me my pee stream is a bit less
"robust" than it once was. And yet somehow my prostate
seems to feel fine too. Could be I'm just imagining
things. -- But the e-dys I'm not imagining, no.)
*

So then. One a.m., nothing's happening. Oh how
I'd love to be able to work down here every night. Drop
my job, live on the inheritance from good ol' Mom. I
could do it. I could survive six or seven years that
way if I could keep my expenses at or below their
current bare-bones level. And this is just what Mom
herself urged me to do. But -- I'd better not. Not
yet. As long as I can hang on to a job as close to
ideal as the one I have I ought to do so. I just hate
to cut back on anything -- reading, workouts, loving,
socializing (which includes some politicking too, now,
though still not much, and definitely nothing in which
my efforts count for anything more than moral support).
Yet I've also got these various writing projects going
and I'd like to be devoting five or six hours a day to
them. -- But I don't want to be overly driven or
maniacal about this, no. -- So just do what I can and
be happy with what I'm doing and -- that's it.

As for this past week, no Kat (I miss her!) but
otherwise splendid. The half-dozen hardy fuchsia starts
appear to be thriving -- we haul them in from the
balcony every night to be sure they don't chill too much
out there. At Z's insistence we took a special class in
stretching with Leola and Gerry at the WOC and then
joined them for dinner at a downtown steakhouse I've

93

walked by hundreds of times over the years -- glancing
down at its throngs of gussied-up carnivores as I climb
the hill from "middle road" to "high road" -- but had
never before entered. Oddly enough, I went for the
halibut, which then not too surprisingly turned out to
taste more like beef than fish. (Alas, Z and Leola are
no longer as close as they were in the "B.G." era
(Before Glen) -- and in fact Z says this is true of her
relations with many of her friends, maybe even most.
Those flexible enough to put up with less attention are
the ones she's still doing well with. The needier ones,
among them Jessica D. ("the other Jess"), Irene, and of
course Aida as well as Leola, are bridling.)

Z's photo has been popping up lately in various
newspapers and newsletters owing to her appointment to a
prestigious national committee on environmental justice.
At the meeting of the county women's caucus she urged
greater involvement in the fight against I-200 and was
promptly chosen as the caucus's delegate to the "No on
200" steering group (where she'll join Aida and Emiko
and several other friends), thus committing herself to
at least two more evening meetings per month. Everyone
wants a hunk of this woman! (Aida, by the way, is still
seeing super-suave dreamboat Colin, and Emiko is still
steamed over being bird-dogged by her, just as Adele is
steamed over being bird-dogged by Emiko over that same
Colin.)

And lest I forget: tonight in talking about taxes Z
revealed that in her twenties she was audited four
straight years because the IRS kept questioning the huge
medical deductions she was claiming for psychiatric
sessions. Each time she convinced them they were legit.
What's more, she swears they truly were. "Just think
how crazy I'd be now if it weren't for them."

-- The perils of support-networking. Saturday
Paula (Z's former compatriot in a radical-therapy group
and current occasional housecleaner) called on me to
help move furniture from storage to her new digs on the
tenth floor of a low-income hotel near the public market
(with a spectacular water/mountains view). Ned, a

longhair in the grand tradition and a former "primary"
lover, Z tells me, of the same therapy group's leader,
provided the wheels, a rattletrap pickup truck, along
with considerable muscle. (Once I lightly tapped Paula
on the back and she jumped a foot and briefly seemed on
the verge of a flip-out or heart attack -- I'd forgotten
she was battered for years in an abusive relationship
and now can't stand to be touched by men.) (Nonetheless
I like Paula and we get along well -- both of us being
veterans of subsidized downtown living who've actually
lived poor, whereas most of the others in the old
therapy group, notwithstanding their admirable
campaigning for poverty-related causes, haven't.)
     And then Wei and I will soon be doing a "boys'
night out." His mother died a couple of weeks ago. I
still have high hopes of our becoming bona-fide friends
(though not quite as high as before -- because of some
needlessly caustic remarks he's made to Z about certain
prag and neoprag heroes of mine). -- Wei and Alison
invited us to come over Saturday for an Easter-egg-
coloring party, but Z begged off; her calendar's already
too full (as it almost always is for those who don't get
to her weeks in advance, myself sometimes included).
     And then June. Sunday afternoon she dropped by
while Z was out and we talked for several hours. She's
so much like Lady S -- their family histories being
almost uncannily similar -- I have no trouble at all
relating to her. We justified the long talk as a
"bonding session." I had helped edit her application
for entry to law school, including an essay on which I
made extensive changes, and she's now convinced I can
read her mind. Like Lady S she's wonderfully spirited,
intelligent, determined, emotional -- she broke into
tears half a dozen times while spilling her family tales
to me -- and also vain, repetitive, and bogglingly
convoluted in her storytelling. Saturday night she'll
be taking us out to dinner as thanks for the help -- to
a Korean restaurant! (I tried to let her know -- gently
-- I don't go for most Korean food owing to the spices,
but she wasn't hearing me. Again just like Lady S, she

gets rolling on her enthusiasms and can't be denied.)

The sad news of the week: Paz and Tobey, after four or five years together, appear on the verge of a breakup. Word has it Paz is lusting after another woman. Tobey is barely functioning. (Yet she'll be attending June's dinner Saturday night. And so will Aida, who wrote a law-school recommendation for June, as did Z. And Aida's boy Charles will be there as well, "for the broadening experience." Aida and June are becoming closer now, perhaps in part to compensate for the diminished face time each has with Z.) (But today Z stumbled in on Paz and Tobey talking intensely in Tobey's office and she thinks a reconciliation may still be possible. Paz, she said, looked every bit as stricken and bedraggled as Tobey did.)

Also this week I finally got around to sewing up the loose stitching on my old brown backpack. The deteriorating condition of my black backpack was the motivator. I bought both packs at roughly the same time and pressed the brown one into service first, but after only a few weeks the stitching for the main side pocket began unraveling. Therefore I "temporarily" substituted the black one. That was about eight years ago. Now I'm starting to use the brown one again and it seems like a new bag, only better. It looks new but it feels familiar, broken in and comfortable (all these years I've been meaning to repair it at the first opportunity because I like the color better). And I take special pride in it because I did the repairs myself.

-- Almost two a.m. So I'll stop soon. This many pages, I'm again very pleased. If I can step up the pace a little more I might finish up this J-book right on time (by the original "random" schedule). And I don't see any reason why that shouldn't happen. (One night at three a.m. as I read in the living room Z stumbled in -- naked except for her new black sleep mask, which she'd pulled up a fraction of an inch for navigation purposes -- and dragged me back to the bedroom because, after a noise from next door awakened her, she found herself "too horny to get back to sleep."

And how delighted I am to be living with a woman who'll
speak up -- and act! -- so audaciously.)
        -- But I haven't mentioned our shopping expedition
to the big-box discount mart. A Saturday too, hundreds
if not thousands of customers jamming the aisles. Z
bought a fancy suitcase with wheels and an extendable
pull handle, not cheap at eighty bucks but a steal next
to the three-hundred-dollar catalog version she'd been
considering. I too went wild, at least by my standards,
forking out seventy-some dollars for bulk purchases of
juice and tuna and the like, and it happened because I'm
now feeling flush after finally asking Lynn to send up
the five K from the deep reserves. The money's not here
yet and so the flush is only anticipatory, but in a way
this makes it even headier; if the money's in hand I
start worrying too much about blowing it and so can't
indulge in the sheer pleasure of having it. (As of now
I've already blown well over half of it in that same
anticipatory way, as reflected on the desk here by a
long list of intended purchases and various obligations
that must be met. But I've actually spent only the big-
box seventy and so I'm not worrying at all just yet.)
        -- Happy happy. And it makes me even happier to
think maybe someday Z will read this entry (and the many
others like it) and be surprised to see just how pleased
I am with our life together. I wasn't just saying it,
Z-goose! (I'm thinking she'd be reading in here because
I'd be dead and gone. One of us has to go first and I
have little doubt it'll be me. And actuarially it will
for sure. And the cause, given my present problems,
will likely be some sort of vascular condition. Well,
in that case I'd want her to know no mere vascular
condition can mope me out as long as she's in my life.
The shamelessly lackadaisical Possum may not be doing
much, but you, Z-goose, have turned my whole life into a
quivering "life hard-on" with frequent "life ejacs."
Sensational ones, too, repeated again and again. Wotta
way to go!) (And I can scarcely believe I've written
what I just wrote. Cheesy, schmaltzy, mawk mawk mawk.)
("Mawk mawk." "Who's there?" "Jyzer G!")

[Deep Jyze]

12

     It's "Bye Bye Blackbird." A familiar version but
who's doing it I don't know. At three a.m. A bottle of
cheapo kosher wine but not blackberry this time (all the
stores we tried were out). Concord grape. And this on
one of the few days in the USAn year when it's actually
of consequence even to non-night people that
technically the day ends at midnight. It's April 15.
The most taxing of days, that's correct.
     Otherwise a fairly typical night. I arrived home
at 1:35. By then Zoelie'd been in bed for hours,
probably since nine or ten. This week she's fiercely
focused on finishing up a grant application that's due
Friday and so we're operating under a TFB -- "Temporary
Fucking Ban" -- between, that is, the hours of nine p.m.
and nine a.m. Signs to this effect are hanging all over
the place. What's more, ol' Possum is still recovering
from a deep scrape suffered during Sunday's sanctioned
playtime. Yet oddly we've been doing more actual
fucking than ever. Nothing invaginally ejaculatory yet
-- or this wouldn't be a typical night at all -- but
closer, ever closer. And one of those times my scrape
wound was still raw and it stung something fierce. So
-- the Big H? It's always a risk.
     Taxes worked me over pretty good this year. A hit
close to seventy percent greater than last year's. Sure
does make me grouchy. Yet I have little real reason to
complain. It's growth in the deep reserves that
accounts for all the increase and then some. Without
those profits I'd've paid fifteen or twenty percent less
this year than last year. (Some of the capital gains

were directly attributable to the ongoing so-called
Asian financial crisis. I shake my head in quizzical
rue -- or something like that -- at the irony of this
and the way the irony keeps compounding, including
financially.)

    And so it is I'm not more euphoric about the
arrival of the check for five K from Lynn. It came in
yesterday, and today I had to send off thirteen hundred
of it to the IRS. That's about nine hundred more than
I'd been figuring. I also wrote Z a check for the seven
hundred I've owed her since December for moving expenses.
Already the five K is down to three. A thousand of that
I'll set aside for our "roots" trip in September.
Several hundred will go for the fail-safe divorce (a
rough estimate). Urgently needed clothes and shoes will
eat up maybe four hundred more.

    What happened to my cushion? In a blink it's
shrunk to thirteen hundred or less! A single bad
month and I'll be right back to living on the edge!

    -- But to hell with it. I shouldn't grumble. As
observed already probably way too often, life's being so
damn good to me right now. Still! (Just ought to be
everlastingly grateful to Mother for laying the deep
reserves on me. -- And would she be pleased with the
way I'm using them? Maybe not, but I like to think she
would. I'm hard at work on two major writing projects,
not including this one right here. I can't deny it,
though: I'm glad I don't have to try to explain these
projects to her. Or for that matter, to anyone.)

    Still boxes galore around here. Our latest plan is
to rent a truck week after next and haul the lot of them
over to the storage unit. After making little headway
using the piecemeal approach we'll try our luck with an
all-out massive assault and evacuation.

    If I turned the radio down a little more I could
probably hear the first birds of morning right about
now. Ten to four. Lots more birds around here than at
my previous place. Not nearly as many night owls,
though, of the human type. And I'd probably look like a
strange old owl indeed, for this or any other hood, if

someone in the surrounding buildings were up and could somehow peek in the windows and see me. I'm wearing just a ratty gray long-sleeve henley and a pair of blue socks; my upper body is sunk deeply into this sagging black armchair and my hairy bare legs are stretched out onto Z's footstool and most of my ass and the whole of my gen set are hanging out for airing in the space between. It does get surprisingly warm in here, especially at this time of night. Why, I still have no idea. (No convincing idea I can back up with hard evidence is what I mean.)

     Z is concerned about my wounded male member. She's disappointed with me for not having the self-control to refrain from pushing it into her even when I know it's vulnerable. (But to me this just shows she's still not fully aware of the psychology of e-dys.) She's also lavishing the invalid body part with extended hands-on "reiki" treatments to make it all better. "Dr. Ooh-Ooh's" shingle is out.

     -- So a kwikjyze bedtime story. When I hear the telltale lead-in to public-radio news, that'll be it; I'll leap to shut the radio off. (And now the first plane of the morning roars overhead. Low. Loud. But so used to the greater noise level of daytime sleeping am I that the planes don't bother me too much. Z they bother quite a bit, just as do a good many other things which I scarcely notice. Constitutionally, as noted before, she's a person of great sensitivity or, looked at differently, has an extremely low tolerance level. "Overactive amygdala" is another term she likes to use for it. Sometimes this condition, whatever it is, is a drawback -- also previously remarked, but still worth repeating -- but it's inextricably tied in with what makes life with her so fabulous, which is to say: her astounding responsiveness.) (And in the middle of that last sentence I leapt to douse the news.)

*   *

     -- The loveboat gets blown about a bit. But now after four days of fairly severe pitching and yawing it finally seems to be back on a steady heading.

100

Sunday night. Hideaway. Blues show on. Z just dropped me off outside (the triangle so dead) after we attended her friend Ryan V.'s thirtieth birthday party at the writers' clubhouse one hill to the north of our own, which is to say on, yes, east hill.

Thursday afternoon I couldn't get back to this jyze because she put the final touches on her grant application earlier than expected and -- surprise! -- decided to take the afternoon off. Home she zipped and in a celebratory amorous mood too; straight into bed we leapt. The only other time-slots large enough for jyze between then and now, late Thursday and Friday nights after my return home (this being once again my heavy workweek), I found her awake both nights upon arrival and each time we wound up talking for a couple of hours or more both in bed and out. Saturday we had Kat all day. Today we lolled in bed until two or maybe it was closer to two-thirty.

-- So all of a sudden the thrill is gone for her. Or so she told me. I didn't believe her for a moment, but that she would say so and make an issue of it was itself the cause of the storm.

Mostly I've been trying to puzzle out what it means for the long term. It must mean something. Yet nothing seems all that different with us. We've even been humping away more than ever (though still "without issue," ejaculatively speaking, despite a couple of delicious invag pre-come tickle/tingles for the admirably rampant ol' Possum). Today she revealed, in cries and whispers, lots of politically improper yearnings. "Story of O" stuff. "Love slave" stuff. It was a hot and for me sometimes slightly uneasy afternoon at the old ballpark. Yet it was relaxed too, eventually, the first Sunday like this in what seems to be months. Waffles with syrup, maple (hers) and blackberry (mine). Z joking about the kinks and quirks of "you Sandefjord boys." (Yesterday she looked up Gail while in the vicinity of the far-south-end library where she works and they had a grand old time comparing notes about various odd Sandefjord-bro traits. Seems neither Rob

nor I likes to be told more than once to do something --
we regard this as "nagging" (Rob) or "hounding" (me) --
and so on.)

Personally I think Z and I are fused at the heart
and none of this foofaraw matters. I can't believe I
might be wrong about this.

And just the other day she was raving about ol'
Possum being irresistibly sexy and gorgeous in the early
morning light as we lay naked and sheetless in bed. She
was hovering just above my crotch, scoping out the area
with her usual larklike early-morning alertness as I
drifted in and out of a doze and ol' Poss lolled lazily
about, stretching and fidgeting at times, twitching,
even at one point swinging up out of his crotchy den in
an arc and then falling dramatically on his back for her
so she could rub his belly. (Such a shape-shifter! she
cried. And then: such a color-shifter!)

Tonight's party, Ryan is a pal of hers from her
environmental-justice group who rented out the
downstairs cafe of the clubhouse for his celebration
because he's also a budding scribbler of the nonfiction
type. Several dozen friends, mostly political activists
of various persuasions, showed up. Z and I were the
presumptive elders and often treated as such in ways
both positive and negative. Odd, because I didn't and
don't feel all that elder and Z doesn't either. I can't
even see we act it or look it. However, I don't deny
for a moment, nor does she, that that's exactly what we
are.

So, a mildly punky bossa nova lounge band played.
I met Z's friend Rose, a flashy Afrusan woman well known
locally as a musician and New Age-ish radio personality,
and she reported having heard all kinds of hot dish
about us. "You must really be something to have snagged
our Zoelie," she raved when Z was away, almost as if Z
had slipped her a fin under the table to do it. (But
no, Z is known far and wide for her exacting standards
and her ferocious "interrogations" of stereotypical
maleness and especially WASPy maleness. And I'd even
say this well-deserved reputation of hers ranks high

among the ten thousand reasons I am indeed so proud of
having snagged her, oh yes I am.)

Ryan is Eurusan, gay, very tall and long-straight-
brown-haired-to-midback and hails from the small-town
heartland about two hundred miles due south of Gatewood.
He's a little reminiscent of cousin Kar in appearance
and manner but without Kar's preppy/suburban patina.
He's heavily into tenants' rights and prison reform and
several other irreproachably good causes. Likable and
admirable. (The political stuff is still a big yawn for
me, though, most of it, as this party kept reminding me.
Doesn't mean I'm agin any of it. I don't even mind
being preached at once in a while as a member of the
choir. I'd just like some livelier engagement at the
ideas level. Some knowledge and realism about the array
of forces, the conflicts, the contradictions, the
priorities, the ambiguities and ambivalences, the odds,
the nuances, the trade-offs. -- And so it is I'm likely
to be seen by some true believers as standoffish, a
maverick, self-involved artist type, intellectual snob
even, though I work hard to avoid deserving any such
labels.) (But here's another big reason among those
same ten thousand I'm delighted with Z. All my life
I've yearned for such a woman, one who's politically
aware and committed, who cares, who's sophisticated
about public opinion and the public interest, who's in
it for the long haul and has a sense of humor about it.
And Z also understands my artist, maverick, and
intellectual sides, such as they are -- and also such as
they aren't. She respects and admires them and not in a
deluded or starstruck fashion. And I'd say this is
because she has those sides herself -- and chops to burn
in all three -- but she chooses to focus much more
intensely and directly on the political.)

-- So how about otherwise? This week in jyze. New
and different ways I want to be shaking out the phoneme
chains just to keep my jyze alive.

This afternoon we swung down to the south-end
branch of Z's usual co-op for what's turning out to be
our weekly Sunday provisioning run. A few weeks ago at

the same branch I surprised her by stealthily buying, as
she shopped for groceries, a red heart-shaped carved
stone, not much larger than a silver dollar, inscribed
with the words "Marry Me" (and marked down by half after
Valentine's Day) and then presented it to her on bended
knee when we got back to the car. "Yes, yes, yes!" she
cried, seeming quite moved. Today it occurred to me she
hasn't recently asked me (again) to marry her, not
formally anyway (in our loose sense of what formal is).
So I told her this, and since then she's asked twice,
also on bended knee, both times. "You know how to put
the pressure on," she conceded. -- And then on the way
back from the co-op today we stopped at the big
corporate supermarket on the main drag down in the
valley. That's where I lay in most of my own grub these
days and also my coffee (at the attached franchise
coffee shop), and did today too.

   Coffee. My favorite cup, the big jazzy hand-
painted twenty-ouncer, is starting to chip badly along
the lip. Lead flakes. Not healthful. Z offered to buy
me a new cup if I would retire the old one. I caved to
inevitability. The only acceptably large replacement we
could find on such short notice was one designed for
tourists, inscribed with little-known factlets about our
city and state, among them one to the effect that eighty
percent of Jyze City's residents recycle. Imagine Z's
delight to see that! She, of course, played a big part
in making this factlet a fact. So today we bought two
more of those cups, one for Z's office and one to send
to Kat's "Uncle Nick" for his birthday. And we're
planning to personalize all three with ultra-markers --
and never mind that the ink in these markers is toxic.
(And even so they've proved so useful to me I now
routinely carry a black one in my shirt pocket and
several more of assorted colors in my backpack.)

   Uh, hello? Can anyone suss out, I wonder, the true
relevance of anything going down in these pages tonight?
Or if not relevance, at least the absence in this
jyzical account of even the slightest trace of
disinterest? (And I thank the greatest living prog

neoprag for some new light he's shedding for me on the concept of disinterest. But in several important respects I think he's wrong. Attempts to minimize personal bias should not be called objective or disinterested. A new term is needed, I decree, much as new terms are needed for the many different varieties of "truth" -- relative, absolute, consensus, scientific, religious, diabolical, and so forth -- though not now nor anytime soon will jyze attempt a clarification or explanation of any such abstruse notions as these.)

About my Jyzer Ink contract work, then, I sense trouble. It's almost farcical the lengths to which I've gone to keep this gig going over the years. I'm now wheeling the grand-jury computer around on a flimsy metal cart (this in the painfully small and cramped new scope office). The computer is antiquated, the program it uses is obsolete. The huge government-required safe, because no place can be found for it in the new office, remains in the old one, which is now unoccupied, its doors to the hall often standing wide open, its floor littered with scrap paper. I have to patch the old computer into the current office system in order to print anything. I have only the vaguest idea of what I'm doing with this patching and must improvise as I go, endangering the firm's entire system (though so far I've done no actual damage to it that I know of). The computer itself is giving out; the monitor screen registers print in blue on a lavendar background and it's barely readable. When I tried to back up some files onto diskettes before I left work Friday night the diskette drive died. Every time I go in I have to jerry-rig a workplace in the computer room. I can't take anything out of the office on pain of potential (however unlikely) government felony prosecution. If anyone ever asks I'm supposed to say I do all the government work on the laptop which I store in the safe and on which it's impossible for me to do scoping for longer than half an hour at a stretch. It's all absurd. How much longer can I push it? (Yet the grand-jury contract with the feds still has a couple of years to run. So -- lots of wrangles ahead, I suspect, but probably I'll be able to muddle on for at least those two years. And then maybe I'll go over to living on the deep reserves so I can escape from all this botheration and focus solely on being the best J-slinger I can be.)

A glance upwards, I see three new boxes of the same low-cut basketball shoes I've been wearing since sophomore year in high school. "Chucks," yes. I'm reloading. But they're no longer available in khaki, the color that works best for me as a big-time walker of puddly or muddy or dusty streets. And I've been unable to find a new sales outlet (the old one closed) for the street soccer shoes I started using a couple of years ago to give my feet an occasional rest from the chucks. I'm still determined to buy a wedding shirt and pair of pants but there's no hurry on those. The jeweler in Z's building is repairing my Russian-made pocket watch, soldering on a new fob ring for the bargain price of five bucks ("because he sort of has a crush on me, I think," Z didn't fail to let me know). And I've laid in a good stock of cheapo kosher fruit wines: it's up to five bottles and counting. Today I came across a cherry flavor for the first time and bought a test bottle.

As for Wednesday and Thursday nights, both produced near meltdowns by the Z-woman. Abundant tears. I loved this: Z wailing "We can't change the world fast enough!" She's also still having an awful time (though not every waking minute) adjusting to the fact that she's actually living with a penis-bearer. As she's the first to say, she just can't get used to it sometimes. The sex thing can be so confusing now that she's getting it every day, or can, or whenever she wants. She's no longer just a weekend warrior of sex -- and waddayaknow, she's discovering her sex drive has limits. By her own account she no longer gets incredibly aroused as she did all last year. (The exception is wake-up time in the morning. Then she almost always does.) Sometimes while I'm in the saddle grinding away she suddenly feels she'd rather be reading a book! (Or be back in good old Centropolis, I suppose.) -- And then after bravely revealing these sad truths she worries I'll want to retaliate! Somehow! Like by not wanting to have sex as much!

Well, I'm surprising her. I'm taking it pretty damn well. Or maybe I'm not but then again I don't need to be, because since our talk about this we've balled twice or more every single day (with each and every round featuring at least some "penetrative action"). And truly I think this is the case. I think her cutting back is likely to have the counterintuitive effect of making us more compatible. I'd even say ol' Possum is showing signs of entering the final stage of recovery from his long-term shellshock. The penis-bearer is becoming, to resuscitate the old pun, a pole-bearer -- and with Zoelie B. the (half) Pole, capped, it bears.

(Should I or should I not be putting quotes around "ol' Possum"? Should I be using the term at all, other than when actually quoting? Is it just too damn coy and cloying? Too T.S. Eliotic? Too downright idiotic? Probably all the above. But I do like it, metaphorically and analogically and for the humor and the fact that Z came up with it. Such a vivid image it evokes, the old member lying lank on its back refusing to cooperate. Yet it's hopeful too -- the tiny paws faintly quivering, the beast only "playing" dead.)

-- So now I'm finally getting it up and in with regularity. Next question is: how can I convince myself it's okay to ejaculate in there? Over the past five days, until this morning, in perhaps a dozen invag sojourns, some quite lengthy by my current standards (fifteen or twenty minutes, say), not a single ejac. This morning's come -- mine -- was a wowser with all that steam behind it (I hesitate to use the hydraulic metaphor and then I recall it isn't just a metaphor when applied to the genital system: plumbing and fluids is exactly what this is about) but it wasn't inside her; it was a handjob just as with all the other ejacs so far (though with a new twist this time, literally, improvised by her, and therefore one of the finest ejacs yet).

-- And why this new twist? Because, as briefly
noted before, one of last week's handjobs scraped the
skin right off ol' P's tender underbelly. It reminded
me of the way my left thigh looked one time in early
teen days when I took way too high a full-speed feet-
first dive into third base. All week we kept close tabs
on the wound's status. Z reiki'd it nightly (and when I
asked her to keep doing so just like that for the rest
of my life, she promptly assented -- but I know she
won't, just because she's not really that much into
snuggling up with the thing for long periods except on
certain high-libido occasions or unless I specifically
request it). (My "manhandling" of her sexual parts
sometimes puts them out of action too, by the way. Ours
is an equal-klutziness sexual deployer. At times this
happens because she out and out demands it -- "Harder!
Harder!" -- and at other times I go overboard just in an
attempt to outshine past triumphs or to get her off in
some new way. Her left nipple is usually the more
banged up. Vaginally her troubles have eased a lot
since she became more diligent in applying the wild-yam
extract but even that doesn't always protect her against
an overenthusiastic three-finger G-spot twanging.)
      -- During the most recent meltdown some
embarrassing things trickled out. Sad things. She's
still worried I'm "imprinted" on Lady U who, being a
dancer, must have had a beautiful body and been very
graceful and skilled in bed, and that must be why I
can't ejac inside her, Z. After all, Lady U is fourteen
years her junior. That makes her roughly the same age
as Aida and also Z's own nephew Jacob. Somehow Z, even
though she's known the essential facts all along, never
quite realized the extent of this age gap -- and maybe
there's some truth to her "imprint" worries, who knows.
Eighteen years with one woman is a long time and Lady
U's body was terrific and she did good things with it
and I loved that body and those good things too, yes I
did. Absolutely! But so what? Z's body is terrific
too in its own highly distinctive and extremely sexy way
and I love it just as much, and still better she's

sexually exciting and excitable and does those good
things like no one I've ever known. The point is -- ah
well, the point is screamingly obvious. But there's Z
disparaging her own body in grossly inaccurate terms.
Breaks my heart. So perform, you goddamn wimpy crotch-
hanger! (Another metaphor of hers I loved. One morning
as I tried to hold her for an extended period in a state
of high excitement on the edge of climaxing she said she
felt like "a Calder mobile about to fly apart in all
directions." Shorn of context that sounds almost
sinister. But with her breath coming hard and her
juices flowing and her body straining and every word or
two punctuated with a moan, ooh ooh ooh....)
     But what else? She loves that pillow talk, yes.
Okay, so then how about the two neighborhood drug busts
in a single day, one directly across the street (six cop
cars, officers with drawn guns, a drug-sniffer dog, and
our living-room picture window serving as a kind of
theater balcony box for viewing all this). The other
was directly behind us half a block to the west at the
very crest of the hill (for which bust Z, home alone at
the time and just getting ready for bed, was startled to
hear a police megaphone -- sounding as if it were coming
from just outside our windows -- warning "everyone" to
keep their heads down). During this second incident she
called 911, worried about my unreachability, and later
she launched another intense lobbying campaign for me to
carry a beeper or cellphone at all times. I told her if
she'd call 911 a little more often they might offer to
implant a phone in my skull for free just to keep her
off their case.
     She also blew her cork twice over beater cars
revving their engines in the next-door driveway for long
periods, spewing dramatically churning grayish-black
clouds of toxic exhaust which drifted straight toward
our south windows. What gripes her most is that
directly confronting these malfeasors would likely be
counterproductive (not to say suicidal) in a hood such
as ours. The solution will have to be technological:
internal air cleaners. More machines! More expense!

More energy use! And such paradoxes! She morphs into
the naive gentrifier, I into the wary street dude.

       Saturday her noon Adopt-a-Street meeting, for which
we had passed out flyers at every house and apartment on
both sides of the street, was a total flop: other than Z
herself, only Kat and I showed up. And yet this has its
bright side: it suggests the hood will stay down and
dirty and dangerous and thus scare away the next wave of
gentrifiers. Therefore the rents should remain
relatively low and the largely poor and nonwhite present
inhabitants might be able to stay put. And of course
this prospect delights both of us -- except for the
danger, the squalor, the low level of city and landlord
services. She relishes the paradoxes too, by the way
-- when they're not driving her nuts.

       I should also mention, or anyway will, that my two
old hardy fuchsias from B-2 have staged a miraculous
recovery. They're out there on the balcony riotously
producing tender new shoots. And this: to thank us for
helping with her law-school application and related
tasks, June not only, as promised, took Z and me, along
with Aida and Charles and Tobey, to dinner at a snazzy
Korean restaurant, but then to everyone's amazement she
invited us all over to her home out in the northern
burbs. In the seven or eight years they've known June,
Z and Aida had seen the place only in photos. It's two
stories, easily twice the size of my own family's
Gatewood house and much fancier, and she lives there all
alone except when her two sons are home from college
(she's been divorced for fifteen years). Again I was
often reminded of Lady S: most notably by the numerous
posh art objects (centuries-old scrolls, statues), the
omnipresent dust (and the dislike of "low-class" manual
labor it implies), the bogglingly convoluted stories of
family disputes told in hard-to-follow broken English.
(Also the super-spicy Korean food at the restaurant
incited a stomach rebellion that took me days to put
down -- but the soju rice wine was excellent and evoked
dreamlike memories of Korea days which, surprisingly
perhaps, I was wise enough to keep mostly to myself.)

[Can This Be Jyze?]

    And? A second new prog-neoprag book, also very
good, hits the stores and on the same day my chairside
reading stack. And a new study comes out showing
vitamin C might not be so good for you after all (and
right after we socked in a full year's supply). And Z
announces for perhaps the third or fourth time in six
months she's had a first vaginal come with ol' Possum
inside (her explanation this time, offered later:
slightly different positions or angles for each and
every one of those previous comes made each a "first").
And an outbreak of low-pitch hums in the middle of the
night (some of them Z could hear even with her earplugs
in) nearly drove both of us around the bend before
vanishing as suddenly as they'd appeared.
    And -- no more. With only this jyze accomplished
for the day -- but why shouldn't it be enough for this
or any day? -- I reverse the controls on this baby (as
on a ferry) and head back home.

                      13

    It's happened. We did it. We're "consummately
joined" (and in the phrasing too, because that term is
Z's -- it's written out, in her hand, with three
exclamation points, on the chalkboard riding the kitchen
counter). (And here on the couch stands her hilariously
obscene conjoined bagel/carrot "organic sculpture" also
celebrating this grand occasion, with a dozen small
banners stuck into it -- by me, using partially unbent
paper clips as lanyards -- proclaiming the likes of
"Viva la Possum" and "N'dow Nails It," and intertwined
through them -- by her -- a "Mobydickus lub strip" ---
                        *

[Deep Jyze]

     And the phone rings, she's leaving the office, will
be home in a few minutes (an hour earlier than usual).
This is because at the crack of dawn tomorrow she flies
off to a distant province for a weeklong convention.
     Consummation Day was Cinco de Mayo. Forevermore it
shall be. A year almost to the minute after our first
roll (in the hay). Who can say now the woman has no
patience?
     And I must stop. Already. Probably won't be able
to return until tomorrow or later (it's another heavy
workweek). But then, when I do come back, I'll be
trying something new. Another experiment. The
apotheosis of kwikjyze. -- But not as kwik as this,
no, or not usually. Nor am I aiming to change the
total production of jyze (as measured in pages for the
year). But -- frequency of subentries will go up,
length of subentries down. -- And gotta split.
                    *   *
     -- Try to be a little thoughtful for a change.
It's two nights later and almost two in the morning.
Z's not here, although the phone could ring at any
moment. It did about this time last night. She's,
what, roughly thirteen hundred miles away to the south/
southwest at a resort out in the desert somewhere. Four
times she called, in fact, but only for the fourth was I
here. It seems reading a certain sexy mystery on the
plane had gotten her worried I might be "carousing."
     Ha! Was ever a candidate less likely for carousal?
Consider my present state: not only crazy in love but
also possessed of an only sporadically functional
carousal organ -- despite the Cinco de Mayo triumph --
and also (though she might not know this) not feeling so
hot today. Laid low by a head cold. (Well, she knows
of its seeming imminence. Before she left I told her I
could feel it coming on.)
     So anyway, a week of solitudinous nights is here,
and in a way I welcome it. It was just a year ago this
week that she went off to the remote in-state mountain
resort for her last big grad-school session and when she
returned our romance took off (starting with the

fabulous seductive sunset dinner in her apartment with the million-dollar view). Ever since, it, the romance, has been flying high and with plenty of exciting turbulence. This is the first real break we've had, the first chance for either of us to pause, collect his/her wits a bit, try to see things from a calmer and more detached perspective with his/her feet solidly on the floor or the ground or whatever's down there.

So here's the bedroom. Ours. Where the triumph went down (and I'll be getting back to that in a bit). Two small lamps shining at the moment, a pair of warm, almost perfectly symmetrical cones and fuzzy truncated circles of light cast upward onto the walls and ceiling. Blinds closed as they almost always are (because they're too hard to get at for adjusting). A cat yowling outside; few other sounds. And for the first time since B-2 days I'm jyzing in -- and also for the first time since then, seated in -- my longtime favorite funky green armchair, its wornness and shabbiness now masked by a large and neatly tucked purple throw-thing of Z's. (Personally I detect little improvement -- but then I thought the chair was just about perfect as it was.)

I'm seated at the foot of the bed, facing it. Only tonight has it dawned on me I could rest my legs on the bed by stretching them straight out, and I'm doing so now. This as I "sit in for," so to speak, my dirty laundry which usually occupies this chair, the pile slowly mounting between laundry days. Earlier tonight I moved the pile to the hall carpet in front of the folding doors concealing the washer/dryer. One thing I intend to get done while Z's away is a major, major load or rather series of loads of laundry, including even some stuff that's virtually clean except it's been moldering for ages inside boxes or unopened drawers. (Also high on the to-do list is the long-delayed final setup of the art worktable in the living room, clearing the center portion for action of various kinds, with the nature of many of these yet to be determined.)

A fine room, this. Books, plants, lamps, carpets, clutter. Atop the four-unit wire cube organizer to my

left, overlooking the bed in a spot where I hope Z will
be constantly reminded of it, is the giant red "Da Troth
& Nuttin But" Valentine's card. And on the middle shelf
of the five-foot-high foldable bookcase to my right, a
cup of the usual kosher wine, cherry flavor this time (I
like it!). Also to my right is the lamp I'm jyzing by,
and its positioning there makes for intricate shadowplay
as cast by J-stick and hand and arm. But because of the
strange angles in the walls behind me the narrow table
on which the lamp stands would fit only to the right of
the chair, not to the prescribed left to enable
unshadowed J-ing for a right-hander.

So -- jyze took a long holiday. Its longest ever,
I do believe. A fortnight plus. No hope now of
wrapping up this first volume of Annal 5 on schedule.
We're already a week past the projected completion date
with a little over forty pages still to go.

During the interim a couple of minor fights, a trip
with Z to the storage unit, and, to repeat, our landmark
first authentic full-service -- yes! -- copulation.
Then, the night before I took her to the airport (along
with her fellow utility employee Kendra) another minor
fight broke out, the most minor of them all but still
disturbing because the timing was so bad. It seemed to
displease her excessively that I couldn't, on such a
meaningful night, come up with a second consecutive
authentic full-service copulation. The way she
expressed this was: "I still can't get used to the way
you are." My style of humping, she meant. It led her
to cite again, as a model of how it ought to be done,
"The Story of O" (whose author, as it happens, died
just last week).

I won't deny it, this statement of her preferred
style pained me, and still does, and it's pain I don't
enjoy at all. I don't want to have to be dealing with
S/M issues again. Isn't one Lady V enough for a
lifetime? But of course I conspire in this too. I
must. Somehow. No, I don't want to explore just how
and why. Been there, done that, learned little of real
import. I'm just hoping I can gradually ease Z away

from any bona-fide S/M yearnings by showing her a better
way of loving. Better, though? Really? Who says? I
dunno, I dunno, and it doesn't matter anyway. It's the
only way I can love, and I do love her. (True, on some
days the word starts to seem almost meaningless. But
our being together doesn't.)

J-slinging like this, suddenly I think of an
ancient protojyze master. The idleness. The zuihitsu.
Brushstroking away by lantern light in the shadowy
nocturnal deeps of a far-off land and time.

Yes, it's good to be reminded of my essential
aloneness. With Z gone I'm immediately reimmersed in
the old solitary B-2 ways. I find myself lingering in
my chair, picking up new things to read, puzzling
meanwhile whether I really want to head out the door so
soon, and this despite having planned to do just that
and knowing eventually I must. But nothing can get me
moving at any particular moment. (This is that other
chair I'm talking about, the black armchair in the
living room. For the past four months that's been my
major perch.) I stretch out the scoping work over more
days -- why not, since I have nothing truly planned
anyway. Makes it that much easier to do the actual
work, even though it can be demoralizing to find myself
doing it Friday and Saturday nights (as I was last night
and tonight).

So I linger. I dawdle. I temporize. I idle. I
ruminate. -- And I love doing all this. That's the
real rub. Even being at loose ends I love it. And yet
it's disturbing as well. I want to blow it all off and
get serious about something. But -- I know that's
ridiculous. And I don't really want it. It's just a
kind of headstrong superficial desiring which needs to
be overcome by a deeper soul-fired desiring which I know
must be there if only I can find a way to tap into it
given all the delicious distractions, including the one
of simply yielding to distractedness.

Okay, never mind. Enough. I no longer have even a
faint idea of what I'm talking about.

-- During the journey to the storage unit I gave Z

a quick tour of my former stomping grounds, including a drive-by of the house where I lived with "that Nora woman" for almost seven years. It was a fairly gutsy thing to do, I thought. Z didn't melt down, thank god. She said very soberly, "Are you sure you're okay with south hill after living in a setting like this?" I assured her that after the novelty of backwoods living had worn off -- which took about six months tops -- I was dying to get back to the city and I love our place here on the hilltop and most of all I love living with her. (All emphatically true!)

We borrowed Leola and Gerry's sturdy pickup for the trip. Hauled a big load of boxes over and Mother's huge stereo console back to the city. Even managed to schlep the console up the stairs here by ourselves (sliding it on a couple of narrow plywood sheets left over from the dismantled loft). Felt quite heroic in doing so, both of us, and what's more without a single pulled muscle or splinter or broken fingernail as far as I know.

-- Well, I see it's after three now and she still hasn't called. Could be she's feeling she overdid it last night and so she'll wait until tomorrow afternoon (when she won't have to whisper because Kendra's asleep in the next room). This is wise and good and it's even smart, I guess, since I'm feeling a few little twinges of miffedness.

The bed here, I'll mention, is not made. Yellow sheets on it, the lumpy indigo denim comforter. The layered futon mattresses, hers and mine, still with that deep valley running down the middle. Our bed. It's home. Where we rut in that same rut, or across it, and sometimes, or at least once anyway, consummatorily. where I slip in in the dark almost every night about four a.m. under the current dispensation, Saturday night usually being the one exception. She always naked. And I think this is just for my benefit. We started out that way, both of us, and now it's required: to be even skimpily nightclothed would send a worrisome message. (She persuaded me to get rid of my old pillow. It still worked fine, I thought, but it was shedding a few tiny

pieces of foam through a small leak. I was accustomed
to the pillow and comfortable with it but I never really
loved it, so what the heck, why not toss it if it means
she'll no longer have to breathe in potentially toxic
foam pieces. But that pillow, I was trying to remember
when I got it and I think it was just over twenty years
ago, when I moved out of the residential hotel, which
supplied linen, to live with Lady U, who as it happened
didn't, and so I had to buy a new pillow (but she
already had one of her own). -- And every day I make up
the bed before I leave the house in the afternoon.
Seems fair. In fact I like to do it -- and also like
to leave Z a note on the pillow, or under it.)

     -- So I think I'm done. For now anyway. Antsiness
is on the rise even as I'm again becoming more tired. I
want to see if the big Sunday edition of the "night
paper" has arrived yet. If it has, I didn't hear it.

     Probably I'll return to these pages for another
session in a day or two. I'm trying to work out this
thorny matter of how to proceed jyzically -- made even
thornier by the fact that I'm now so far behind schedule
-- and I'm thinking an odd-days approach may be the way
to go: first, third, fifth, and seventh day of each
eight-day J-week.

*   *

     Yup, two days later. Same room, same chair, same
lamps on, same maroon sweats on me (it's cool again at
night after a couple of uncommonly mild weeks). And
just about the same time. Three-thirty a.m. or so.
Sometimes the birds have begun warming up their pipes by
this hour -- especially if a crime copter hovers
overhead or nearby with floodlights glaring, as happens
maybe once every few weeks -- but not tonight.

     So then -- the first consummatory fuck. Why'd it
finally happen? Two important contributing factors
spring to mind. First, meltdowns stopped, or almost
stopped. Z herself noticed this. Second, I think I
finally managed to get across to her the importance to
me of finding a groove, building a rhythm, ratcheting up
together. Apparently she hadn't really understood when

117

[Deep Jyze]

I'd mentioned these things before, and especially what
I'd meant about slowing down when she was getting close
to -- argghh, I don't know, the whole thing's probably
way too complex for this kind of analysis.
     I don't even want to be trying to break it down.
Why am I doing this?
     -- Probably because I'm nervous about what'll be
happening next with us. When she gets back I'll likely
be a stranger to her again. Every other time we've made
progress in the sexual realm it's stirred up high
expectations on her part only to be followed by a bad
meltdown when they weren't swiftly realized. I'm afraid
we're by no means out of the woods on this matter. (And
it's no fun at all going through such an ordeal just
when "the erection pill" is the talk of the land.)
     (The tone of this jyze seems to be changing, I've
noticed. Why, though, I don't know. I don't think it's
reflecting a shift in relations with Z. I suspect it
has more to do with searching for a sustainable
perspective on the relationship as it settles into long-
term form and maybe even authentic copulatory form.)
     Today she called during the noon break of the
recycling conference. The talk seemed awkward. (I
tried not to show I felt it was, though.) Before
leaving town she gave me an envelope to open each day --
each one so far containing a roll of organic hard candy
-- peach, cherry, and butterscotch, my three favorites
-- and a picture postcard bearing a brief loving message.
I wish I'd done something equally mushy for her. (But
overall I don't feel we're out of balance on such things
-- at least not yet.)
     -- It's almost as if I'm waking up after being in a
trance for a year. Bedazzled. A love tornado picked me
up and whirled me madly around and finally it's dropped
me here. -- Me and my whole life. Where am I? (Sounds
a whole lot like her "Who are you?" I admit it, yeah.
But does this mean I should tell her about this?
Wouldn't doing so make her even shakier?)
     Yesterday, I should note, was Mother's Day.
Tonight I was reading about the growing incidence of

fatal lung cancer among women, especially those who've
undergone hormone replacement therapy while smoking (as
Mother did). The sadness of this. Also, as happens
from time to time, another possible new cancer cure,
"the most promising yet," is grabbing headlines. Would
it have saved her? (I also wonder if it might save me
someday. Can't help it. I'm my mother's son! What
took her down might come after me too! And if I can
just hang on for a few more years -- meanwhile keeping
myself out of the docs' clutches -- I might have a
pretty good chance of racking up a normal life span and
thus have enough time left to complete my lifework.)

   This is horrible. Tonight I'm utterly uninspired.
Again! What the hell is this? Is it a kind of post-
First True Fuck letdown?

   Day after tomorrow I'll be starting a new jyze
entry. That'll be the night before Z returns. Maybe
I'll do better then. (A distant bird is cheeping. Just
one. And I can hear the ticking of the clock on the bed
headboard, and it too sounds like a distant bird, albeit
a more mechanical one, like the cuckoo of a cuckoo
clock. I suppose this may be because my own clock here
is perched at the back of the small square "soundproof"
compartment I built into the headboard and which now
serves as a kind of echo chamber.)

   -- So I think I'll go try to shrink the periodical
stack.

14

   First test of the newly revamped jyze. It is
indeed Wednesday night, and hereafter for the rest of
the year J-day will fall without exception every eighth

day (barring emergencies, of course). On those J-days I
figure I'll always be able to eke out at least a few
pages. Later on in the eighter I'll fill in the rest of
the allotment with odd-day kwikjyzes as necessary.

Will it work? Can this -- this right here -- be
jyze? No way to know just yet. But a good sign: I'm
already kind of liking it. The pressure seems eased.
Forty-five minutes, wot the hey, even on a very bad day
I can vamp for that long (vamp at the revamp).

So here. Sizzle of light rain. Twenty after three
in the a.m. A distant train whistle, a not-so-distant
car alarm (almost every night I hear at least one or
two, and sometimes also a shattering of glass preceding
the alarm). -- And I've returned to the black armchair
in the living room.

I'm wondering how Z will see this place after
staying in a fancy hotel room and also for a night at
Nick's very large apartment, which she says he keeps
compulsively clean. (Yes, this is Kat's "Uncle Nick,"
former husband of Manny's daughter Ruth.) Could be
she'll be hit by a kind of reentry shock. She's already
told me she wants to devote Sunday to straightening up
the place so Nick won't be too boggled when he stays
with us week after next.

Today five cards from her arrived in the mail. A
short note in each. She's worrying too, as I know also
from her call yesterday. "You still love me???" She's
quick to agree she'll see me as a stranger at first.
(One card says she has a couple of "aha!s" to offer: on
"coming" and "looking.") And she didn't fail to
contrast my behavior this past week to what it was when
she left town a year ago, when I sent off those wildly
impassioned special-delivery letters.

But -- I'm actually feeling better today. I've got
my vision back, my worldview or maybe I should say my
life view. What matters above all is loving the Z-woman
well. Making sure she feels it. That's the absolute
key. (One of her cards says traveling is different for
her now because she knows she has an "anchor" back
home.)

[Can This Be Jyze?]

       What helped me most was looking through a box of
her old photos I'd never seen before. (She said prior
to leaving that it was okay to do this. Imagine, asking
permission for such a thing! But I did.) A number of
them touched me deeply, including several where she's
with some unidentified boyfriend of bygone years. (I'm
not saying the boyfriend pix don't also make me insanely
jealous. But, in fact, they don't. Not insanely. But
jealous enough to goad me into staring them down, one
after another, yes -- until the guys in them blink.
Hard. Or at least that's how I see it.)
       I also came across, in the same box, an old
instruction sheet from a certain Centropolis charity
hospital for crippled children. For a moment I felt
with real-life intensity at least some small part of the
horror that same hospital held for her as a child and
all the way into her late teens as she returned for
follow-up exams and demonstrations of her reconstructed
gait for the assembled interns (and in her nightmares
she experiences this right up to the present).
       (What am I proudest of? That I've been able to
calm most of her anxieties at least somewhat. Maybe
even all of them at least somewhat, since it seems
pretty clear they run in packs and when one eases, they
all do. -- Of course before long they all come back to
pretty much where they were, or most do, although each
succeeding round their bite may be a bit less troubling
to her and so also to me. If that makes sense. I
guess what I'm trying to say is it's a long and very
gradual process of anxiety-relieving we're involved in
-- or I hope that's a significant part of what's
happening here.)
       -- Tomorrow I'll be picking her up at the airport a
little before one in the afternoon. I'll have to scrape
myself out of bed at ten or so in order to shower,
shave, make coffee, eat, and then allow plenty of time
for the drive to the airport and parking. I'll take
along a book. (And I know in advance I'll be strongly
reminded of the many times I picked up "Nora" there,
most of which involved turning my night into day in much

the same way.)

    Meanwhile how are things going? Seems I'm always in a mad scramble just to keep up on newspaper and periodical reading and this past week's been no exception. Otherwise I've accomplished little beyond hustling the usual meager living, working out several times, making my meals and doing my chores (laundry and the like -- all done!). Normally I walk downtown every day; this week I've also been walking home. (The nighttime hikes through the Asian quarter and up the hill, while far from tension-free, aren't half as bad as I'd expected. Probably they're safer than riding the bus.)

    -- And so my time's up. For the first vamp of the revamp, good enough. Tomorrow after her return Z will be taking the afternoon off from work: should be a trip (and a whole different kind of trip from the trip she'll be returning from). Unfortunately this is again a heavy workweek for me (relatively speaking, of course; even the heaviest are still rarely more than twenty-five hours). But Wednesday night through Friday night I'll have to be scrambling.

    Well yeah, so?

    Just want to say I hope the awkward reacquaintance period won't go on too long.

    (The newly cleared worktable over there, I'd like to be doing some real work on it. But several other projects come first. Most of these are the domestic-chore type, and Z devotes nowhere near as much time to this kind of thing as I'd like. I don't want to be doing them all myself; I want us to tackle them together (in parallel in most cases, I suppose, she tending to hers and me to mine). Evidently she's never been too big on the homemaking thing. And ironically, though she might like to be a little bigger on it now -- when she's finally got a real domestic/romantic cohabitation scene going here, truly the first of her life -- she has less time than ever. The network of friends she built up to help cushion the pains of living alone has compiled a large backlog of unfulfilled claims on her over the past year and she feels she must respond to them.)

*   *

Quick! Quick! It's half past three already and
bedtime is four and she's "hongry" -- for me! A couple
of notes say so! And she could amble out here at any
moment (naked as usual at this hour except for her black
sleep mask, which she lifts just enough to make sure I'm
not sneaking up to tickle her). And we're on a roll
too. Almost shocking to me, and to her too no doubt,
ol' Possum has pulled off a second straight full-service
ejacoshag.

And me wearing right now just a sleeveless black
henley ("Z-shirt"), naked otherwise, ready for action --
even a bit genitally flushed and swollen and tingly and
elongated in anticipation -- "lunkerish" -- but getting
in a few licks of another kind first. J-licks! The
black armchair once again.

"The struggle of jyze to regain its equilibrium as
it enters a whole new conjugal era."

(My newest plan to make more time for personal
projects -- jyze included -- involves leaving home every
day at one p.m. no matter what. Breakfast and all the
other "morning" ablutions, including newspaper reading
and chores, I'll cut back to no more than an hour.)

Tonight I hit the scope office an hour earlier than
usual -- at about half past six -- and busted my ass all
night but still couldn't get everything done. Three
nights is no longer enough for two full days of grand
jury -- not if I have to be catching the last bus home
so early, i.e., 1:15 a.m.

(Then again I'm feeling a little more secure about
finding new work for Jyzer Ink should Naomi decide to
drop out of the business or do her own scoping. For the
second time in just a month someone tried to recruit me
-- was desperately in search of an experienced scoper.
It seems as the demand for scopers shrinks, the supply
is shrinking even faster, meaning for those few of us
foolish enough to remain in the business things are at
least momentarily looking up. -- But I don't expect to
need more work for the next year or two. Of course

123

Naomi could fall ill, something like that. The truth is
J. Ink is depending on a single client now and therefore
its sole proprietor has very little job security. But
now at least he can feel a little better about winging
it, which is what he'll be doing regardless. -- Talkin'
'bout this jyzer going at it right here and now smack in
the middle of the very last sentence of this lengthy
parenthetical stalling paragraph, correct.)

So Z returned. It wasn't as bad a homecoming as I
was fearing -- and it wound up a triumph -- but for a
while things were quite awkward, as expected, and then
came a brief but intense squabble. The mad dash for the
airport, the long wait for luggage, the drive way up
north to drop off Kendra (and tour her impressive fixer-
upper house -- for seven years she and her son have been
hard at work upgrading it), stop for a late lunch at Z's
favorite gourmet burger joint and another for groceries
at the co-op, then home -- and just inside the door she
started bawling because no flowers or balloons or
posters were on festive display to welcome her back.
(Earlier she'd been cool toward me, again as she'd
warned me to expect, yet also had complained because I
hadn't swept her into my arms at the airport -- yet
she'd explicitly asked me in advance on the phone to be
discreet in Kendra's presence.)

Yes, sometimes she can be more than a little tough
to take. This breakdown before she'd even gotten her
coat off hit me like a fist in the gut. It also felt
like a shameless manipulation. (But I liked Kendra for
saying first thing when we were alone for a moment at
the airport, "She missed you so much.")

It took about an hour to get past it. "Dour
Norwegian." Three times she did a high-drama cutoff and
stomped out. But we did learn something, I insist. We
even spelled it out. Right now, however, I don't want
to be trying to remember exactly how. The main thing is
this: in the future when she pulls this stuff I intend
to call her on it. Challenge her. No more Mr. Grimace-
and-Bear-It. No more Mr. Rope-a-Dope.

So then to the bedroom and now only an hour

remained before I had to leave for work, though it stretched to two and then three (when she offered to drive me downtown -- and this as the very last episode of her favorite TV show was about to begin). Lo and behold, the old male apparatus wasn't feeling dour at all. Three separate times we humped invaginally, and the third was a charm. "We've finally," she crowed, "begun to fuck for real!" -- And she even said (also), "Hey, we can fuck good!" I'd like to think she hasn't seen anything yet. (But I don't want to jinx us either.)

The third round left her too sore or we would've gone a fourth. She admitted she used to get torn up this way fairly often with some of those other guys, it's not all that unusual, but then again aging and thinning vaginal membranes may be a factor. She's vowing to apply more of the storied wild-yam abstract (she's supposed to be doing it three times a day but has let it slide, so to speak -- gloop! -- to something like three times a week or less).

As I walked down the hill this afternoon she spotted me from her bus and hopped off at the next stop and came trotting back (in those proud new yellow chucks of hers) as I reversed direction (in my proud old black-and-white chucks) and we met in the middle of the high bridge. She asked then which would be better for nookie, tonight when I arrived home or early in the morning (later in the a.m. she has plans). I said I might be brain-fried from work so we'd have to see.

-- And here we are. It's ten after four but I'm feeling pretty good. Might just give it a shot in there, yup. Three in a row would be quite something. "Consolidate your gains. Strike while the iron's still -- iron!" (And hot too, yeah. For real! I just checked!) -- Well, we'll see.

*   *

Taking this up at quarter to four in the a.m. on the next odd day of the eighter. And why not? Seems destined to become routine, at least for the life span of the current experimental odd-day kwikjyze regime.

125

Black armchair. Jazz radio. Wine. No pants and
of course no underwear since I don't even own any (and
so at this moment I sit not in but atop a pair of
ancient blue gym shorts so as to protect the chair from
any inadvertent emprinting of asshole asterisks (yuck)).

What's new, I'm nibbling at a stack of graham
crackers. This afternoon Z urged me to go ahead and
have at the box of same which I bought for her last fall
when she was sick. "Gam cackers." And what we pull
over us on cold nights is at least sometimes a "banky."
Baby talk, a fair amount of it -- she apologizes for it
from time to time -- but it doesn't bother me. (It
recalls certain Korean men snuggling up with kisaeng:
letting their inner child out. Z had a tough early life
-- all those operations and hospital stays, not to
mention inner-city working-class deprivations and
maternal sexual abuse and racist insults from Cawkazoid
schoolmates and others -- and even as a child she had to
learn to clamp down on her own inner child.)

It's been a fine couple of days. Lotsa lovin' and
even a little cleanin'. (Will a time ever come when I
want to jyze about something other than the matter of
whether I've succeeded in boning my sweetie? Let's hope
so. Right now, though, it's still without question the
lead story. -- So yes, I did so succeed, but I did not
succeed at squeezing out any fresh jizz for her. Not
inside her. She still got me off, in fact twice, but
both times by hand. And she emerged with a "pookie
pussy" and sore nipples as well. We were catching up.)

A big gang showed up for the slide show at Wei and
Alison's. Other than the hosts we knew none of them and
pretty much kept to ourselves. We mulled whether
we'd've hit on each other had we attended such a yawner
of a party as singles. I loved her a lot and was struck
time and again by how fabulous she looked. Just might
have something to do with those days in the desert sun.
"Seeing her with fresh eyes." (And a fine moment
tonight, surprising her in the bedroom with as soulful a
gaze as I know how to work up -- and I wasn't even
trying! It just happened!)

[Can This Be Jyze?]

     Yesterday, which is to say late Friday night and
early Saturday morning and then again early Saturday
afternoon, we went at it three times in all, well over
an hour each round, once at the beginning, middle, and
end of my night, and it was after two p.m. when I
finally staggered out of the bedroom. In the late
morning while I slept she slipped out to have her nails
done, toes included, using a gift certificate Jess and
Gwen gave her. Orange toenails. I think she expected
me to rave about them more than I did (but I did suck
her clit and her fibroidectomy scar and also laved out
both of her armpits and reveled in all the funky
aromas). And then again last night (before our
ritualistic Saturday-night reading in bed, which starts
at around ten or eleven or whenever we get home and goes
on until four a.m., though she's often asleep well
before midnight) and then again this morning. So what's
that altogether? Five rounds, that's right!
     We're very happy. Can't get no satisfaction? Hah!
Turns out we can get quite a bit and on both sides of
the M/F divide, at least on certain righteous occasions.
Whooeee!
     -- But she's starting to push me about setting a
wedding date. Grumbles that I'm less interested now
than she is. (So last night when she least expected
something like this I hooked her little finger in mine
and looked her hard in the eye and said gravely, "I
marry thee, Zoelie B." And she seemed moved, but by
this morning the effect had completely worn off.
Tonight she proposed a wedding date: March 29 of next
year (that is, our second Meet Day anniversary).
     I'm chewing on it. I dread all the hassles and
rigmarole, but what the hell.
     -- And I dread Sunday, May 31st of this year.
That's the date she pinned me down on a few weeks ago
for resuming our long-postponed "conversation" about my
health: diet, doctors, dentists, proctologists,
sexologists, penisologists, and more. Could be the next
ten days or two weeks will mark the end of an era.
Matters could be about to get a whole lot more fraught.

[Deep Jyze]

     -- See, it's late. Almost half past four again.
This is the trouble with last-thing jyzing. And so
maybe I should try to do it first thing when I get home
and move the reading and chores later. As it stands now
I'm too wasted by this hour. But if I've been working I
need to wind down first upon arriving home. Decompress.
So maybe I'll aim for somewhere in the middle.
     (Birds clamoring magnificently -- the full mighty-
throated chorus now answering the earlier soloists, the
isolated practice-room warm-ups of an hour ago.)
                    *   *
     -- Suddenly the walls seem to be closing in. A
message from reporter Verna awaited me when I got home
tonight (at the usual time, 1:35 or so, after the usual
fortnightly light-work Tuesday evening of cranking out
GJ finals). She's starting her new job at the county
on June 1st, Verna is, much earlier than she'd expected,
and she wants Jyzer Ink to do her scoping, as I long
ago promised her it (I) would. But do I actually want
this to happen? And do I owe it to Verna to keep my
word to her after she was so bad about keeping hers to
me at that crucial juncture three years ago -- in fact
at two different crucial junctures?
     Some serious weighing lies ahead. The scales.
Fears and hopes. Scruples. Narrowing timelines.
Loving. Projects I badly want to complete or at least
get down and grapple with.
     A values crisis! Interrogate all those opaque
principles and desires and ethics until you drop!
     Meanwhile it's three-twenty and Z's awaiting me in
bed. It's a designated nookie night. She's feeling bad
because she had to cancel our workout at the WOC
yesterday and our normal Tuesday dinner at home earlier
tonight. (In fact we set up tonight's nookie session at
the end of this morning's, which she had to call to an
abrupt halt after getting hers several times but before
I'd gotten mine even once. But in truth I was far past
getting mine anyway, even a small part of it, and quite
pleased merely to have been able to crank the requisite
body part up and in for a pretty good churn against all

the odds: tiredness, a heavy WOC workout yesterday,
light eating all day, two cups of wine before bed -- and
I'd been asleep for an hour, which seems to be just
about the worst length of sleeping time for me to try to
quickly rouse myself from, sexwise or in any other way.

   -- Nope, no excuses here. Just observations. And
I loved it regardless, I always love it when she awakens
me for loving.

   Black armchair. A rushed reading of the evening
paper, also part of yesterday morning's paper, also the
whole of our very fine local radical fortnightly, not to
mention a lengthy note from Z composed in the form of a
labyrinth with the handwriting gradually shrinking as it
spirals ever inward (loving note too, really loving,
proposing we get married every Friday and make every
weekend a honeymoon). And I reheated some lamb
leftovers she brought home for me from this noon's
luncheon honoring June (who's been officially admitted
to law school). And about an hour ago Z herself ambled
out naked for some brief conversation during which her
black sleep mask rode her hairline like tipped-up
sunglasses.

   -- Possum is excited too. Again. Earlier I
checked: how's the ole Eliotic appendage looking up
close after all the hard workouts lately? Stretched it
out and twisted it around this way and that and examined
it real good. Looking all right, I decided. "Shabby
but not too shabby." Slightly swollen and even flushed
a bit like a much younger, spryer marsupial. Eager to
go another round. And ready too, I do hope. A three-
day buildup of vital fluids: that should do it. But who
knows. Full confidence is not yet back. (Jyze rules
decree another exception on "Eliotic," which I may have
failed to declare earlier after using the term.)

   -- Also complicit regarding the time crunch, I love
to leave her notes. Three of them this afternoon: one
in the hall, one on her pillow, one on the chalkboard.
And a fourth, come to think of it, pointing out the two
new magnetic "kitchen caddies" I bought yesterday from
the bargain bin at the big downtown office-supply store

and slapped onto the side of the fridge above the
microwave this afternoon, matching his and hers, "Z" and
"G" emblazoned thereon with silver ultra-marker and
spray-on glitter (and then turned the fan on because she
regards the marker as being toxic) (and it is).

And I love to try to keep myself updated on
political and arts-world doings. And I love to walk and
work out. And I love to be very easygoing with Z on
weekends and whenever she wants to talk. And I love to
be laid-back about time in general, when possible.

Something's gotta give even if Jyzer Ink doesn't
take on Verna.

It's almost four. I'm wondering if I've done
enough here. -- I'd like to scribble out a reply to Z's
labyrinth note before I wander in there. This, that,
the other. Wheeee! Jyze, you're barely scraping the
surface. Is this how it's gonna hafta be? And we in
our first Deep year? (Tonight's headlines: India sets
off test atomic blasts and the grossly hypocritical
boss-of-the-world U.S., brandishing its massive nuclear
arsenal, squawks. The feds hit our local corporate cash
cow, the software behemoth, with a huge antitrust suit,
if that matters (and in the long run it probably won't).
Indonesia seems ready to blow as its economy collapses
under the strains of U.S.-driven corporate/"neoliberal"
globalization. -- Which reminds me: Aida's sister
Serafina and her family have finally fled Djakarta and
are due to arrive at the Jyze City airport tonight.)

So, news. -- But do I have enough energy to gear
up and still get done the things I want and need to get
done? And while at it still love life? Love the life
it'll make for?

Well, play with it. Check it out.

(Or am I wedded to an outmoded self-image? And
would I be upsetting relations with Z to shuck it?)

-- So three kwikjyze sessions and now a new J-day
looms just forty hours ahead. As yet I have no real
sense how this new protocol is working out.

But it's nookie time. Up and at 'em, you scruffy
joy toy you!

15

    And it's the new J-day. Oooeee, such a good one.
Truly we're over the hump on humping. Lots and lots of
humping now. And get this: today we consummated twice.
I mean each complete with ejac. In-bagel ejac. Two of
'em in one day. Whoop-de-do!
    (And I laffed like crazy after the second. Spoofed
myself as the swaggering stud. Z'd never before heard
me yawping quite so barbarically. Don't know if I had
either. "You must've really been under some pressure."
"Hey, lemme tell you" -- and then more crazy
cachinnation.)
    We figure it was probably the lamb that did it.
"Eat lamb, be a ram." "I got plenty of mutton, and
mutton's plenty for...." "Ewe, Ewe, Ewe, I'm in love
with...." -- Talking about the lamb leftovers she again
brought home from a fancy downtown restaurant. Truly
they were tasty and red-meaty. (Another factor, she's
been on jury duty the past couple of days and so hasn't
had to worry that being a little tired in the morning
would lead to grief at work, and therefore I haven't had
to worry about it for her either. And she's been
excused early each afternoon, meaning she could hurry
home and we could "take a nap" and "bonobo big-time.")
    Now I'm lolling at the hideaway. 'Long about, yup,
midnight. A very light workload at the scope office
tonight; it took only about forty minutes to crank it
out, and that included dragging the computer from one
end of the suite to the other and back again on its
creaky frozen-wheeled cart. This after Z dropped me off
downtown at seven p.m. on her way to the co-op to pick

up snack goodies for our upcoming weekend at the ocean,
which has been planned and replanned over a course of
many months although I don't think I've ever mentioned
it before. (I'd've been here much earlier tonight but
I blew a couple of hours browsing at the two main
downtown chain bookstores.)
     Oh how sweet it is. Even if it only happens this
once and never again, still, it's just the thought it
could happen again that matters (and I bet it will
happen again -- lots and lots of times) (here I'm
confirming I'm just one more of those infamously
mindless U.S. male macho blowhards, no question).
     -- She read aloud a couple of hot passages on
lesbian love which she said come close to describing her
own feelings (except for the lesbian part, and even on
that score they're not too far off, because she does
sometimes fantasize about hanky-panky with women) --
especially a phrase about orgasms lined up "like beads."
-- So now I'm multiple too, ha. So take that, Ms. Polly
Morphous Perverse!
     Meanwhile she's not too pleased with my decision,
newly reached, to sign up reporter Verna as a client,
even though it's only provisional. "We're a couple now
-- shouldn't this be a collaborative decision?" And so
it will be, by and by, but not before I see whether it's
feasible at all. My hope would be to do most of the
Verna work in the afternoon or early evening, and when I
told Z this she seemed relieved. (And truly she has no
right to complain given her own time-gobbling job and
the many additional hours she devotes to political
causes and to get-togethers with friends and her
surrogate family (the D's, Nurse Betty and Kat). My
guess is the weekly Jyzer Ink workload for Verna and
Naomi combined would average thirty hours or less.)
     Other issues? Nothing really major and for that
matter nothing much minor either. Just the usual
velleities (ooh do I love that word). For instance: I'd
like to see her read more of the serious books I lay on
her (even if it meant cutting back on whodunits).
Meanwhile she'd like me to arrange my reading lamps so

they don't bake my pituitary gland (as this one here
is doing right now). No shortage of items like
those two -- but then that's almost always true.

On the surrogate-family front, Serafina and her two
daughters are safely back in town, with husband Dak soon
to follow. Z's thinking things will be different now
with Sera, the eldest of the D-clan siblings, and for
pretty much the same reason they're different with Aida
(middle child of the five): Z won't have anywhere near
the time she had before to devote to Sera and Sera will
be miffed and relations will sour. (Each week brings
news of some new spat with Aida. And a friend of
Kendra's who works for the state confides that Aida has
already gained a reputation there for being extremely
hard to work with and "too authoritarian." Z says she's
trying to help Aida work on this and it's not the first
time.)

Ho hum. See, Kat and Betty need her, Z, as she
says, and Sera and Dak and the kids don't; they've
already got way more extended family than they can
handle. Same's true for Aida, really, except Aida's a
single mother with a hyperactive ten-year-old boy on her
hands two weeks out of every month. ("Ho hum," why'd I
write that? Because all this is largely repetitious,
that's why. Same issues as last year. But of course
this doesn't mean they won't be just as important this
year. On the contrary. Maybe even more so with Sera
and family living here to thicken the plot.)

-- But nonpersonal hot issues we're talking about a
lot? I-200, the initiative campaign to end affirmative
action in our state. The deepening housing crisis and
its effect on our hilltop hood. (This crisis is
national in scope. Kat's "Uncle Nick" flew in two
nights ago and during a layover en route in my former
city No. 2/7 picked up the most recent issue of my old
alt rag and then passed it along to me, and it happens
to feature a long piece on the housing crisis down there
-- vacancy rates under one percent, rents zooming out
of sight, thousands of folks "couch-surfing" -- that is,
sleeping on friends' couches.) -- And an article in one

of the dailies here describes the burgeoning "hobo
jungles" in the greenbelt on the flanks of our hill,
scores of chronically homeless folks camping there under
abysmal conditions -- one irony however being that their
growing numbers serve to insulate the hill somewhat from
the citywide rent pressure. They're like our own ragtag
guerrilla army guarding us against the gentrifiers. Of
whom, from a different perspective, Z and I in our
different ways and also in our similar and combined ways
-- some of them -- could be seen to be exemplars
ourselves, as noted before, like part of a vanguard or
fifth column.)
     -- Eep, I see it's a couple of minutes before one.
Last bus to the hill is, as always, one-fifteen. I'm
sure I've mentioned this before but here it is again:
this is now one of the major constraints on my life.
Don't want to try to run the gauntlet of that ragtag
guerrilla army on foot night after night even though I
think on balance they see me as an ally of sorts (and I
know just from the facial expressions of some hilltop
residents that they think I could myself be a soldier
in that same army -- especially in the late afternoon
as I in my street camo come loping down the north
slope past homebound hilltoppers near the points where
the footpaths lead down into and up from the "jungle").
-- But can't dawdle here.

*   *

     With ol' Possum on the comeback trail. A strategy
session for the chief trainer and makeover strategist.
     This at the far end of a four-day gap. Down at the
ocean not a free minute for jyze. Or rather to clear a
few would've caused too much disappointment, and not
just for one terrific little eight-year-old girl but
also for her even more terrific subaunt, my super-duper
Last Chance Romance, I mean Big Big Big Time. (Have
said it all a thousand times before but just can't say
much else these days and can't say it any less smarmily
and that's a fact. -- Though I'll keep trying.)
     So now my fingernails are painted yellow, and each
one features either a red "Z" or a purple "K." Kat did

134

them all. And later I touched them up myself because I
like to show them off wherever I go.

     (Hoofing it down to the hideaway tonight, an hour
before sunset, I watched a huge rainbow materialize --
and also incendiarize -- in a light mist as the sun
broke out over the mountains. One end touched down in
the low-income housing clustered on the southern flank
of east hill some four or five blocks to the north, with
the arch then sweeping up and over the greenbelt and the
high bridge and the huge orange-brick castle -- also
known as the old marine hospital -- which rides the
northern prow of our own hilltop. I mean, a scene of
sublime corniness even beyond the Ozian. Surely only
jyze would dare touch it.)

     Three-hour drive back, surprisingly fast, cutting
over from the coast to the freeway, squalls off and on
all the way. Big bag of organic popcorn. I'm driving,
dipping my hand in the oily bag or sometimes Z's finger-
feeding my face. No need to be a passing fool as I
occasionally did have to be on the drive down (but not
to anything approaching the extent Nick was such a fool
and then some on Saturday night in zipping us twenty
miles on country roads to a fancy seafood restaurant --
I still shudder to think about it).

     The resort -- a fine old "big house" (also known as
"the lodge") funky with art and books and plants, a
grove of tall firs surrounding it, just a five-minute
walk from the beach. The six of us stayed in an
outlying cabin, an immobilized and even more funkified
mobile home of the classic aluminum streamlined type,
one of a dozen or so on the resort property, and happily
the very one where Manny and Betty did their honeymoon
four or five years ago. Since Z and I were the only
couple present we drew the "master bedroom." And we
made the most of it during two long loving nights with
rain at times pattering loudly on the flat low metal
roof. The fucking, yes, is still fine. (Which isn't to
say I'm coming every time or am likely to ever again.)
But three times each night and then one more when we got
home this afternoon. We're fuckin' fools! And laughing

fools too!   (How many times did I actually come? Three.
She? Maybe seventy or eighty. Same old Z, orgasmically
prolific beyond all amazement.)

     -- And so we stopped at an upscale supermarket down
in the valley this afternoon and Z came out with the
makings for a surprise dinner: lambchops. To refuel the
resurgent Possum. We broiled them tonight. Gobbled
them with our eyes gleamingly locked and hungering just
like the celebrated scene in "Tom Jones" -- now a cliche
so potent it's even capable of penetrating jyze.

     Back to the resort. Memorable moments. Kat flying
her kite on the beach, scampering crazily along and
laughing delightedly as it seemed the winds might carry
her aloft like, yes, Icarus. Z and I walking into town
Sunday night and feasting on fresh-caught fish at a
caboose diner gorgeously overgrown with nasties
(nasturtium) and hardy fuchsia. Nick taking grief from
everyone owing to his irksome fastidiousness (always has
to be cleaning and washing and putting things in their
proper places and reminding you to do the same and
better hurry up or he'll do it for you). Z informing me
she was jealous because women were eyeballing me at the
grocery store and the diner (I noticed this too, and
most likely it was triggered by my painted nails and
hand-decorated workshirt and freshly washed shoulder-
blade-length hair -- "Hollywood-style big hair," as Z
cheekily described it -- all of which made me stand out
a bit among the mostly super-straight tourist types; or
then again, possibly owing to my ratty garb they
thought I was about to rob the store or the diner).
Kat, Betty, Nick, and Wanda (Betty's neighbor, a
registered nurse close to Nick's age who joined us for
the weekend, Betty trying to play matchmaker according
to Z, but no match ensued) -- all four riding by on
horses with some twenty others on the windy beach and
suddenly the wind blew off a rider's hat, a horse
panicked and reared as the hat skittered between its
legs, the young girl riding the horse (right behind
Kat's) took a nasty tumble (but after some anxious
moments, as all nearby life froze, was pronounced okay).

    And: Kat in her nifty dark-blue pajamas stretched
out on the couch raptly watching a video of "Oklahoma"
(bringing to mind my own mother playing the same
soundtrack on vinyl when I was a kid) (and such
unmitigated schmaltz it seems now!). "Old Sid," the
charming South African, white-bearded and -- according
to Z -- the very image of Manny as he'd look now were he
still alive -- "Old Sid" chatting with us about the
rooms in "the lodge" after we'd toured several of them,
at Z's urging, in search of a prospective honeymoon love
nest of our own for next year (and we're thinking we
might go for the garret suite that's almost like a
deluxe yet also hyper-funky treehouse on the top floor).
Arnie and Zeke, the two dogs, a black cocker mix and a
dalmatian, both of them gentle and friendly, tugging us
here and there on leashes. Nick putting his new SUV
through its paces in the sand, scarily doing twirlies on
the beach and powering up through the dunes. Nick, Kat,
and I playing catch with one of Z's incandescent green
tennis balls on the beach before a spectacular pink
fractured-clouds ocean sunset (and Kat effortlessly
playing Nick and me off against each other, putting up a
terrific battle against ever going back to the cabin).
    And: Betty's startled look as she opened the door
to our bedroom Sunday morning and caught sight of our
naked upper bodies in a just barely postcoital moment
(surprising, this, because she'd been cracking raunchy
all along about the hijinks in there so you'd think she
would've knocked; but as Z said, maybe she was lost in a
flashback to her honeymoon nights in that very same
room and bed with Manny). And: all my usual little
love-gushes for Z as I watched her playing with the
Katgrrrl, reading a mystery in an armchair, singing
along with "Poor Joad Is Daid" on the video, waiting
outside the local grocery store with Arnie the dog as I
shopped inside (Betty says Z's so far gone on me "she's
becoming more Norwegian every day").
    Said Z to me: "This is such a change, for me to be
the one in the group of women with the boyfriend"
(talking about recent years, before we met, she was, but

surprisingly she didn't specify that). In lovemaking
she had a hard "but interesting" time because she felt
she had to keep quiet too much owing to the close
quarters and thin walls (and I was restrained too, but
more because the bed made considerable noise and the
whole trailer began to creak and rock). (But Z did keep
up a nonstop whisper regardless -- including, once when
I was inside her, "This is heaven -- you can't know what
bliss this is" -- and then apologizing because she
couldn't keep herself from coming again and again rather
than "ratcheting up to a big symphonic come-together
come," as she knows I'd like her to do at least once in
a while) (but I'm not pressing for such results, in part
because I'm afraid if I did ol' Possum would rebel and
refuse to participate at all -- head for the exit and
take his pouch of matched rollers with him).
     And still more little things. While lunging for
one of Kat's tosses I took a totally undignified dive on
the beach and for the rest of the weekend sand was
grinding everywhere inside my clothes (low water
pressure prevented us from showering the last two days)
-- and yet somehow none of this grit ever got into Z's
inner works. Z led me on a "short cut" through the
dunes (having visited the resort a couple of times in
the past, she couldn't resist playing the knowing
veteran) which took us ever deeper into marshy sands and
finally landed us in someone's very large backyard --
guarded by a violently barking and salivating German
shepherd, fortunately restrained by a heavy chain --
and this probably close to a mile from the declared
destination. Nick called me "sir" several times, much
to my chagrin, and said I looked like a "hippie freak
from the Summer of Love," which of course I liked (but
Nick also showed a kind of hypermacho side which clashed
oddly with his fastidiousness and sensitivity and took
him puzzlingly out of focus for me and Z both, to the
point where she was wondering aloud if I thought he
might be gay or bi -- and I'd say he might, which could
help explain his strangely awkward behavior with Wanda
-- but he was married to Manny's daughter!) (and

Saturday night he dutifully roared off to attend an AA
meeting thirty miles down the coast, the nearest
available). And: with his crewcut and angular Teutonic
profile he reminded me physically a lot (and always has,
though it took me a whole year to pinpoint this, in a
eureka moment) of my grade-school buddy Karl B.

-- But just as Kat started to turn ornery whenever
she was overtired, so did Z as the long holiday weekend
wore on. Nothing really bad -- just the resurfacing of
certain small vexations which I suddenly realized had
been absent the first couple of days. Her focus was no
longer quite there. She had calls to make, e-mail to
check, clothes to lay out. And on the last day she and
I had to be leaving well before the others -- because I
had scoping to do back in the city (though only about an
hour's worth) and it had to be ready to go out first
thing in the morning. Vacation over. But both of us,
I'd say, feeling closer than ever before thanks to it.

On Friday, by the way, I got a taste of what Z
faces with Serafina. Aida's computer was down so Sera
called up and more or less announced she'd be dropping
by to use Z's. When she showed up -- with husband Dak
(who arrived back in town from Djakarta the same
morning) and kids Dalisay and Tala in tow -- she camped
out in front of the computer and had scarcely a word to
say to anyone. When I emerged from the shower and
stepped into Z's room in my robe to say hello, Sera
looked up and chirped "Long hair!" and turned right back
to the screen; and that was it for her interaction with
me. Shortly after that Z and I left to see a movie --
this had been planned for days -- and upon return found
no trace of Sera and family and not even a thank-you
note.

Z's theory is that Sera is used to having Z dote on
her kids and be at her beck and call and perhaps already
senses their relationship may no longer be what it was;
and this sounds plausible to me. So I suspect the times
ahead with Sera may resemble the ones we've been going
through all along with her sister Aida. -- One
difference, though: Sera lived with Z for a year or two

and she should have a better idea of Z's ways with men and therefore be more comfortable with them -- and with me. I hope. (And note this too: Z was present in the operating room for the birth of both of Sera's daughters -- even snipped Dalisay's umbilical cord.)

*   *

And now a setback. The ups and downs. So goddamn what if I'm dispirited.

The offending line was: "Will you marry me even if we're incompatible?" It was the way she said it. It came after ol' Possum had staged a classic foozle. This in turn was inspired by her sudden demand just after I'd managed to work my way inside her under less than optimal conditions: "Fuck me fast and hard!"

Fast and hard has never been my thing. Once in a while I like it, but this was definitely not one of those times. I wasn't ready. Not even close.

-- But why the attack? Why so cruel? What about the breakthrough of the past few weeks -- she's ready to say that means nothing?

After a while she "took it back." But by then she'd done new damage while arguing her case -- how it hurts her to realize she'll just "never be satisfied." Her "insecurity" makes her say such things, she explained, and they're not "intended" to be cruel. And she has a theory: what it's really all about is (1) my rebelling against my mother's attempts to control me as a kid, and (2) her (Z's) fears of abandonment by her father. Yes! It's all because of things that happened decades ago! What's more, she "knows" I'm fighting against "something" and she thinks it might be an unwillingness to admit I find her "only superficially attractive and too demanding."

So it's back to square one. And now on returning home tonight I find a note from her saying we're "already to square two." Oh yeah? I doubt it.

What actually caused the blowup? Probably my yielding to her pleas to show her the rest of my photos, the set from Glennarian Stage II (that is, from my twenty-eighth year onward, right up to last year). I

140

hauled them out for her at the hideaway before we
walked home last night. At the time she seemed to
take them pretty well, but I was fearing a meltdown
anyway (just as has actually happened every other
time I've shown her photos and also many of the times
I've revealed in other ways anything at all about my
life with other women, and especially the one who
dominated most of Stage II, Lady U).

And then I woke her up when I went to bed. Simple
horniness prompted this (but the loving kind -- as a
hangover from the weekend I was still feeling
exceptionally close to her -- and by the way, she also
blamed her outburst on what she herself calls her
"phobia" about intimacy and things going too well --
she thinks a little argument is called for to clear the
air after such a super weekend).

This afternoon I met her at the hideaway to help
crop and frame a photo of herself destined to become a
birthday present for her mother. Unexpectedly Jess P.
was there with her -- already inside oohing and aahing
and maybe snickering a bit over some old photos of mine
which Z was showing her when I arrived -- and so we
couldn't deal with any of the issues. And maybe they'll
just fade anyway. Z asked me to let her do "power
sleep" the rest of the week because she lost too many
winks last night. (Bawled too. Loudly and raucously.
Felt "attacked" when I tried to fill her in on how her
"even if we're incompatible" question sounded to me.)

I told her she can't stop believing in us now.
Whatever happened to "unconditional cherishment"? And
this morning she left a note on my chair: "I know. My
satisfaction is guaranteed." Yes, I think it's sincere.
But I don't think she really understands. To put things
in a nutshell: I can't relax into lovemaking with her if
it seems a mere off-night "e-dys episode" will lead to
another major attacking kind of meltdown like this.

It's painful. Humiliating. Mortifying. -- And
not just for me, I know. And knowing this (and usually
being aware of it) just makes matters that much worse.

Four a.m. I'm feeling so low right now. Yet I

know this is the worst of it and things will get better.
It's not the end for us by any means, nor do I think
there will ever be an end. Our sex life probably won't
be permanently damaged. But I fear it might be. Too
many reckless words and attacks could do it. Yet I'm
also trying to maintain the faith: believe in us. Isn't
this what a Deep oughta do? Isn't it written right
there in almost the same words in my "Troth" card?
                              *

     -- And so, on to a new volume, the second of this
fifth jyze annal and the fourteenth of the entire Jyze
Age. Almost a month behind schedule, this transition,
or call it a matriculation (fingers crossed), but I'm
pleased because jyzically, at least, things seem to be
back on track.

BOOK II

[Jyze to the Bone]

16

Did I ever do this before? Seems I did, but a
quick riffle through the previous volume fails to
confirm. It's the new scope office, the conference
room. The direction the windows face is new also.
East. First time ever for any of the downtown offices
I've worked in. The ones here in J. City, that is.

About half past eleven on a Friday night. The
second day of grand jury turned out to be mercifully
short and now I've got an unexpected free ninety minutes
on my hands. (Something else unexpected on my hands is
the set of colorful "Z" and "K" fingernails, or at least
so they still strike me. Whoooeee, lookie here!
Where'd these come from!)

Meanwhile it appears we've already put paid to the
"incompatible" incident, Z and I. As she observed at
the WOC this afternoon (unusual day for a workout, but
we both recognized the need after the long weekend
during which we did little else but canoodle and stuff
our faces) -- she said, "Don't you think we're doing a
lot better now at conflict resolution?"

Well, yeah, I guess. This time we talked it out in
our separate chairs in the living room within an hour of
her arriving home last night. The upshot: from now on
we'll both try to "go toward the other" rather than
withdraw if we're feeling hurt or insecure. And I
assured her it's fine with me that she likes sex fast
and hard once in a while. And it's even finer with me
that she expresses her sexual preferences, even if it's
slightly risky to do so; and as long as ol' Possum is
obliging, I'll certainly do my best to fulfill them.

And she in turn will do the best she can to remember to
dial back a bit every now and then and let herself
slowly ratchet up into a "symphonic come."

And so this morning we were at it again. She atop,
ratcheting and voicing what she was up to. I didn't
come myself (drat it) but otherwise it worked out pretty
damn well, I'd say. And she'd say too, or so I believe.
And with plenty of supporting evidence.

She told me some other little things. On parents'
night at Kat's school last night she, Z, filled in for
mom Betty, who had to work (as did I), and Kat tried to
hide when she saw Z coming. It stung her, again meaning
Z. She was reminded of the days when she was chased
home from gradeschool and taunted for being a "Jap" or a
"Chink" or a "crip" (or a "Jap crip" or a "Chink crip").
I assured her that Kat was probably just doing her usual
eek-eek-hide-and-seek thing, but Z was not persuaded.

Kat's school, by the way, is impressively diverse
-- it's toward the southern end of our hill -- and yet
she too faces racial taunting, including from her own
classmates and friends. "A white boy will never marry
you," one of her best girlfriends razzed her -- and the
girlfriend's a Latina/indigene mix herself. Kat's
ambivalence about her own brown skin and Guatemalan/
Mayan origins is something Z and I both try to help her
work through. And I try to help Z be less critical and
"tough-lovey" with Kat, more cuddly and physical and
praising. As an only child, in effect, Z rarely had
anyone younger to play with, and her fears about her
mother's intentions taught her to be wary about being
physically warm with family members. And her very
strict father forbade her at age five ever again to run
around the house "half naked." And about her mother she
says: "I was ashamed of her at school. I never thought
she was as cool as the other kids' mothers." And of
course Z's childhood problems with her feet often kept
her from being physically active and so she now has
trouble at times relating to Kat, who's as lively a kid
as I've ever come across, male or female. Kat loves to
run, play ball, ride horses, spin in the air, get dizzy,

get tickled, and most of all to wrestle. One of the
most touching moments for me at the resort came in
watching Kat and Betty frolicking on the couch as
"Oklahoma" played on the tube, Betty trying to lick
Kat's nose and Kat trying to ward her off, the happy
laughter pealing from both.

*

So jyze away. Where's it gonna take me? I'm
glancing across the street at a huge wall of ice-tray-
fluorescent-lit windows. In all those office interiors
not a single person is visible. To both sides of the
building itself rise the middle and/or upper portions of
numerous other brightly lit skybusters ranging into the
distance. Above the farther ones, and in the spaces
between some of the nearer ones, hang a few odd
geometrical puzzle pieces of glowing off-black sky. And
that's it, the view from this office interior right here
at nightscoper break time.

My repaired pocket watch, tied by a cord to my
backpack, is laid out on the tabletop just to J-book's
left and ticking audibly. A glass of water stands next
to it (glossy red metal mug, actually; I keep it hidden
atop one of the cabinets). My funky green hooded street
jacket is tossed over my bag on one of the chairs.
Propped against the jacket, this week's "bus book": a
maverick Japanese anthropologist takes on the cultural
weirdness of the U.S. Hugely entertaining!

One new vexation here: earlier tonight the monitor
for the grand-jury computer croaked. This forced me to
patch the hard drive into the office system, a time-
consuming and risky business, especially considering --
as noted more than a few times before -- I know next to
nothing about the mechanics of computers. I'm just
hoping the backup monitor Jyzer Ink bought last year
(it's over in my storage unit right now) will suffice as
a fill-in and thus I won't have to ask the firm to cough
up for a replacement. I still figure the less I remind
them of my presence around here the better off I am.
This is the strategy I've pursued all along and I'd say
for the most part it's worked well. For sure I'm not

147

about to abandon it now.

-- So do big work-related changes loom? I still
haven't talked with Verna, but jobs could start coming
in from her as soon as next week. J. Ink's total
workload might increase by anywhere from a third to
maybe two thirds. I'll have to learn an advanced
version of the transcription software I'm using now and
add a new courthouse stop to my nighttime circuit or
extend the circuit hours backward into the afternoon on
some days. Financially I'll be more secure but the loss
of free time could hurt a lot. On balance I doubt I'll
be better off. Yet I still want to try it. Why? I
don't even know. Maybe just on the off chance it'll
turn out to be a step up from my present gig.

And then this is the weekend Z and I are supposed
to get down and dirty on my health and medical "issues"
-- the things she volunteered last June not to talk
about for a year (true, I said that's what I'd prefer;
but I didn't ask her to do it). My hope is she'll be
wise enough not to press too hard on any of this stuff
and especially not on the e-dys enigma.

(Meanwhile I was wearying so much from hearing
about her friends jockeying to take charge of our
wedding reception -- and of course never bothering to
ask for my views on the matter -- I jokingly demanded
that she tell any inquirers on this score they'll have
to run their requests by me. To my surprise she
immediately agreed. So now I figure I'll at least be
hearing a lot less about the topic. -- And who knows,
maybe she'll gain a little relief too.)

-- Tonight she's visiting Serafina; it's their
first real get-together since the family's return from
Indonesia. (Sera's sister Aida is one of the ones
bucking to do our reception.) Aida, meanwhile, seems to
be turning ever moodier and feistier. Today she failed
to show for a luncheon engagement with Z and didn't call
before or after to explain why. Beneath the surface a
new round of major shifts in the delicate balance of
Z's friendship circles may be taking place. She's just
too short on time to keep everyone happy. Lee M. is in

town too, for the first time in months, and he proposed
dinner for tonight as well, and Z had to say no. She's
having to say no to lots of people these days and she's
not at all pleased about it.

And now? Now it's two minutes before eleven.
Almost time to march back in there for the stretch run.

At home tonight I'm expecting some hot loving to
make up for the couple of days lost to the fight.
Compensation swyving. Reconciliation swyving. This is
how things oughta be! -- Just drives home the truth of
that rusty old saw: by the time you learn what to do,
you can hardly do it anymore. -- But no, I'm not
conceding defeat. I'm still believing things are on the
mend. I can still do it, she can still do it (lord can
she ever). And so: we can still do it. Goddamn right!
                    *   *
Hideaway some forty-six hours later. Half past
nine in the evening on a Sunday that's also the last day
of the month. I've just returned from dropping my rent
envelope through the building manager's mail slot on the
third floor.

Before that I took a hike up to the main post
office to mail my monthly rent check to the storage
company (stopping for dinner at the double-stack joint
and for dessert at the yogurt-cone joint, and also for a
browse at the nearer and more browser-friendly of the
two chain bookstores). When I got back here I was
nearly blinded by an array of klieg lights set up in the
street near the side entrance. Turned out they were
preparing to film a beer commercial. For a while I
joined scores of others gawking at the squadrons of
Hollywood crew functionaries scurrying about, the
massive makeup trailers, the whining air conditioners,
the rain machines, the tangles of wires like hoses at a
five-alarm fire, the rent-a-cops grumpily herding us all
back back back. I'd probably still be down there gaping
right now if there'd been any sign of real action.

And before all that the trek in from the hilltop
where my last act before leaving 203 was to write out
this month's "rent, etc." check to Z. Came to $486.70,

it did, including my portion of the resort-trip expenses
as well as those for last night's outing with Jess and
Gwen (fish and chips out in the Scandi quarter, drinks
at a nearby bar, video rental -- this the very first
video-rental double date of my entire life).

So, yes, Z and I have cleared another major hurdle.
Today was "Health/Medical Showdown Day" and it turned
out to be a lot less traumatic than I expected. Because
Z earlier this morning had agreed to meet Olwen at two
for an arboretum walk, she hit me with the big questions
right when I woke up at noon. No rages or meltdowns
ensued, her side or mine. It was all over in less than
an hour, and that included a quick nipple-tweak session
at the end. (It started with a mock-seductive "Should I
bring them out?" I love when she does that.)

The essence: she'd like me to undergo a full top-
to-bottom, inside-and-out physical exam just to make
sure I'm not harboring any conditions that will prevent
my reaching age 105. And she'd like to understand
better the basis of my long-term policy vis-a-vis
avoidance of professional health care of all kinds
except in emergencies.

Best of all, the matter of sexologists and
penisologists and little blue hard-on pills never even
came up. It seems we really have gone around a corner
on such things. Or at the very least she's feeling bad
about the "incompatible" outburst -- so maybe in the
long run that will turn out to have worked in our favor.

I did say -- acknowledge -- I'm hugely grateful for
her acceptance of me "as is" and also said I hope it
continues, just as I intend to keep accepting her "as
is" (a fact for which she'd already expressed gratitude
-- and she again offered to have her moles burned off
and her fibroidectomy scar "vitamin E'd" if I'd like,
and also to try out the new experimental herpes drugs
(available through a free program at the U); and again I
said that although I wouldn't outright oppose her doing
any of these things if she so chose, I certainly
wouldn't dream of asking her to do them and in fact I'd
prefer she didn't).

And we talked wedding dates. She'd now like to go
for the warm season next year -- preferably but not
necessarily late June. Olwen, who's ordained in Z's
Sufi order, would do the honors. And: Z would like some
ritual. "Can't we have fun with this?" I liked the way
she put that; it won me over instantly. But I let her
know I'd rather we not write the vows ourselves. That
sort of thing, I said, always strikes me as gaggingly
pretentious (although in truth I really hadn't thought
much about it before today, or at least not in recent
years). She seemed okay with leaving the vows to Olwen.

Meanwhile the physical loving is again going less
well. Imminence of the health/medical showdown might've
had something to do with this, or maybe not. In any
case ol' Possum has again been lying low and lank. (She
proposed renaming the beast Mercutio.) Now in an effort
to make up for earlier unkind statements she's saying
she's grown as attached to finger-fucking and nipple-
tweaking as she ever was to full-bore penile fucking in
the grand old days -- meaning before me -- and she's
making no more demands for "hard and fast" (but I'm
still hoping to fulfill her true desires on that score,
assuming I can ever discover what they really are). She
continues to toss off O's with casual abandon and
usually at least seems, and what's more declares herself
to be, sexually satisfied. And as has been true from
very early on, she's sexually loving me more attentively
and intensively than anyone else ever has. (The way she
kissed and caressed and licked and nibbled me from head
to toes this morning at nine to wake me up for the first
round -- sensational!) -- From time to time she still
asks whether it troubles me that she "loves to fuck so
much" and is so "insatiable" (her words) and of course
it doesn't, none of that, I love it, I'm wild about it,
and I've let her know this in every way I can think of
-- but as long as ol' Possum/Mercutio/Slacker/N'dow
fails so often to rise firmly to the occasion she'll no
doubt be needing frequent reassurance.

One thing now, she's no longer worrying about
vaginal pain. The fit is fine, even when I'm in my most

supremely rampant auxiliary-tank torqued-and-craning
state). She chalks this change up to not just the wild-
yam extract and the finger-stretching but also to the
fact that having an actual penis to clamp on makes her
"meliferate" (that is, produce that good love honey)
even more bountifully than usual. (She thinks she
may've inherited this ability from her mother. All
those years they were sleeping in the same bed she often
noticed her mother's powerful sexual aroma. -- And
never said a word about it to her, by the way.)
    -- So now it's twenty past ten. A good kwikjyzin'
fifty minutes, Herr Professor, yes, I think so.
    What next? When the calendar page flips at
midnight it'll be exactly one year since 20K Day. And
I've got some resolutions in mind, almost as if a new
year really were starting instead of merely my 20,366th
day on the planet. I have fierce resolutionary intent.
For the summer months: work out hard three times a week,
save lots of money for the "roots" trip, zero in on
personal writing projects. And do all I can to love the
Z-woman the way I want to be loving her, which is to
say: with everything I've got. (And if this be pure
corn, any or all of it, I say okay, fine, where Z and I
come from corn's a staple and we both feast on it.)
                    *   *
    Closing it out at No. 225 two nights later.
Stopping in briefly at the hour when I'm usually
leaving: one a.m. The street outside the night entrance
(where the commercial was filming last time) is now all
torn up for construction and so I had to park around the
corner. Ironically the only open spot was right in
front of one of the dance clubs (a "bloozy" one, typical
for the area in all the time I've been coming here, one
of the dozen or so on the "joint admissions ticket") and
even at this late hour it was still rocking out. It's
the best indication yet that we're moving into tourist
season. Yippee! (Seriously.)
    Some kind of day it's been. A boink session at
four a.m. last night, another at eight this morning (Z
was taking comp time and going in late), another at

eight tonight. She's wondering what's come over me --
suddenly I'm "randy G" again. (And I say in reply
nothing's different except for the fact that this is a
"nada week" for her -- little to do at the office --
and therefore I feel free to let the 'mones take over
whenever they want to. But then this itself is very
different for us: as far as I can recall it's only her
second "nada week" in the whole time I've known her.)

     And this afternoon I drove over to the storage unit
to pick up my backup monitor to replace the one that
blew out at the scope office. In effect Jyzer Ink's
donating it to the cause, and solely in hopes of heading
off any new dealings with reporter Fran (who's
technically the owner of the burned-out monitor, but
from her cutting-edge vantage point it's obsolete anyway
and I'm sure she wouldn't give a hoot about its fate;
she just enjoys making life miserable for her former
underling the RIF'd salaried-staff nightscoper).

     While at the storage place I grabbed a few other
items, including a redwood armchair -- unupholstered --
which should just barely fit on our tiny outdoor balcony
overlooking the street. Also some old photos, an atlas,
and my boyhood scrapbooks (which Z wants to scope out).
And I moved some stuff around (with Z's items added to
mine over there, the place is literally packed to the
rafters). And I fell into a trance of nostalgia while
glancing through a file drawer of Mother's photos and
didn't emerge from it for an hour or more. How sad it
is to see all those carefully sorted and labeled black-
and-whites (mostly of her childhood family and friends)
which it's now unlikely anyone, except maybe brother
Rob, will ever want to look at again. I hate to think
of their probable fate: some stranger briskly flipping
through them and tossing the lot into a dumpster. But
of course this is what fate's all about for just about
everything and everybody at all times, sooner or later.

     -- And the newly yclept Mercutio? He's up, he's
down. Yesterday was one of his finer days in a while.
Some genuinely half-decent yes-fuck fucking that
actually went on for a fairly protracted spell. I'm

starting to feel proud again. And Z may be feeling
something new too. She says it's dawning on her this
really is for real. Or since she's said that before, as
she admits, "Let's just say it's sinking in deeper and
deeper." (After our evening together Jess and Gwen
agreed that Z and I are "like two pods in a pea" --
something like that -- and it's an absolute miracle we
found each other. Of course some self-congratulation
was involved since in a sense Jess and Gwen were the
ones who "found" us for each other with the ad they drew
up on Z's behalf and at first unknown to her -- an ad so
fine it was like a good hunting dog, flushing the wild
jyzer-bird from his squalid inner-city bog.)

Yesterday at the WOC a touching moment. Z had been
impressed by an article I'd clipped for her on the
absurdity of trying to cover up little signs of aging.
"So will we accept each other's aging and grow old
together?" I loved the look in her eyes as she asked
this. It's just what I'd hoped for (but never dreamed
I'd really find) back in the early post-Lady U days when
I decided to try to hook up with a woman closer to my
own age. (And that despite our aging we can still be so
physically drawn to each other, so sexually insatiable
even when less than fully capable, as it's turned out,
at least in my case -- and only in my case -- all this
is truly truly miraculous, yes.)

And what. Today the city delivered a load of
recycling bins to our garage and Z left one in front of
each unit's door along with a little personalized note
explaining how to use it. She cares! She's fabulous!

And I just brought out the bag of antique
silverware Mother left me. For the past three years
it's been sitting in a metal lockbox, most of that time
right here in this office. Despite my promises to her
I've never polished a single piece. (But they all look
pretty much the same as far as I can see.) -- So now
I'm tempted to take the bag home and give it to Z. Or
say to her: "Now that our fates are linked forever, what
should we do with this?" It's worth a bundle, maybe
five grand or more, which means, I suppose, we shouldn't

keep it in 203, where it would be the only item of any real monetary value. Just as I feared in the past and tried to explain to ol' Mom -- though in the face of her final illness I softened -- its main effect would be to force us to worry more about break-ins. -- Well, so let's see what Z says. My hunch is she's more sentimental about family connections than I am. Maybe she'd like to have this kind of stuff around.

Driving over to the storage place I heard the supreme jazz singer of the century (I'd say) warbling out "Our Love Is Here To Stay." Wow. And what a moment. A few big-thump heartbeats later the station started fading as I crossed the bridge to the peninsula (into, that is, the old Lady U turf) -- mainly because the aerial on the Z-mobile broke off months ago and under my mingy influence she's decided not to replace it. -- But of course the fade portended nothing. Our love is here to stay, yes. I'm still shaking from the unexpected power of that moment -- meaning maybe it was my own equivalent of Z's "sinking in deeper and deeper" moment.

17

Just up from a two-hour nap snatched on the hideaway rug. Not that the Katgrrrl ran me ragged or anything this afternoon. (The backs of my hands right now bearing notes from her printed in bright red ink. Love notes, no less, with word-for-word copies in my drawer at home, those also scribbled by her shortly before I left in case I couldn't read the originals on my hands. And I couldn't, and still can't.)

A fine day all right. But this is not J-day. I'm

a day late. Saturdays it's just about impossible to
squeeze in any jyzin'. I thought maybe I'd be able to
do it after Z fell asleep -- it's a ritual now, my
reading in bed with her for hours on Saturday night --
but I couldn't. And in truth it was because I was
enjoying the reading too much. Or rather: the whole
scene. Bedside radio playing softly, Z stretched out
naked next to me looking so good in the bed lamp's soft
light. One of the first warm nights of summer.

Three big personal news items from these past five
days. Or four items maybe, with the fourth being my
long-delayed talk with reporter Verna. But that one --
which could easily turn out to be the biggest of all (or
not) -- that one I won't try to tackle in here until
later.

So the first undeniably big item. And that is, it
was a heckuva lucky week for Zoelie B. Not only did her
Deep bring home a bagful of antique silverware, but the
very next day a check for five thousand bucks and change
arrived in the mail, totally unexpected, from her
godmother's estate. Although Z's decided to send a
thousand of this to her mother and to apply most of the
rest to her considerable credit-card debt (just how
considerable it is I don't know, but I do know it's only
a fraction of her education-loan debt of close to 60K
including interest), it still put her in a binge mood.
At the top of the new shopping list: an air cleaner, a
screen door (for the balcony), and some new lingerie.

-- Which leads into the second big item, because
the lingerie included a thong, the hot new style of
women's "unners" dominating the media in recent weeks.
Friday evening I happened to stay home later than usual
and when she arrived she slipped into her new thong, a
black one -- "Should I model it for you?" -- and it
definitely did the trick: we hopped into bed and (yup)
fucked a real fuck around and through the thong, which
remained on (the underpanel easily slides to the side)
and (wottaya know) I even ejacked inside her! How 'bout
that! I'd even say it rivaled some of the studlier if
not the studliest of the studly acts of my studliest

days of yore -- not that I'm crowing or anything.

(Then again, last night she wasn't interested at all, nor was she this morning, and both times I was. It's possible she'll be cooling off sexually more than I expected. This cooling could even have something to do with my heating up, that is, my reviving capabilities. She says she's not cooling, but I still suspect otherwise. Her story is that she's only slowly becoming accustomed to the unending availability of sex after the long drought, meaning the self-imposed six-year one before we met. And she still often reminds me that living with a man is something new to her and, after all, she's been doing it with me less than six months.)

-- Today Betty had to put in a twelve-hour split shift (with four hours of study time in the middle) and by prearrangement she dropped Kat off with us at nine a.m. (At this point we're watching her for a full day once a month.) This was the third big item.

Z took charge of Kat during the morning hours while I slept. Then I became the main diverter as we shopped for the screen door and later for groceries, with stops along the way at one of our local hilltop parks, the usual valley co-op, the environmental home center, and no fewer than three big-box discount marts. Everywhere Kat rode on my shoulders much of the time. This is almost a necessity because she's so quick afoot, darting hither and thither (and all too often to a thither where you can't find her). She loves to race ("Beat you to the corner!") and is forever wheedling away at us to buy her this or that while simultaneously delivering a droll running commentary on goings-on as she sees them. Laughs a lot, cracks wise, flirts, goofs, mimics, yells, teases, queries, preens, makes faces, does sudden somersaults and quasi-cartwheels on hard tile floors which might easily crack open her skull. Once in a while she turns cranky, mostly when tired, and too often she's bored and lets you know it. But the simple truth is she's almost always a delight to be with.

The complicated things with Kat I won't even try to go into now. Just to name some of them, though, in most cases no doubt not for the first time: The effect of being adopted, and by a farm-raised (and very loving) heartland Eurusan woman. The effect of Manny's death (her adoptive father) when she was five. The effect of her being brown-skinned and strongly Hispanic-looking (Mayan actually) in a predominantly Cawkazoid northern city (and of course culture). Then the effect of way too much exposure to over-the-top consumerism and TV.

Then the matter of her relations with Z (who's sometimes tough-lovey with her to a fault, I'd say) and with us (maybe I'm too easygoing and let her get away with too much) and how she plays us off against each other and how Z and I deal with all this and interact with Betty about it. And then of course just around the corner is the matter of puberty and sexuality (and not least owing to the sexual abuse in both Z's and Betty's childhoods we're already into this stage in a sense, and also because Kat herself is dazzlingly attractive, seductive and sensual and sexy, as all acknowledge and relish, although of course warily so).

-- But, yeah, best not to pursue any of these matters too much further right now. Best, instead, now and later, to take a jyzey approach and deal with them as they arise and define themselves more clearly. And I do think this will happen because almost certainly Kat will remain an important figure in our lives. Or anyway we're hoping she will and determined she will. And if she doesn't we'll both be crushed.

Then finally that last big news item, the talk with Verna. She called on the very day she began her new full-time job for the county. In a nutshell, Jyzer Ink will now be handling all her scoping on a trial basis. The scoping site will be her office in the courthouse; she'll be providing (and owning) the computer and printer. Since most of the work for J. Ink will stem from appeals of court cases, it's not likely I'll have much to do until, say, September or October. But sometime in the next month or so, as soon as she sets up the computer, I'll go in and familiarize myself with it as well as the transcription system she uses. Since

it's an updated version of the one I use with Naomi it
shouldn't be too hard to pick up.

My best guess right now is that taking on Verna as
a client will increase my total workload by about half.
Ironically I'll be finding myself in the very situation I
was hoping for three years ago when I set up J. Ink and
started into the current freelance scoping phase: working
full-time for Verna and Naomi, with "full-time" defined
as doing all their scoping and being available to take
work whenever called upon, every day of the week except
Saturday. And I suppose there's a small chance the time
requirements could be greater than anticipated. But if
they are, I'll worry about it then. Clearly this setup
is worth a try. If for no other reason, it just might
turn out to be close to ideal.

-- All this from the brown chair on a quiet Sunday
night with the six-hour blues show playing on the jazz
station (but now, post midnight, back to jazz). Next I
head up to the nearest bus stop, straight east, across
the street (known as "the high road" for jyze purposes)
from the county courthouse and right in front of a big
low-income housing center. That area's always a bit
dicey this time of night. (A few nights ago my string
of arrivals up there during which I found either an
arrest or a medical emergency in progress finally ended
at five straight.) I read and try to look both tough
and unthreatening, both alert to and unconcerned about
anything going on around me. I try not to let anyone
see any money or Z's bus pass when I'm carrying it, as
tonight (it's a yearly pass worth hundreds of dollars).
Of course the way I dress is "street" enough for me to
fit in fairly well, and I've been walking the late-night
downtown grid long enough to know how to blend in and
just what the danger signs are. But still, I'm always a
little worried. Sometimes more than a little. -- And
yes, this is how I want to live (given how the world is
and how our times are and what I hope to accomplish as a
jyzic interpreter and memorializer and occasional
culture-jammer of it and them). And I'm plenty happy to
be able to do this the way I've been doing it and hope

to continue handling its inevitable drawbacks and difficulties at least passably well.

*   *

Twenty-four hours later, same seat. Since the gap between sessions this time is only one day, not two, I guess this entry isn't a true kwikjyze under the current definition. But kwik is what it'll be regardless, because in forty minutes the last bus rolls.

Mondays are now my best bet for an easy day. An off day even. A day on which I'm usually free to concentrate on my own work or whatever else I want to do (unless a back order comes in, which happens only occasionally, maybe one Monday out of every five or six on average). So how have I used the time so far today?

Not wisely or well. Yet not all that badly either. Up a few minutes past noon, I prepared my usual breakfast and read the usual papers in the usual place, the black armchair. Before leaving the house at two I also tidied up the kitchen, made the bed, talked briefly with Z on the phone about stamps she needed, and watered the plants, which takes even longer now with the wooden flowerboxes set up on the balcony -- about fifteen minutes in all. (I made shelves for them while we had Kat and then all three of us worked on planting the dozens of small potted flowers we'd just bought -- geraniums, marigolds, petunias, lobelia, verbena -- that is, all the usual low-cost suspects.)

Then I walked north down the hill and followed my standard route westward through the Asian quarter straight down (farther down) to the old "south pole" and then a few blocks northward again to the triangle and up one flight of stairs to this office (I'm delighted I now have all this routine to fall back on with greater or lesser mindlessness, thereby freeing me to dwell on other matters, if I want, as I often do, as I trudge along). Here I picked up my gym gear and half a sheet of stamps for Z and then hurried straight over to the WOC (just one short block east and two north), arriving at ten to three, thus giving myself a few minutes to grind out some sets on the weight machines before Z's arrival at three.

[Jyze to the Bone]

     Then our workout together, starting with stretching
and twenty minutes of speed walking on adjacent
treadmills during which we talked nonstop (on which more
later). Then we split up to work on various machines
for another twenty or thirty minutes, drifting together
every now and then as our paths crossed, with little
chats and touches and smooches in out-of-the-way places
and even some in-the-way places. Then she left, to
shower and return to her office, and I stayed on for two
more hours, until six, hitting all the machines of my
favorite brand for three or four sets of fifteen reps
and a few other machines of different brands and some
freeweights as well. (I mean, I'm working hard now.)
     Next a long shower, shave, dress, and then, still
carrying my workout gear (in the black shoulderbag I
salvaged from the B-2 dumpster last fall), I walked
uptown where I stopped first at the nearer of the chain
bookstores for an hour or so of browsing and then hit
the usual fast-food joint for dinner, consisting of two
ninety-nine-cent "double stacks" with lettuce and tomato
only, no cheese, and a can of guava juice which I
smuggled in because the drink selection there is so
poor. Next a hike two blocks north and one west to the
other usual fast-food joint for dessert, the standard
large vanilla softie cone (meanwhile reading at one of
the cramped fixed-seat metal tables near the restrooms
-- the only seats in use at that hour with the upstairs
closed -- as a constant parade of street people, most
relatively unobjectionable -- that is, same category as
I probably fall into myself -- but a few truly obnoxious,
shuffled by to use the restrooms, and the whole time a
fully armed cop kept a wary eye on all of us from his
perch on a stool by the door about fifteen feet away).
     Then the walk back here (slowing down to scope out
the new concert hall, whose construction has moved into
a near-final phase, the high fences finally coming down)
-- arriving about nine-fifteen. And then two hours of
reviewing notes for a writing project and a one-hour nap
(again I couldn't resist, second day in a row after
months without a single nap) and then this jyze.

No time for more. Not now. Next entry I'll be back for a true kwikjyze. Or maybe not -- maybe I'll try to finish up this "chapter" No. 17 tonight at home.

*   *

-- And now doing it! Surprise!

At 3:11 a.m. after zipping through tomorrow morning's newspaper so as to free up more time in the afternoon to work on hanging the balcony screen door.

As I was walking to the house from the bus stop half a block to the south the delivery man for "the night paper" rolled up -- in the same noisy little red pickup I now often think I might be seeing in other parts of the city -- and handed me the paper through his half-open window. A first. (I've seen him only one other time, so I was surprised he recognized me. "Ah, so you're just getting home from work?" Vietnamese roots, I'd guess, from his looks and slight accent.)

Tonight's note barrage tells me Z sacked out at 8:45 and set her alarm for 5:15 -- "nookie time." Or as the note also says, she's ready to "consolidate some beachhead." This refers to something I mentioned as we treadmilled today: how I'm surprised she hasn't seemed eager to do just that now with ol' Mercutio finally launching fairly regular amphibious landings. (Some such hooey.) Is it that she can't stand the prosperity or that her 'mones are no longer raging since she can score a chunk of that good good lovin' anytime she wants to? She laughed but more or less dodged answering. I suspect she's struggling with the question herself. But I also think she'll work her way out of any real puzzlement she may have.

Eh wot? I dunno. Her main expressed concern these days has to do with racking up more quality sleep. A recent study in the news -- clipped and now posted on our bedroom door -- has convinced her she needs to be doing much better at this. One solution she proposed calls for me to go to bed at six a.m. and sleep until two. I'm supposed to be thinking this over. Meanwhile she's apparently decided on her own to try a different approach in which she hits the sack earlier -- perhaps

as early as eight-thirty. But I don't see her being
able to stick with this over the long haul or for that
matter more than a few days. She has too many evening
commitments which keep her out until nine or later.

Also at the WOC this afternoon she said she'd been
blue all day over work-related concerns. During a long
morning meeting with three of her overlings, all Cawk
dudes, she'd felt awkward and excluded, rejected,
"unacceptably different," just as she often did when
she was the brown-skinned little girl growing up in a
Cawkazoidal hood. Her eyes teared up as she told me all
this. She's unhappy in her job, bored. She's applying
for another opening elsewhere in the utility but her
heart appears not to be in it. In addition, it's
bothering her quite a bit that our "parenting styles"
with Kat differ so much and she can't seem to move
beyond seeing the difference as a function of class
background. (I'd say it's at least as much cultural,
tied in with the Catholic/Protestant split.)

"But I always love you no matter what mood I'm in.
I don't forget how incredibly lucky I am to have you."

She said that. But it also could've been me saying
it to her. Yup, the mush is once again flying thick and
heavy these days and we're both loving it. And so:
Q.E.D.? Q.E.D.

Ten to four. Birds are hard at it already (and now
a fiercely yowling cat). I crane my neck to see if an
orange crack of dawn is opening along the mountain
skyline. Nothing visible yet. Might be the obscuring
effect of the bright streetlight which dominates the
left half of the window scene, blotting out much of the
distant view. Lotsa glare from my present angle.

Officially summer's still twelve or thirteen days
away. This jyze volume, however, will be largely a
summer volume regardless, because if things work out
right the last entry should go down just before Z and I
leave for Mentoka and our "Deep Roots Road Trip," as
we're now calling it, the first official week of autumn.
Hopefully this will be a quiet summer for me, dedicated
mostly to the matters noted earlier: fixing up the

apartment, working on my writing projects, saving money, shaping up another notch or two at the WOC, and consolidating still more of that high-profile erotic beachhead. And to more and better sleep as well, for both of us, absolutely.

If this isn't exciting enough, well, so be it. For the rest of this year I refuse to be worrying about the JEQ: jyze excitement quotient. Next year with its nuptial and calendrical celebrations I expect to be different, a truly wild and crazy annum. This year is a year of (relative) rest, a year of preparation, a year of easy-as-it-goes (or sometimes doesn't go) "Deepening" in as many realms and senses as we can manage.

Now three minutes after four. Still need to reply to Z's stack of notes. Sometimes, it's true, I wonder if I'm draining too much writing energy into these note exchanges. But then again I don't want her to be getting any funny ideas -- say, for instance, that I'm losing interest in her or us.

And so, Mercutio/Possum/N'dow you Slacker you, you ready to go tonight? I suspect not. Friskiness I do not detect down there (as I sit here naked, the writing board covering my lap). More than three and a half days since the last round -- way too long. Self-consciousness returns. And even if it didn't, today's heavy WOC workout may've taken more out of me than I realized at the time.

--------·

18

--------·

Again I pick myself up off the floor from a nap. At the hideaway on a Sunday night.

This week I'm strongly under the influence of those

great Chinese poets of millennium-plus yore. Or at
least I'd like to be and am trying to be. But I've also
been bushwhacked by an unusual early-summer cold. At
Leola and Gerry's barbecue party yesterday out in the
burbs I was, in Z's words, "My deep-nose snuffler."
(Because we arrived early to help with preparations, and
also because I so memorably humiliated myself in croquet
at last year's L&G party, I was put in charge of setting
up the game this year and then serving as the expert on
the rules. At both of these I did all right, I think,
but at the game itself I showed little improvement,
coming in dead last two out of three and not much better
on the third.)

So I'm weak from the cold, and also tired from it
even though I slept almost nine hours last night (when I
wasn't snuffling and coughing), and also feeling bloated
from all those good eats at the barbecue, including a
dynamite rhubarb-peach pie (and usually I don't much go
for rhubarb). After staggering back home last night Z
and I were both so stuffed we could do nothing but groan
and fart (and in my case snuffle and cough too, yeah).
To be able to read in bed we had to sit upright. (For
the first time I showed her my blowfish-stomach trick
and she was gratifyingly amazed -- had no idea I was so
talented.) (My new name for her during such virtuoso
flatulence displays, by the way, is "Swamp Mama Z." She
can effortlessly outdo me. Fabulous volume -- a single
spark and whole city blocks might burst into flame.)

Also I'm weak sexually. Ain't got no pop. Since
this bug's first bite on Tuesday I've been unable to
come up with anything better than a rubbery semi-hard-
on. And yet, because for once I can offer a decent
excuse, I don't feel too bad about this. (Cold, flu,
virus, I don't know what it is. Likely picked it up
from Kat last Sunday. She'd been laid low all week by
what Nurse Betty is now calling a sinus infection.)

-- But wait, exciting news! Yesterday Z decided we
had to have a new couch on which we could sit together,
read, snuggle, canoodle -- the whole dang kit and
caboodle. My old brown loveseat just wasn't cutting it

anymore: it's too small, too uncomfortable, too precarious with its makeshift repairs (its cushions riding on a canvas sheet suspended trampoline-like on springs reattached with baling wire -- by me -- to the wooden frame after the last collapse roughly two years ago). Worst of all, it's too reminiscent of (or in Z's excellent phrase, "intimates too much about") the Lady U era. She, Z, had been wanting to binge anyway with her inheritance from her godmother, so why not a new couch to solve all the loveseat problems at a stroke?

This afternoon we drove down to a furniture emporium and picked out a fancy futon-style piece (for a mere seven hundred bucks including all the trimmings and tax). To my surprise we were able to stuff the components into the back of the Z-mobile, tying the top-hinged rear door down with canvas strips, and once home to assemble it -- this job fell to me alone -- in under an hour just as advertised.

And it's gorgeous! And I love it! And it was tough tearing myself away from it to come down to work!

In choosing a pattern for the cover we discovered our tastes in such things differ dramatically. I'm not sure what bad words she'd use for mine but I'd say hers tends toward the dark and garish. I had to exercise several vetoes, and she, not to be outdone, rejected out of hand a number of my suggestions. (She was paying; I couldn't do much more than suggest, I felt.) In the end we wound up with what seemed a reasonable compromise, a large modified checkerboard pattern, each square about six inches on a side, fairly light without much contrast, cream and two shades of a slightly minty tan or -- I don't know what it is. Not bad at all, though, especially for a compromise. Once I had the thing set up in 203 Z grudgingly admitted the lighter colors worked fairly well. (Though at the time she was still in sticker shock mixed with a kind of forbidden-pleasure consumption giddiness; after all, the only two material items on which she'd ever spent more were her wagon and her computer.) -- But I'm afraid when her head clears she might see the colors a little differently.

[Jyze to the Bone]

     And I can report this. Z was talking with her
friend Olwen about Olwen's son Trent, who's soon to hit
a big decadal birthday and is going through a kind of
"men's passages" crisis. Olwen thought it would be
good for him to talk with a "sensitive older man" and I
was one of the men she thought of (or maybe even the
only one). Z prefaced her revelation of all this by
saying "Olwen had a sweet compliment for you." When she
explained what it was and laid out the list of Trent's
problems -- he's not successful with his writing, he's
not living up to his hopes for fame and fortune, his
hair's falling out -- I told her I could definitely
relate. So now we're all set to meet at a street fair
in the Asian quarter a few weeks from now, and Olwen and
Zoelie will slip away for a while, I gather, and at that
point I'll be expected to impart some wisdom to Trent.
"Trent, let me tell you about something that just might
save your ass. It seems to be working quite well for
me. It's a crazy little thing called jyze."
     My new life. It's different. I like it. (And I
like Olwen. She's a refined poetic type and yet she
can, and does, do rad/prog politics too, and she has a
hearty profane streak that's quite amusing, as is her
laugh that sounds something like a hoarsely barking
seal. Years ago she and Z both mowed wide swaths
through the fields of love and romance around this town,
sharing -- at different times -- at least two lovers, Z
tells me, and possibly several more. They also both
worked during more or less the same period as home
energy checkers for the electrical utility, each driving
a truck. Olwen carried insulation panels in hers and
the formaldehyde they were laced with triggered a nasty
chemical-sensitivity episode whose aftereffects she's
been struggling with ever since. Before seeing her, Z
and I must be careful not to use soap in the shower and
we can't wear deodorant, aftershave, or anything else
containing "unnatural chemicals.")
     -- Right now the pressure's on at home because
we've invited a number of people over for dinner this
summer. Z's feeling it too -- we gotta get off our

duffs and make this joint presentable! -- and she thinks
this might be the reason her temper's erupted several
times in the past week over what she herself calls minor
matters (none when I was around, I'm pleased to say).
     But next session for more about that. Bus time.
                    *   *
     On yet another day during which we've successfully
copulated, invag ejac included! It happened not long
after Z arrived home from work at half past five. This
was our first at-home Tuesday evening since we've had
the new couch, and it was also our first chance to
realize the fantasy which inspired its purchase: reading
while sitting next to each other in physical contact,
hands exploring, genitals twitching and swelling and
juicing up.
     For an hour or so earlier this afternoon I moved
small pieces of furniture around and rearranged the
futon so it would sit just right on the frame (and also
opened for the first time since our move-in the small
screened portion of the corner window facing the street;
this whole time that sliding window had been jammed but
I was finally able to figure out how to free it up).
The chair/couch area now is roomier and with the blinds
open on a sunny afternoon it was (and will be!)
pleasantly comfortable and attractive -- especially with
the door open also, the one to the balcony with its
railing-top boxes of profusely blooming flowers).
     However, we didn't use the couch for its fantasy
purposes this time, or at least not beyond simply
sitting next to each other and stretching our legs out
onto the large wooden footrest/coffee table (this is the
same table that came with the loveseat as part of my
half of the "living-room set" divvied up at the end of
the Lady U backcountry era, and it's made of varnished
two-by-sixes, strong and sturdy, but never before while
I've had it has it been used for feet; so I guess it's
now been demoted). Z was feeling bad because of
problems with a contract at work -- she had failed to
ride herd on it as closely as she should've -- and
wasn't in a particularly affectionate mood.

But I was. Last night she'd left me a note saying if Possum (in our bedroom lingo the marsupial's suddenly back on top) -- if Possum was feeling healthy again, this would be a good night to awaken her when I came to bed. Well, I never know about Possum, but I was feeling pretty good myself and I did awaken her and did start into loving her and after a while Possum did begin livening up. But by the time the beast was ready for the plunge Z was close to rapturing up from a finger-fuck (this in the dark and she with dabs of zit medicine on her lips and therefore unwilling to kiss -- and those dabs eerily glowing, I swear it, white with a purplish undertone) and I was feeling less than totally confident about Possum's firmness condition and therefore opted to stay with the finger-fuck, and after she'd come (powerfully and rambunctiously, to the point where I had to pin her down with my shoulder to be able to keep the hand motion going) -- after that she was panting and exhausted and took quite a while to recover and meanwhile Possum said to hell with it.
    -- But it had been a full week since our most recent roll in the hay (Kat's "sinus infection" having laid me low) and so I figured I'd be horny all day and we'd go at it again tonight. And I socked in a good night's sleep (intentionally remaining in bed an extra hour, until one p.m.) and then stayed home and puttered around in just my blue shorts and the whole time I was indeed feeling unusually horny, "loaded for Z-goose."
    But when she came in after work she wasn't much in the mood. So I had to seduce her. Had to let her see the semi-aroused state Possum was in (hanging down out of the leghole of my shorts indeed something like a possum dangling upside down by its tail from a tree limb, and all bloated too the way a possum is when it plays dead, and veiny to boot -- or better to lick) and then invite her and all but push her backwards step by step like a football lineman rushing the passer down the hall into the bedroom and bringing her down for a big -- gain! She in a thigh-length white T-shirt and white unners, and those I slipped off as soon as she started

responding to insistent kisses (after first holding me
off with talk and laughter) and because I was instantly
turned on in a way I felt pretty sure would last (and
she tugged down my shorts as soon as I went after her
unners) I did something I'd never done before with her:
spread her legs and knelt between them with my torso
straight up so I could watch while working the beast's
head up and down within her vulva, against her clit, up
and across her muff so she could take a gander, down
again on the outside of the lips -- standard stuff, no
doubt, but it sure did look fine and sexy as hell after
all this time of my being reluctant to try anything
remotely like it for fear of foozling. -- And then
fucked the real fuck. And after only a short while knew
I'd be able to go all the way: that telltale pre-come
tickle appeared. She moaning loudly and coming twice
herself before I let go. She: "I can feel it so good"
(and I could too, because those auxiliary side tanks
were again pumped full to bursting) (as they were, that
is, one morning a couple of weeks back when I was
maximally rampant, feeling deliciously huge and powerful
to the point of unwieldiness -- and yet that time I
wasn't able to come). She: "I'm in heaven...." And she
again, after: "I was really noisy. The whole building
knows we were fucking."

    -- For a while longer I'll probably be doing this:
making a big deal out of mere fucks. I can't help
myself. It's been a long, excruciating fuckless spell
-- several years when it comes right down to it. In
fact three years almost to the day.

    (Afterwards I had an annoying itch in my ear and
went after it with one of her cotton swab sticks. We
were standing in the half bathroom at the time. Then
the phone rang and she went to answer it. When I pulled
out the swab I noticed the color of my ear wax was very
close to that of the dark yellow bar of soap on the
sink. A gremlin whispered into that same ear that I
should break off a globular chunk of soap roughly half
an inch in diameter and press it against the cotton on
the stick until it, yes, stuck. I did that, and then

lined it up inside the outer portion of my ear and
wandered over by the dining table, where she was just
hanging up the phone. "Geez, I think I found what was
itching so much," I said, twisting the stick about
like a shovel in a rocky garden and then levering out
the chunk. "I think I got it here. Hey! Mama mia,
willya look at that!" She nearly passed out.)
     Fun and games.
     But yes, truly we're into a new stage now, and
loving it. (We're real fuckers!)
*
     Meanwhile: I'm in an exceptionally good mood for
other reasons too. For one, my attempt to work myself
back into half-decent shape at the WOC finally seems to
be showing some results. Deterioration in most areas
appears to have slowed or stopped and in three or four
spots I believe it's actually been reversed. Of course
I realize any improvement is only temporary -- good for
a few years, five or ten or maybe fifteen or twenty at
most if I keep working very hard at it and luck is with
me -- but I'm enjoying it while I can. It's to the
point now where I may even be showing some development
and/or "definition" in places I never had much or any
before (mostly parts of my chest and upper back). It's
ridiculous to make a big deal of this -- vanity's always
relative, and the sorry group to which I can vainly see
myself as having become physically superior to in any
way at all is tiny and shrinking by the day as those
poor souls rapidly die off -- but I'm definitely feeling
more body confidence and this can only be a plus.
     (Yesterday for the first time I began jogging, not
just speed-walking, on one of the WOC treadmills. I'd
prefer to be jogging outdoors on solid ground but in
this rainy city it's not realistic to expect to do so
regularly. Better to have a program I know I can stick
with even if it is indoors. So I'll try to build up
gradually to jogging two miles three times a week at the
end of iron-pumping sessions. This will be in addition
to the twelve to fifteen miles a week I'm already
walking out on the streets. -- And today my calves and

171

the back of my thighs are gratifyingly sore in a
way they haven't been since the final unglorious
days of rec-center pickup hoops more than a decade
back.)

    Also I'm unusually pleased with the reading I've
been doing lately. More than ever before I feel clear
about where I stand on the issues of the day, how my
ideas and values hang together (in those scattered
places where they do), which thinkers and artists I most
admire, what I want to be doing with my own work.
(Being able to do it, of course, is something else
again, but at least as of this moment -- perhaps merely
as a matter of contagion from the other areas -- I'm
feeling pretty good about that too.)

    (This jyze right here, by the way, is once again
going down at the hideaway. It turns out to be another
of those Tuesday nights on which I have no scoping-
related work to do -- though come this fall as the job
with Verna starts to kick in I expect nights like this
will be much scarcer. -- I would've waited to do these
pages at home, but June will be staying with us tonight,
crashing in Z's room, and much like Z herself she tends
to wander out into the living room at odd hours -- but
modestly robed, not naked -- unable to sleep, wanting to
talk, and I do like talking with her, which is actually
more a matter of listening to her and tossing in a
question every now and then when she momentarily loses
steam.) (Just now I've stopped to measure the amount of
space available behind my left shoulder for a chairside
floor lamp. I'd like to bring Z's lamp down here and
move this one up to the apartment since its extendable
swing-arm will be better for reading while we're lolling
together on the new couch. But I'm afraid Z's lamp with
its large round fixed shade won't fit in the space
behind me: I'm guessing it's about two inches too wide.)

    -- Going back, then, I wanted to be sure to mention
how touched I was this weekend by Z's decision to buy
the couch. For hours afterwards she remained in that
same state of giddy/guilty sticker shock. "Love made me
do it" -- something like that. The symbolic dimension

of this decision may've broken through some unconscious
resistance in both of us. More than ever before I feel
she needs me and depends on me and wants to please me.
I also sense she's accepting this herself to a far
greater degree than before and this is changing the
nature of her ways with me. (Giving rise to a chicken-
egg question: is the successful sexual-loving
breakthrough part of the cause of this change or part of
the result? -- But of course it's probably both, with a
mutual feedback ratcheting effect, or at least I'd sure
like to think so.)

Also touching, today I finally reached Rob at the
bookstore to invite him and Gail over for dinner on the
Fourth. He'd just returned from a long bus trip to
attend Zach's graduation. With much amusement he told
me about the small gesture of rebellion staged by
Zach's graduating class (of just twenty-nine): they all
donned sunglasses while marching in. Naturally this
sight spurred memories of Rob's own high-school
graduation with its (his, really; in the end the others
all chickened out) antiwar protest. -- My brother the
newly anointed official book buyer. He sounded happy
with the promotion and also with his new set of
coworkers and bosses. Meanwhile I'm ordering a copy of
the "lofty essays" of B-2 days for him as I begin to
try to restore some balance in the matter of gift-
giving. Ironically, I'm ordering it through him to
take advantage of his large employee discount, thirty-
five percent, for which I'm eligible as an immediate
family member. (I told him I'll add the savings onto
the check I'm sending Zach as a graduation gift.) In
the months (and I hope years) ahead I expect to be
doing a lot more book buying of my own through Rob, and
a big chunk of it will be for Z (we're Deeps!).

Clock? Two minutes to one. Jyzer JIT shows his
stuff again. (JIT: that's just in time.) -- And he,
this same jyzer, even has a moment to mention he finally
got around to unpacking the half-dozen boxes of supplies
he hauled down here from B-2 at the time of the move.
Seems almost spacious in here again.

[Deep Jyze]

--------.

19

-------.

    Can I do this? It'll be interesting to see.
Maybe. -- Or more likely it won't mean a goddamn thing.
Yet then again it could. Years down the road I might
look back upon this as the start of a whole new phase in
my life. Or if not me, someone might. But -- probably
not. Just a slim chance. Exceedingly slim.
    Several days ago I "dinged" my back while sliding
behind the wheel of the Z-mobile and unexpectedly
sitting at an odd angle on, of all things, the log-
shaped back support Z uses while driving. Today on a
weight machine at the WOC I somehow redinged -- but much
worse -- that same spot. And now any movement I make
must be extremely cautious. Left lower back, sharp
stabbing pains. Not inevitably with any movement, but
even very slight bending of the back in any direction
can do it. Just which direction, however, I can never
be sure in advance.
    I managed to undress, shower, towel off, dress,
make it up the hill and down the road to do scope
finals, then catch a bus home. Now I've been sitting
here in the black armchair for a couple of hours, having
hit on a fairly comfortable pain-minimizing position.
Reading. And now the same position's working just about
as well for jyzing. But when I stand -- ouch. The
stiffness caused by sitting too long in one position
makes matters worse, and using what little flexibility I
have left -- surely not much more than a mummy's when
hauled up from the crypt -- I slowly try to bend myself
back into a position more or less upright.
    Oh well. I'm hoping this'll clear up within a week

or so. That's been the approximate recovery period for
all my previous lower-back dings. This one, though, is
without doubt the worst yet. So who knows.

And lots of work to do in the apartment over the
next few days. Cleanup time is here with a vengeance.
This coming Saturday we welcome our first dinner guests
to No. 203, Wei and Alison. And before then Z's friend
Paula will be putting in a full day's worth of
professional, or at least paid-for, cleanup. What Z and
I are engaged in now is pre-cleanup cleanup.

Gusty night, sweeps of pelletlike rain, and the
windows are open behind the closed blinds because, until
things changed suddenly around ten p.m., this was a fine
warm tranquil early-summer evening. Now those blinds
are billowing inward at times and outward at other times
and occasionally breaking into fits of rackety clacking,
sort of like dancing skeletons. Meanwhile saxes battle
on the radio at low volume and lamps shed pools of warm
light. And a few feet to my left stands the magnificent
new futon sofa. (It's truly big. We didn't realize
just how big until we had to wrestle it up the narrow
staircase and squeeze it through the front door and hall
and finally set it up in here. It's on a larger scale
than anything else in the room, something like an SUV
parked in a lot full of compacts.)

And it's been an interesting eighter. (The old
"interesting" standby, if I lift the black cloth on its
cage even a fraction of an inch it squawks yet again.)
An unorthodox week. Not wildly so, but -- indeed. And
with events. Yesterday, for instance, was the summer
solstice. Or maybe it was Saturday; I never did see the
date specified in the papers. And this by itself is
unusual. But as of the solstice, whenever it was, Z and
I entered a new era: we've now known each other all the
way through all four seasons. Because we met a week
after the vernal equinox last year, we didn't put in a
full spring until this year. (And we're coming up on
another milestone. As of July 1, she'll have lived with
me longer than she did with Arvin. And Arvin, of
course, is, with the unsurprising exception of her

175

father, the only other man she's ever lived with. So
she's heading into uncharted territory, and I'm heading
there with her. I expect it'll be plenty -- interesting,
yeah. Indeed. SQUAWK!)

What else stands out this eighter? Friday and
Saturday Naomi had all-day rush jobs and so for a change
I had to buckle down at the scope office over the
weekend as opposed to during the workweek (and the jobs
themselves were unusual, involving a lawsuit filed by
the magazine division of a huge publishing house against
various small companies peddling cut-rate subscriptions
to the publishing house's magazines and using
computerized demographic data, often obtained by shady
means, to compile their mailing lists; I realize now
I've unknowingly bought several of my own subs through
companies like these). And for the past four or five
days the lobby door here at 1511 has again been broken
-- we can get in by key but can't get out at all through
that door; we have to use the garage pedestrian exit --
and so at night I must go down and all the way around
via the front sidewalk and the side passageway to pick
up the newspaper, which the delivery guy tosses just
outside the lobby door. And one night while doing this
I scared a cat stalking rats in our building's small
front yard next to the dumpster by the garage entrance.
And it's good indeed to know those rats are no longer
going unchallenged (we had noticed before that this hood
is long on dogs but short on cats).

And: the next street over to the east, the main
drag up here -- but forty or fifty feet lower on the
steep hillside -- was closed for repairs most of the
week and our street was the official detour, and traffic
was heavy and the air was not good and it triggered
plenty of grousing from everyone, with Z of course
leading the pack.

And: for the second year in a row we rocked out at
the big charity bash for AIDS victims, on Saturday
night, but only briefly (because the music was so bad
this time -- mostly techno, as if for a gathering of
robots). We bought two more wooden flowerboxes for the

balcony along with flowers to fill them and also a cheap
electric drill so I can speed up the hanging of our new
metal screen door, also for the balcony, as well as
install chain locks for the existing doors. I finally
met Felicia, our Afrusan next-door neighbor who Z thinks
is quite beautiful -- and I'd say she's right -- and we
had a pleasant chat, Felicia and I, as she smoked a few
feet away on her balcony while I watered the flowers on
ours, once missing the box entirely as she queried, "So
what've you been doing with your life so far?" "Not a
whole lot," I lamely admitted, as the water splashed
thunderously on the dumpster lid below. "Oops!"
(Reminded me of trying to pour wine for Z during our
courting days and entirely missing the glass.)

     And much much more. But now's not the time to go
into any of that; now's the time to see whether I can
lift myself up and out of this chair by sheer arm power
(here's where all those thousands of dips I've been
doing over the past year might pay off) and then make my
way gingerly into the bathroom and then the bedroom and
then the bed. Without doubt each step along the way
will be a challenge. -- But best first to reply to the
notes Z left out for me. And it's already almost half
past four. On one of the shortest nights of the year!

                    *   *

     Just to keep a hand in. Same time, two nights
later. The injured left lower back is still hobbling
me. Lots of my normal daily tasks I can do only very
slowly or not at all. It's a big painful ordeal to put
on socks and shoes, slide behind the wheel of the Z-
mobile, stand up after sitting back for too long in this
black armchair right here or any other chair. But --
I'm noting some improvement. Yesterday I gobbled five
doses of ibuprofen; today I've resorted to only three,
and the most recent was four or five hours ago.

     (Why didn't I start in earlier on jyzing? Why'd I
have to go through both of today's local newspapers
first after arriving home, and also skim tomorrow's
"far-coast paper," and also read one of the alternative
weeklies and a few more pages of my current bus book,

the diary of a certain highly meticulous British
fictionist? -- Not to mention indulging in a dish of
peach cobbler Z left for me in the fridge.)

    -- After all our crazed preparations for Paula's
cleaning day, she calls in sick. Today was supposed to
be the big day. Z's now thinking Paula's health has
become too fragile to permit her to do the job on a
regular basis. And her understudy, Sally, can work only
mornings and since that's when I'm trying to sleep,
Sally's not all right with me, and so Z wants to pick
someone from the ads in the co-op newsletter. Z makes
the big money (relatively speaking), this is how she
wants to spend it, she's not pressuring me to pony up
for a cleaning person or to do the cleaning myself (that
is, do it up to her standards; I already do most of it
but only up to my own sorry norms for the most part) --
so why not go along with her on this?

    (True, too much one-sided going along and I might
turn queasy. But if that happens, I think she'll be
willing to negotiate some adjustments, although maybe
only with our attorneys present.)

    Last night a surprise. At half past three she came
padding out in her usual sensational summer-night's way,
naked except for the black sleep mask, moaning about
being unable to sleep. She pleaded with me to come to
bed early so she could vent a bit on the fallout from
the latest invoice snafu at her office. I did, she did.
Meanwhile we drifted into a canoodling session, and I
was fine so long as I kept my body motionless -- was
even actually turned on -- and then after inducing a few
comes for her I made a foolhardy attempt to "mount" and
almost instantly collapsed back to the mattress like a
fallen cavalryman (a naked one) as flaming arrows of
pain shot through my hip and back. But -- the talk was
good. Living with me, she said, is like having her own
therapist-in-residence, and I honestly think she meant
this positively. Then this morning's slateboard message
from her called me her "Center Peace," which was a play
on the song "Centerpiece" which we've been goofin' with
lately, and I liked this a lot.

[Jyze to the Bone]

Much of the afternoon I gave over -- in a move
almost as foolish as the bungled bedtime "mount" -- to
shifting books around among the bookcases. We're trying
out a spare folding bookcase of Z's in the hallway.
This is my idea; she doesn't like it very much because,
although she reads a great deal, she thinks having too
many books around is oppressive. So I put a card from
the ORB (only real bookstore) atop the bookcase when I
set it up. "A room without books / Is a room without
soul" -- but I added "or hall" with a caret after "room"
in both places. After seeing it she said the card had
persuaded her to let the experiment proceed.
-- And it's quarter past four. Time to stop. I'll
mention first, though, it's frustrating that I can't
keep up with my program at the WOC. If I have to stay
away from it too long it'll be like starting all over
again. More pain! -- And I did a provisioning run in
the Z-mobile on the way in to work last night, picking
up a large load of two of my personal food staples, tuna
and cornflakes, both on sale. I was too lazy -- maybe
even too smart -- to try to "mount" the stairs with
them, so they're all still sitting down there in the
back of the wagon.
-- A note for Z to find out here, then bed.

*   *

The hideaway throbs tonight. It's Friday night but
another summer's rolled around and the whole quarter's
rockin' again because the tourists are back for sure.
(Too many folks around here take them for granted and
often seem to despise them even while depending on them.
Just as in historical tourist spots everywhere, I
suppose -- why not? So then how precarious is the
future of our quarter here? Quite, I'd say, but less
from deterioration itself than from the restorations and
new construction projects announced recently. At this
point a general upscaling of the area looks almost
inevitable. A few years hence this could easily lead to
mass evictions of subsistence-living scribbler/dauber/
jyzer types such as myself from our low-rent offices and
studios.)

179

[Deep Jyze]

     The trouble with reading sober, serious diarists
like my current British bus-book bloke: I turn sober and
serious myself. Especially in these pages right here.
My sentences tend to become even more earnest than
usual, not to say leaden. Wheels spin. -- I don't want
to be doing rewriting in my head before the first
thought has hit the page! Or anytime soon thereafter!
It's a serious violation of the jyze creed!
     Meanwhile I'm still hobbling. My back's only
marginally better. Yet this morning I defied the odds
and tried another "mount" and this time it worked. One
of our best shags yet! (How horn-doggy I was beforehand,
lord. The poor Z-woman was soundly asleep at four-
thirty a.m., lying naked on her side with her back to me,
when I spooned in close and launched some exploratory
moves. Touches as light as I could make them but soon I
was ratcheting up myself. How sweet it was! (Never
again will I take a plain old erection for granted, I
swear it.) -- And then I couldn't be so subtle with
those touches anymore.)
     The soft early morning light. Purple sheets
frosted gray. The deep curve and twist, knowing from
the start that this time I would come and even be able
to wait for her as long as I wanted (elementary indeed,
but still what triumph). Also such a load to pump (four
or five days' worth) and such rapture when it gushed
inside her.
     Later she confessed she's been having a hard time
getting used to my sex change, so to speak. "Thrusting
into a new phase." The pleasure, she says, "is so much
more spread out." No longer does she have to be
wondering if it's my bad health or her own
"unattractiveness" (sic!) that's making me e-dysfunct.
Then she wrote me a poem expressing a kind of nostalgia
for the simpler bygone times when ol' Poss reliably,
not just sporadically, refused to perform.
     (In the paper I read about the rare blooming of a
phalluslike titan arum flower in a greenhouse on the far
coast. The story quoted someone who compared its stench
to that of "roadkill possum" and said it draws "sweat

bees" from miles around. So I made Z a special card
featuring a fellow named G with a titan arum labeled
"non-roadkill possum" blooming from his lap as he sits
on an overstuffed couch and a condor-size "bee" labeled
"no-sweat Z" alights next to him -- I bought the card a
week ago by a lucky chance and now I drew in the titan
arum and the labels on it; all the rest was already
there. I was applying the finishing touches when she
arrived home from work this afternoon. She'd left me a
card too. She was surprised I was still there at that
hour. She admitted to feeling "hickety" and didn't know
quite why. Soon she asked if I'd like to lie down for a
while before leaving for work. I said I'd like that.
We did it. We got it on again but didn't go all the
way: she was worried that "prodomo" rumblings portended
a herpes outbreak. At her request I did an inspection
with a flashlight. Looked like a minor abrasion to me,
not an outbreak, but she insisted we not take any
chances. Besides, it had been too long since we'd been
able to indulge in "open-ended pillow talk.")
     (Oh, and she told me I'm really something. She
can't believe she's snagged me. Earlier this week she'd
said she realizes she'll never have as good a body as I
do -- which I say is absurd, and which is absurd, but I
let her know I'm plenty pleased to know she's finding me
more attractive these days and I'm even more pleased to
hear her say it out loud. Today she said -- again out
loud -- "I don't know how you do it. You have such a
scathing intelligence but you don't turn it against me."
"But I love you!" -- And this compliment too I'm
finding oddly gratifying. It's as if I'm an awkward
high-school kid all over again. And I think I'm
reaching her and moving her and affecting her in deeper
ways now. Her resistance is fading. She's letting
herself go, she's trusting me far more than before. She
looks at me with melting eyes much more often.)
     And my gimpy back? She'd like me to see a doctor
and asks often if I'm doing better now. She worries.
She cares. (I tack one of my favorite Kenneth P.
picture-poems onto the entrance bookcase: "Caring is the

only daring -- Oh you know it.")   She helps me put on my
socks and shoes if she's around.   She urges me to
partake of certain exotic herbal ointments and tinctures
whose names are so odd I can't even remember them.   She
tells me Wei thinks it's my "duty" as an officially
registered Deep to use my city health benefits as much
as possible and urges me to do so.   She still doesn't
"get" my sadly stereotypical "Paleolithic stoic male
attitude" about all this.   But she does seem a little
more resigned to going along with it.

Meanwhile I've bought another cheapo three-shelf
"stacker" for the art worktable and I've put it
together and cleaned off the table itself and placed
the stacker atop it in the corner of the recessed space
opposite the old stacker, which is slightly smaller.
For the first time since B-2 days the table boasts some
truly open space.   That's where I worked on the titan
arum card this afternoon.   The apartment's feeling more
and more homelike now.

Earlier this week Z and Aida were talking, during
their regular weekly luncheon, about Z's loss of
interest in pursuing the kind of independent consultancy
the two of them had schemed for years about starting up
together.   Z was saying she didn't know why she couldn't
work up the drive to go for it.   "It's because you're
getting laid!" Aida cried.   "You're happy!"   Z's telling
of this tale launched us into yet another long analysis
of the status of her relationship with Aida and the
changes Aida herself seems to be going through.   Her
boy, Charles, has just been diagnosed with ADD,
Attention Deficit Disorder; her former lover Kavi is
again "clit-teasing" her, as Z put it to me (and
apparently they routinely talk this way between
themselves); her big sister Sera is up to her old
imperious tricks and putting all kinds of pressure on
her; and her new job with the state is very demanding,
which is her excuse for the reputation she's getting
there, Z tells me, as being "super-pushy" (and Sera's
rep is similar).

I offer Z my opinions on such matters if asked but

in general try to steer clear of anything having to do
with Aida. I'm still smarting from her treatment of me
last fall and her continuing coolness now. She's never
come up with anything faintly resembling an apology for
the unending series of slights back then or attempted to
explain any of them. So...that's how it is.

And my loveseat is gone. June came by last weekend
to pick it up for use in her new apartment near the law
school (she'll be living there, a mile due north of us,
during the week and returning to her home in the
northern burbs for the weekends). It was while her off-
and-on boyfriend Wade and I were hauling the loveseat
down the stairs to his pickup that I dinged my back for
the second time (which I forgot to mention earlier) (and
by the way, June met Wade through an ad a year and a
half ago, not long before Z ran hers, or rather Jess and
Gwen did). -- I'd become sentimentally attached to that
loveseat, I admit, but I never did use it for much of
anything beyond a place to stack magazines and books and
I doubt I'll be missing it for long. And I still have
its mate, the brown armchair, which I'm sitting in at
the moment as I jyze this hideaway jyze (at ten before
one a.m., with strains of live soul mixed with rap/hip-
hop coursing up from below as has been the case for most
of the evening), and also its matching hassock, and also
the matching low table which itself has become a kind of
hassock in front of the black armchair and the new sofa
at home. Nonetheless I feel I've symbolically cut loose
from another big chunk of my past. (This might be why I
dreamt of Lady U several times this week, and all of
them nightmarish enough to wake me up.)

*   *

-- This going down in the scope-office conference
room on a Sunday night which will flip to Monday a.m. in
thirty-four minutes. And being still somewhat under the
influence of "The Wild Old Man" (written by a fine
Chinese poet of antiquity) I'm thinking: at least some
of what's solid does indeed melt into jyze. Praise be!

See if any of this will so deliquesce. Last night
we threw our first dinner party as a couple, Z and I

183

did. I tossed the salad and dished out the dessert and
saw to the drinks, she tended to the main course, but
none of this was overly demanding because virtually
everything was premade: the salad and the peach pie came
from the co-op, the adobo and other main-course dishes
from the hilltop Filipino buffet, and the drinks from a
couple of bottles of merlot. It was a fine summer
evening and the apartment looked, I daresay, at least
minimally presentable in casual/funky fashion. Oddly
enough Wei showed up dressed almost exactly as I was,
tan pants and a blue workshirt (but his shirt was
button-down and sure did appear, unlike mine, freshly
ironed, although he insisted with mock ire it wasn't).

Triumphant the evening was not, however, and the
fault was largely my own. For one thing, I let myself
be drawn into an argument with Alison about current U.S.
policy regarding Tibet, and worse yet, I argued poorly,
hemming and hawing and fumbling and stumbling and
stammering and yammering. Z agreed: "I've never seen
you like that before. Were you drunk?" (I'll say this
in my defense: my hemming and hawing, etc., didn't
necessarily stem from confusion about my own views
concerning the issues under discussion. More to the
point, I was caught between wanting to say what I really
felt, on the one hand, and wanting not to appear
belligerent or contentious or overbearing on the other.
In short, I was trying too hard to be the affable host.
-- And only after saying all that will I admit I may
have been a little hammered, yeah.)

The other gaffe was worse: during after-dinner
conversation I called Z by the wrong name. I called her
"Jang." Fortunately for me she didn't flip out over
this as she might easily have done. She's been teasing
me about it at irregular intervals ever since, and I did
find it politic to talk in depth about what I thought
the deeper cause of this boo-boo might have been and the
ways in which she, Z, is similar to and different from
Lady S. Also it may have helped somewhat that I could
remind her of the several times she called me "Jerry"
last year, although she's now disputing that she ever

did so even once (but she does know her memory's not too good on such things, and it's definitely not good in this case if she's being sincere -- and I believe she is).

The underlying cause of the botch? No doubt it was partly the intense argument about East/West religion/politics/philosophy with Alison and Wei (eventually he jumped in too) which was a great deal like the arguments I used to have with Lady S and her eldest brother, and this was what I said was the likely cause. But I'm sure it also stemmed from the reading I happened to be doing the previous evening in my own protojyze about the breakup with Lady S, and this I decided to leave unmentioned. At least for the time being I think it's best to keep private all jyze/protojyze matters not bearing directly on the Z-woman herself.

And then today, "Mulan" with Kat and Betty. Here again the subject was China (and the character Mulan herself looked quite a bit like a cartoon blend of Lady S and Kat (and thus Lady V)). I enjoyed it: could easily see why the critics and even many Chinese are raving about it. -- This, by the way, being Kat's "Gotcha Anniversary": on this day eight years ago Betty first "got" Kat: picked her up in Guatemala. (And Kat was unhappy with me today: my gimpy back kept me from roughhousing with her and carrying her around on my shoulders and racing her to corners: made me into just another boring old geezer, as she was probably itching to say out loud but for some odd reason didn't.)

And I can toss in some truly small stuff. Like, I chopped off a few protruding tufts of hair on the sides (and Z says she likes my "look" better now) but I didn't touch in back and there it's longer than ever. It tickles her at night, it's a hassle to dry, it makes my nape and shoulders break out in a prickly sweat on unusually warm days, but I'm sticking with it.

And then not so small, or at least so I suspect: Z decided to withdraw her application for a substantially higher-paying job having to do with sustainable building materials. We talked it over in advance and only a day

later she announced her decision and said she felt much
better: the stress had greatly eased. It would've been
too demanding, that job, and not interesting enough. My
own hope is she'll now move toward greater involvement
in art, politics, or (best) both, possibly while staying
with her present job (trying to change its nature from
within) or better yet by switching to something totally
different (even though this would likely cause financial
problems because of her heavy debt load).

What else? Her herpes fears persist, but I towsed
her anyway last night (after she'd drifted off as I lay
reading in bed next to her as usual on Saturday nights,
jazz playing on the radio riding the old wooden
footstool, the small air cleaner humming) and then knelt
above her in semi-tumefied "lunker" state in hopes of
being able to ease on in for some meat-and-potatoes
humping and she had to shove me away, more or less --
and then at dawn she did me manually in return, and
exceptionally well, from behind as I lay on my side,
coaxing me slowly out of my dreams oh so lovingly,
caressing chest and inner thighs and lower stomach and
buttocks, tantalizing -- gently pulling my "rollers"
(her amusing term) up and down by fingertip scrotum tugs
from above -- then alternating slow and fast cock
pumping, light and strong, finally causing me to spurt
so deliciously in several long loops like lariats tossed
up above and around my navel (I had slowly twisted onto
my back) -- and the whole time she was wearing her black
sleep mask! Just like "The Story of O"!

And I should note (abruptly shifting realms here)
this week the city bestowed upon her a fifteen-year
service pin. And the living room is now festooned with
flowers, including a huge bouquet from Wei and Alison's
garden, two potted yellow daisies from the hilltop
supermarket, and a scattering of miscellaneous annuals
cut from our own balcony flowerboxes. And: Wei helped
us get the color TV/VCR working for the first time ever
(this is the one I foolishly bought two-plus years ago
at breakup time with Lady U) and we watched a video of Z
delivering a speech and I agreed with her assessment of

it: "I thought I looked really cute!" And: we learned
she'll be going off to D.C. at the end of next month to
attend the first meeting of the new national committee
on environmental justice. And: she promised she'll do
tandem jyze with me while we're cruising along on our
"Deep Roots Road Trip" in September. And: I ate way too
much pie this weekend, first the peach and then today a
strawberry humdinger Betty baked and brought over --
fresh strawberries too, from her garden.

20

   A slice of moon hanging above the bay. A slightly
chill wind whistling up the old "middle road" as I
stride along (but it's not enough to coax me to don my
jacket). A floodlit Stars and Stripes rippling and
slapping atop the building across from Z's office
window, maybe about fifteen stories up (the flag, that
is; her office is on the fifth floor), and because I've
never noticed that flag up there before I'm assuming
it's on display just for the week of the Fourth.
   Most of the clubs in the triangle are closed
tonight (Tuesday) but the one that isn't is packed, with
all seats occupied in its fenced-off sidewalk cafe.
Farther down by the hideaway building a guy is brazenly
pissing into one of the window wells; while still at it
he crooks a finger at me as I'm trying to slip by: "Hey
man, c'mere, I got rocks, check it out."
   Uh, no thanks. (And exactly what is he peddling
there anyway?) -- Round the corner, punch in the
combination, head down the corridor, through the lobby,
up the staircase (shaped like a tilted, mirror-reversed,
squared-off question mark), down the hall: I'm here.

[Deep Jyze]

No. 225, world headquarters of Jyzer Ink.

(The diagonally patterned bricks of the patio outside the federal office building, crossing them tonight triggered a Marcelian moment. The ancient brick and stone walkways of the triangle sometimes have a similar effect. And I'm thinking how odd it is that a big pile of bricks could be the cornerstone, so to speak, of a great literary work. And: why is it I don't have much interest -- almost none, really -- in delving into memory or history in my own work? -- All right, so then does the fact that I write mostly about things more or less as they're happening in my own life mean I'm just a no-account narcissist? Will anyone ever be able to see jyze as being anything but fluff? And do I care? Should I care? It, jyze, is the only way I can write that doesn't bore me to tears and seem a colossal waste of time. To me everything else looks simpleminded -- too one-dimensional and contrived. Too lacking in texture. Too false in its rhythms. -- Well then....)

Okay, enough. Midnight now in my own garden of mostly short-term remembrance. Fan on. And I notice some dirt under my fingernails from working on the balcony flowerboxes this afternoon. I was out there wielding a watering can when Z unexpectedly appeared on the sidewalk down below. She: "Hey good lookin', how 'bout a date?" (Sinking my fingers into flowerbox soil up there did unearth a few additional quasi-Marcelian memories, I'll confess, of similar planting sprees of earlier eras.)

Z's thinking things are a little "hickety" (which I've always thought should be "hinckety") between us right now and have been for a week or two. "Interesting how it's different," she says, "once we start in on the second year." She's of the opinion -- even comes right out and says this -- I'm criticizing her more. "I don't have you as wrapped around my finger as I used to," she asserts. I tell her she's nuts. (She tells me, "You're the funniest man I ever met. The goofiest too." She also suggests I sometimes push the attempts at humor too far -- anything to spark a laugh or wriggle out of an

188

awkward situation -- and even if she didn't feel this way, I do myself. But not too often. And in any event, it's how I am. And in general because she responds so well and goofs right back it seems to me we perk along without any serious problems most of the time -- and certainly without worrying too much about whether the proportions are just right.)

Yesterday I was late for our joint WOC session because an errant golf ball had fractured the front windshield of my bus near the driving range farther south on the hill, before I got on. To avoid straining my back I was taking an inbound bus from the hilltop for the very first time. Half a block after I boarded it, the bus, a trolley, lost all power. I wound up walking in after all.

Today, happy to say, my back seems much improved. I'm thinking maybe I've lucked out and dodged the bullet (golf ball) this time. If so, let this still be a warning about overdoing it. (Same subtle warning my ruptured left Achilles tendon imparted a quarter century back.)

Z left a hunk of peach pie in the fridge a bit too long. I thought she'd lost interest in it and ate it myself without seeking her consent. This touched off an exchange of quirky notes (in one of them I bestowed upon myself the "Ol' Possum Restraint Prize" for having resisted temptation as long as I did). Also I left her a card showing a cartoon cat conked out in a hammock with "Z"s hovering over its head, and I mixed in some "G"s and then tacked on a caption: "Z Gettin' Perky."

After I came in from the balcony and washed up, we stretched out together on the new couch for the first time. Later, having retired to the bedroom for a while in the interim, we did dinner at Z's old dining table, just the two of us, also a first (and Z's infamously frail wooden zebra was occupying half the tabletop, lying on its back, legs sticking some twenty inches straight up, because I'd glued it back together for her earlier this afternoon and was afraid moving it too soon would break the bond). Ol' Possum was frisky beneath my

blue shorts -- I did like leading Z back to the bedroom
with the shorts majorly tented (as has been the case so
rarely in the past year) -- but in bed it wasn't quite
frisky enough. Why, I don't know. (This morning it was
plenty rampant, but after she'd come a few times she
realized the hour was late -- and probably feared
getting me off by hand would take too long -- and asked
me to "save it." Tonight I was the one who said I'd
keep on saving it. -- And then took a quick nap, ten
minutes. A surprising wave of tiredness had rolled in,
probably caused by the cup of wine I drank at too early
an hour (it brought on a headache too).

After dinner we drove down to her office to pick up
the new air cleaner (which she'd had delivered there so
I wouldn't be awakened by a morning delivery at home --
and I never had to ask her to do it!). This air
cleaner, a souped-up version of the one we already have,
is another benefit from her unexpected inheritance.
-- On her way back home she dropped me off near the
library (I returned "The Wild Old Man") and then I
walked up the street a few blocks to the scope office.

Today's the last day of June. End of the
emblematic first six months of living together. At this
point we expected to be sailing into uncharted waters,
but yesterday she suddenly recalled that her time with
Arvin had gone about three weeks past six months. Just
like us they began living together on January 1; they
broke up on Bon Odori weekend around the third week in
July. She remembered this because Arvin had dropped off
Z and a friend at the festival and was supposed to pick
them up after a certain period; when he didn't show,
that was the last straw: she "evicted" him. (And later
she had to go for a restraining order to keep him
evicted.) (And as it happens, I was present at Bon
Odori myself that same year. Lady U was one of the
dance leaders. Z and I were probably trudging along in
the big circle of dancers, maybe even at the same time,
maybe even right next to each other, maybe even, who
knows, flashing lusty depraved glances at each other --
though if so the memory has somehow slipped away on both

sides.)

*   *

Midnight now, three days on. Twenty minutes ago I set off at a fast clip, tan summer raincoat clutched in one hand and a batch of letters in the other, hoping to arrive in time for the midnight pickup at the main post office. A misty Thursday night and I was feelin' pretty damn good. And still am. What's more I came panting up to the big curbside mailbox well ahead of the deadline -- had a pickup actually been scheduled. Unfortunately, none was. Maybe none had ever been scheduled at that hour. Maybe I imagined the whole "midnight pickup" thing just because I like the way it sounds.

Doesn't really matter. Kat left a long letter on my chair saying she missed me a lot during her visit to our place last night (I was at work) and I made her an elaborate card featuring schools of colored fish swimming in a sea of "thank you"s, the fish made by adding eyes to triangular slashes of factory-inked calligraphy brushes of various hues. I was hoping she'd receive this card tomorrow, but even with a midnight pickup it might not have gotten there that fast. (Now that I think of it, I'm sure it wouldn't have. The six p.m. pickup is the last one for which next-day in-city delivery is guaranteed. Just shows how long it's been since I was trying to beat the last pickup to send off all those urgent courtship cards and letters to Z.) -- And all the other "letters" in tonight's batch were bill payments and none were particularly time-sensitive.

Today I finished hanging the balcony door. That's another matter I was happy about. (Actually it's still only half hung; I've yet to put all the hardware on it. But since it's hanging there, I figure I can say it's hung.) And Z took the afternoon off and we hanky-panked a bit, and that was fine too. (Tonight she's scheduled an "orgy" for us. Tomorrow's the official Fourth of July holiday. So the morning should be good as well.)

And maybe I'm happiest of all because my back seems fully healed and I've finally returned to a full-scale workout regime. -- And that's another reason I decided

191

to walk up to the post office: just for the exercise.

So at this point I'd say the long buildup is over and the last constraints are off. I'm ready to go all out on whipping myself into optimum shape. (Why, good for you, sonny boy! Yet another gold star for you!)

After hanky-panking this afternoon the lady and I went over the lifetime list of her major lovers to give me a better feel for her romance history. It turns out the longest she's ever been faithful to one man may have been only about two years, not the two and a half I'd been thinking (she was confused herself). That one man was Jerry II and it ended with him nine years ago this coming Thanksgiving. The other heavies lasted between a year and two years. (Jerry II, by the way, she also met through an ad. For Christmas one year a group of her friends of that era presented her with a batch of letters in response to a personal ad describing her and run, unbeknownst to her, in the same weekly paper where I saw another ad drawn up for her by a different group of friends -- or just two actually, Jess and Gwen -- a little over a decade later.)

Yesterday morning she went off on a verbal fantasy trip as we got it on for the second time that night. In her fantasy I was the Norwegian sailor shipwrecked on a Philippine island, she the native initiating me into local mating practices (that is, she was her own great-great-grandmother whose husband actually was a shipwrecked Norwegian sailor, or at least so family lore has it, and Z's pretty sure it's true if for no other reason than that her father always insisted it was).

Ha -- and this: I'm still giddy from impulse book-buying. A hardcover, three paperbacks, and a couple of new lit journals. Couldn't stop myself! And was proud not to be able to! (And tomorrow night I'll be writing Jim Q., to apologize for the long delay in answering his Christmas card, and also brother Jeff to let him know Zoelie and I will be visiting Lahontan this fall.) (And I don't believe I've mentioned the latest revision in our wedding plans. It's now tentatively set for sometime next summer. Olwen will do the honors in her

backyard, or inside her house if it's raining (her
chemical sensitivity makes any other place too risky).
The reception will be either at Jess and Gwen's or at
Aida's. That's up in the air until the status of Z's
relationship with Aida -- and mine with Aida too --
shakes out a bit more. Z's now thinking Aida really is
"a lot meaner" than she used to be, and that the likely
culprit is her graduate education at the leadership
training institute. And this same Aida will soon be
bringing Charles over for dinner at our place "so he can
get to know Glen better." -- Not that Aida's ever asked
whether Glen wants to know Charles better. But so it
goes. -- And I'm sure it's June, who in the past year
has become almost as close to Aida as she is to Z --
it's June who's nudging Aida to try to patch up her
relations with me. Among all Z's friends June's the one
who seems to think most highly of me and also, ipso
facto (to be sure), the one I most enjoy being with.
-- And Z confessed she doesn't like my talking so much
with June late at night while she, Z, is sleeping: so
maybe she is a little jealous after all. And I say
that's probably a good sign. -- And June will be
joining us for dinner and fireworks-watching from our
hilltop park on the Fourth along with Rob and Gail.
Invited herself over, she did, and we wouldn't dream of
turning her away, be Z a little jealous or not.)
    -- Z, meanwhile, is temporarily assuming the unit
manager's position Jess held at the utility (before Jess
ran out of patience with her section boss, Dale, and
transferred elsewhere). It means a big pay boost. In
effect Z is now Dale's second in command. I may've
helped encourage this move by persuading Z that Dale's
not the male-chauvinist Cawk monster she'd been thinking
he is. Now I just hope he doesn't blow it and prove me
wrong. She and Dale have a fraught history at the
utility going back a decade or more. (And Malcolm, a
guy at the WOC who knows Z -- she briefly intro'd us --
came up later and raved about her to me, about how
"special" she is, how she's widely known for fighting
for her beliefs under even the thorniest conditions and

always letting you know exactly where you stand with
her. "Highly principled." Malcolm himself is a
consultant (Eurusan) in diversity training who "makes
big bucks at it," Z says. He's also gay, she advised
me, which was scarcely necessary since he's quite
straightforward about it -- or "queerforward," as he'd
probably quip with his trademark disarming chortle.)
    -- But the bus will be along soon and as always
it's the last bus. And since stopping now means I can
leave a little space in here for the Fourth, I'll do it.
                    *   *
    -- The scope office is becoming my own private
downtown late-night picnic ground. If the fast-food
joint across the street is too crowded to find a seat at
this hour -- and it often is, because they close down
the big basement dining area at night -- I bring my two
double-stacks with lettuce and tomato (costing together
two dollars and sixteen cents, tax included) up here.
    Super kwik tonight. Make my quota for the eighter
and that's it. The rest I'll save until next J-day.
    This afternoon I set off for the hideaway at five
o'clock and while passing under the freeway (whose
massive support columns have recently been painted
bright orange and yellow and decorated with huge line
paintings of carp and dragonflies) I realized I'd left
my keys at home. I knew Z, who was home when I took
off, had a meeting scheduled at six and so as I hustled
back up the hill I was watching for the Z-mobile on its
way down even though I thought it had probably passed by
already (Z being no less than ever the ABE type, "always
be early"). Luckily, though, this time she was delayed
at home by two phone calls and I found her still there.
    Why'd I forget the keys? Probably because I was
distracted by something unusual: for the first time in
more than a quarter century I was putting my hair up in
a ponytail. Yesterday I bought a bag of little elastic
loops for that purpose. They come in two sizes and lots
of colors. (Rob said my new 'do "looks great." Nobody
else has mentioned it at all, not even at the WOC where
I was expecting to get some grief about it.) ---

21

Wednesday night it is, and late. I just polished
off a big bowl of ad hoc strawberry/blueberry shortcake.
Three nights in a row I've done this, and I can't deny
I'm probably eating too much, but I'm almost compelled
to do so. When Z asked if she could pick up anything
for me at the discount mart, I said, "Maybe some fresh
strawberries or blueberries if they have any." She came
back with an entire flat of each. Worse yet, but from
another standpoint better yet, she won't eat a single
berry herself, either kind, because they're not organic.
It seems discount marts don't do organic berries, or at
least this one doesn't. And even if these were organic
I think they'd still be proscribed by her blood-type
diet (this is the diet she insists is keeping her
disease-free and making her feel good).

I say the shortcake is ad hoc because I toast up a
corn biscuit and toss it into a big bowl along with a
scoop or two of vanilla ice cream (left over from
Saturday's feast -- and it's organic too). Then I throw
in a handful of cored strawberries and a cup of
blueberries and top it all off with some blackberry
syrup. And I pig out.

So far I've made myself four of these shortcakes,
including one for breakfast yesterday. Amazingly they
haven't given me the runs or caused any other kind of
digestive upset. (Z was surprised by this too. But
even more she's been surprised by how I've plugged the
toilets several times over the past few weeks. I insist
these unit 203 toilets are unduly sensitive, but then I
can't refrain from mentioning the toilet-plugging

exploits of my youth. Now she's taken to calling me
"the Paul Bunyan of Poop.")

   She's in bed now, as she should be, presumably
asleep. Recently it's reached the point that most
nights I'm turning in just as she's waking up, and in a
way this is good. It's not intentional, incidentally;
in fact I was intending, and still am, to move my
bedtime a bit earlier, to half past three. But if I
don't watch myself I'm likely to get hung up on reading.
And sometimes I'd rather not watch myself, and
especially late at night. -- In any event, this way we
can indulge in more pillow talk, which delights us both,
and also I'm a better lover (unless I'm too beat to
start with when I go in there). The trouble with the
arrangement, obviously, is I must sleep in until quite
late the next day, and even then -- say at one or one-
thirty in the afternoon -- it's probable I won't have
slept enough. And if it's Monday, Wednesday, or Friday,
it's all but certain I won't make it downtown early
enough to put in an hour or two working on my own stuff
at the hideaway before hitting the WOC.

   So it goes -- the cycles. We're on the third or
fourth round now (referring to the whole past year),
first trying my turning in early, then late, and along
the way experimenting with various times in between.
It's a grass-is-greener type of thing, even though we
know, or should know, this particular grass never is
greener. Or if we do know, just say we tend to forget.

   And today's distinguishing marks? Z scrawled a
message on the kitchen chalkboard complaining about my
having left her only a single note last night (that was
a short quasi-poem taking off on the fact that Jess P.'s
half-deaf and rather strange father, during a brief stop
we made at Jess's on Sunday, somehow misheard Z's name
as being her land of birth -- "New Zealand," as he
thought -- and took to calling her "Kiwi" and wouldn't
stop. Z also left me a short poem of her own describing
the "sly" smile I'd given her in bed the past couple of
days, what she called the "Possum on the rise" smile.
(And she said she'll call her chapbook containing

196

current poetic works "Domestic Shock Poems.")

So then before leaving the house I dashed off a letter thanking her for various "small things" (hunting me up a handsome wooden box, for example, suitable for my wormlike cache of ponytail loops) and augmenting her description of that "sly" smile. And because I stayed home later than intended to write the letter, I didn't show up at the WOC by the time I'd assured her I would and thus her attempt to surprise me there failed. This is the third or fourth time it's happened. Her note on the stove says, "I never raise you at the WOC!" (This in turn refers back to another exchange over the Kiwi business, she with a pun about Auckland/Awkland and me with one on zealotry/Zoelietry. We're both aware this private language we're slowly evolving is becoming ever more impenetrable to others -- and once in a while confirm this when someone happens to encounter it. June for one finds it totally opaque, not to say nutty.)

What else? A potpourri. Z brought home some awful photos of us taken at the dance a couple of weeks ago. Malcolm, her gay friend at the WOC, mentioned he'd like to talk with me about editing a book he's writing on workplace diversity. Jess and Gwen arrived home from Borneo almost a full week early (preceding their postcard to us by several days); when we heard they were already on their way back we worried that something had gone seriously wrong, but it turned out they were just bored from too much beach-sitting, and the ocean in that area was polluted anyway. And Serafina sent an e-mail from Surabaya describing the chaos there, with minority citizens of Chinese descent under attack by the native majority.

Enough, almost, and I haven't even started in on the events of the Fourth. But those I'll shelve again (never get to?) and instead say a few words about the pair of fine ejacoshags that lit up the past few days, especially since neither was the standard kind (for us, that is, so far). The first, Sunday afternoon, was a side-lier (for me), she on her back, our bodies arrayed at ninety-degree angles, and it was one of the few times

I've ejacked inside her when we weren't in missionary posture or something close to it. The second, yesterday morning, I surprised her with a quickie on a day with a high perkiness index indicated on her meter outside the bedroom door, meaning she needed to be alert at work. "Gotcha." (That was one of the elements I said she'd missed in the smile, already mentioned, that appeared for the first time immediately afterward.)

*   *

Here's a sudden change and not a good one.

Guess I'll say we've hit a rough patch. But -- I'm afraid it's worse than that. I'm afraid it's the end of the honeymoon. (She's said this herself several times before, but I think this is the first for me.)

It happened last night. Again I'd been working on drilling holes for handles on the new balcony door when she arrived home from work. We'd gone two nights without loving, the first because she'd set the clock alarm incorrectly, the second because of another high perkiness index (this time I thought I'd better honor it all the way). So I was feeling frisky, and this was one of our two weekday evenings together. Further, time was short because I'd have to be leaving for work not too long after seven to start in on this week's grand jury.

She, however, was in one of those inexplicable seeing-you-as-a-stranger moods: personable enough in a neutral way but seemingly trying to keep me at arm's length and not responding to anything physical. A couple of attempted kisses drew the wooden-lips treatment. I didn't like the blatancy of this, and I liked even less the strong impression she was trying to push/manipulate/control me by withholding affection. Why do this now? It was off-putting, insulting, offensive, bewildering -- not immediately or all at once but cumulatively as she kept up the resistance and with a growing irritation of her own to match mine.

This was one of her worst "stranger" attacks yet. Even so, I should've been better prepared for it. I had let myself forget about these episodes and how painful they can be. Maybe I was fooling myself. In any event

198

I left myself wide open. And it hurt bad. We didn't
actually fight, but by the time I left for work I was in
an extremely downhearted state.

Later we did fight. When I returned home at one-
thirty I found a long series of notes laid out on the
floor. A glance at one was enough to reveal they were
further complaints about my alleged failure to accept
her "difference"; and being brain-fried from work as
well as even more bummed out than before, I set the
notes aside to read in full a bit later after I'd eaten
something and had a chance to wind down and gain, I
hoped, some emotional equilibrium.

But I never got to them. After thirty or forty
minutes she charged out in a fury demanding to know why
I hadn't awakened her, as one of her notes had asked me
to do; then she flew into a rage when I said I hadn't
even read the notes yet. A full-scale attack followed.
This eventually caused us -- her -- to haul out our
fight agreements from last year. By this point I was
too dismayed to do much but sit glaring at her. She
announced she'd be seeing Olwen alone Saturday afternoon
instead of with me as planned. Three different times
she stormed out of the living room and then returned to
take up the attack again.

Stomp-out No. 4 she didn't return from. She did go
back to our bedroom, though, rather than close herself
in her room, which she'd done during our two previous
major battles during our time in 203. After a long wait
I finally read her notes (one said she'd been hysterical
about my safety because a car had been vandalized
earlier that evening right in front of our building).
Then I wrote her a lengthy reply, almost two full pages,
explaining my view of what had happened between us while
also trying hard to avoid saying anything to upset her
further. I joined her in bed and attempted to take her
in my arms but she pulled away. We wound up sleeping as
far apart in the bed as possible.

This morning she slipped out of bed after bestowing
a perfunctory peck on the back of my head, then an hour
later delivered a similar peck, but even shorter and

lighter, before leaving for work. When I awoke at noon
I found no response to my two-page note and no sign
she'd even read it. Payback, no doubt. Before leaving
the house I wrote another note almost as long
apologizing for not having handled matters better the
night before and proposing we talk it all over Saturday
night if she wanted -- but also saying I thought we'd
thrashed it out enough. We both knew what had gone
wrong and we both knew what we could do to avoid or tone
down any similar episodes in the future. And tried to
make all this sound as hopeful as possible.

    However. I know we're in trouble. I must figure
out how to protect myself better during such incidents
(really two separate ones). I'll have to be more wary
and so less spontaneous in loving her. -- In short, I'm
coming down out of the clouds. I can't go on pretending
she'll change. I must be ready for her to reject me as
a "stranger" at times (she herself estimates it happens
a quarter of the time after we've been apart and unable
to talk for more than a day). I'll have to hold my
romantic/emotional expectations in check. She'll be
attacking me over what I regard as trifling matters. I
want to be able to hang on and I won't be able to do it
if I keep leaving myself wide open to her.

    -- I suspect this is a major turning point for us.
Hope I'm wrong. But even if I'm not, I still think we
can make it. It's just that this match won't be as
sensationally good as I was thinking (or dreaming).
-- And yeah, it's still pretty goddamn disheartening to
realize this.

    (On a Friday night at the hideaway. The usual
throbbing music down below. A big throng milling in the
triangle owing to the warm weather, this year's massive
tourist influx, and tonight a baseball game letting out
around ten o'clock just six or eight blocks up the
street, at, that is, the usual domed stadium. -- And so
what awaits me at home tonight, I wonder. Probably more
attacks. The main thing is to hang on to my cool --
don't let her provoke me into lashing back, or we'll be
in far worse trouble.)

[Jyze to the Bone]

*   *

    Now Sunday night, the same hideaway brown chair. Z
and I have made up, as of this afternoon, and we've even
gone shopping for cabinets at the huge mall just south
of the city and seen a movie with Jess and Gwen ("High
Art"), but it still looks as though my earlier
impression was correct: things won't be the same.
    Friday night nothing much happened. She'd left me
a note before going to bed, and it had some conciliatory
parts, but for me what mattered most was her statement
in it that she'd wanted to make up but after reading the
note I'd left her that afternoon (the apology!) she no
longer did. In bed she ignored me again.
    Saturday afternoon I confirmed I didn't want to
talk until after she returned from the Evan W. party
(Olwen, whom she was to meet at three, canceled owing to
dental troubles). This she disliked because she'd been
counting on my escorting her to that party (and I'd been
looking forward to it too) and so she invoked the
"moskstraumen" clause -- meaning this was a serious
emergency -- and so I agreed to talk right away.
    We had it out for a couple of hours right there in
the living room. A typical showdown for us: she was
getting extremely upset and letting fly with nasty
remarks, I was stuck in the grim "rational" role. This
cycle in which she flies off the handle and attacks and
I play calm and cool and withdraw into sadness ("go
dour," she calls it), thereby upsetting her even more,
causing me to pull back even further, was itself
something she wanted us to come to grips with. I agreed
to try out her idea that we call a "five-minute time-out
(with a hug)" if either of us spotted the cycle starting
up again. (To me this plan seems almost preposterously
high-schoolish, but if it works, who cares.)
    When upset she says a lot of very harsh things.
Even if I don't think she really means them they can
hurt a lot, and often it's hard to be sure just how
seriously I should take them. This time, among other
charges, she said I treat her in a condescending way
(also implying I'm classist, racist, and sexist, though

later she qualified all of these slightly by saying I do better at overcoming these alleged traits than any of the other benighted Cawk males she's known, and of course in her eyes every last one of them was just that: benighted). She said I remind her of her hated leadership-institute teachers and that my working with legal transcripts all week has made it impossible for her to communicate with me. She also said my insistence on her abiding by the "rules of dialogue" which she herself had insisted we draw up made me a cold rationalist and "just like Tom," Aida's ex-husband who supposedly "would never let her get mad."

And lots more. No doubt all three of the above charges contain at least a grain of truth, but I'd say not one is even close to fair or deserved. Even if they all were, it's hard to see how the alleged bad behavior on my part could compare in nastiness with the way she lashes out at me. And she goes to such extremes! Because I subjected one of her notes to a supposedly overclose reading, she's now decided we should stop exchanging notes, period. The only exception will be messages which are "completely innocuous."

When, at what initially seemed to be the end of all this, I told her I was still refusing to accompany her to the party because "I couldn't live with myself if I did that after what's happened" (referring to her threat to cancel the outing along with the one with Olwen if I didn't yield to her demands), she blew up again. This struck her where it really hurt, she said, reviving childhood fears about her father leaving home. But eventually, in a tearful scene (both of us tearful), she did let me leave the house (I had said I'd be going down to the hideaway -- where I am now -- rather than to the party). And she did it without throwing another big scene.

Drama and big scenes: as she proudly reminds me, that's her style. Self-restraint and calm dialogue -- nunh-unh. (Then she goes sarcastic: "Of course your way is the preferred, proper, so-called 'civil' way. Of course we're both well aware of that.")

[Jyze to the Bone]

So anyway. She went to the Evan W. party by
herself. As it happened, but probably not by
coincidence, she ran into Aida there and wound up crying
on her shoulder at a beachfront restaurant ("I wanted to
be near water"). Aida told her, as Z reported to me
later, "You're still the happiest I've ever seen you" --
and did not take Z's side against me. (I'm happy to
hear this but can't help finding it hard to believe.)

I'd told her I'd be home by nine and I was. She
pulled in at eleven and had nothing to say to me. I'd
bought her an illustrated copy of newly translated works
by her favorite classic Sufi poet (thirty bucks!) while
I was out; she took it into her room and for an hour I
heard nothing more. I assumed she'd crashed in there on
her couch -- probably opened it up into a bed -- but it
turned out she was reading. Then she came to the end of
the hall, coolly said, "Thanks for the book," and
without another word went off to bed in our room.

When I joined her there at the usual time she again
ignored me. Same thing this morning. Then around noon
she came back to bed. When I said, "Won't you ever be
ready to make up?" she warmed up a bit; and slowly, step
by step over a couple of hours, we managed to work our
way back to a fairly friendly state and to decide to go
ahead with our previous plans (we were late in doing so
because of the talk, so I skipped what she calls "your
usual get-up rituals" -- coffee and reading the paper).
But there was no lovemaking, no passion, no fiery
reconciliation. Much of the ground we lost earlier in
the fight remained -- and remains -- lost.

*   *

Tuesday evening, some forty-seven hours later.
Hideaway. I read a bit of this, a bit of that, putting
off until almost the last possible moment tonight's
grappling with jyze. It wasn't this way before, or at
least not very often, and in theory it shouldn't be now.
It's just a matter of not worrying too much about where
I should try to go with the upcoming entry (beyond
noting the major things that've happened since the
previous one). -- And the "this" I was distracting

203

myself with was a tome on solitude, the "that" was
poetry of another ancient Chinese master.

Meanwhile it appears the lady and I are finally
finding our way out of the bramble patch. At five this
morning when I went to bed I pulled her close from
behind as she lay sleeping on her side and when she
didn't push me away I snuggled in and gradually became
strongly aroused (meaning my goddamned joystick
functioned properly -- hooray!). Gentle kisses as she
turned toward me, then when she began breathing hard
(and querying aloud, presumably as much of herself as of
me, "why's it happening now? Why's it happening now?")
and I found her abundantly juiced up, I knelt between
her legs and again took great pleasure observing my cock
(my fingers pushing it downward at the base) quivering
at vein-popping full mast as the head nuzzled in her
sweet little bushy brownish-red vulvar zone and then
slowly pushed on in until the shaft was fully buried in
her and my fingers were gently pressing her puckering
outer lips against it -- such a lovely sight! And not
long thereafter she had a "big, big come" but alas I
never had one at all. So it goes! And even so she said
later she was flashing on that loving all day. (What in
particular? I asked her that. Said she: "I don't know.
More like the whole gestalt -- or the whole G-stalt.")

We met at the WOC at four, worked out, then did
fish and chips for supper on the waterfront. (Her right
knee was hurting and so we walked even more slowly than
usual. My back, her knee: looks like decrepitude is
closing in on us, we agreed, or at least the early
warning signs, the first creaks and shudders presaging
the eventual and inevitable structural collapse. -- So
best to live it up and of course screw like minks while
we can and to the extent we can, we agreed, yet again,
wholeheartedly, or at least so it seemed to me.)

Then an attempt at conflict resolution. After some
verbal rassling we came up with, at her insistence, a
detailed "working agreement" aimed at easing the tension.
Hopefully its four planks are well-balanced: she won't
stomp out without first giving some warning, I won't

withdraw into gloomy silence without giving some
warning (that's two planks). And: no voices raised to
the level neighbors would be likely to hear them. And:
apologies and conscientious damage repair for hurtful
statements made in anger. In short, being more loving
with each other and showing more care on both sides.
     But still I know hard times lie ahead. She's
intimacy-phobic probably to about the same degree I'm
intimacy-philic. She's hard-ass just where I'm needy
and vice-versa. For myself, I must be prepared to go
through periods when I'll be stung a lot and dismayed a
lot. I'll need to be ready to cut her plenty of slack.
I'll need to try to deepen my empathy and learn to see
with x-ray eyes the vulnerabilities lying beneath her
shows of city-girl toughness and pushback. See the girl
(and woman) who was different, ostracized, highly
sensitive, wounded, deprived in many ways, who grew
strong and resilient through her own determined efforts.

22

     A return on foot to the most recent of my former
hoods in this city. And now I've gone beyond it, or
rather to its far boundary, the old "north pole," where
I'm presently holding forth outdoors at the "plastic
oasis" on the upper deck of the local urban mall (with a
huge upscale corporate supermarket taking up the whole
first level). It's a fine balmy summer night along
about eleven p.m. And across the street, slowly
spinning at roughly the level of my eyes, the brightly
illuminated freestanding parking-lot sign, maybe ten or
twelve feet high, for brother Rob's bookstore.
     Went in to work early tonight thinking I'd be

tackling an all-day job, but it turned out to be only
sixty pages (or about a quarter of what I was expecting).
So why not use the resulting free time, it occurred to
me, to scope out the old stomping grounds. While doing
that I could rack up some extra walking mileage (I'm
aiming for at least thirty miles a week this summer),
check the availability of certain books (Rob's been
shunted to another store this week, so I can't just call
and ask him), and shop a bit at the drugstore I'm now
sitting in front of (where the canned chicken, which I
sometimes use to "beef up" my chicken noodle soup, is on
a rare two-for-one sale).

And best of all, I could break out of my rut and
sling some jyze at a new venue. Or, as it turns out, at
one of last year's venues. I also considered the digi-
cafe, the old coffee bar, and the old semi-retro bar,
but the first two were about to close by the time I
arrived and the third looked too crowded -- it was
unlikely or at least problematic whether a table with
sufficient light for jyzing would be available by the
time I could return after running my errands.

I hadn't thought of this deck with its white
plastic outdoor furniture as a potential site (as now a
trolley bus glides to a halt almost directly below). A
dozen chairs, all empty; four tables, all unoccupied.
From time to time a human head pops up facing this way
at sidewalk level maybe thirty feet to my left and then
its body sprouts to full size beneath it atop the
escalator and then head and body conjoined peel off into
the drugstore, which is open twenty-four hours (one of
its great attractions to me when I lived less than a
mile to the south). What's best, nobody's angling for
the tables here. And you don't have to buy anything.

I'd wager Rob comes up here fairly often during his
breaks. The fairgrounds a block to the east may offer
better spots -- quiet, grassy -- but at times he'd
surely find the convenience of this location hard to
resist. In the chairs by the railing he could light up
his pipe with no worry of offending anyone.

After leaving the scope office I hiked the zigzag

northbound route of B-2 days. The relatively early hour
-- before ten p.m. -- made the walk seem different,
although not really all that different. A few minor
changes here and there reflected the ongoing slow morph
of the hood from artsy backwater into upscale downtown
highrise residential district with a vibrant nightlife
scene. A sign in the window of a once-thriving grunge
record shop announced a move to the public market
(meaning, I guess, it's given up even trying to appear
to be anything but a tourist draw). What I took from
afar to be a new radio tower turned out to be a huge
construction crane rising above the site of yet another
massive condo project. "Luxury living!" trumpeted the
sign. A few of the smaller new condo projects in the
area are already far enough along to start renting,
including the one on the site of the former "Jello-mold
building" (for a period visible from my windows in B-2)
where my favorite funky postmod restaurant was still
slinging its souped-up hash as recently as a year ago.

"Change usually occurs in discrete [surely not
discreet] increments." And even the ones I'm noting
here don't seem all that conspicuous overall. At least
for me the feel of the area remains pretty much the same
in most places. Punky bars, sidewalk cafes, fancy
restaurants, art galleries -- but just as before, very
few establishments I'd want to visit myself. Even if I
were a few decades younger I doubt I'd go for it all
that much, despite its occasional points of interest.
It lacks the kind of easygoing cafe life which I've
always considered essential for the truly livable hood.
(I'm not saying our hilltop area has this. Its interest
is of a different kind. And it offers easier access to
districts boasting a somewhat better cafe life -- the
Asian quarter and the eastern outskirts of the old
"south pole" or historic quarter.)

So I took a hike along the hillside alley and stood
right outside B-2. A light was on inside but the vines
on the high chain-link fence were so thickly overgrown I
could see nothing but a faint greenish glow where I knew
the windows to be. No one was around in the alley, but

it looked unchanged. A few paces farther north, though,
where the paved alley road turns to gravel and,
paralleling the viaduct, begins curving uphill past the
vacant lot (while the viaduct plunges into the tunnel,
with a stretch of ever steeper bare hillside in between)
-- there the fence was down and a construction shack
was in place and work was clearly about to begin on the
eight-story (not ten-story as I'd thought) condo project
announced for that site last year. I was surprised it
wasn't further along than it was.

Z often asks if I miss living alone in B-2. The
truth is I rarely do. What I miss most about it is a
seemingly trivial feature: the nerfhoop attached to the
loft. The new apartment offers no comparable space for
jumping around; and even if it did, the ceilings are too
low for serious nerfing and I'd worry too much about
disturbing the people living below, whereas B-2 had just
a crawl space down there. Otherwise, I really didn't
like the solitude of life in B-2. Felt too isolated.
Nor did I care for living in subsidized housing; it had
a corrosive effect on my spirit. Even though the
location was close to ideal in a number of respects --
proximity to work, downtown attractions, transportation,
among others -- I doubt it was ever in the cards for me
to be truly happy there. I think of it now as more a
place of exile where I tried to work out some elementary
conundrums -- was forced to face them head-on, along
with the grief caused by losing Mother and Lady U in the
same year -- before I could move ahead with my life.

-- And then in wandering up here to Rob's store I
passed the main fairgrounds arena as a big country-music
concert blasted away inside. A dozen stretch limos
lined the plaza sidewalk outside, engines idling as if
the stars might come dashing out at any moment.
Twanging guitars, soaring yodels, whooping applause and
whistles.

It's Thursday now, by the way, two days on from the
last kwikjyze of the previous entry. Z's book group met
at our place tonight. I took off just moments before
the first guests were due to arrive. (Does she wonder

why I don't join the group? But the only reason I ever
would've even considered such a move would be in hopes
of meeting someone like her!) The "great room" was
looking good: cut flowers adding color here and there,
a fancy takeout Thai spread simmering buffet-style on
the dining table.

Supposedly tonight's gonna be a hot one in bed.
But I dunno, whenever she leaves a note implying this,
as she did last night in informing me she needed to be
perky today, it doesn't pan out. It seems she
completely spaces out the contents of these notes.

But yesterday morning was a humdinger. Another
ejacoshag! She loved it and so did I. "Geez," I said
without undue modesty, "I always figured things would
have to start coming together sooner or later."

So are we out of the woods, then, after our nasty
fight of last weekend? I'd say probably so. She might
say otherwise, though, and mainly, I think, for
superstitious reasons having to do with the fact that
Bon Odori's rolling around this Saturday. To repeat:
before, her one previous experience living with a man --
with the charming sociopath Arvin, sixteen years ago --
came to an end on Bon Odori weekend. Therefore if we
can hang on into next week we'll be safe, at least for a
while. That's the theory anyway. (The final barrier
for her, she says, will come at the two-year mark,
because that's the longest -- this by the revised count
of a few weeks back -- any relationship of hers with a
man has lasted. And on this one we still have about
nine months to go. And if we do manage to survive that
long, we'll be moving into a new kind of uncharted
territory with excellent timing: just as the wedding
approaches. Or at least that's how it looks now.)

-- One additional note about Arvin. Though Z talks
about his having been "violent" with her, it turns out
the only actual physical "abuse" was a single shove
which caused her to stumble backward "just a little."
Yet it was that shove which did it for her; his failure
to fetch her at Bon Odori was only the proximate cause.

I'm wondering how late it's getting. Don't want to

miss that last bus. The nearest stop's a mile away, not
just the usual block or two. So better not take any
chances.

*   *

     -- I did make the bus, though just barely. The
clock inside the drugstore at the mall said it was three
minutes to one, much later than I'd thought; the bus
would be pulling out at quarter past the hour. It was a
high-speed forced march, sometimes breaking into a trot,
straight up the old "edge road," right past the B-2
building and the parking-lot driveway directly across
the street which was the site of the storied first kiss
of Z&G (in the Z-mobile as she was dropping me off at
the conclusion of our fourth date, I believe it was).
     And now it's two nights later and here are a couple
of new firsts. For one, the jyze thing is going down
atop the futon couch. For another, it's going down on a
Saturday night at almost three a.m. shortly after the
jyzer has slipped out of the boudoir. What's more, the
slip-out was a sanctioned one. (I've finally had to
admit -- to myself for starters, and then to Z -- the
setup in there is not conducive to long stretches of
reading in bed. This was not easy to tell her, because
I created most of that setup myself and above all for
the purpose of being able to do lots of reading in bed.)
     A warm night. I'm lolling about in the usual blue
gym shorts and green henley (the "new" one Mama U sent
me four or five years ago; all my other short-sleeve
henleys are at least ten years old, and for that matter
so are the sleeveless ones -- also called Z-shirts --
and all but two of the long-sleeve ones). The balcony
door's open. The air cleaner is on (it's standing atop
the dining table) and churning out, as always, quite a
lot of noise along with the purportedly scrubbed air.
(But as much noise as produced by the revving auto
engines next door? From my perch here, yes, at least as
much.) And the radio by the black armchair is playing,
though just barely audibly. Piano jazz right now. With
a back line? I can't even tell.
     The room's still strewn with the detritus of Z's

book-group meeting. She'd intended to clean up this
morning, but after arriving home last night "feeling
pookie," as she said in a note left on my chair, and
then waking up this morning with much the same feeling,
she decided to cancel all engagements for the rest of
the weekend and also to take Monday off from work. Thus
we didn't, after all, babysit for Serafina's kids today
(the parents have returned to Indonesia to retrieve
their household goods), nor did we attend Bon Odori with
Kat and Betty this evening. Instead we had our first
truly relaxed day together in quite a while. (The least
relaxed moment of the day, I'd say, came when we
discussed just why it is we're so rarely able to have
relaxed days together. In short, it's mainly because,
as Z is the first to admit, she has a hard time saying
no to all the friends and organizations clamoring for
chunks of her. Nothing new here -- in fact she says
it's been this way all her life. And I told her I have
no trouble living with it as long as she can.)

     She attributes her current "pookieness" to several
factors. One, stress regarding the book-group meeting.
Two, stress regarding the Bon Odori "significant date."
Third, and this one I hadn't heard before, stress
regarding our purchase yesterday of round-trip plane
tickets for our "Deep Roots Road Trip" just nine weeks
from now. It seems she and Jerry II planned a similar
venture a decade ago so her mother could meet him, they
bought tickets, and then Jerry "punked out" on making
the journey and soon they were history. And six or
seven years before that, much the same happened with her
and Brian S.: though they did manage to get airborne,
they hit the rocks shortly after returning.

     But soon she was feeling better. In midafternoon
we wound up back in bed and a fine hot roll in the
sheets ensued, including a GCC (Z's abbreviation -- not
an acronym! -- for a Glen consummatory come) in a new
position for us, me upright on my knees straddling her
right leg and holding her left leg aloft as she lay on
her side. And I liked very much, I must say (and do!),
slowly dragging my "rollers" up and down her inner

thigh before they tightened up for ejac. (But even so
I must say I'm still not fucking very well. It's as if
the Good Ship Lollipop is undergoing sea trials after a
complete dry-dock overhaul during which only ill-fitting
used parts were installed. I'm still trying to figure
out what I can and can't do. And I've told Z as much,
because I dislike the thought that she might be
supposing this is the best I'm capable of. Vanity
showing itself here, definitely. And why not? Go for
bold! Because the lady likes bold!)
     Later we launched a mad search for a book she's
burning to read ("Arousal," an extended revisionist
"sex-positive" feminist essay, from what little I know
about it) but all three of the nearby bookstores we
tried were sold out, and we decided not to hit any of
the downtown stores owing to the massive crowds expected
for nearby events (a "bite" food festival and a big
country-music concert at the fairgrounds just to the
north, a high-interest baseball game just to the south).
Then to the co-op on east hill (Z was craving red meat)
and then home. Followed by a quiet night reading with
the blues show on and the bedroom air cleaner blasting.
     Yesterday she took off early from work and we
picked up the airline tickets and then I accompanied her
as she did some shopping, including a spell at the large
department store where Lady U also liked to sample the
wares (and I did some reading while waiting for Z
exactly where I ofen did the same while waiting for Lady
U). Z said she found me remarkably patient and well-
behaved. Then we worked out together at the WOC. So
much physical exertion on a warm day might've been too
much for her; she cited it belatedly as another possible
cause of her "pookieness."
     -- And I should mention one other slightly bad
moment. It came earlier this afternoon when she
wouldn't stop complaining about exhaust fumes wafting in
through the balcony screen door. To me they were barely
detectable (the wind was blowing steadily away from the
balcony), but that wasn't the point. We'd talked about
all this before moving in and she'd agreed to put up

with it, or otherwise we wouldn't even be living here.
But -- stoic acceptance is not her style. Worse, lately
she's been reading a book called "The Highly Sensitive
Person" about people who react strongly to industrial
chemicals and various types of pollution (as, for
instance, I did myself six or seven years ago to a
certain kind of printer toner which caused me to break
out in welts on my hands and feet). And if this book
weren't enough to prime her, then an article I gave her
on how industrial pollution shortens life spans in low-
income neighborhoods -- that was. She roared: "I don't
deserve it! I've paid my dues!" But after a bit she
cooled off, and later she bought a new cloth face mask
to wear when the balcony door's open, although conceding
"it's just a placebo." (True, this came only after I'd
pointed out that the label on the box said the mask was
useless for anything but dust and pollen.) -- And
tonight when we were reading here with the balcony door
open she didn't even bother to don the new mask. (Maybe
she'll limit its use to the mornings when I'm not up?)
     Sometimes she does overdo this stuff, sez I, and it
starts to get to me. I just have to remind myself of
her specialness, though -- would she, just as an
example, be so responsive sexually and emotionally if
she weren't also so responsive to noise, smells,
distractions? -- and I'm okay. So far anyway.
     -- I finally finished the English novelist's diary.
I'm still wondering: does this kind of reading cramp my
jyze style? The man's writing is so slow, so careful,
so measured. I admire it. Unconsciously I may be
trying to imitate it, and this may be why I seem to be
bumbling about even more than usual in these pages.
"Slow and careful and measured" is not me, not the way I
usually go at it, though the sentences do sometimes read
as if it were -- as does this one right here for sure
and any number of its predecessors. -- So then let's be
done with the jyze for tonight, I hereby decree.

*   *

Now Monday night. This from the hideaway, my feet
riding the hassock, my joined knees propped to the left

213

against the armchair arm to form a jyzing platform.

First, life with Zoelie B. Some sixteen months
after meeting her this is still all-important. Most of
the time when I'm not with her (and not working, and
sometimes not reading -- for much of my reading also
relates to her) -- yes, in one way or another it's all
still caught up with her. During the hour a day, give
or take, I'm walking I'm usually thinking or daydreaming
about her or some aspect of our life together, and I'm
doing the walking in large part to nudge myself closer
to good health for her -- to being aesthetically more
pleasing, even, if possible. Same's true for the long
workouts at the WOC. She likes strong arms, so let's
pump up these arms. Let's get this heart pumping better
too, in hopes not only of a longer life with her but
also a better-pumped-up Possum and for longer stretches
as well, and in both the space and the time senses of
the term. And so on. I could describe just about
everything I do in this way, and at this point it would
be the primary and most accurate description.

Will this be the case forevermore? Maybe not
always to such an extreme degree, but by and large I'd
wager it will, yes. And aver it will make for a
splendid life too. I can't even imagine a better one.
I think I might feel just about as the venerable Chinese
poet I'm now reading did after he gave up his career in
government service and returned to his home village. He
had poetry, wine, and family. I have jyze, wine, and
Zoelie. And Zoelie is so fine there's really no need
for wine other than as an occasional ceremonial gesture.
So maybe I should say jyze, sex, and Zoelie?

Today we bickered a little about her sudden urge to
schedule an appointment with her longtime counselor,
Anita. It's that ongoing problem she has about
"accepting happiness." I'm trying to coax her into
seeing that since by her own testimony she's lasted
longer with me (living together) than she has with any
other man and she's been happier than ever before, why
take a chance on messing all this up by letting a
counselor tinker with it? Besides, she'll develop more

confidence in her ability to keep things humming along
with her sweetie if she does the tinkering (or call it
fine-tuning) on her own. But she thinks I'm seeing
things in a male, Protestant, suburbanly and colonially
Cawkish way. And as a corollary of this, I suppose, she
thinks I'm trying to impose that same way of seeing
things on her. And maybe in a sense I am. But I don't
want to have a third person flitting in and out of our
private life. What kind of intimacy is it if a
professional interloper is part of it and what's more
has a monetary interest in backing the views of one of
the parties? I don't want to be trying to figure out
which of Z's views are really Anita's and which are
truly her own. I don't want to see Z become a manipulee
of some dubious psychotherapeutic system. (I wouldn't
mind half as much if something like this happened
through the reading of psych books alone. In that case
Z would at least be the active agent. And if I wanted
to look more deeply into what she was saying and doing
by reading the books myself, I could do that.)
     Then again, if her "inability to 'accept
happiness'" is truly making her miserable -- and in my
view that's not the case just yet -- I'm prepared to
give in and honestly support her quest for outside help.
And in the end she'll be the one who decides about this.
She's encouraging input from me but not really all that
much. If I'm not careful she'll decide to see Anita
just as a way of driving home the point that the
decision is hers to make. But I don't think I need or
deserve this kind of reminder. I've been careful and I
intend to continue being careful.
     And must note this: my semen from the Saturday leg-
straddler caused her vagina to burn. It hadn't happened
before with me, she said, and very rarely with others.
Was it maybe something I ate? Did the unorthodox
fucking position cause unusual abrasion? Is this an
instance of age-related thinning of vaginal membranes
actually affecting sexual practices? She'll be asking
her naturopath, Lorraine, about all this, and maybe her
mainstream doc, Karen, too. (I tend to think it was my

own unusually vigorous "thrusting" toward the end that
did it. This itself could be interpreted as an effect
of aging. In my younger days I wouldn't've needed to
pump away like that in order to come, nor in most cases
would I have found it anywhere near as pleasurable as
small-movement or no-movement fucking. But I'm still
hoping to recover the ability to love her up for longer
and longer spells in those venerable ways -- gradually,
incrementally, yes, but also emphatically and undeniably
and thrillingly. I mean, why not go for it?)

--------·

23

--------·

        Oh yeah, the throbbing "south pole." Midnight and
I just hiked down after finishing up this week's scoping
an hour and a half early. A warm evening and the summer
threads are out with a vengeance. Microminis and hot
pants -- some even on females. The entertainment zone
around the big hotels near the scope office is more
upscale and thus more sedate and then on the middle road
on the way down here I pass a few fancy restaurants --
young valets sprinting off to fetch luxury autos as
grossly overdressed customers fidget on the sidewalk,
grudgingly making way for passing riffraff such as
myself -- and I then land in the triangle with its
battling bands and surging pagan crowds (beneath the
rustling trees, the shining three-ball lamps, the stoic
statuary, the towering totem pole).
        And up into my lonely building. How that thumping
bass from the club directly below makes all this
solitude rattle. It's a wonder the old brick walls can
take such a beating week after week, year after year.
Sometimes I feel I too am crumbling under the assault.

And this has been especially true of late. For months
now it's been the same bands every week, the same tunes
(mostly) and I don't know the name of a single one nor
can I say I've ever heard any of them elsewhere. Mostly
mediocre hip-hop stuff, sounds like to me.

But yeah I'm doing fine. A bit sore across the
chest from grinding out lots of push-ups today, numbers
even a fanatical convict might be proud of. My henley
is orange; my hairstyle is starter ponytail. Once in a
while I catch a reflected image of myself and I think of
brother Rob, whom I seem to be resembling more and more
as the years go by. -- And why so many push-ups?
Because today I ducked my WOC session. Figured I needed
a day off. I've been worn down lately from stepping up
the workout level (among other reasons) and since last
Sunday's double-pop day ol' Merc hasn't done a thing and
I was thinking maybe the break would rejuvenate the
brute for later tonight. It's a hope anyway. Next week
Z will be flying to the far coast for her star turn at
the EJ conference and so over the next few days I'd like
to focus on racking up some good good lovin' we can both
be relishing in memory loops while she's away.

For her it's been a tough workweek. The newsletter
she's edited for almost nine years is folding. It'll be
merged into something much like it that will cover all
parts of the utility rather than just one, but it will
be out of Z's hands and thus no doubt far tamer. She
was bored with the newsletter anyway and wouldn't have
put much into it even had she stayed at the helm
(because her new job duties assisting Dale leave her
little time for anything else). But still she's
hurting, and not least because she's receiving little
recognition for her long and highly successful run as
editor. She wants us to do a champagne party at home.
(And if I were more adept as a social organizer I'd be
setting up ceremonial last rites for the publication in
its current form, no doubt soon to be dubbed classic.
Maybe I'll suggest the idea to one of her work friends.)

Also Dale, her boss, ran into a sexual-harassment
accusation from his secretary, Gloria, who happens to be

a Filusan and therefore first broached the matter to Z.
When I saw Z at the WOC shortly afterwards she was ready
to lead a lynch party to Dale's office. I tried to cool
her off a bit and I think succeeded fairly well. And a
good thing too, because the offense turned out to be
wholly a matter of mutual semantic miscues. Dale's
explanation, when Z asked for it, made sense. Gloria
also bought it when Z passed it along to her. But for a
couple of days it appeared Z might have to support
Gloria at a hearing of some kind and undermine her own
reborn relationship with Dale almost before they've
begun working together.

At home, meanwhile, the heat is upon us, of the
weather kind. If nothing's done to cool the apartment
it turns into a broiler on hot summer days. Nights too.
Therefore this week I've installed chain locks on the
entrance and balcony doors so they can be left cracked
open for air circulation when we're not around, I've
finished (truly finished this time, yes) hanging the
balcony screen door, I've done lots of experimenting
with fans and air flow. The two air cleaners are going
full blast nonstop, and at night we move the larger one
from the dining area into the bedroom. With one cleaner
roaring on each side of the bed it's something like
sleeping in a wind tunnel. Even so we can't touch each
other without becoming drenched in sweat.

But we'll figure something out, I'm sure. And this
is still a northern coastal city, so even at its hottest
it's not all that hot, and the season of heat doesn't
last very long. (But this will almost certainly be
changing as global broiling dials up -- of course.)

DOOM-bumma-DOOM-bumma-DOOM-bumma -- the relentless
rhythms throbbing from below. Next time I want to be
sure to mention my new janitor pal B-Jay, whose self-
produced rap tape rides in my bag. Same kind of music
as what I'm hearing now, I suspect. (If I'd come along
in this era -- as a high-schooler, say -- I'd probably
be doing honky rap of some sort. Most of my best stuff
back in the day, bad as it was, was a kind of proto-rap:
"Alley-Oop," "Stranded in the Jungle," "Too Much Monkey

                    [Jyze to the Bone]

Business," "Hot Rod Lincoln" -- and many more!)
                    *   *
     Today's a scorcher. And the next few days may be
worse. "I guess it really is too hot to fuck," grumped
Z. And then asked brightly: "Do I shock you when I say
'fuck' like that?" Well, no, except occasionally when
I'm caught in the mindset of some innocent lost self
(and I do have a bunch of those -- they may be invisible
to the outside world, or at least I sure do hope so, but
every so often they clamber up to take me over for a
while -- as at the end of the previous paragraph, say).
     Left home around eight p.m. Z was planning to
crash before nine so she could get up at half past four,
which would be half past seven back east, or in other
words her projected wake-up time for the conference
she'll be attending later this week. "Jet-lag prep."
     (Pausing now to savor a marvelous scratchy
recording of Memphis Minnie doing "I'm Sailin'" on the
six-hour Sunday-night radio blues show.) (Clang clang
clang -- another Memphis Minnie jyze-rules violation,
just like last year.)
     Surprise as I was passing through the Asian quarter
on the way down: a parade. Floats, bands, platoons of
prancing majorettes. Sidewalks lined five to ten deep
with a mostly Asian crowd -- and I love to walk through
such crowds (takes me back to Korea and Japan days).
This time I happened to bump into Z's Japusan friend
Adele who was in a hurry to photograph her niece whose
Girl Scout troop would soon be marching past the review
stand. Even so she paused for a moment, apparently
startled, I suspect because she'd never seen me looking
so stubbled and, in Z's term, "Stanleyish." It's my
Kowalskian black-henleyed persona that does it for her,
Z, though maybe not so much for Adele. (No clang-clang
clang for Stanley or Kowalskian, of course, because the
man's fictional and therefore allowed in by jyze.)
     An "interesting" afternoon and evening for Z and me
yesterday. (Squawk!) After running several errands,
including picking up a cotton shower curtain at the
environmental home shop (which is her favorite consumer

                            219

emporium of them all), we stopped by Rob's bookstore and went on a PMS ("printed material syndrome") consumer mini-binge to take advantage of his thirty-five percent discount. As I talked with him in the book-cluttered back room (a special privilege frisson to this because a sign on the door says "Employees Only") I suddenly realized he now has the ideal job, and not just for him but for me too. Every time we see Rob, Z remarks upon his viewing me as a "mentor," and it's true I've played that role for him at times over the years, but now as the age gap between us shrinks evermore (in percentage terms) I feel we're more like mutual stabilizers and supporters and inspirers. -- A touching moment afterwards as Z and I sat in the wagon in the bookstore parking lot and Rob strolled by, not realizing we were still there (after first seeing him we'd done some ancillary consuming in the nearby mall drugstore). It was just the relaxed, easygoing way he ambled along, the raggedy casual clothes, the long hair blowing in the wind -- and from behind a small bald spot visible at the back of his head. My little brother I used to carry around on my shoulders the same way I do with Kat now.

Then over to east hill and the Catholic university for a fundraiser held by Indonesian foreign students. Hundreds of people showed up for it, outdoors in the central plaza, traditional food and entertainment. Even though Indonesians and Filipinos are closely related culturally, it was hard for Z to feel that closeness in this setting (one possible reason being that most of these students are the highly Westernized sons and daughters of the rich). Then she nearly lost it over a long wait at a fried-rice booth. "I can't stand it," she fumed, "when Asians do things that make Asians look incompetent." (And then a pushy Cawk woman insisted she'd been waiting even longer than we had, although she'd apparently left the immediate area for several minutes, and now she reappeared and barged in front of us in line. Sometimes I have to act as Z's restrainer and this was one of those times. Later Z apologized: "Sorry if I embarrassed you by being so impatient. And

then with that lady, it was just too much. I absolutely
hate being taken advantage of!" No doubt she'd be
pleased if I too blew my top over such incidents. But
I'm not likely to do that unless the stakes are a bit
higher. Over a plate of fried rice? I don't think so.)
     Then we hiked a few blocks down the hill to see
"Smoke Signals," and this film turned out to be notable
for several reasons. Topping the list, it's the first
feature movie made entirely by Natusans -- written,
produced, directed, acted -- and it involves lots of
local people and much of it was filmed here, with one
scene taking place at a corner I cut across most days on
my way in to work. Second, it's basically the story of
a kid whose father "abandons" him at a young age, told
through the kid's eyes, and for most of the picture I
was wondering how my own kid's view of his father would
differ from that of the kid in the movie. Probably not
by much, I concluded. (And never mind how wrongheaded
this would be, I insist.) And then third, the actress
playing "the other woman" in the film is almost a dead
ringer for Lady V. What a shock when she first appeared
on the screen! (I waited a day to tell Z about this.
"Did you feel any twinges of regret?" she asked. I said
no, and it's not that far from the truth. But seems to
me -- to sap out to the max -- if you've truly loved
someone it's not possible to extinguish all regret over
losing contact with that person. In what I consider
normal and healthy and proud ways my feelings for Ladies
V and S and U and K, and also Karen A. and Briana T. --
among others! -- are still alive in some deep chamber of
my heart and I suspect always will be, and though that
chamber usually stays locked, I always know it's there
and I'm glad it is.) (And do I hope the same is true for
Z with the men she's loved? Absolutely. -- Doesn't mean
I'm not jealous of these men and the love she still feels
for them. But I can live with it and do and only
occasionally is it a little painful.)
     And also to report: more good sex. Yes! This was
early Saturday morning. And it came after a classic
Possum foozle -- the worst kind too, post-entry, just

when things seemed to be taking off. But Z handled it
well, no meltdown, and we drifted off to sleep, and
maybe an hour later, around dawn, I woke up and found
myself turning on again as I lay behind her, both of us
stretched out on our sides, naked, coverless in the
sweltering room. What caught my eye in the dim silvery
light was the way the old wanger was drooping, the skin
lightly sticking to her tush until a tumescent twitch
caused it to jerk away, and then it slowly fell back and
stuck again until another twitch caused a similar
reaction, with several more rounds like this before it
finally pulled away for good, becoming fully aroused --
a delicious feeling, so fucking sexy I couldn't believe
it. -- And then finally pushed on in slowly from behind
in that same position, legs intertwined a bit but torsos
moving farther apart until they were almost at right
angles, and then a long luxurious deep-going churn, Z
lying on her back now so our eyes could meet, she coming
several times as I surprisingly stayed hard and was able
to hang on the edge for an extended period -- ooh ooh
ooh, so scrumptious, as good as it's ever been -- and
waddayaknow, I was even able to come like that.

Does this mean I'm all the way back? Probably not.
Almost certainly not. No -- certainly not, period. I
won't ever be twenty-two again, nor thirty-two, nor
forty-two. Fifty-two, maybe at isolated moments. But
I'll be plenty pleased if I can love her like this just
every now and then. And she will too, I'm sure. We
both know what to do to keep the fires burning the rest
of the time (and just a few hours later, before we got
up, she proved again she knows, getting me off a second
time, by hand, and to me anyway that was almost as
surprising and delicious as the earlier triumph).

So: what will it take to be able to love her this
way just every now and then, but still often enough?
Fitness consciousness. Sexual concentration. Soulful
attentiveness (to her soul and my own). Eating right.
Sleeping right (knowing when to be extra-rested).
Staying alert about her times and degrees of
receptivity. Keeping a sharp eye on schedules. (All

this just for the occasional great fuck? U betcha! I
should be so lucky! -- And so why not keep on acting as
if I just might be? -- And she too, of course.)
                         *   *

     Two days later and the unusually intense heat keeps
baking away. The last I heard this afternoon it was
ninety-seven out there and since then it might've ticked
up a few more degrees. Even with all the fans on and
the doors open the apartment was so hot I couldn't work
up the energy even to read. Soon I felt ready to drop
-- "heat exhaustion." Dragged myself into the bedroom
and stretched out on the bed, the air cleaners roaring
on both sides. Stayed like that for over an hour --
dozed off at times -- and when I got up still left a
dark spread-eagled "sweat angel" on the purple sheets.
     Now I'm holed up at the hideaway and it's midnight.
Even without air conditioning the thick stone walls here
keep the place fairly cool, just as they keep it
passably warm on winter weekends when the heat's off.
     What's new? For the past several days Z's been
gradually packing for her trip. She's also been
dragging herself out of bed at four-thirty a.m. just as
I'm hopping in. No sex during these days -- in part
because of the heat, in part because she's fearing a
herpes outbreak is on the way. And she's wearing those
same intentionally unsexy pink H-rag "unners" to bed
with a sanitary napkin tucked inside because she's
using suppositories to try to "toughen up" her vaginal
skin a bit more and the liquid tends to ooze out. This
suppository treatment was suggested by her naturopath,
Lorraine, as a way to deal with the "stinging semen" (to
my relief Lorraine's diagnosis was about the same as
mine). And I suppose I should fess up to detecting a
little surge of studly pride (in my own self this is
now, I say, as this confession twists into grotesquerie)
when Z first bought those panty shields for a different
purpose: to soak up the flow of oozing semen. (But
geez, I ought to have the right to crow from time to
time in these private pages after what I've gone through
over the past fifteen months. -- And she should too,

and in fact I wish she'd do a little more such crowing
instead of seemingly just taking it for granted that I'm
finally able to function sexually in at least somewhat
satisfying full-service fashion -- sometimes anyway.)

Before leaving home tonight I finally got around to
playing "Nigga Out The E-town." This is the hip-hop
tape made by B-Jay, the twentyish Afrusan janitor who's
been working our floor at the scope building for the
past several weeks. He performed and produced the thing
himself (using a commercial drum tape) and sent it off
to a self-publishing music outfit that made him five
hundred copies which he's now selling for five bucks
apiece. As he warned me, it's "a little raw" (for a
Cawk fossil's sensibility, he no doubt meant), but I'd
say it's not bad at all. Two cuts are about smoking
dope, one's about hip-hop groupies lusting for his body
(or maybe he's just dreaming), the fourth's about "no
free rides" (aimed at unspecified people who want to
grab part of his "business"). He's a sweet guy,
friendly, he's got a couple of kids by a woman he's
estranged from living fifty miles north of here in "E-
town." Best of all in my view, he often raps aloud as
he's dusting and vacuuming. (And maybe I'll rip off a
phrase from his title too: call this jyze thing here, or
some future volume, "Cawk Dude Out The J-town.")

Tonight for the first time I walked along what
under the old naming scheme would be the "very, very
high road" on my direct route from home to work.
Usually I stick with the next avenue down -- the "very
high road" of course -- since it's the most direct of
the major routes and it involves less of a climb. This
new approach takes me right by the county jail, a huge
facility (ten stories?), and on a hot evening like this
the windows were all open and from blocks away I could
hear the shouts and screams of men locked up inside.
Why they were making all that noise I don't really know.
Possibly it's just a heightening of the usual level
owing to the heat, with the open windows making it more
public. Also I think maybe some of the inmates could
see women stylin' about in skimpy high-summer clothes

on the sidewalk below. Not too many days in the year
could they witness that (and maybe the windows would
have to be open, as they rarely are).

     As I hiked by I was half-expecting some comments
directed at me to come floating down, but it didn't
happen. Nonetheless I was nudged into remembering what
an outrage the "War on Drugs" is -- how it's torn apart
a generation. And this recalled Z's observation of a
few weeks ago, arising suddenly apropos nothing: how
fortunate it is that neither of us fell prey to drugs.
Interestingly, she's also suggested several times over
the past year that we ought to do some weed together.
The fact that this hasn't come up lately suggests she
probably originally proposed it thinking it might help
with my e-dys. But I also think, as she says, she'd
just like us to have the experience together -- a
different way of being intimate. (I'm game. Yeah, and
a little wary too, as always with any kind of drugs.)

--------·

24

--------·

     It's cause for thought. Or at least I think I
ought to be thinking on it.
     "It": being alone. For only the second time since
moving in with Z I'm temporarily and partially returned
to the state I was in for a couple of years before she
appeared in my life. (And also to the much earlier
state I was in when Lady U went off on one of her dance
or theater gigs or her visits to her family, but I don't
think I'll be looking back that far. And of course I
could be wrong about this. In a sense, given these
words, I already am. In another sense I can say that
same wrongness will stop for good when this parenthesis

comes to an end, like now. If I'm not confused here.)

It's Saturday night, first day of August, half past midnight. This is Z's last day at the conference; tomorrow afternoon I'll be picking her up at the airport. (And with a wince I recall how she fell apart on her last return from out of state when she saw that the apartment was not decked out with flowers and balloons and "Welcome Home!" posters. Melted down, she did -- and I haven't used that phrase in a while. Or have I? Certainly it's not surfacing as much these days. -- But should I rustle up some sort of homecoming commotion for her this time? Sigh. Maybe. But this loving can be hard work sometimes, it sure can. And yes, I wouldn't deny I should be working even harder at it. Possibly this is so for the simple reason that, to repeat, I'm a few decades less young and tender than I once was. Possibly also it's a matter of my having fallen for a woman who's complex and demanding. I insist it's no shameful thing that I occasionally need to be reminding myself of this. I wanted a stretch and I got a stretch. Without doubt it's one of the best things that's ever happened to me. If not the best, period. And I think I'd better stop right there.)

This is also the night of the big summerfest torchlight parade. In prior years it was always held on a Friday night; this year, for reasons having to do with new air-show requirements and ever-growing traffic snarls and ever-evolving cultural habits and needs, it was changed to Saturday night. And I failed to check it out. I've seen enough of them on my way in to work on Friday nights in past years -- always just a tiny portion of any particular one but still, enough. And also more than enough. I know just what I'm missing. And I'm fully prepared to go on missing it indefinitely.

Instead I walked all the way over to the far side of the next hill to the north -- again, east hill -- to see a movie. Turns out it's not a movie I'd recommend that anyone walk five feet to see, much less five miles (round trip). Terrible, horrible movie. But for me it was thought-provoking anyway because of the subject matter. It's about writing. The protagonist is a self-proclaimed novelist who's been working for years on an "opus" which no one's ever seen and when someone finally does see it, it's revealed to be no damn good (sort of like the plot of a certain celebrated nonfiction book). The guy could even be me, I suppose, except I proclaim myself to be a jyzer and I've been at it for much longer than the celluloid guy has.

-- And so what thoughts did this travesty provoke in me? Oddly I can't think of a one. Or no, one. I realized at least I've got some dignity left. Yes, I insist I do. I'm proud. I refuse to deny that at times as I sat through this clunker I was seeing myself as a crusty old warrior of sorts, maybe even not unlike one of our militant local indigenous heroes of a century and a half back standing proud until the end against the invading "Bostons" (as Cawks were called by those same heroes and their besieged tribal compatriots).

(This movie was showing in one of my favorite cinemas from the old days, in the smaller of its two theaters, upstairs. Over the years I've seen dozens of films there -- almost all with Lady U -- but none for a decade or so. And I was sorry to discover the theater itself is falling apart. Foam innards were poking out of the top of the seat in front of me and a jagged patch of floor tiles was missing a few feet to my right. Worse, a faint whiff of what I took to be mold mixed with stale semen hung in the air. I was also amused to see that, of the fourteen people in attendance, no fewer than eight were male singletons like myself, widely scattered, all of us betraying certain conspicuous writerly characteristics. What little laughter the movie evoked usually seemed nervous or hollow or, once in a while, overwrought and hysterical.)

It had been my intention to do some jyzing after the movie in a cafe somewhere along the nearby entertainment strip, but I found myself in no mood for that. And I don't think this was solely because the movie was so bad. I think it was also that trendy east-hill crowd. I've never liked it much up there and now I

find it harder to take than ever. It's a seriously gay
and largely young and punky and artsy crowd -- in short,
neocounterculturish -- and therefore I ought to feel
fairly comfortable with it, but instead it strikes me as
appallingly snooty. Even the people who obviously lack
money still act snooty, as if to fit in with the many
who are flaunting it. Except for a brief stop at the
handy outlet of our No. 1 local fast-burger chain for a
bag of fries -- actually two bags, both contained within
a larger single bag, and all three bags grease-soaked --
I walked straight home, down east hill and then up
south hill, nibbling on those fries most of the way.

Earlier this afternoon Z called. I hadn't heard
from her at all since the airport drop-off -- which
after all was just Thursday morning, only two and a half
days ago -- but still I was starting to wonder if her
silence was payback for my failure to call her or to put
up "Welcome Home!" signs for the earlier trip. Well,
just possibly it was, but if so, she wasn't pounding the
message home during the call today (and I didn't press
her on it either). She said, "I've found myself
thinking 'I miss my mate,' and that's something I never
thought before. I didn't think of Arvin as a mate or
any of the others either." Then she turned a little
pouty when she thought I wasn't being mushy enough.
Immediately I tried to be mushier. It wasn't at all
hard except for feeling I'd been squeezed on it a little
too quickly and so didn't have a chance to be extra-
mushy spontaneously. (But okay, this is nonsense.)

Tomorrow, by the way, another heat wave is due to
roll in. Should I say when Z leaves the heat goes off
and when she returns it snaps back on, and in more ways
than one? -- I will say neither of us is great shakes
as a hot-weather lover. And this could be another
symptom of our being recently minted Third Stagers.
Maybe. But without doubt this is the hottest apartment
or house I've ever lived in. (And also by the way, Z
caved in on cooling measures. "I surrender!" When I
came home on Tuesday she'd opened all the windows and
doors and set up a newly purchased fan in the bedroom.

She swore she'd hit half a dozen stores before finding
one with a few larger fans still in stock. -- And so
the matter of trade-offs regarding ecology/class/
consumerist issues may not be about to come to a head
for us after all -- or at least not immediately.)

     Flowers laughing out there on the balcony. The big
new futon couch looking fat and sassy. The red shorts
I'm wearing needing a good wash. A baby somewhere in
the building tantrumming alarmingly.
                    *   *
     Where was I? Well, since last jyzetime two days
ago, lots of places. But not too many of them new. On
several occasions in previous incarnations I waited for
someone at Gate N2 at the airport. Never before,
though, did I park in slot 203 (our apartment number!)
in the metered parking garage. Otherwise I'd say same
old same old is as descriptive as it needs to get.

     Where I am now is seated with surprisingly good
posture atop the new futon couch. It's three a.m. and
then some. Summer night, warm but not too warm. The
big potted plant standing to my left (it happens to be a
peace lily) is thriving and Z credits this to my
scrupulous watering regime -- says it's never before
been treated so well. (It was originally hers.)

     -- But she's back! And all's well again! Notes
are flying! We've already balled once (alas, sans
ejac) and "nookied" for hours (with one ejac).
There've been phone calls and trips to a deli, the
same one twice (at the co-op). There's been some
classic kvetching by the lady about the weeds
growing too high near the dumpster, offering shelter
for the rats (and I do see rats occasionally and they
do appear to be thriving). And ooh ooh ooh, she's
given me some melting-eyes loving looks to die for.
And in a card she wrote while away and then hand-
carried back she says up until now she hasn't really
let herself go vis-a-vis loving because she's been
afraid she'd lose me the same way Betty lost Manny
(and I suspect the different way she herself lost
Jerry II and Arvin and Brian S. as well, though she

hasn't said that), but now she's insisting to heck with
it, she'll love me all the way, let it all hang out.
(It's true she's insisted something very much like this
several times before. She seems to go in cycles on the
matter as she does on "storming" and many other of her
romantic behaviors. But even so I continue to believe
we're moving deeper with each cycle, "spiraling upward
and inward ever deeper and Deeper." And I was very
touched by this card and still am. Something brave
about it too -- maybe having to do with her willingness
to write platitudinously at times. This may sound odd,
but I really do find it admirable and another sign of
her strong character.)

     -- Speaking of ejacs, we had a rough few moments
last week, before her trip, when the topic of female
ejacs came up (initially prompted by the book "Arousal"
she was reading -- we finally found a copy) and she tried
to pin me down on whether I'd "ever known anyone who
could do it." Somehow she got me to admit I had -- well,
I know how: by assuming it, then going "Aha, I was
right!" when I didn't deny it (this being a favorite
rhetorical trick of hers) -- and then she started pouting
and getting all hurt and demanding to know who it was.
But I wasn't about to let this go any further and after a
while she dropped it. After all, we've agreed numerous
times not to let ourselves be drawn into the invidious-
comparisons trap, and this was definitely one of those,
and I could see she was itching to snap it shut.

     (The paper just arrived. THWAP! Suddenly it's
coming later. It's not the same delivery truck either;
the little red pickup with the loudly knocking engine
and squeaky brakes no longer shows up out there. But
this delayed delivery poses a problem: it makes me stay
up too late. If I don't, chances are unacceptably high
the paper will be pilfered by the time Z gets down there
in the morning. And when I've finally set up a "dual
alarms" system for us and I'm trying to go to bed
earlier -- now it happens!)

     And I did start back in yesterday on the typing of
what will someday be Annal 3 of The Jyze Age and then

continued with it today. So I'm feeling pretty doggone
good. Firing on all cylinders. Loving, working out,
writing, revising, typing things up. Apartment in good
shape. Schedule full on socializing nights. Income
adequate. Health (as far as I can tell) good. Diet
passably nutritious and yet still quite tasty at times.
walking from here to the hideaway and later onward to
midtown almost every day. Feeling more robust. Deeply
happy with Z despite (and sure, in many cases because
of) the abundant frictions.

A peak time in my life, no doubt about it. Most
times can't be like this. Things can't stay in such
marvelous balance for long. -- But knowing they've
been like this (and might be again) can fuel lots of
forbearance during times when they're not.

(Am I experimenting with my own ability to write
platitudes? Not consciously, no. -- And besides, I
already know I can do it and go on and on with it. The
protojyze of yesteryear was one place where I felt
perfectly free to do it and in fact did do a great deal
of it, I'd say roughly half the time at the very least.
But since then I may've lost some of that early
boldness.)

*   *

Running way late. It's four days on and it's also
past four in the morning. Here I sit in my old green
armchair in the bedroom for a change (again), because
Z's not here tonight (also again). wei and Alison asked
her to take them to the airport tomorrow morning (less
than two hours from now, in fact) and she decided the
easiest way to do it would be to stay over at their
place tonight. It's my "heavy week" anyway; she
probably figured she wouldn't be missing out on much.

Not true! She's missing out on a lot! She's
missing out on way more than she'll ever know! -- But
I'm okay, I do believe. I'm hangin' in there. And I
suppose she probably is too.

Purple sheets back on the bed. The white comforter
is folded at the foot of the mattress. That's our
summer blanket. A couple of days ago the weather turned
much cooler and we've needed that comforter. (I make up

this bed every day; have I mentioned that? A super-
quick job, nothing anyone would be proud of except maybe
me, slightly.) This cool front blew in right after Z
had completed another major "reorg" of her own makeshift
cooling system, which now consists of four fans and two
air cleaners. At this point I'm just going with the
flow, as I like to say to her. Sometimes she gets a
little crazy about this stuff. And there's plenty of
it, a whole wide spectrum. She admits this herself
(which doesn't necessarily make it any less crazy).
    Meanwhile it's the main weekend of the big
summerfest and the air show is back. Low-flying jets
spewing ear-splitting noise as they rehearse -- same
maddening cacophony as when I was in B-2 the past couple
of years. They wake me up! They set off numerous car
alarms! They make sleeping impossible! I hate them!
    And lots of loving. Every morning this week, five
days straight. A couple of those mornings I outdid
myself -- gave Z a big fat album of sexy images to flash
back on during the slow hours at the office. And if I
do say so, myself too, yeah (but she came up with the
phrase first -- "big fat album" -- and so I figure I'm
covered this time, the crowing all but ordained).
    And what? While Z's boss Dale is on vacation she
becomes boss. Mainly so far she's noticed she's had to
attend a lot more meetings than before. She's sort of
going against type (her own, that is), trying to act like
an exec rather than a rabble-rouser. Well, why not:
that's what the grad-schooling was supposed to be all
about, "learning leadership." Still, though, she's a
little afraid she's being seen by some of her friends as
a sellout and I'm a little afraid she thinks I, because
I'm cheering her on, am trying to deradicalize her --
make her nice and safe and middle-classy. I say no, huh-
uh, I want to support her however she wants to be. If
she wants me to, I'll try to help her be more effective
at the bossing, though I also insist she recognize in
advance that I might not know much about the current
approved ways to do it. And so far it appears she still
wants me to try, to "offer insights and support." And

just in case I might get carried away, she works in a
reminder every now and then that she's her own woman.
And she does this quite effectively.

    -- I'd better stop here. Big day tomorrow: Aida's
coming over to 203 for the first time. And Z once vowed
Aida would never ever EVER set foot in here. And I'm
bushed from the "heavy week," from working out and
walking, even from the reacquaintance talkathons with Z
-- not to mention all the late mornings of loving. Most
days this week I haven't gotten to sleep much before
seven a.m. -- and then the air-show jets have rudely
awakened me at noon or earlier. No going back to sleep
with them around. It's shocking to see them fly by so
low and nearby -- just barely above the level of our
"great room" windows, out over the valley a few blocks
to the east. Seems you could easily toss a cherry bomb
their way and knock them out of the sky (don't I wish).

    So I'll have to do some catchup next J-day, which
is Sunday. Day after tomorrow. I definitely don't want
to be falling any further behind in page count. I'm a
reformed jyzer; if I do nothing else in life I do my
allotted pages of jyze. (But not this time, not all of
them, no. Real reform starts next round. "Next Time
the Jyzarope.")

25

    -- So it's the last day of summerfest, Sunday, the
evening thereof, a few minutes before midnight. I'm
leaning back in the brown armchair at the hideaway. The
building is utterly empty as it almost always is at this
hour -- or anyway as it almost always appears to be at
this hour, because who knows what's actually going on

behind all those closed doors and darkened windows.

Red short-sleeve snap-placket henley, bluejeans, black chucks. Hair in the now-customary starter ponytail and newly trimmed at the temples. Z says she likes the look. Admittedly this makes me a little nervous, and she knows it too. "I hesitated to tell you it looked good because I figured you'd probably rebel and want to change it." So at first she just told me she was "startled" by it. That in turn startled me.

But ooh ooh, are we getting along well now. And I attribute it all (or a great big chunk anyway) to my suddenly upgraded male plumbing. Z talks as if she scarcely recognizes the main appendage. "It's so much bonier all the time!" she raves. And it is! At times it feels almost as if I've received the world's first successful penis transplant and it came from a randy teenager who drove his hot rod into a tree and willed his organ to the neediest elder on the list.

This morning, after a couple of late rounds in the sheets last night (fucking-type rounds this time, real fucking) she kindly let me sleep in. But this afternoon between cups of coffee we slipped back into bed for a quickie. For the, what, maybe eighth or ninth time this week I managed to get my refurbed wanger both up and in. Not that it's always stayed up and in for long, but maybe half the time it has, and several of those times I actually ejacked. And two or three other times I've ejacked when she's done me by hand. Three, I think.

Sounds like sheer fantasy. Preposterous! The old jyzer's lost it! How could he think anyone would believe this incredible turnaround tale for a single second? The miraculous rebirth! The Resurrection of Jyzeboy Sandefjord!

This afternoon's session didn't produce a come (for me, that is; for her, several, as almost always, at minimum). No surprise to me; I figured I had already fully shot my wad for the week and then some. A couple of days of recuperation would probably be necessary. Even at my studliest peak back in prime youthful days that might've been true after a streak of such semenic profligacy.

Following the quickie and also my second cup of coffee, we two satiated Glennarian Third Stage boinkers did a grocery run. On the way back we stopped at the home-improvement big box down in the valley and scored the large white cabinet we've been eyeing for weeks or I guess months now. It didn't quite fit in the Z-mobile; we had to tie down the vehicle's back door with newly bought bungee cords (and also we purchased a small stepladder for the purpose of slinging towels over it in the large bathroom, where the previous tenants ripped both towel racks from the walls and now the racks can't be remounted because their removal left jagged holes in the plasterboard, which holes we try to keep hidden from the view of any overly judgmental visitors through strategic placement and stocking of bathroom shelves). This new cabinet was unexpectedly heavy too; in degree of difficulty for wrestling it up the narrow and twisty 1511 staircase it approached the new futon couch. (And also, to complete the bill of goods for this latest consumerizing binge, we sprang for a large three-trunked palm on sale for thirteen bucks at the corporate supermarket -- "The ultimate green air-cleaning machine!" hypes the tag -- and that bio-machine's already taken up sentry duty just inside the balcony door, since the bad air from the street comes in mostly that way. "Head it off at the palm.")

Last night then, Aida's visit. Worked out pretty well, I'd say. She arrived just about on time (looking quite fetching, I thought -- and Z agreed -- in white sundress and her hair newly cut short, somewhat like Z's). She was obviously being careful, saying nothing even slightly controversial, but after a while I sensed we were out of the danger zone and decided to risk some direct talk about our tensions from last year. Aida acted as if they'd never existed -- what, what, I had thought she was upset about something? -- and that was fine with me. She'd just been very busy for the past ten or twelve months, that's all, is how her story went now, and also waiting for Z and me to "settle in

together." At one point I flat-out told her I'm sure
she and I can talk openly about personal matters without
putting any pressure on either relationship, Z's and
mine or Z's and hers, and Z nodded in agreement, and
Aida said that was just what she wanted. But will it
happen? I'm highly doubtful. (And I never mentioned at
all, nor did Aida, the biggest source of tension between
her and both Z and me, individually and collectively:
her pulling the rug out from under us on renting the
upstairs apartment last fall. The closest I came was
when I said, "Well, Aida, if it weren't for you we
wouldn't even be living in this building." She laughed
but quickly turned the conversation elsewhere.)

    We had talked about catching a movie after dinner,
but in the end none were appealing enough to pry us out
of our chairs. We wound up playing Scrabble on Z's tiny
metallic travel set (a gift from her mother, I think she
said, to take along on her world trip thirty years ago
next spring). The older I get the more I dislike
Scrabble, but it's hard to avoid nowadays because Z's
been playing it with friends for ages and they're not
about to give it up. But she said I did well at
disguising my real feelings about the game. And then Z
and Aida both roundly whipped me. How embarrassing!
"Gee, I was sure you'd kill me," said Aida, who won by a
mile. "Two big intellectuals like you guys!" (She also
urged me to get to work on my book. "We want to see
it!" she cried. I thought I detected a slight
skepticism in her tone. But then I'm paranoid on the
subject, and doubly so where Aida's concerned.)

    One oddity. Aida was talking about her parents'
long-running moral disapproval of certain hang-loose
qualities of her brother-in-law Dak, Serafina's husband,
and I was suggesting maybe some of his perplexing
actions of recent times could be viewed as a kind of
rebellion against that same disapproval. Then this
morning Aida called Z with a big secret which I boldly
pass along here: Sera had just asked Dak for a
separation. Big doings indeed! And the proximate cause
was Dak's failure to show up today to help Sera with

some shopping as he'd said he would do; instead, without even contacting Sera about it, he'd gone off to play tennis with a buddy. "Sounds like classic male rebellion to me," said Z. "Glen may be right."

(So, what's my point in all this? I'm clairvoyant or something? Maybe I'm trying to suggest I could be useful to Z and Aida both -- could add a different kind of perspective to their discussions -- if they didn't keep me walled out. -- And mainly it's Aida I'd like to realize this. But Z too sometimes needs, I think, to see she misses things because she tends to view everything from an overly skewed female vantage and doesn't look deeply enough into emotional motivation on the male side -- including my own, of course. -- Not that I'm setting myself up as being wiser than she. No way! I'm merely trying to be evenhanded. I want some balance here and any other concerns are strictly minor.)

*   *

Four days slide by.

First to set the scene and catch up. "Old business and new business."

Hideaway. Midnight. Ninety-degree-plus weather is back and even up here it's hot. (My shirt's off; just now a bead of sweat trickled down my chest, after condensing in the torrid zone where my chin's pressing into my neck as I tilt my head forward while leaning back -- the ergonomics of this ancient low-riding armchair being less than ideal for jyzing.) -- And unusual for a Thursday night, a band is playing live at the club one story down and about forty feet to the north, and it's some sort of retro heavy-metal outfit, which itself is a surprise. I'd thought that kind of music was pretty much extinct around here. Guess it's intended as a nostalgic draw for a new breed of tourist. In any case, it sure does get the bricks bouncing.

Old business. Only after capping the J-stick last session did I realize why I'd been J-ing about the Dak/Sera separation rumble. It was because it moved Z to worry about our own fate as a couple. "Let's never, ever separate," she pouted with a brow-knitting frown.

237

"Couldn't possibly happen," I assured her; "we're
hitched for life." "You broke up with Jang. You broke
up with 'Nora.' You broke up with Valerie. And you
loved them all and they loved you." -- For a day or two
she worried aloud almost incessantly about this. But
also we were both reminded of not just how fragile
things can be but how fortunate we are to have so much
in common. And we've both been around the block enough
to appreciate this. (Not that we're smug about it. No
chance! We gotta keep plugging away! Take nothing for
granted! Gotta work fanatically hard just to keep on
keepin' on!)

Dak and Sera, meanwhile, are "talking things over."
And for the first time I was able to exchange a few
words with Sera myself. She's been coming over to use
Z's computer to keep up with her e-mail while awaiting
the arrival of her own machine, now crossing the Pacific
on a slow boat from Indonesia. Z had asked for my okay
on Sera's doing this while I'm home during the day,
whether awake or asleep, cooped up in the bedroom or
wandering around half-naked, and I had given it. When Z
told her this, Sera quipped that she'd already seen too
many of Z's boyfriends naked. So Z (who didn't hesitate
to pass on this remark to me) assured her I always wear
at least a pair of shorts.

Yesterday Sera showed up with her two daughters in
tow, Dalisay (about six) and Tala (four), and I found
the little ones almost as irresistible as Kat. For an
hour or more the three of us goofed around in the "great
room" while Sera tended to her e-mail in Z's room. Both
girls seemed to think I was wildly funny, "just like Mr.
Bean," who's the clownish title character in a British
movie I'm unfamiliar with, but Z took Aida's Charles to
see it a while back and she concurs I'm "a little Mr.
Beanish at times." Sera herself is tiny, bright, quick,
cute, and famously hard-charging (sobriqueted "the
Bantam Fighter"), a couple of years older than Aida,
politically well to the left on most issues, apparently,
but still not someone I feel naturally in tune with.
For one thing, she seems devoid of interest in anything

that falls outside the realm of city politics and her
own domestic/family (D-clan) scene. As of now I doubt
we'll become friends any more than Aida and I have.

Speaking of whom: it turns out our Saturday dinner
didn't go down as well with Aida as I'd been thinking.
What a shifty one she can be! To my face she says she
wants us to be friends, but then she turns around and
makes a point of telling Z (at lunch yesterday) she
wants to be her friend and not mine. She's said things
along this line several times before, months ago,
including once to me directly (when she phrased it "Just
remember Zoelie is my friend first if any problems come
up"), but to have her talking this way again now after I
made a big effort to clear the air between us is the
last straw for me. From now on I'll be including myself
out whenever possible for things involving Aida.

What else? There was Z's amusing dream, in which
she found herself naked in bed with a work colleague,
Libby F., whom she suspects to be a closeted lesbian,
and in this dream it turned out Libby had a penis and Z
was fascinated because it "looked just like yours except
it was really, really white, like chalk." (Cawk chalk,
I presume, as in "The Caucasian Chalk Penis.") (She
gave no direct reply when I asked if, in the dream,
she'd been able to make it rise on its hind legs and beg
as she now regularly does in reality with ol' Merc.)
-- And in another of her dreams she and I were visiting
Lahontan and I was giving her a hard time, boasting
about various women I've known there and trying to look
some of them up. (Pure guilt on Z's part, I figure.
I've never had a single lover there -- excluding one or
two spirited in for a quick visit from Mentoka Falls --
whereas she's had plenty, during both her grad-student
days at U.M. and her two years as a social worker with
the Mentoka tribe in Coutawa an hour's drive to the
northwest, not far from Mentoka Falls.) -- She usually
tells me her dreams if she remembers them, even, or
maybe especially, when they put me or herself in a bad
light. A couple of times I've worried she'd try to hold
me accountable, meaning punish me, for something I did

in one of her dreams -- as Lady S sometimes used to do,
more than once nearly driving me bonkers with the
practice -- but so far it hasn't happened.

     And last Saturday was a terrific loving day. Did I
mention this already? If so, it's worth repeating. A
three-shagger. The third and final one was in a kind of
side-straddle position coming at her from the rear, me
on my knees with back straight up, a fine, well-lit view
of the action. "The best yet," she declared. "Please
remember how you did that and do it lots more." (This
gets me to thinking about a sexy card she left out for
me in my chair the next evening describing how "Peaches"
was feeling "not just peachy-keen but peach-cobblery
keen" for hours afterward. And this in turn recalls,
I'll just note here, what a sensational couple of weeks
it's been for fruit -- real fruit I'm talking, fresh off
the bush or tree or vine -- including peaches, one of
which I've been slicing into my cereal every day along
with, at times, fresh strawberries and blueberries and
raspberries (neither of the last two sliced, of course)
and the usual banana (sliced!). Every afternoon I'm
euphoric as I dig into my heaping cereal bowl, which
just to maintain appearances always has at least a few
cornflakes sprinkled in with all the fruit.)

     -- And I learned some new details about Z's other
lovers during her time here in J. City, mainly from Aida
at our Saturday dinner but also from Z herself, who
listened delightedly as Aida dished and couldn't refrain
from tossing in a few juicy tidbits herself. Jerry II,
the last before me, not only was a millionaire and had
hard-ons that went on forever (as I already knew) but
also was very muscular (as I'd sort of guessed). "You
shoulda seen the biceps on that man!" chortled Aida.
"Of course he was a fireman." (Like her brother Ray,
that is, who's also a hunk.) And then more on ex-fiance
Arvin's asinine doings. He loved to put people on. He
would lie to their faces, for example one time bragging
to Serafina about his extensive credentials in urban
planning (when in reality he had none). He must've
known that the people he was hoaxing would eventually

learn the truth and some would be infuriated, but this never deterred him. Z put up with his shenanigans when she was the one he was lying to -- "I had vowed to make it work and I was determined to hang in there no matter what" -- but when the lying started getting flagrant with her friends, that was the end. (Or rather yet another cause of the end; she's already told me about several others.)

     -- And I should mention this. Sunday's paper reported two shooting incidents in the city Friday night. Both were downtown. One was at the bus stop across from the post office, the stop I use when I'm working late at the scope office (the area was still swarming with cops that night when I arrived at a little past one a.m., some ninety minutes after the incident). The second was at my other main downtown bus stop, the one across from the courthouse just up the hill from the hideaway. (The point here being that I'm aware of the risks I'm running to live as I do. If I go down as a fool, so be it, but I don't want to go down as an ignorant fool.)

     -- And now with this disclaimer firmly in place, I'm about to set off for the second-named of those two bus stops.

*   *

     Next night, Friday. Hideaway again, and this is one of those rare times I have wheels. It's one a.m. I was lucky to find a parking space a mere six blocks distant. Nightlife is at its summer peak in the quarter right now and this year the peak seems higher than usual (or maybe I'm imagining things, seeing what I want to see: because I do want this area to prosper in its current form). Lengthy lines snake along the sidewalks outside the clubs with live music. All amps are cranked to the max. Lots of horsing around and frayed tempers. Pulchritude, whoooeee, it's everywhere! Fleshy display is audaciously in vogue this year (and often of the enhanced tattooed or pierced or hennaed variety).

     Earlier, at home, the birthday dinner party for Paz and Tobey came off without a hitch. Our favorite

241

hilltop Filipino buffet provided most of the eats as
usual. Jess, Gwen, and June were also present. Lots of
yuks. Seems to me all four lesbian ladies -- June being
staunchly hetero -- are now pretty much comfortable with
themselves in front of me. (A good many of the yuks had
to do with Jess's fear that their fancy SUV, parked all
shiny and white down around the corner near the women's
work-release house, would be stripped to a skeleton by
the time they got back to it. But it survived without a
single blemish -- we walked down there with them and
checked it out at two a.m. before seeing them off.)
     And by the way: even though we've enjoyed doing
this entertaining of various friends over the past
couple of months, we're now agreed we've had our fill of
it for a while -- say about twenty years. All the major
friends Z felt obliged to invite over have come by. We
can kick back and/or concentrate on other things -- my
own birthday, for example, coming up a week from Sunday.
     (A few details. Gwen was sexy but perilously
underdressed for the hood in short-short denim cutoffs
and a strapless black camisole top just like the one she
and Jess gave Z for graduation last year. In showing us
a bruise on her upper thigh Jess flashed some pubic hair
and Gwen scolded her for being so shameless. June was
proud of an article about her law-school admission
appearing in a local pan-Asian weekly (the same one Z
does book reviews for); it included tributes to June's
sterling character from Z and Aida and several other
friends. Tobey, who's Afrusan, let us know she wasn't
afraid to go down on the street unescorted at night:
"These are my people" (actually only a few are; Asians
and Hispanics predominate at this end of the hill and
even we carpetbagger Cawks probably outnumber Afrusans).
Paz leafed through Z's stack of catalogs for much of the
after-dinner period, occasionally breaking in on the
talk to read aloud hilarious blurbs hyping yuppie gear.
During dinner itself the weather abruptly changed: what
had been a very hot day morphed into a gusty cool
evening, and we shut off all the fans and air cleaners
-- wow, such sudden stillness in the night!)

26

Well, it's still going on, the miracle comeback.
Saturday Z and I "quadrifucked" for the first time ever
in a single day. True, only one was ejaco, but all four
worked well enough to produce at least one O for her and
went on long enough to be considered (I'd say) normal in
duration for a good contemporary USAn fuck (which may
not be saying much by Tantric or Kama Sutra standards,
but we'll take it).

Then first thing Sunday morning Z stiffened me up
again by hand and we could've gone yet another round.
Instead she tried to take it all the way manually
(probably because she was a little battered from
Saturday's bountiful offering), using her normally
failproof reach-around-from-behind torquing technique.
This time, alas, it failed.

-- And guess what. Historically today's a good one
for jyze to be churning out such a lubricious account.
This is the day the president of the USA and thus de
facto dictator for the rest of the world testified
before a grand jury about his "inappropriate sexual
conduct" involving a female White House intern less than
half his age. Shortly afterwards he apologized to all
his subjects in a TV address which I missed because I'd
gotten the wrong info; at air time I was in the WOC's
locker room taking -- aptly enough, I suppose -- a long
hot soapy shower.

-- Meanwhile it was an interesting weekend in other
ways too. I'll try to get back to them next session,
because now it's already bus time.

*

[Deep Jyze]

(Oops, another "interesting" slips by unscathed.
So should I just silence SQUAWK instead? Maybe!)
                    *   *
    Today's a little goofy. I've had to improv a bit.
Accordingly I find myself with a free hour on my hands.
And I can use it. This going down in the hideaway
again, but at the desk for a change (otherwise who knows
why). And it's four in the afternoon.
    It's Friday too, and four days after the previous
installment instead of the usual two (but then this is
starting to happen often enough that the two-day gap
shouldn't really be described as "usual" anymore). At
five or so the Deep will be showing up here and we'll be
making our way up the waterfront for a jazz/blues
concert. (This is the same gorgeous Deep featured in a
display of no fewer than seven photos right here on my
desk. See, I'm in lo-o-o-ove. I'm Deeply attached.
I've once again gone off the Deep end into the sea
of total sappiness. -- And it seems quite clear I'm
no longer the confirmed isolato I used to be.)
    I'd planned to work out at the normal time this
afternoon but wasn't able to wrench myself out of bed
early enough. By the time I got down here I could've
done little more at the WOC than undress, shower, shave,
and redress. So I decided to try again tomorrow
instead, on a Saturday. I'm becoming fanatical, I
guess, if only temporarily so. And besides, we (the
Deep and I) have to be in this area again tomorrow
evening for a hip/alt/New Age-style wedding involving a
member of her book group. In theory at least,
witnessing this ceremony will help us figure out what we
want for our own wedding next summer. (It's a topic
that's been coming up a lot in recent days.)
    Also this surprise, which is of the serves-you-
right variety: yesterday Z hit me with a couple of pent-
up complaints about our sex life. I guess I've been
focusing so fiercely on my own attempted sexual rehab
that I've missed numerous hints from her regarding her
sexual needs. She first mentioned this yesterday
morning in bed -- at five a.m. just after I'd crept in

with yet another hard-on already shaping up on its own
before I'd even gotten to the bedroom door -- and we
agreed to talk things over during dinner here at the
hideaway last night. She would give no more than a
brief preview of what she wanted to discuss. In
addition to sexual needs, she said it would pertain to
certain concerns about a new kind of performance anxiety
she thinks she's developing now that we're yes-fuck
fucking pretty much regularly.

We did go over those two matters last night. Both
turned out to be much less dire than what I'd been
girding up for in imagination all day. -- But later for
more on this. Time's again getting short here.

Real quick a word about why last weekend was
unusual. Mostly this involved Kat, whom I hadn't seen
for some time -- could it have been a whole month? But
Saturday we were unexpectedly called upon to watch her
while Betty filled in for a sick nurse friend at a
summer camp, and Sunday we took her on a speedboat ride
which Z purchased last spring at a charity auction. One
unsettling moment Saturday: while doing our usual
"rassling" in the bedroom Kat suddenly started showing
a new level of interest in sexual matters (volunteering
that she'd seen a boy's "thingie," asking if I'd ever
seen a girl's, wondering if I was wearing underwear
under my blue shorts, even glancing up the outside of my
thigh to confirm I wasn't) ("Glen! You're so bad!") --
and I realized she and I will soon be moving into, or
already have, a whole new era. (By happenstance an
article on this very topic -- pubescence and how parents
can deal with it -- appeared in the next day's paper and
was helpful for both Z and me. While being cautious
about maintaining boundaries, it advises, we shouldn't
withdraw from all physical contact with our "pubescent";
in fact, it's important that things continue more or
less as before, although with certain very reasonable
cautions. Z agrees about this -- and here she is now.)
                    *   *
The hideaway desk again and it's Sunday night two
days on. Earlier this week local media reported that

last week's pair of matched bus-stop shootings stemmed
from a new outbreak of drug-related gang warfare. After
hearing this, Z implored me to avoid the stop just up
the hill from here. Yet to my surprise, when I
explained why doing that would be almost impossible and
the alternatives would likely be worse, she accepted my
reasoning. -- Or no, she didn't go quite that far, but
she did ease off on her insistence and eventually
dropped the subject entirely.

     (Tonight, though, and regardless of all this, I'm
intending to be doubly bad. I'm planning to break a
promise I actually did make and walk all the way home at
two in the morning. And for an utterly trivial reason
too: just so I can get in a little more exercise today.)

     Meanwhile the weekend's gone by. The blues/jazz
concert was fabulous. The wedding in the Chinese-decor
room some forty stories up in the great white tower --
it turned out to be New Agey all right, a quasi-Buddhist
ceremony with lots of froufrou added -- the wedding, I
say, was picturesque and moving but also sobering.
Today's lovemaking, like last night's, was long and
delicious, even though the damnably erratic Mercutio
wasn't worth much for most of it. But afterwards Z
assured me I'd done okay on the all-important matter of
tending to her newly amended list of sexual needs.

     -- Last weekend then. Just a few high points and
low points. During our three-hour speedboat ride (with
a port stop for ice-cream cones near my old far-province
stomping grounds) (and this on a gusty day in which we
hit a couple of potent squalls) I took an awkward spill
in the back of the boat (wotta buffoon!) and then hours
later tumbled again while spinning Kat in the parking
lot at the camp where Betty's working. The two of us,
Kat and I, flew out of control and crashed into some
bushes. I think I managed to make it look less serious
than it actually was (or could've been, rather, since by
good fortune neither of us was hurt -- but if the bushes
had been of a different kind, or say a big blackberry
patch, the medics might still be working to extricate
us.) -- And then later that same evening, very

movingly, Betty announced my promotion from subunk to
full unk.

Also a dramatic moment at the ferry dock. We
started walking out onto the ramp too early, mindlessly
following the lead of a small group in front of us --
this during what turned out to be a brief pause in the
car-loading -- and the ferry's foghorn blasted, whistles
blew, lights flashed like dance-hall strobes gone wild
as ferry workers shrieked at the whole group to "Get
back! Get back! Get back!" Z was so startled she
stumbled and nearly fell off the ramp into the water.
Afterwards she declared her nerves to be shattered and
for the next couple of hours was scheming up ways to
"Get back! Get back! Get back!" at the ferry system.

Okay, enough about the weekend. (Or no. We did
finally check out the new grocery on north hill. It
turns out to be a kind of corporate natural-food chain
store offering many of the same items the co-op does and
often at considerably lower prices. I was especially
pleased to come across creamed honey that I've found to
be almost as good as the whipped honey I used to buy
(it's no longer available locally). As Z pointed out,
the place was very "Euro/West-Coasty" in both decor and
clientele: upscale, hip, Cawk. French, Italian, German,
and Russian were all being spoken as we waited in line
at the checkstands.)

And finally those earlier discussions about sex,
that is, ours, Z's and mine. Mainly she was just
wanting to let me know she felt I was sometimes pushing
her along a little too fast in recent weeks, and once in
a while a lot too fast, as if I wanted her to 'gasm
immediately, and this was making her feel pressured and
anxious -- even inducing a kind of performance anxiety.
This took me totally by surprise, but it wasn't too
upsetting because I didn't, and still don't, foresee any
problems arising from it. I think what's actually
happening is she's slowing down a bit and her needs are
becoming less urgent as she grows more accustomed to
having an active sex life and this time one that's not
just confined to weekends. Getting her off is a little

harder than before and so I was trying harder. But it
remains ridiculously and delightfully easy. She was
afraid she was letting me down, but she never was.

     (Of course the truth is the reverse: I'm the one
who's letting her down, even now, with my sporadically
dysfunctional wanger. Ironically, though, the fact that
the functioning has been so much better in recent weeks
has also made her anxious, because now she worries about
whether she should 'gasm quickly when I'm inside her
before I lose (maybe) my hard-on and also about whether
any change in her movements, however slight, might cause
a foozle. I tried to encourage her just to be her
natural splendidly carnal self and not worry about it,
and that's what she said she'll try to do, but I don't
foresee any easy solution here. The best we can hope
for is continuing incremental improvement, with some
inevitable, but hopefully temporary, foozly backsliding
(literally sometimes) mixed in. Because after all we're
both Third Stagers now and who can really know what
might happen. So just keep loving each other up and
hope for the best and be grateful as hell if "the best"
actually appears once in a while -- or a little more
often than that, if possible.)

     -- And that'll be it for today. I think I'll catch
the bus after all and drop the idea of walking. It's
1:02 right now -- blink, 1:03. I'll bank the remaining
pages to put towards next week's birthday entry.

--------.

27

--------.

     I've left just thirty minutes for jyze but this is
the appointed day and so here goes.
     At the hideaway (as per usual, mostly, it seems,

recently). The desk. Twin desk lamps blazing. Distant
sound of the ancient elevator door screeching on the
first floor, then eight or ten seconds later the even
more distant clank of the metal bar that opens the
building's night-entrance door being pushed hard
(because it sticks) -- and someone's outta here. At
this hour the odds are high I'm the only one left in
the building who's not (illegally) living on the
premises. Those odds were high before this departure, I
should say; now they're even higher.

And so begins yet another Jyzer G birthday entry.
The day itself is still five days off (four technically
since we're now into early Wednesday morning) but the
celebrating starts right now.

Zoelie's making a big deal of the occasion as she
always loves to do with birthdays (and loves every bit
as much to have done for her, to be sure, when hers
rolls around). Upon her arrival at home tonight it was
"Close your eyes until I say you can open them." Her
room's been off-limits to me for a week now (or rather
even more off-limits than it usually is). She's taped
a "Birthday Countdown Schedule" all the way across the
upper cushions of the futon couch. She's asked me to
bring my swimsuit home Friday night and to get lots of
sleep that night and to fast as much as possible before
then. Saturday we take off for parts unknown, "and it's
not where you think" (which she keeps saying because
Aida, during her dinner visit earlier this month, let it
slip that the destination would be the same mountain
resort where Z was attending an intensive grad-school
retreat when we exchanged our very first messages.
"So," Aida blurted, "have you two done the big getaway
up at Slee --" at which point Zoelie stopped her in
midword with frantic flashing eye and hand signals.
Ever since then I've been insisting, "I didn't hear
anything, I know nothing." And she's been rebutting,
"You think you know but you don't know").

Meanwhile she's experiencing a mild herpes
outbreak. This is reminding her once again that she too
brings a kind of handicap to our sexual life and she's

acknowledging aloud that our two handicaps, thanks to
ol' Possum's revival in recent months, now come much
closer to balancing out. -- Anyway, we're happy with
the loving, if maybe also a little privately frustrated
once in a while, so what difference does it make.
(She's even vowed to drop entirely her periodic remarks
implying we might not survive as a couple. "You mean if
we last that long?": phrases like that. Down deep we
both think we've "got the chops" to last a long time --
as long as we ourselves last, or rather the shorter-
lasting of us lasts (and of course actuarially that's
much more likely to be me despite the fact that she's
eighteen months older). So then, I insist, why not act
as if we believed it?)

Her very hot amorous spell on Sunday she's now
crediting at least in part to a six-pack of Peruvian
passionflower cola she bought on impulse last week. A
friend of hers who's even more up on herbs than she is
has told her passionflower contains a powerful
aphrodisiac. My comment: "Thus the name, am I right?"
And hers: "You're such a lawyer's son."

And now -- the bus.

*   *

Later the same night. Like four a.m. later. What
the heck am I doing back at the old pop stand? (Here
referring to the black armchair at home.)

Kwikjyze, that's what.

First off I'll note that June burst onto the phone
during one of Z's calls from work today with a piece of
legal advice: "Glen! Get divorced!" It seems bigamy
was the focus of one of her first law-school classes.
Z, of course, is pushing the divorce project herself,
but she doesn't want to be accused of hounding. She's
also talking, again, about moving the wedding date up to
March 29, our Meet Day: exactly seven months from this
coming Saturday (my birthday eve). And she's reversing
herself and saying she'd better take a pass on our doing
another tandem jyze spree -- like last August's --
during the "Deep Roots" trip next month. "The pressure
would be too much. Will you forgive me? Don't worry,

250

you can still do yours. Just tell me when you want to
get into it and I'll wander off by myself or take a nap
or something.")

Betty called too, at Z's suggestion. She'd like me
to come over and help her decide about Manny's old
stuff: what to keep, what to sell, what to toss. We'll
be making a date of it; I'll go over for dinner the
weekend Z's away for Jess P.'s big all-female birthday
celebration (that's September 4, same date as sister
Barb's birthday -- just as last year, waddaya know).
Betty told me a touching little tale of how Kat popped
out with a boast one day -- when some of her friends
were talking about their exotic relatives -- that she
has a "real Norwegian uncle." That would be me.
Declared by Kat apparently with a straight face.

Now I can go to bed.

(But first should scrub down real good. I
unthinkingly massaged my tired eyes and now they're
stinging and I see that newspaper ink is blackening my
fingertips. Z has noticed similar blackenings at
various times and let me know she doesn't want ink-
stained fingers visiting any of her parts, public or,
still less, private. Not much chance these fingers of
mine will be visiting either kind of part tonight, true,
and especially the latter kind, but still I wouldn't
want her to see them looking like this when her alarm
goes off less than an hour from now. Or almost as much
my undoubtedly blackened eyelids. -- Ink-stained jyzer
wretch, get your bedroom act together!)

*   *

Hiding away again. Thursday night now. What's
unusual is someone's at work in the adjoining office.
Or maybe he's sleeping, I don't know. He just arrived a
moment ago -- a few minutes past midnight. Slipped by
my open door without saying anything and before I could
catch a glimpse of him, though I did hear him pulling
out his keys. I'm assuming it's the same fast-talking
middle-aged Afrusan dude who stuck his head in the door
a few days ago and asked if I might happen to have an
extra telephone lying around. The one he'd just bought

was already on the fritz, he said; it was one of those drugstore cheapos. He moved in at the beginning of the month, I think.

     -- Yeah, I'm pretty sure he's sleeping. I just checked -- had to stand up to see over the nearer of the desk bookcases -- and the light's out in the transom window above the plastered-over doorway which constitutes almost half of the hideaway's interior east wall. In theory I could stand on my tiptoes on top of the desk and scope out the action or lack of same in most of his suite (it's five or six times the size of mine) but in practice it would be way too risky -- too many things might come tumbling down, including the desk itself and the jyzer with it. And what if my new neighbor spotted me up there peering down at him?

     So this is intriguing. How many other nights has he been sleeping in there, I wonder. Of course I used to think it was quite possible I'd soon be needing to do the same thing myself in here. And then: along came the fabulous Zoelie B.

     Earlier tonight I picked up Wei and Alison as well as the Deep herself at her office at closing hour and we made what we're calling our second semiannual joint shopping trip to the biggest of all this burg's many big-box discount marts. There I became an official mart member, complete with farcically bad photo ID. (Could that crazed geezer possibly be me? Not in my worst nightmares!) I also blew more money than I should've on items such as a bulk package of wintergreen mints (a dozen tins), a huge five-buck bunch of (or rather bunch of bunches of) red-flame grapes, and next year's public-market wall calendar, with an extra four months tacked on at no extra charge (and the first of those months starts next Tuesday!). After going through the checkstand the four of us sat down to a ballpark-type dinner in the concession area (hotdogs, popcorn, ice-cream sundaes) and engaged in lots of the usual sort of anticonsumerist joshing and gibing as we stuffed our faces and our overloaded carts circled the table to protect us from the howling mobs -- or more likely to

protect them from us. We joked about celebrating Wei's
upcoming birthday by hennaing some tattoos on his shaved
dome (and Z let fly with a groan-inducing pun about it
making him look "henna-pecked"). The hennaing idea
popped up because we'd been talking about the rage for
tattoos currently sweeping the nation. Among the
hundred-plus shoppers on view in the big-box concession
area, however, we could spot nary a tattoo, and what did
this say about our city which likes to think of itself
as riding the foaming crest of any new wave of hipster
fashion out there? So then, to uphold J. City's honor I
used a marker to draw a tattoolike blue heart on the
back of my hand and wrote in it "G.S. & Z.B." and
pierced it with an arrow -- awwww....

Then Z and I dropped off W&A in the parking lot
outside the county jail downtown (Alison counsels
inmates there part-time) and we went on to the hot new
north-hill grocery for more consuming. This time we
were seeking just a single item: that aphrodisiacal
Peruvian passionflower cola. Z wants to have plenty on
hand for our birthday celebration up in the mountains
this weekend. And I too think that's a terrific idea.

I saw her off at the market, having decided to hike
into town for the exercise. Along the way I did some
browsing at Rob's bookstore. He's on vacation this week
(as I knew beforehand), but I'll be meeting him tomorrow
night for the first of our two annual birthday dinners.

Next came a stop at the scope office to crank out
some finals. Two pieces of bad news awaited me there.
First, B-Jay the rapping janitor has been fired,
probably (according to his replacement) for being caught
"sloughing off," which likely means tinkering aloud with
his raps. And he's without doubt the hardest-working
janitor I've ever seen there or anywhere. Also one of
the friendliest. I'll miss him! -- And second, after
years of promises and snafus, the security card system
for the elevators is finally up and running. Now I have
to be able to prove I'm legit four times before I can
get to my workplace. And that's before I unlock the
safe and my lockbox and type in my computer password.

So seven degrees of security. Or as it should appear from any sane perspective, insecurity.

And then I hoofed it down here.

Last night Z was having trouble sleeping and stumbled out sleep-masked and otherwise naked as per usual, seeking herbal relief. After she dosed herself I escorted her back to bed and lay down with her for a while as I usually do on such occasions, and this time it turned out to be a long while: more than two hours. She again brought up the matter of my divorce -- not wanting to be too much on my case, to be sure, but it seems every last one of her friends is concerned about it. She asked a number of hard questions, and in the end I went much more deeply than ever before into the Lady S and Elgie story. Several times she was in tears over it, and I was not far from that myself, but the main effect (as she confirmed today) was to draw us closer together. We also talked about her past, herpes, the curious parallels in some of the things we've gone through and our consequent ability to understand each other as no doubt very few others could understand either of us. She wailed at one point, "I'd much rather stay living with you and not be married than get married and lose you" -- and she was imagining all sorts of grim scenarios, including one in which Lady S and Elgie, singly or together, came after me with "Korean Samurai swords or whatever they call them there." An exceedingly remote possibility, I assured her. But still, fear of stirring up a hornet's nest is probably one of the reasons I'm not moving faster on seeking the divorce (the fail-safe one, that is, just in case Lady S never did make it official herself as she vowed several times ten years ago she would soon do). It's also a simple matter of laziness and procrastination on my part. And old patterns: habits. But also: intuition. In any event I assured Z I'll be doing it because, yes, I absolutely do want us to marry and to be sure the marriage is legal and that's jhat. -- And with that settled (that that's that and that's it), over and out for tonight.

*   *

The "Slee" resort it is. Six-thirty in the morning
now -- on my actual birthday -- and Z's snoozing away in
the big double bed to my right, though restlessly astir
from time to time, probably because it's already past
her normal wake-up hour. I'm sprawled out on a huge
overstuffed armchair, feet propped on a hassock, and
I've pulled back the curtains the better to gaze out on
the campsite. I see tall evergreens with clusters of
red-roofed A-frame cabins scattered among them, high
wildflower meadows (not natural, to be sure, but allowed
to grow more or less naturally and certainly looking
natural or even almost supernatural) and then through
the trees the steep gray granite slopes of a couple of
the mountains that tower over the site close-in to the
west. It's an impressive scene. Spectacular even.

And "the last day I'll ever be of an age when I was
at least partially a Glennarian Second Stager" is over.
This is it. Exactly one year after the adult-life
"Absolute Pinnacle" birthday I'm finally Stage III all
the way, which is to say: fully on the decline. And of
course this downward slide picks up a little more speed
each and every day and will stop doing so only when I
stop existing.

Ergo do what you can while you still can. Always
an apt B-day slogan. And more so than ever this year.

Last night Z showed me what she called "the place
where I fell in love with you." (Oops -- the radio just
burst out with some schmaltzy music, very well timed.
"Will you shut it off, please? I didn't realize I'd set
it." -- She's saying this amid chuckles emerging from
deep beneath the quilts. It's a little chilly right
now. The mountain air. But this is the eastern part of
the state and they have authentic summers over here.
The jaggedy-edged tree-branches-filtered pieces of sky
up above those granite peaks mentioned before are all a
rich summery blue. An hour ago while still in bed I
thought I heard rain, but it turned out -- as I
discovered in pulling back the curtains -- the
sprinklers had switched on. Clearly they're at least

255

one source of the supercharged vividness of the
wildflowers.)

   The fall-in-love spot, I was about to say, was the
deck outside another cabin in another cluster where she
was staying during her last institute session here some
fifteen months ago. That was where she read the long,
intense, love-you-forever letter I express-mailed up.
(She likes stories. She tells me this. She likes to
reconceptualize her past through storytelling. She's
often asking me to do it too, on the spot and off the
cuff and out loud, with my personal story and also with
our joint one. Retelling the stories or making up new
ones, she believes, is much better than merely
remembering. I'm different, though. I prefer more and
more detailed elaborations of the stories I've already
settled on. I don't like discarding the old stories.
But on the other hand I do like moving on to new ones,
sure. But...not always, no.)

   She was pleased with her success in keeping me
uncertain we were actually coming here (despite Aida's
blurt) until the moment the resort's entrance sign swung
into view. -- Hey, she's the sleeping maiden herself
right now! And does she match the profile on the very
first card she sent me, also from here? The eponymous
mountain pictured thereon stands out of sight to the
southwest from this window (but from the deck right
outside the window it can be seen as an improbably busty
woman lying on her back; and I'd say there's some
resemblance there, no question, except for the
"improbably" part; here, with Z, we're talking -- Your
Deepness, are you hearing me? -- we're talking JUST
RIGHT).

   (Now the phone rings and it's our wake-up call
coming in an hour early. Grounds for a major complaint
to resort management? I ask. Possibly a partial refund?
"This is a maniacal place!" she laughs and rolls back
over, apparently still hoping to sleep some more.)

   Early last evening I clambered to the top of a
rocky nearby hill which afforded a fine view of the
area. Z was wearing slippery sandals at the time and

decided to stay down below and meditate. I could see
her sitting cross-legged on a relatively flat rocky
outcrop above a boulder-strewn creek celebrated for its
whitewater rapids and sports fishing. Far above her to
the southeast on the far side of the creek was a long
ridgeline still blackened and virtually treeless in the
aftermath of a major fire several years ago. Down in
the valley to the east the lights of a little Bavarian-
knockoff tourist town were starting to twinkle. To the
southwest the maidenlike mountain -- itself actually
more of a ridgeline but a much higher one -- stretched
out alluringly (untouched by the fire); to the west the
creek roared out of its canyon, with the massive gray
mountains, or gray massif I guess, looming above.
        A romantic time we're having. Extended nookying on
the bed here right after we arrived (complete with "male
boundary marking": an array of semen stains almost like
calligraphy brushstrokes or painterly "white writing").
An excellent buffet-style dinner featuring salmon and
roast beef at the dining hall above an outdoor music
amphitheater carved into the hillside. Swimming at
midnight in a rocky heated pool beneath blazing stars.
Hunkering down on the same brocaded couch (outside the
gift shop in the dining hall) where she scribbled that
first card to me. (And as if to confirm the epochality
of this trip for us, while napping I had a dream about
Lady U. In it she and I rendezvoused for some reason at
a schlocky bric-a-brac shop in the little Scandi tourist
town not far from where we used to live in real life and
she told me, "This is it. This is goodbye.") (Yes,
this is a true story even if just a dream.)
        -- And now Zoelie whispers poutingly from under her
quilts, "Where's that pretty Norwegian bartender? I
have an order I want to place." It's a joke I'll have
to explain later.

*   *

        -- "Then we had a fight on his birthday." That's
how Z says she'll start the postscript to her earlier
journal entry (which she wrote while I was taking a nap
after breakfast).

257

[Deep Jyze]

     "Nah -- why you call that little nothing squabble a
fight?"
     We're sprawled on a couch in the big camp meeting
hall awaiting the lunch bell. The microtiff was of the
familiar JIT/ABE type, my "just in time" penchant
clashing with her "always be early" resolve. Checkout
hour was eleven but she didn't want to linger in bed
past ten. I teased her about it. I never dreamed this
goofing might carry any real sting, but when we met back
at the car to load up the luggage after she'd paid the
bill, she was in tears. "I don't want to be seen as the
one who's always hounding you."
     But I think we worked it out all right. (As usual
I was startled by the intensity of her emotional
reaction, which to me seemed like boggling overreaction.
-- Or not "as usual" but rather "as happens every now
and then." But when it does happen it definitely seems
overdone to me, as in histrionic to the max. Reminds me
very strongly of how things used to be between this
jyzer right here and, yes, ol' Mom. Life was always
more vivid with her around and the same's true with
Zoelie B. Nor do I have the slightest doubt this has a
good deal to do with why Zoelie B. and I are together
now.)
     On the other hand a minor disaster came to light
when I looked in my bag for stamps for the postcards
we'd been writing. My leatherbound checkbook was
missing -- and it contained not just checks and stamps
but roughly a hundred bucks in cash and various coupons
and photos and other items I'd hate to lose. My best
recollection is that the thing was last out of the bag
on Friday night when I wrote a check to Rob at a
sidewalk cafe near the hideaway. Maybe I left it there.
We'll look for it when we get back to the city later
this afternoon. Meanwhile it's remotely possible
someone's drained up to fifteen hundred bucks from my
checking account. If so, it's almost certainly too
late to do anything about it now.
     And it's my birthday. I don't want this day to be
spoiled! (As Z plows ahead in the novel she's reading
about USAn corporado villainy, she still seems to be

pouting a bit over our so-called fight. Am I perhaps
doing something like that too? I hope not. But if I
am, I'm gonna yank myself out of it right now and that's
a stone fact.)
     The dinner with Rob turned out well, by the way.
The big hardcover collection of "lofty essays" which I'd
ordered for him -- the complete works of the purported
inventor of the essay himself, Western or Occidental or
European kind -- had finally come in and Rob brought it
with him, at my request, so I could add an inscription.
He also had a book for me (along with a bottle of
scotch), a collection of excerpts from a different
translator's version of selections from the very same
essays, with introductory remarks by a fine modern
protojyzer (one of the rare times anyone's ever come up
with a gift book for me which I didn't have already and
had never heard of but was eager to read -- he spotted
it at the big half-price bookstore out in the Yuke).
     And lots of good talk with Rob which I'd like to go
into if Z weren't pointing out -- fully in character for
sure -- that the lunch buffet will open in ten minutes
and we oughta git on over there to beat the line. And
I'm heeding her advice. (Peace must reign! ABE rules!)
                    *   *
     So now just twenty minutes left in my big day and
I'm back at the hideaway in Jyze City. The checkbook
appears to be lost for good. After a thorough search,
including stops here and at the two cafes Rob and I
visited that evening, I called the bank and had them
stop payment on all the missing checks. Fortunately my
account had not been invaded at that point and so I
won't have to open a new one or anything like that. The
bank will charge me eighteen bucks for the stop-payment
service. I'd braced myself for a lot worse.
     Otherwise all's splendid. Seriously. Immediately
upon arriving home Z and I took a two-hour nap with
nookie at both ends (no true fucking, though, because
the Big H quarantine is still in effect, as of course it
also was up at the resort). Our Sunday newspapers were
not awaiting us, but as of the time I left the house we

didn't know if this meant they'd been ripped off (as has happened almost without fail whenever we've left them outside after eight a.m.) or that Doug and Thuy had brought them in as per our request but kept them up there (D&T had been out all day, apparently, and still hadn't returned as of my departure time tonight).

The drive back was scenically spectacular. The highway we chose parallels the intermountain route of the east/west passenger trains I've ridden several times in the past, but both the weather during those trips and also the viewing hours on the trains have always been unfavorable and so it was as if I were seeing the area for the first time. Z's stomach was acting up at first (we had to make a couple of semi-emergency stops) but after gulping down a gallon or so of bright pink antacid elixir she was fine.

The best part of the drive was a detour of ten or fifteen miles down a winding, hilly single-lane logging road -- more like a goat trail -- near one of the high mountain passes. A rocky whitewater creek burbled and sometimes roared nearby most of the way and the forest canopy was so thick we glimpsed only a rare dapple of sky. The light was a marvelous limpid green and thanks to a brisk breeze the mountain air was bracing despite the long line of exhaust-belching vehicles we were caught up in (bumper to bumper nearly all the way, like a jeep convoy groaning over the Burmese hump in some old war movie).

-- And so it goes. This as my very first Post Peak Prime Time birthday joins all the others whizzing ever deeper into antiquity (already it's eleven minutes gone and, of course, counting); and meanwhile, but headed in the opposite direction, Z and I whiz ever deeper into Deepdom.

*   *

All right, I'm embarrassed. No doubt about it: I'm a blockhead. All along the wallet was right here in the hideaway, somehow inadvertently shoved out of sight in the inch-high space under the lowest shelf of the right-side bookcase standing atop the desk. Probably

this happened when I laid out my old leather briefcase
on the desk to pack for the trip. What's more, I
should've known it was there, because I'd written my
rent check from it on the desk, and that was after I'd
seen Rob on Thursday night and come back here. Totally
spaced that out, I did. Idiot! -- On the other hand
I'm now $93 richer than I'd been thinking for the past
two days, that is, while I was trying to reconcile
myself to the loss. So -- whoeeee! (And it turns out
I love the old wallet. How fine it is to have it back!
And all the stuff that was and still is in it as well!)

     -- And rather than push on for another page or two
of birthday kwikjyze coda, right here's good for the
wrap. This is it, super kwik. (Or could call it flash
jyze -- maybe even all such entries from now on.)

--------·

28

--------·

     Here's an abundance of wood at three a.m. Wood and
greenery. It's the far end of the futon couch by the
table lamp and the peace lily. A curlicued blue ribbon
is tickling my left wrist, dangling from a birthday
balloon tied to the futon arm (and Kat made me a big
blue-beaded stuffed cat for my birthday and gave it to
me tonight).
     I'm stretching out the time between J-days. This
is so I won't have to start a new volume before we leave
for Mentoka toward the end of this month. Instead I'll
do a separate volume for the trip itself in a smaller
blank book that will travel better. Then when we're
back I'll start up a new full-size volume to coincide
with the opening of the "truly settled-in" period of our
life on the hilltop. Or that's the latest plan anyway.

[Deep Jyze]

    This in the early-morning hours of the 6th, and
also on a late Saturday night. And it's Labor Day
weekend as well (it falls very late this year), and
because Friday was Jess P.'s birthday, Z has joined a
group of women at another mountain resort (that is, not
the one she and I visited last week) for another
birthday blowout. That's where she is now.
    I regard Jess as my friend too -- though not quite
as the sister surrogate I kid her about being since her
birthday happens to fall on the same day as my real
sister's -- but Z thought I'd probably feel out of
place, and Gwen did too, at what would otherwise be an
all-lesbian gathering (Z excepted, at least as far as I
know) and I agreed. So I stayed home and tonight joined
Betty and Kat at a belated birthday dinner they threw
for me at their place.
    (This weekend's birthday resort for Jess, by the
way, is on the same route as ours for me was last week
but it's even more distant, and for a while it seemed Z
would have to drive out there by herself. The thought
of this scared the hell out of her and also me. In the
end she decided to stay on at the cabin a little longer
than she'd wanted to so she could ride out and back with
a carload of Jess's friends.)
    And thus it is I'm alone again tonight in the
apartment, as I was earlier this year for a few days --
twice, including just last month -- when Z went off to
conferences, and also several more days for other
reasons. I have yet to leave her alone here for a
single full night and I expect it'll be a rare occasion
when I do. On the other hand I leave her alone here for
a partial night five or six times most weeks (but then
she also leaves me alone here for a partial night -- by
my reckoning of night -- five or six times most weeks).
-- So is there any point in mentioning all this other
than to highlight once again the fact that, despite all
our proud similarities, we lead vastly different lives?
I have to think a second about what it might be, because
there must be something.
    Maybe I'm worrying a little bit more than before

that my fondness for turning day into night and working
odd hours will cause difficulties for us. Admittedly
this fondness is partly a form of selfishness and/or
self-sacrifice on behalf of art, that is, "artyrdom."
And admittedly, too, it might unconsciously be a way to
prevent a love relationship from becoming overwhelming,
by arranging my life in such fashion that a certain
number of hours stay free for my own work almost by
default. But whether the latter be the case or not, I
think it's probably acceptable to Z, whose need for
freedom to lead her own life seems to be every bit as
strong as mine. And therefore I also think I shouldn't
be worrying too much about whether my night-owl penchant
is causing us problems. But of course that doesn't mean
I can just automatically stop doing that.

    Well. It's just about time to call a halt for
tonight to all this ratiocination. Rather than crash at
Betty's I drove her car home and tomorrow I'll have to
get up fairly early (for me) to return it. And yet the
main reason I decided to come home was to make sure I
could retrieve the Sunday "far-coast paper" before it
could be ripped off again, and it hasn't arrived yet. I
don't want to rack out until it's here.

    It was a delightful evening with Betty and Kat and
also a poignant one. From eight o'clock until well past
midnight I helped Betty go through dozens of boxes and
shelves of Manny's books, deciding which to try to sell
and which to keep or toss. Manny was every bit the book
hoarder I am, and by inspecting his library volume by
volume all the way to the end I felt I came to know him
in a way probably not too many people, if any, did while
he was alive. His interests were extremely broad, far
more so than mine (and I like to think mine are broad).
I couldn't help but feel almost brutal as I made snap
decisions about which books would stay and which go. I
also couldn't help but imagine someone trying someday to
make the same sort of decisions about my own books.
-- Or then again that person may simply say toss 'em all
or sell 'em by the pound.

    For dinner, meatloaf and mashed potatoes followed

by one of Betty's fabulous homemade pies, raspberry this
time, ala mode, and also topped with real whipped cream,
and this too homemade by her. Four red-and-white
barbershop-striped candles burning atop the pie because
they were all she had on hand. Before dinner, a romp
with Kat at a nearby park. How she loves to spin on
that grungy old tire suspended on a chain. And loves to
play hide-and-seek, which at times seems a bit strange
for a kid eight and a half years old -- does it maybe
have something to do with her being adopted? Betty
told me I'm now the main male figure in Kat's life --
"you da Man." And I'm delighted to be, though I suspect
it'll be a while before I can stop worrying about
becoming too attached to her. What would happen, for
instance, if Betty remarried, as she's told Z she hopes
to do? Despite her best intentions, the new man might
not welcome Z's and my presence as much as Betty does
now, if at all. Or the new family might move to a far
corner of the land or even somewhere beyond that.
     We also talked about Kat's looming "pubescence."
Betty thinks the kid's breasts will be budding any day
now. I hope I successfully eased any fears Betty might
have about how I'll interact with the sexually blooming
Kat -- for example, that I might morph into a Humbert
Humbert. (I assured her I hate motels.) (Actually I'd
be more concerned about Z's fears than any Betty might
have. But the whole issue worries me less than it did
last year when Z was making such a big deal about sexual
abuse of kids -- including what she and Betty had gone
through -- around the time we saw "The Pillow Book."
Since then we've never really grappled with the issue
but rather it's simply faded, presumably because she's
come to trust me more as she's gotten to know me better.
Nonetheless on a few occasions I've sensed it simmering
just beneath the surface. And this too makes me
hesitate to become too attached to Kat.)
     -- Going back to the resort last week, I should
mention the second reason Z wanted me to see it: its
state-of-the-art ecological consciousness. It's owned
by a socially prominent and left-leaning "pioneer"

(i.e., settler-colonial) Cawk family from our city, and its primary guiding spirit, one of the deceased patriarch's daughters, lives in a chalet which stands directly across the celebrated creek from the campsite. She travels back and forth on a tow line which crosses the creek gorge about fifty feet up. We saw her do this twice and bumped into her several other times, including once at the resort's rocky heated outdoor pool under midnight starlight (she was not naked; and because she wasn't, we decided we'd better not be either, though we'd hoped to be). On the truly crucial matter of environmental justice, however, Z views this woman and her family as having a long way to go. In fact they're near the top of the list of elite Eurusan enviros Z considers her collective bete noire.

As for the "Norwegian bartender" remark of Z's, some years ago this same patriarch's daughter met a "beautiful young Russian guy" who was mixing cocktails somewhere and she scandalized everyone by marrying him even though he's less than half her age. The women of the leadership institute used to gawk at him nonstop, Z told me. We saw him numerous times too, though never with the patriarch's daughter; and to me, though he was wearing a black Russian fur cap with the earflaps down (yes!), he didn't look particularly like the star of the Hollywood version of "Dr. Zhivago," though that's how Z's group saw him (inevitably, I suppose) (even though that star is Egyptian). Twice while we were sitting inside the A-frame that serves as a nighttime gathering spot he came bicycling up to fetch drinks. I pretended to be jealous of him because of the way Z mooned over his "prettiness." Said she: "I'm talking about how I saw him before March 29 of last year. One glimpse of my very own Norski bartender at the magazine shop that day and Dr. Zhivago was nowheresville." (Well, that's what she said. We'd both had a drink or two at that point.)

-- Still no far-coast paper but it's past four now and I'd probably better crash.

*   *

It's come right on time for the symbolic turn into

265

autumn. Late afternoon of Labor Day, after weeks of fine weather, a big dark menacing cloudbank appeared above the mountains to the west. By eleven-thirty tonight, as I walked down to the hideaway from the scope office (where I finaled a two-hundred-page rush job, a brambly expert deposition involving slot-machine gambling on a so-called Indian so-called reservation), the temperature had dropped maybe thirty degrees and a gusty wind was carrying strong rain scent.

Now midnight. Quiet building. For once the new guy next door in 231 (the numbering system here is bizarre; I'm in 225 and all the numbers between his and mine appear on doors on the far side of the floor) -- for once, I say, the new guy doesn't seem to be around and his lights are off, though of course he could be in there sleeping or doing unspeakable things in the dark.

The Labor Day turn also means we're moving into high politics season. Some interesting (no SQUAWK!) and frightening stuff is happening. The stock market took a big dive over the past couple of weeks and it appears the world economic system is facing a spell of severe turbulence. Even for the gun-bristling tanklike U.S. juggernaut the good times might be about to grind to a halt. Meanwhile the juggernaut's chief mahout is being pressured to step down because of a sex scandal (which to my mind sounds trivial enough that all the brouhaha looks preposterous). And -- and what? This isn't enough? But our local elections are heating up too, including the big matter to be decided in November, I-200, the initiative to end affirmative action in our state (eyes of the nation will be focused here because of this, and Z is still deeply involved in the anti-I-200 campaign, as are many of her friends).

So that's politics. For the time being I'm still just a curious observer and not planning to become more directly involved. In fact I'm not a player at all. I'm not even registered to vote, nor have I been ever since I made the mistake of signing up in peninsula days and then faced a weeks-long night worker's "daymare" of haggling during daytime hours to obtain an exemption

from jury duty. I figure I'm just being a realist now
-- not to mention a pragmatist -- not to mention those
old bugaboos, a relativist and a situationist. And
besides: to make the slightest short-term difference in
today's massively corrupt U.S. political climate you
must be ready to devote huge chunks of time to the cause
or to fork over lots and lots of bucks. I can do
neither. I'm committed elsewhere -- long term. (But in
an emergency I'd pitch in, absolutely, if I thought I
could make a difference. And in an emergency maybe I
could, even if only a tiny one.)

As for daily life, Z arrived home from Jess's
mountain birthday soiree at two a.m. last night. She
was several hours late but didn't bother to leave me a
voicemail message, figuring I wouldn't check for one
anyway. She was wrong about that. And I was not
pleased that she'd figure or assume as she did. But I
decided to drop the whole thing. I was too happy to see
her and I didn't want to ruin things.

And so most of today we rutted. Four times, not
counting a quickie later tonight just before I left for
work. (A tale there. I stripped off my shirt to try on
the infamous blue canvas one from last year and prove to
her it really does fit. She decided I looked sexy. We
tumbled into bed. She suddenly fessed up that maybe the
real source of her blue-shirt hysteria last year was the
fact that she was beginning to fall for me that day.
-- And the shirt does fit, yes. But she says this is
because I'm "buff" now and I wasn't then. But this
itself is a kind of triumph: it's the first time she's
even acknowledged I've trimmed down. Though, yeah, it's
true, I admit it, I have -- but unfortunately not all
that much. But then again I'm sure my all-out shape-up
effort has helped give me some, and maybe even all, of
my revived sexual pop.)

Time's a-runnin'. I vow right here to start the
next entry with a few words on Z's weekend at the cabin
with Jess and friends (her, Z's, concerns about racist
resort personnel, twenty-something women with "six-pack"
abs, uneasiness among strangers, the oddness of being

one of only two heteros, as it turned out -- this is
what she says -- among a passel of partyin' lesbians).
And also words on this evening's return to Kat and
Betty's to deliver a couple of scrumptious cinnamon
rolls that Z hauled all the way across the mountains for
them. (I know about the scrumptious part because I
gobbled down a third such roll myself. And a fourth
awaits me at home, which may have something to do with
why I'm moving on right now.)

*   *

Sure enough it's four days later, which is to say:
it's the originally scheduled J-day, the one that I'm
supposedly skipping. And am actually skipping despite
the mildly paradoxical fact that here I am jyzing away
on that very day. But at the end of the year there'll
now be one fewer J-day than the original (revised)
schedule called for and that's the real gritty of this,
yeah, nitty.

The same old hip-hop group is booming out the same
old tunes (ha!) down below. The vibrations up here
aren't as bad, though, because the weekend crowds
hitting the quarter post-Labor Day are considerably
smaller and therefore the amps needn't be cranked so
high. (what happened to the heavy-metal incursion of
last month I don't know, but I will say hip-hop is now,
after heavy metal, sounding relatively good.)

So what else is new? Well, the time for our Deep
Roots Jyze Road Trip, as I'm now calling it, is rapidly
approaching -- we take off two weeks from today -- and
the final arrangements are falling into place. It
appears the airline strike that broke out last week will
be ending tomorrow (when the pilots will vote on the
latest offer), meaning we won't have to scramble to make
new flight reservations. Brother Jeff and I have talked
on the phone and the plans with him and Angie are all
set. Meanwhile June will be staying in 203 much of the
time we're away; she'll water the plants and try to make
the place look occupied to any potential burglars or
squatters. Naomi and I have come up with a scheme for
handling the (wouldn't you know) unusually large number

of jobs she's already been assigned for that time.

Meanwhile the word's in from the deep reserves: my
account lost twelve thousand dollars, or roughly fifteen
percent, in the recent stock-market collapse. The truly
bad news is that the worldwide economic situation looks
even worse than it did a few days ago. Impeachment
proceedings against the U.S. president seem ever more
likely, meaning this country, ergo the world, might be
virtually emperorless at what could be just about the
worst possible time. (For escapists there's been a
baseball home-run derby for the ages to focus on. The
old record is now shattered. Joy and awe reign supreme
in every Mudville in the land.)

What else? All kinds of stuff. Big stuff and
little stuff. For big stuff, Zoelie got all worked up
over a run-in with Jess (the very same birthday girl)
concerning, at least originally, diversity planning for
city events, and later expanding into a number of
obscure personal matters -- and I lost plenty of sleep
trying to console her, because she's very fond of Jess,
and I nearly lost my temper a couple of times too -- but
now the matter's resolved and all at least appears well.
(Just this afternoon we bumped into Jess working out at
the gym in her baseball shirt and all three of us
chortled perhaps a bit uneasily over various mishaps and
miscues of the preceding days.)

For little stuff, let's see, I oiled our front-door
and hallway-door hinges and now I can slip downstairs at
four a.m. to pick up the night paper without feeling I'm
awakening the whole building. June sent over another
delicious bag of plums from the small orchard in her
very large suburban backyard. Z revealed Aida is about
to go out on a date with one of Z's former lovers from
way back in the dreamtime, Kirk M. (younger brother of
congressman Ed M.) -- seemingly yet another instance of
Aida's retribution for Z's taking up with this no-
account jyzer right here (or seriously-diminished-
account jyzer, speaking of the bank variety, could say).

And other items. Z hit me with killer garlic
breath when I climbed into bed the other night and she

269

got a big kick out of the way I keeled over and
collapsed on the floor. Also, I spilled a bowl of
cereal on her cherished Nepalese dragon rug (but cleaned
up meticulously and decided not to tell her, since the
rug looked about the same as before and she was stressed
out over Jess at the time -- lucky excuse for me). And
the same afternoon I knocked over a filterful of wet
coffee grounds in the kitchen -- it was one helluva
klutzy day for me.

And I gotta say: I'm struck over and over by the
comical irony of the fact that I'm approaching the point
of almost regaining my youthful body shape at the very
time all the bodily decay processes of aging are about
to kick into high gear. (But regardless I'm mighty
pleased with my progress, yes I am. -- In another
irony, though, Z might not be. She's starting to
complain I'm becoming too skinny! During her weekend at
the resort the other women talked, she told me, of
nothing but food and body-beautiful maintenance. "I
never want to hear the term 'ab crunches' again," she
grumped. But today at the WOC she was asking me to show
her what machine would be best for ab crunches. "It's
all your fault," she moaned, "that I have to do this!")
(In reality she's been hitting fitness clubs for fifteen
years or more. And she's the one who shamed me into
joining the WOC. She created this monster!)

--------·

29

--------·

Once again I've failed to leave myself the hole I'd
hoped for -- this time it's just forty minutes. Then a
dash to the bus stop outside the new concert hall (this
week's the grand opening and a few hours ago on the way

in I saw flocks of very large penguin-like creatures
wearing somewhat realistic human face masks waddling
around amid a row of fancy champagne-dispensing tents
pitched behind high wire fences with armed guards
patrolling just inside on the sidewalk where my normal
scope-office bus stop is supposed to be and usually is).

Somehow it's Friday night again too. This means I
probably won't have a chance to sling any jyze when I
get home. Even if I do -- if Z doesn't lure me into the
bedroom, that is, as she often likes to do on Friday
nights -- and thank the goddess for that! -- I'm so far
behind on my periodical reading I think I'd better
devote the time to, yes, that (because for sure I
wouldn't want to feel anything less than pretty damn
well informed, because then what would I have left to
pride myself on, intellectually speaking, in these
revolting times, politically and apocalyptically
speaking?)

Okay, so then here's the week in short, though I'm
hoping to be able later -- probably Sunday night -- to
expand on at least a few parts of it. Last Saturday
night Z and I did dinner and a movie with another pair
of old friends of hers I'd never met before, Fred and
Eleanor W. Sunday we visited Olwen and Trent and played
Scrabble (Z won in a blowout) after scoping out their
backyard in which we expect to be married next year.
Also on Sunday, Betty and Kat brought over yet another
freshly homemade raspberry pie to replace the one they'd
intended to lay on me for my birthday (a second one,
"just for you!") but then had demolished themselves when
their visit was delayed (and later in the week Betty
added me to the "emergency call" list at Kat's school
and I'm very proud of that).

And: Z and I had a good week, for the second week
in a row humping four times on Saturday (but again with
only one G ejac) and then maneuvering our way out of
several tricky situations, any one of which might've
triggered a brawl in earlier days. The first of these
involved trip preparations -- Z had promised the
daughter of a coworker who's dying of cancer (and Z

scarcely knows this woman) we'd pick up a couple of the
woman's favorite fuzzy collectible toys (the hottest
such fad in years) which are available only, supposedly,
at a certain fairytale village deep in the Mentokan
outback, and to do this we'd have to drive almost two
hundred miles out of our way and the schedule for the
only day that would be possible, in theory, is already
impossibly tight. The second involved a breach of an
earlier accord in which she thought I was chaffing her
too much about all the air cleaners she's buying (but
she did say yesterday she now feels much better about
living in 203 -- and even so she's arm-twisted me into
agreeing to consider the possibility of moving upstairs
to the other side of the building before next summer so
she won't have to put up with another heat season of
noise and car-exhaust fumes from our rowdy neighbors in
the old house to the south -- and at the same time she's
dropped the notion of our moving into a cohousing
project being built four or five blocks to the northeast
(but off the hill, near its northeastern base), being
persuaded by Olwen's tales of woe about the time demands
posed by that particular form of group living).
     Third of the potential fight triggers was the
general situation with Aida. Not only have I taken a
pass on a couple of outings involving her (one of these
would've had me building a treehouse for Charles and I
was never even consulted!) but I've also given my
blessing to a three-day out-of-town art-viewing trip
proposed by Aida for her and Z alone (and Z jumped at
this when I said it was fine with me, so I think she too
has been missing her old relationship with Aida).
     And the last of the potential triggers had to do
with -- surprise! -- sex. Again a careless goofing
remark of mine was the cause, at least proximately.
During a couple of long loving sessions she was totally
passive except for grabbing ol' Possum at the start and
then hanging on as if the creature were just, as I said
in a steal from "Last Tango," "a subway strap." She
disliked it that I (gently) called her out on this. The
next morning she left a note saying she wanted to talk

about our ways of loving, and that evening we did. She
pleaded tiredness as her excuse for the "strap-hanging"
incidents and then we went deeper on the ways of loving
-- eventually reaching our usual bedrock (or rocking-
bed?) stances, and with no significant new strata
revealed along the way as far as I know -- and yet I'd
also say everything at least appeared to come out quite
well.

*   *

     -- Two days later almost to the minute and I'm
here to do what I said I would do. But then again I'm
doubting I'll do it. So much else has happened! And is
happening! I always think I'll want to go back and fill
in the details rather than deal with the new stuff. Why
is this? Probably it's just a form of avoidance.
Laziness. Procrastination until it's too late. Also
it's possible I like to foil myself just for the sheer
perverse fun of it.
     Today the nation's agog over the release of
videotapes of the president's evasive testimony before a
grand jury about his affair with the voluptuous White
House intern. I find I can't get into it at all -- and
I don't think it's just because I've spent a good part
of the past twenty years reading the testimony, evasive
and otherwise, of witnesses before grand juries.
However, this doesn't mean I'm about to take a crack at
describing the truly important goings-on in the world --
the unfolding economic crisis, the burgeoning AIDS
crisis, the ever-exacerbating long-term run-up to
several different kinds of ecological catastrophe. What
would be the point in trying to do something like that?
As before, I'll allude or refer briefly to the grand
historical forces and events and trends going on out
there, at least as I see them or think I do, while
focusing for the most part on things happening in the
near vicinity that matter most to me and could be
described by no one else (except by the other people
directly involved, of course, and then only from their
perspective, obviously, and involving only the shared
fragment where their story and mine overlap).

273

[Deep Jyze]

    So never mind the jyzic self-justifications.
Better to ask: what's new and different? Then, if time
permits, go back to what's a little older but still
different (mostly trying to avoid that which involves a
difference already superseded).
    Try some little things first. Last night Betty,
Kat, Z, and I did dinner at another fifties-style
nostalgia restaurant (not to be confused with the one we
visited a few weeks back; this one is a notch or two
funkier and yet also a notch or two more upscale, even
though it's still gratifyingly downscale) (and Kat rode
in a kid's Batmobile which sounded like a cement mixer
and caused rows of kitschy tin lunchboxes hanging
overhead to jangle amusingly). And the dinner of
meatloaf and mashed potatoes at this same time-warp
eatery was most excellent and so was the roast turkey
with stuffing (I ordered the meatloaf and Z the turkey
and we wound up swapping half and half). Truly both
meals were so good in such an almost forgotten yet
familiar respect that, for me anyway, we might almost
have been sitting at the Sandefjord kitchen table of my
Gatewood boyhood. And the same applies to the cherry
pie dessert; and even the big overflowing scoop of "ala
mode" vanilla was a knockout blast from the fifties-
supermarket past.
    Saturday night we, Z and I, saw "Closely Watched
Trains" at the big indie video shop out in the Yuke.
Only six people attended and yet the tiny upstairs
theater was half full. The movie reminded me vividly of
hanging out in the Mentoka Falls train station during
grad-school days, no doubt in part because I first saw
the movie back then. But I'd forgotten that it was,
among other things, a tale of a man who slices his
wrists because he can't perform sexually. At least Z
seemed to come away from the viewing with an expanded
awareness of why a fellow -- someone of her acquaintance
even -- might be frustrated and near-maddened by an
almost yearlong nonstop bout of e-dys. (Her favorite
scene in the film, though, was the famous one in which a
woman force-feeds a goose by straddling it from behind

so that the goose's neck and head become a serpentine
phallus emerging from her crotch. Never have I seen Z
laugh so hard or for so long. As she noted later, "That
movie gave a whole new meaning to the term Z-goose" --
which is one of my pet names for her, as one of hers for
me is "G-duck" -- and sometimes we reverse them. What
the original spark for those names was I can't even
recall.)

Then this morning she woke me up to say she'd been
unable, after trying on and off for a whole day, to
reach her mother by phone. This had never happened
before. Did I think she should call the police? I
played the calming role. She brought the phone into the
bedroom. Luckily, one last attempt to call succeeded.
Mama E had been in the bath for a long spell Saturday
afternoon, it turned out, and had taken out her hearing
aid; and all of Sunday she'd been visiting a friend. Z
and I vowed to come up with a plan for keeping better
tabs on her from a distance when we see her in person in
just two weeks (like her daughter, she's very prickly
about her independence). Later Z wrote a note thanking
me for my help -- "Each day / I'm grateful for your love
in a new way." At the WOC at five, as we vigorously
strode along going nowhere (as per usual) on our
adjoining treadmills, she emphasized how much she meant
what she said in this note. (And it meant a lot to me
that she wrote it and then wanted to emphasize its
contents. What's more, her doing this reminded me I
ought to be expressing the same kind of thought to her a
bit more often, though in my own way to be sure.)

Erotically, sorry to say, it was a dismaying
morning and a poor weekend. Although I managed to do
the manly thing twice on Saturday morning -- fuck her
until she came, not to put it too crudely or anything --
I didn't come at all myself all weekend and haven't
since a week ago. Late last night before going to bed I
thought I was ready to rock'n'roll again (we had talked
about taking advantage of her earlier sleep hours --
she's again trying to preadjust to jet lag -- by getting
in some early-a.m. loving). But when push came to shove

-- or rather in fact before either could be an issue --
I wasn't able to produce a decent hard-on. And then
pathetically tried to push on in anyway with an indecent
hard-on, which was scarcely a hard-on at all, and
couldn't manage it (did get in, should say, but then
quickly deflated the rest of the way -- "melted" just
like the guy in the movie, I suppose, or "foozled" or
"fribbled" in jyzespeak).

     -- And that's it, no more time. Hope I can squeeze
in a session Wednesday night but it might be tough with
all the trip-prepping still ahead.

*   *

     -- Well it's tough all right but here I am anyway.
Gritty guy. Midnight. One hour to perform the jyze
act.

     For a big chunk of the evening I've been putting
together a sheaf of material on Carver and La Chevalle
counties, Turtle Rapids, Mentoka Falls, Coutawa,
Wachute, Lahontan, 45 X 90, Centropolis, Gatewood.
Later it'll go into the suitcase standing open on the
dining table at home. But right now I'm just staggered
to rediscover how much research I did over the course of
a full decade for the Mentoka series, and all to no
avail. Seemingly. It's true I've been toying with the
idea of giving "Jyzer" or even "Mentoka Dreams" another
whirl from a somewhat different angle. But if I do
this, either of them, it won't be happening anytime
soon. Several other projects have moved ahead of both.
And in the meantime it might be a good idea to forgive
myself, if possible -- and for sure it won't be easy --
for wasting all that effort on the research and
planning.

     Oh well. At least I've got a life again. (And
that ain't just chopped fiction. Though to be sure it's
partly that. It's gotta be! Life in the Jyze Age --
anyone's Jyze Age -- can't be otherwise!)

     Meanwhile some good news. Yesterday I finally
managed to pump some seed into my sweetie. Hallelujah!
Not long after she arrived home from work we hit the
bedroom "for a little nook" (the usual Tuesday-evening

276

thing). When I found myself cranking up almost immediately I rushed her a bit, I suppose, into a quick nipple come (which, as she kindly reminds me from time to time, is a fail-safe way to lube her up) and then plunged in. At a couple of points it was a little iffy -- a phallic "melt" seemed imminent -- but then I found a groove in an unexpected place, from an unusual angle, with ol' Merc about halfway in and moving only slightly, and went with it. Before long it triggered a surge of priapic growth. Yay-hoo! A spate of the true deep churn followed -- quite a long and delicious spate -- and then a big funky raw-edged explosive ejac. -- And I apologized afterwards for going off on my own like that, and I don't think she liked my doing so -- apologizing I mean. (In retrospect it's easy enough to see why. She's right, I shouldn't've said anything. To her it had to sound as though I were suggesting she too ought to be apologizing for all those times she's gone off on her own own, as it were, and there have been hundreds or maybe even thousands of those. And in fact sometimes she does apologize when she does that, and I always tell her she shouldn't.)

Incidentally, Z, after reading that creatine in beef may boost men's potency (this in a series of stories triggered by the revelation that both of the sluggers in this year's wowser of a home-run derby -- they're tied at sixty-five apiece now with a week to go -- use pills which act like male hormones) -- after this, I say, she bought me half a pound of "organic" roast beef at the co-op. She did it partly as a gag but also, and likely in bigger part, in hopes it would work. And late Monday night, because I knew her motives were worthy, I gobbled down the whole half pound. (I discount the effectiveness of this, though, because I've been eating beef in the form of double-stack burgers quite regularly and I'm not at all sure it's made a difference. Then again, I do think going without red meat entirely for an extended period -- say a week or ten days -- can have a negative effect. But I haven't been doing that. -- Nor have I tried "organic" beef

before. And one thing I'm utterly certain of: none of
that double-stack ground beef is organic. It's probably
closer to pure petroleum.)

     And so my hour's just about up. Time left only for
a few quick notes. Like, yesterday was the autumnal
equinox (and Z conducted a ceremony which I had to miss
because of work) (but I did leave her a colorful
homemade autumn leaf cutout inscribed with a mix of
mawkish and raunchy apothegms: the "Leaf'a Lub"). Like,
Doug and Thuy will take care of our mail and newspapers,
June will water the plants, Wei will drive us to the
airport, Betty will pick us up there when we return.
Like, Kat looked fabulous modeling a batch of brightly
colorful Guatemala-made hats a friend of Z's brought
back from a visit to Central America. Like, I've had a
bad couple of weeks for spills: first the water and
cereal on Z's Nepalese rug and the coffee grounds in the
kitchen, then black ink in my backpack. (For years
I've feared the top of the ink bottle I always carry
with me would come loose and it finally happened, and
even though the bottle was, as per usual, tucked in a
plastic baggie, lots of ink escaped -- the baggie had
tipped sideways and wasn't fully pinched closed -- and
some of it soaked through the brown canvas-like material
of the backpack, making me readily identifable from
fifty paces as an ink-stained wretch -- and even days
later my hands are still dappled with fading patches of
black.)

     And like I gotta go. (And tomorrow's gonna be hell
on wheels, with scoping work starting up in midafternoon
-- first time in more than a year for this kind of job
-- and going until maybe three or four a.m.; and
shortly after that, at seven a.m., we leave for the
airport.)

BOOK III

[Deep Roots Road Jyze]

30

A quick one from the airport. It's nine a.m. and
we've been sitting here for over an hour with at least
another hour yet to go. A misty, overcast morning. The
supremely annoying airport news channel blares in
surround-sound -- the impeachment uproar, the home-run
derby, the stock market's latest spike -- the same
indigestible bites over and over and over.

And here's Zoelie B. back from the restroom.
"You're going to be my husband," she says with maybe not
entirely mock apprehension. "I'm going to be your
wife." Looking foxy indeed, yes she is, in tight black
jeans, a purple jersey, yellow chucks. -- And now
cackling over some lines in a book I brought home last
night, an anthopologist's exploration (a homegrown one
this time) of the "American cultural construction of
middle age." -- What's amusing her, she tells me, is a
paragraph about "introduction of the term 'virile bulge'
into contemporary discourse."

Good seats here, right up against the window. The
nose of our jet looming just outside recalls ancient
posters for the movie "Jaws." The lower part of the
shark's head is white, the upper part (with the pilot
windows as eyes) dark gray, the top of the head blood
red. Farther down the long tubular fuselage a
distinctly sharklike tail fin slices upward, also blood
red.

Z wanders off. Before going she asks: best not to
be talking too much right now? Best, yeah, sez I, just
this once for a few minutes if she wouldn't mind.
Because I'm sputtering along on half a cylinder. By

current Nightscoper Upside-down Time (NUT) it's three
a.m., which by local Gregorian Daylight Savings Time
happens to be exactly the hour I got to bed last night.
Ninety minutes' sleep tops before it was time to leave
to be sure we'd be here in what to the Z-woman is barely
enough time, to me way too much time. And before all
that, seven harrowing hours of scoping with Naomi often
hanging over my shoulder slavering for more pages. A
lot of years since I've had to endure anything like
that. What splendid timing!

Z wanders back. Says she's not upset or anything
but it's true, isn't it, that I'm a little cranky this
morning?

What, on ninety minutes' sleep? Sitting here in
glary raucous daylight in the middle of my night? As
jets roar and TVs bray? I tell you I'm at my merry
best!

For some reason it suddenly occurs to her we didn't
bring along any of our "fight agreements."

Hmm. -- But I say out loud, "Who needs 'em? Have
you forgotten we don't hardly fight anymore?"

She says in fact she told Lorraine this very thing
-- Lorraine, her naturopath -- but put it to her a
little differently: "I fight less but cry more."

"Not true!" I object, genuinely startled. "You cry
less too! So...you know what? You did it again, you
misled that poor woman."

And her reply: "But have you forgotten that I gotta
have drama?"

-- And suddenly we're about to start loading. The
shark is grinning.

*   *

Now some nine hours later. I'm stretched out in
just my same old blue shorts on our bed at the Hotel La
Chevalle. We made it! Zipped across five and a half
states, some fifteen hundred miles plus. And this the
same bed in the same southwest corner room (No. 5) I
stayed in for several days just a week short of five
years ago. But that time I was traveling alone and
there was no drama at all of the type my Deep's so damn

good at provoking (not to say inciting).

Two windows wide open, propped up with driftwood
sticks provided, I'd guess, by a previous occupant.
Dinner crowd still noisily chowing down on the deck one
story below. River flowing darkly and immensely by. A
couple of times we've seen heat lightning. Crickets
are chirring (or cree-cree-creeing) and trains roaring
by every so often on the riverside tracks maybe seventy
or eighty paces to the southwest. Comforting roars too
-- even Z says so. And comforting vibrations as well,
the whole joint shaking like the hideaway back in Jyze
City on dueling-bands night, only much more so. At
times you'd think we might shimmy off into another
dimension. Or already have.

Creaky wooden building almost a century and a
quarter old. Eight rooms up here on the second floor
(which is the top floor), all about the same size, all
austerely furnished pretty much as in frontier days, and
the going rate per room is a preposterously low $31.50 a
night. Everyone shares a single communal bathroom and
the skinny little hook-and-eye lock on the inside of its
door is the same one, I'd swear, that seemed about to
pull out of the wood five years ago, and still does, as
Z nervously took note of.

"Not to worry," said I; "It's probably been like
that for a hundred years."

And she: "Ya didn't think I was going to leave my
amygdala at home, did ya?"

Tonight only five rooms are occupied. And we
lucked out: a room's unexpectedly opened up for tomorrow
night, so we can drop the motel hunt from tomorrow's
agenda. We'll be able to stay here three straight
nights (though tomorrow night's room will be facing away
from the river).

We've both been a little testy, I cannot deny,
though only for short periods and at well-spaced
intervals. For her, she tells me, it's mostly the
enforced confinement of travel that does it. For me
it's mostly the nerves frayed by fatigue far beyond mere
tiredness. -- And here she is now. Just returned from

the small upstairs lobby where she was reading.
Supposedly I was crashing. But no. First got to, got
to, just got to jyze it up.

"Garlic farts," she chuckles. During dinner at the
restaurant downstairs she almost single-handedly
demolished a basket of garlic bread. -- And now she
slides between the sheets. Ooh looking so lovely.
wearing Jess and Gwen's sexy black gift teddy. Naked
feet slipping right beneath this near-virginal dwarf of
a J-book, Special Z toes wriggling lasciviously even if
under wraps. The bed, with its lacy white coverlet,
shaking and squeaking and jangling. Already!

Must mention this first before saying to hell with
jyze: it was some spectacular drive down the river
road. On the sunrise side. In our hot little
candyapple-red rental car. On the far "wild west coast"
of Mentoka. Fall foliage splendidly aflame. (And now
another rumble -- a big freight thundering by outside
and in here it's shake rattle and roll all over again.)
(The big bluff looming maybe four hundred feet almost
directly overhead and slightly to the north does
something odd to the sound -- seems like the train's
flying up there, could say, much like the jets back
home. And that's two major "back homes" with jets for
me: the Jyze City one and also the one I grew up in,
Gatewood, which now is just a few hundred more miles
down those same railroad tracks out there.)

Gonna quit right here. (Love her though. Love her
a lot. Wanna make that real clear, for the jyze, yes,
but even more for the lady herself, verbally and by
touch, "embodied," even consummately so to the extent
possible under conditions of extreme exhaustion. -- And
to be repeated often too, verbally and embodiedly both,
and "by heart" to be sure, over and over all trip long.)

(Day 2)
Talk about deja vu! Jyze holding forth at the
picnic table under the "Velkommen" sign. Sky darkening
and wind picking up -- threatens to rip this J-book
right out of my hands. Z's scribbling too, churning out

postcards while perched atop a kids' swing maybe twenty feet away, next to the U.S. flag memorial bearing the names of local fallen Eurusan colonial-settler warriors, and every last one of Norski extraction and many of them relatives of mine, often bearing my surname. Across the street the same three big old houses dominate the center of town, all three owned for most of the past twelve or thirteen decades by my small-pond-big-frog ancestors -- or better to say big turtle, what am I thinking? -- and slept in by me numerous times during visits here as a boy. To their left the small bank and the old general store, also owned for that same period by the same Sandefjord/Jondahl bunch (as was the bank and much else around here) and source of my all-time favorite baseball cap when I was seven or eight.

Inside the store an hour ago I learned that just yesterday this town had another visitor with our family name. Like Z and me this visitor was checking out the cemetery, in fact was doing tracings from gravestones up there. "Barbara, I believe the first name was." Sister Barb! It must be. Never heard of any other Barbara Sandefjord -- except for, of course, our long-gone Gram she's named after. But how wild! (Is brother Jeff cooking up some sort of reconciliation surprise for our Lahontan stay, I wonder?)

Then as I posed for a picture in front of Great-Gramp Bendyk's former home, a big car came creeping down the driveway. The man behind the wheel, it turned out, was Emil W., octogenarian younger brother of the current owner of the house, Myron W., and like him a lifelong resident of the area but to my surprise completely unknown to me. He emerged from the car and proceeded for a good twenty minutes to chew our ears off about current and former town and S/J-clan doings as Z fidgeted at my side or nearby.

Another odd coincidence. At this very moment a hundred yards to the west a work crew is tearing down the old mill. It's already about half gone as two men perched precariously on tall ladders pound away with sledgehammers at ancient wooden beams. Loud thuds. The

yard around the mill piled high with splintered timbers.
The old dam standing next to it, which powered the mill's
grinding wheel for a century or so, has been condemned
by "state ecology," Emil W. informed us. It's slated to
be demolished next year unless the town agrees to spring
for massive repairs. Emil then asked if we'd be willing
to contribute ten thousand dollars. (I had to decline,
of course, speaking for both Z and myself. But I said
I'd do the best I could to preserve the old mill in my
own way, and I was referring to these very words going
down right here and right now -- and maybe more words
like these later in other J-books, whether of the JIRT or
JIFT variety -- but then again maybe not.)

Meanwhile that blond kid I saw flitting around in
green overalls on the hilly wooded bank on the far side
of the creek a few minutes ago, he could almost have
been me in my chrysalis stage. Summer vacations -- get
out in that barn and rattle them cows and pigs! In all
four directions from where I sit now, farm fields
visible, also the domed upper reaches of two big silos.
-- And the town still likes to play innocent. Says a
highway billboard on the outskirts where we drove in:
"Welcome to Turtle Rapids - Where Everyone is
Important." Population 307 or something like that.
(But the sign's looking a lot shabbier than it did when
I first saw it five years ago.)

For lunch Z and I sprained our jaws on a couple of
enormous burgers at the former Dew Drop Inn, right
across the street. It's now the Wild Horse Saloon. As
one born in the Year of the Horse I heartily approve.
Four or five locals -- farmers, I'd guess, and all
probably within a decade of our ages one way or the
other and all male -- were watching a Mezzu football
game on the tube. Paying not the slightest attention to
the strangers in town, except of course for some not-so-
surreptitious scoping-out of the Z-babe.

Now onward to Buena Vista, just a few miles up the
road. Then across to Carver County and tooling down the
Mentoka Road and when we hit Mentoka Falls more
excitement than Z's amygdala ever reckoned on. (But I

must note the loving's going well. The road trip must
be rated a huge success so far. The only really bad
moment today occurred in the parking lot of the cemetery
a block east of here when the gearshift knob of the
rental car came off in my hand. For a while we were
unable to reattach it. Z was about to freak out at the
thought of being stranded here in this tiny isolated
Cawkazoidal village, possibly forever. But then a lucky
nudge -- hers -- "Let me try one time" -- clicked it
back into place. Damn! Later I told her my mother had
experienced a similar kind of panic regarding all the
Norski strangeness during her first visit here with my
father; and after that she, Z, seemed to feel at least a
little better about things.)

(Day 3)
See what I can do here. Perched on an iron bench
in a small wooden shelter near the north end of
Wachute's big waterfront park. Stretched out on the
bench to my right with her triply beringed left hand
resting on my thigh, the innocently snoozing self-
proclaimed "jyze widow" Zoelie B.
Breezy autumnal Sunday afternoon. U.S. flag
flapping, river water sparkling as a small stern-wheel
tour boat churns by maybe thirty feet offshore looking
almost like a child's wooden pull toy. Outflow of the
Mentoka -- "Where the Water of Fathers meets the Father
of Waters." Twenty-five miles downstream from La
Chevalle, 50 due south of Turtle Rapids, 50 southwest
(also downstream, but the stream's a different one) of
Mentoka Falls, 60 miles due west of Coutawa, where the
Z-woman once worked social for two years with the
Mentoka themselves, and some 225 miles due east of the
picturesque little country church where this jyzer right
here once, yes -- own it! -- got hitched. (One-year
starter type only, though, it turned out.)
So now we're precisely located. No GPS needed here
-- or wait, can't say that: I'm GPS! (That's an old
joke for me, at least with respect to recent years, but
new to jyze, I'm pretty sure.)

[Deep Jyze]

    A few blocks to the south, the old suspension
bridge frames a row of big downriver bluffs. Straight
west across the narrow boating channel lies the small
wooded island where the biggest S/J-clan scandal of them
all took place. Exactly a hundred years ago, give or
take a few days, the bodies were found: white Roar and
black Sadie and little tan Petie, with the murder weapon
(or maybe love-suicide weapon) still clutched in Roar's
hand. For sure the first racially mixed couple ever in
the family, or maybe I should qualify that and say at
least on Dad's side and in post-primordial times (Roar
being a younger brother of Great-Gramp Bendyk). "So
you're linking up with a glorious tradition here, Ms.
Z." Which is old news to her, to be sure, as is much of
this clan lore I've been re-laying on her and for that
matter much of the stuff to come on Mother's side as
well, because we've talked about it all a great deal in
the past year and a half. But it does take on some new
contextual shading and trenchancy in its original
setting: oh does it ever. And that, of course, is
exactly why we decided to make this trip. Or one of the
reasons anyway.
    "Killer Cawk blood" -- ha. But very serious
history, yes. And there are many more sources of what
rattles her in this ancestral turf, that's quite clear.
And in this jyze I intend, as I've let her know, to come
to grips with and vanquish them all -- at least to the
extent possible.
    -- We walked here from the central downtown. This
after breakfasting at the celebrated Mr. G's (no
relation) and checking out Gram S.'s big old Fritsch
family home and the nearby small frame house where Dad
lived during most of his grade-school years. How did
Gramps the Turtle Rapids boy meet Gram the Wachute city
girl, Z (of course a proud city girl herself) wanted to
know. And I, the burban boy, couldn't say for sure,
except fictively, that is, the story I made up for
"Jyzer." But we do know the Fritsch company was a
major supplier for the Turtle Rapids general store where
Gramps worked summers during his student years and

288

presumably he assisted in picking up wholesale orders
from the Fritsch yard here in Wachute, where Gram
sometimes worked in the office. And to that extent the
story I concocted is at least somewhat reality based.

We also stumbled across a natural-food co-op, at
the sight of which Z whooped with relief. And then we
scoped out the new restaurant in the old Fritsch
hardware store downtown -- an official historic building
now and festooned inside with ancient black-and-white
hardware-store photos, including several showing the
magnificently mustachioed Great-Gramp Vincent -- the man
for whom I was named for a few hours at birth and whose
first name just happens to be an English-language
variant of Z's father's first name, Vincenzo (source of
the "Zo" in her own self-chosen name); and in that
sense, and maybe others (her remote Norwegian ancestor
for one), we may even be a tiny bit related ourselves.

And is all still going well with the road-trippers?
Yesterday did kick up a spat, but we worked our way
through it quickly last night and I hope with no lasting
damage. Afterwards Z commended me: "Honey, you still
got those good conflict-resolution skills." (She's
dozing on. And here's a swirl of her hair, mostly black
but with a few flecks of brown and gray sprinkled in.
And her sunglasses cord. -- My feet heating up as the
sun creeps in under the shelter roof. Autumn leaves
skittering fitfully by, a trace of leaf-burning smoke
wafting in.) -- And some gangbuster loving at the Hotel
La Chevalle. Once at bedtime and again in the morning,
and both long-lasting, and for the a.m. a jyzer ejac
like a snorting bronco, wild Year of the Horse type.
Yee-ha! Exhaustion becomes me! (But can I make it
three straight tonight? Dunno, but almost certainly
will be going for it.)

Last night we shifted rooms twice. First to No. 7,
facing away from the river and toward an ominously large
kitchen roof vent (shaped like a huge black chef's hat);
then, when a second cancellation occurred, to No. 1 back
on the river side. All evening until very late a fancy
wedding reception with live country-rock music romped

and rollicked in the yard down below. Two large white
tents were pitched there for the occasion. We had the
equivalent of a theater box view of it all, almost like
the county-market scene in "Madame Bovary."

Mostly we stretched out on the bed reading. And
every thirty minutes or so another long freight roared
by. (The perfect time for tumultuous 'gasming, these
lengthy roar-bys, and this morning Z made the most of
one such opportunity. And later informed me she can't
clench her teeth anymore when coming during this trip
because she thinks she cracked one during that same
raucous roar-by, so she'll go back to biting my shoulder
until she can see her dentist back home.)

But the spat. Too much touring or too much
togetherness or too much Jyzer G family and personal
romantic history or just what? We followed the Mentoka
Road from Turtle Rapids down past picturesque Silver
Mound to where the road meets up with the Mentoka River
and then on into Mentoka Falls where I showed her the
jyzer's pads of the student era -- including the site of
the house where the fictive version of jyze was born,
though the house itself is long gone (an expansion of
the old strip mall devoured it) -- and did a drive-
through of the Mezzu campus and checked out the chichi
new quarters of the writing program (a former mill
owner's Victorian mansion overlooking the reservoir and
the falls) and along the way I pointed out the site of
Karen A.'s fatal motorcycle accident (Z had specifically
asked about it) and referred a few times, though in
every case only briefly not to say trepidatiously, to
Ladies K and S and C, the massively lamentable "starter
marriage" and various other student-days fiascoes.

Then, since we were well ahead of schedule, I
proposed a quick side trip to the old 45 X 90 resort
where the mother and father of the man Z will someday
not that far off be marrying did their honeymoon ("Heart
of the Western World") -- and that, oddly enough, is
when Z freaked, at the prospect of being "cooped up in
the coupe" for another hour or two. And from there,
fuming and scarcely speaking, we returned to the hotel.

(But via the same road paralleling the river and passing
the Mentoka massacre site, which she'd never even heard
about before, despite living for two years less than
forty miles away -- and before this trip we're on now
she's never ventured west of Coutawa, mainly because all
her friends were in Lahontan in the opposite direction).
-- And we also saw some spectacular badland scenery on
the way back, as she agreed, though only much later.)

   While we were dining downstairs on the deck last
night (still somewhat caught up in the spat) a cheer
arose from the wedding guests outside. We looked up to
see a huge white ocean liner, as it seemed, bearing down
on an apparent collision course with our tiny hotel.
Turned out to be a majestic old-fashioned wooden
steamboat passing by just a few yards offshore, its red
stern wheel (by itself close to the size of our hotel)
slowly spinning. The last major upriver voyage of the
season, the server told us. The entire vessel brightly
lit up, all five or six decks -- so close to us we could
almost lip-read the "drat"s and "dang"s of on-board
gamblers bent over roulette tables. (And Wachute now
styles itself "Steamboat City," I noticed earlier
today.)

*

   -- I stand up to stretch and Z wanders off toward
what we're guessing are the park restrooms. Before
leaving she asked, "Did you write anything about our
fight yet?" "Too minor to mention," I scoffed. And
wasn't lying! -- "But I'll try to squeeze in a word or
two, just so the record's complete."

   But not really. Because this fight truly wasn't
much. Going back, even before we got out of La Chevalle
County after leaving Turtle Rapids, Z turned grumpy and
began to carp about being in the car too long. And this
even though in cumulative-hour terms we'd been in it
much less at that point than we'd been in other cars on
a number of other occasions, including our mountain-
resort trip just last month, as I pointed out to her,
thus turning her still grumpier. (And now she's slowly
making her way back across the green. My babe. How the

291

sight of her ambling along, this time in her powder-blue
jeans and little green top, can still -- or to be truly
accurate I'd have to say can more than ever make the old
ticker go thumpety-thumpety-thump.)

Spat then. Not just being cooped up in the car.
Overdosing on in-law and previous-romance info, yes, she
admitted, but even more the overlays of fictive names on
unfamiliar real names with way too much tangled history
behind them all, real or fictive and often both at once.
And overwhelming her with must-sees and must-dos. And
far too many cemeteries with virtually illegible
Lutheran gravestone inscriptions and skeletons rattling
and ghosts moaning and trolls snarking just barely out
of sight. And maybe other stuff too (so many candidates
here -- overdose of Cawk folks and Cawk ways, unrelieved,
surely being another major one, though for some odd
reason she left it off the list this time).

So after dinner a long walk along the riverfront
road. Leading to the national park with its French
explorer's cabin and the celebrated "floating mountain,"
which we could only just barely make out in the dark.
And by the time we returned to the hotel the spat was
all settled, just like that. Somehow.

And better shut down this jyze for the day.
Restless Z. Reading now but also sort of subliminally
scowling. Understandably! Because we'll soon be
pushing up against the two-hour absolute limit on road-
trip jyze sessions which we agreed to weeks ago (and I
said I'd try to keep them to an hour or less).

-- But Buena Vista, can't stop without mentioning
that. The hilltop lookout. A dark stormfront rolling
across the hills to the north, sunbeams slicing down
through the skimpier clouds to the west and emblazoning
prodigious slow-moving light-and-shadow patterns on
patchwork farmland in the valley. First a silo lighting
up here, then a barn a couple of miles to the west, as
when spotlights single out celebrities in the studio
audience. The monument to the "learned hermit" not in as
bad shape as I'd been fearing from brother Rob's
description of it. The grove some forty or fifty feet

downhill where Dad's ashes are scattered is much more
impressively grovelike now. -- And there, as promised
way back when the idea for the "Deep Roots" trip first
came up, I introduced Z to Dad's spirit. And tears ran
down her cheeks and mine as well. -- His last rites
right there twenty-two years ago this past June. End of
an era as it turned out, and to a far greater degree
than any of us anticipated back then.

(Day 4)
Jeff's farmette. Everyone else has gone off to
bed. I just now finally found a light I could figure
out how to turn on. The parlor. It's still in the
early fix-up stages in this classic fixer-upper of a
farmhouse. Jeff's been working on it in his spare time
for years. And the parts fixed up thus far, including
the first-floor bedroom where Z and I are sleeping and
the living room with its resplendent draperies and
furniture covers -- Angie made them all, she being a pro
seamstress who works independently for interior
decorators -- everything looks terrific.
Earlier a leisurely walk through the yard. Up past
half a dozen ramshackle outbuildings and the big old
barn, now in working shape again. (Cows were sloshing
in the corral at five p.m. when we drove up -- Jeff
rents it out to a neighbor.) And then up the hilly
gravel driveway a few hundred yards to the main road and
back again. Marvelously sweet air. Bright, clear
stars. Crescent moon ducking in and out of an isolated
flotilla of kayak-shaped black brushstroke clouds.
Truly a vivid and idyllic pastoral scene. -- And yet
Jeff himself is helping to develop subdivisions just the
other side of the next big hill. Centropolis "exurban"
sprawl is creeping in from the southeast along with
Lahontan suburban sprawl from the northeast and Jeff and
Angie are themselves part of both invasions, though
probably a good half decade ahead of the main forces.
They're somewhat like Z and me, I'd say, as gentrifiers
on our own little hill some thirty-odd longitude degrees
west and a few degrees north of here.

[Deep Jyze]

    With Jeff and Angie all's going well. (Uh-oh,
what about between Z and me? -- But later for that bad
news.) We met Angie and her frisky twelve-year-old
daughter by her first marriage, Steffi, at their new
rental house in Lahontan at three this afternoon. A
quick tour of the house, seeing so much in it that was
familiar from my own childhood, each item giving me a
small or in a couple of cases a quite large Marcelian
tug. Then we followed Angie out here, twenty miles to
the southwest, stopping along the way to meet Jeff at
the real-estate office where he works part-time. This
in an old-timey Swiss-themed tourist town. Z and Angie
retreating to an ancient saloon to chat amid impressive
history murals dating back over a century while Jeff and
Steffi and I hit the local market to pick up the makings
for dinner. Touching to see how affectionate and
playful Jeff and Steffi are with each other. Jeff
himself, though aging in the standard ways (like who
isn't?), seems reasonably happy with his life and looks
healthy and is as quick-witted and amusing as ever. The
man's been through a lot, though, no question, and
changed in perceptible ways as a result. It's also
obvious Angie has played a big part in keeping him in
one piece.
    Angie and Z hit it off from the start. I'm pretty
sure Angie and I did too (before today I'd been in her
presence only once and for no more than ten minutes).
After downing a few cups of wine she even leaned across
the table and hugged us both at once and announced, "I
really like you two!" As with Z she's a lapsed Catholic
and her live-wire side nicely matches Jeff's and reminds
me a lot of ol' Mom in her middle years (as do her
frosted hair and even her facial structure from certain
angles). Oh yeah -- she also said I was looking great
several times and raved about what working out seems to
be doing for me -- so how could I not go for her in a
big way?
    Earlier during the drive down from La Chevalle Z
and I stopped for our scheduled lunch and quick look
around in Coutawa, the town where she served for two

years as a social worker, mostly for Mentoka tribal
members (her fellowship at U.M. required that she take a
state job for two years immediately after graduation).
We were frustratingly unsuccessful in our search for the
house she lived in a few miles outside of town -- she
concluded it must've burned down. The turkey sandwiches
we ordered for lunch at a diner in town -- she had no
memory of it -- were terrible "but real," that is, real
turkey but also real old turkey. At the new Mentoka
casino she did a sixty-second spin through the two main
game rooms and went straight back to the car. (Earlier
still, on the way to Coutawa, she'd refused to get out
of the car at all during two scheduled stops, one at a
cemetery and one at a historical site. Two other
scheduled stops we skipped entirely.) -- The only new
thing I learned about her Coutawa days is that one of
her major Centropolis squeezes, Bob, after riding up on
the train to visit her, was felled by appendicitis and
she had to nurse him through the aftermath. A few days
of that were enough to convince her they were "totally
incompatible"; soon she moved to Jyze City. (She'd been
conducting a two-year long-distance on-and-off "side
romance" with a guy who lived there -- Kenny, her only
Asiusan lover -- and fallen hard for the area during
her trips to the coast to see him. She met him when he
was a guest lecturer at her social-work school at the U.
in Lahontan.)

*

Okay, the falling-out -- ours I mean. Three hours
of it, seventy-some miles, two stops along the freeway
to Lahontan with Z each time stomping off into the high
grass (recalling Lisa in "Jyzer" days). We barely
managed to patch it up before meeting Angie. I still
fear lingering effects. The issues seem pretty much the
same as before, whatever those might actually be. To me
Z's reneging on our travel deal, that's what it comes
down to. Acting like a prima donna. Can't or won't
make the compromises necessary for compressed-schedule
explorations as we've talked for months about doing.
To her I'm pushing too hard. Refusing to accept

295

she can go stir-crazy and information-overload-crazy and
lose it emotionally without being "culpable" of
anything. Obviously, though, there's more to it than
that.

What matters most to me, all right. We're losing
the chance to do more than a drive-by of anything. My
Lahontan childhood, her Lahontan student years. Many of
the most important spots we'll have to skip entirely,
just as we did in Coutawa. It's likely to be a long
time before we'll have another chance, if we ever do, to
see all this together. Yet she's gotta make a huge fuss
and fiercely stand her ground even if she's breaking a
big batch of implied and actual promises from before the
trip -- when we came up with our detailed itinerary --
and even if it ruins our brief time here. And this
hurts a lot.

How bad was it? So bad I was seriously thinking we
both might be better off if I left the car with Z at her
friend Terry's and took a bus back to Jyze City
tomorrow. Was trying to remember exactly where the
Lahontan bus station was. I would've preferred the
Mentokan -- the train -- but I couldn't swing the fare
without borrowing, and most likely that would've had to
be from Z herself; Jeff and Angie probably couldn't come
up with that kind of scratch on such short notice.)

Yeah, she can be -- a load, exactly. The hated
sexist words! But when she loses it she's about as
gnarly as they come, male or female, and that's just how
it is. And I'm not the only one who says this; her
friends all say it too. (All? All! For that matter Z
herself says it and what's more she takes great pride in
it.) -- Nor is any of this a big surprise. I've known
from day one, the fight by the bridge at the end of our
very first meeting (and as it happens that was exactly a
year and a half ago tomorrow). Even before that, from
the word "feisty" in her ad, I knew, or at least
suspected. Have always believed I could deal with it
and was doing so and in general things were working out
splendidly. And here we are nineteen months later
(meaning after the ad). Do I still believe I can deal

with it? I'll just say the belief's taken a beating
today. -- And stop there.

      (Day 7)
      -- So a sixty-hour break in the action and we're
now into Thursday, which is also the 1st of October. At
about noon on a fine, blazing-blue-skied autumn day.
The jyzer going at it outdoors at the sidewalk cafe of a
coffee shop in a suburb fifteen or twenty miles south of
the one where he grew up (mostly) -- and ten or twelve
miles southwest of the city neighborhood where jyzee Z
grew up (entirely).
      This coffee shop a franchise of the gargantuan
chain headquartered in our current home city. One of
the thousands of such shops now neocolonizing the world.
We headed first for a locally owned indie coffee joint
we were told about but it turned out to be defunct as of
two weeks ago -- no doubt driven out of business by this
one right here opening last year just a block up the
street.
      Z's off touring the creations of the celebrated
architect who used to live around the corner. I might
be exploring the childhood home of the equally
celebrated novelist who grew up nearby -- the museum
consecrated to him standing almost directly across the
street from our hotel, which itself is a kind of shrine
to him and a few other superstar scribblers -- but no.
Gotta feed the jyze monster. Ninety minutes or so to
do it before Z meets me here. Then we go to pick up her
mother and then onward to their old family hood in C-
town itself, the near northwest side. There we'll see
if Z can drive me as crazy with her own "Deep Roots"
tales as I drove her with mine up in western Mentoka.
      Two big days to cover here. No hope of doing it
with anything but extreme sketchiness. (Show a little
grace under pressure, jyzer dude, as that same superstar
novelist might advise. Or just do what you can do as
circumstances allow, yeah, and thank your lucky stars
for the chance.)
      Despite fine dawn lovemaking (side positions laid

out crosswise) the following drive back into Lahontan
from Jeff's farmette two mornings ago was extremely
tense. Same issues again, whatever they actually were
(as I said before -- and I'll probably never know their
real nature beyond what I've already noted). Finally we
stopped a few blocks from "4202," the Hutcheson family
home where Mother lived from age fourteen until a year
after she met Dad some six years later and where I was
brought from the hospital a few days after my birth and
lived for a couple of years while Dad was overseas in
the war; and then over the next two decades I stayed
there frequently during personal or family visits. To
thrash it out one more time, me and Z. Got plenty hot
with her, I did, just as she did with me. Yet the peak
torrid period lasted only about twenty minutes. Because
-- I'd already decided to make the supreme concession.
(This decision coming shortly after I beseeched the moon
for counsel on the farmette porch following the jyze
session in the parlor there the night before.) Proposed
that we drop Gatewood from our itinerary and devote all
our time in Centropolis to her side of things. This to
balance the three days at the start that went mostly to
my side. Lahontan we split more or less evenly, her
years there as a grad student pretty much equaling mine
as a tyke. Entirely voluntary, this idea, not something
she extracted (though it was plain enough she wasn't
about to settle for the status quo). And it seemed to
win her over. She even insisted we also drop our
scheduled afternoon at the U. of Centropolis -- her alma
mater -- so we could relax a bit more, and I not too
grudgingly, I hope, agreed.

     True, the itinerary we put together before leaving
home is now kaput. We had laboriously mapped and timed
it out together to include the places most important to
both of us. She had agreed to it all. But like it or
not, midcourse corrections are sometimes necessary no
matter how excellent the preliminary plans: and surely
I, the neoprag fanatic, could see the neoprag virtue in
such a (sententious -- not to say desperate) thought.
And this was clearly one of those times, yes indeed. No

question. And so that's how it is. (Or to put it even
more simply: be, jyzer, as flexible as you fucking can.)
     Pulled away from the curb assuring each other we
were back on good terms. Neither of us totally believed
it at that point -- of course. But later (she spent
most of the day with her longtime friend and former U.M.
classmate Terry, who lives with her husband, Frank, less
than a mile from Jeff and Angie's place) -- later, I
say, she apologized for having "lost it so badly" and
"acting like a spoiled child." Was Terry's influence
behind this turnabout? If so, thank the divines for
Terry. Because ever since then all's at least seemed
okay. May even be okay. Which is my tentative reading
as of the present moment: it's probably okay. And for
sure I'll be doing everything in my power to keep it
that way.
     And the sex subplot update? Here all's far better
than okay and no doubt about it. Her wry comment:
"Possum really seems to like being back in his old
hunting grounds." Having our hours in sync has
something to do with this too, we're agreed. So does
all the rich food, I say, though on this she demurs.
But I point out that even her own favorite nutrition
gurus advocate vegetarian diets in part because they
supposedly diminish sexual desire, so shouldn't the
converse also be true? In any case: a long humping
session of the invag type every single morning on this
trip and another most nights. Every single day an
ejacoshag. Only once more than one in a day, but then
I'm not asking for miracles. And besides, plenty of
non-ejacos too. If this be my long-term Glennarian
Stage III limit -- yayhoo! Even if the limit only
sometimes gets reached, not to grouse! And she: no
longer can she doubt the jyzer's savage deep-down
bestial desire for her (as opposed to mere crazed
romantic love and all that fluffy regressive patriarchal
hoo-ha).
     (Moving inside now because the sun's too bright.)
                            *
     All right, the two days. Given her always-be-early

proclivities Z might show up at any moment, so summary
first. (One thing she's "already come away with from
this trip," she says, by the way, is that I'm far more
a detail person than she is. Believes she lacks the
patience to attend to detail in my "seriously serious"
fashion. Thinks I might look down on her because of
this. And of course I say not so. I say I love her
talents of which she's got so many -- because it's
simply and obviously true: that's who she is. I say if
"seriously serious" detail's not her thing, we can work
it out -- because we've done so all along. Just don't
be so quick, I plead, to assume the worst. -- And
what's more, on its flip side not being a detail person
is another kind of talent. "Hedgehog and fox." She
prefers to think of it as gestalt and -- something.
-- All this part of the curbside battle in Lahontan.
During which she was raging as I've seen only a couple
of times before during our year and a half together.
Or even more as in her infamous "fire-breathing
feminist" news photo from a couple of decades back,
which I was reminded of over and over again. Evil was
in that car and it was sitting in my seat! I was it!)

     So Tuesday then. Z went off with Terry, I hung out
with brother Jeff. He took the day off and we met at
his favorite cafe. Wasted half an hour looking
fruitlessly for the house where my best childhood buddy
Kevin lived, near the zoo, before he died of leukemia at
age ten. Drove down the nearby secluded lane where
Mother and Dad first kissed (Jeff hadn't known the exact
location but I did, give or take a car length or two,
having asked her about it during my last stay with her
three years ago). Then revisited various major sites:
the apartments and aforementioned small home of my
nursery-school years, the big old tree-swaddled homes of
both grandparental sets (just three miles apart), Aunt
Shel and Uncle Vern's place, a favorite drugstore (still
much the same), the duck pond, the arboretum (where
Tuesday afternoon we took turns climbing atop the big
sandstone gates and striking statuesque poses as the
other snapped photos from below), and a lakeside park

near the last apartment where ol' Mom (or young Mom
then) used to take me and Barb (who was riding in a
baby carriage) after Dad's return from the war while she
was pregnant with Jeff. And now as we walked out to
the shoreline in that park I was visited by a flickery
yet powerful lost memory of being there with them back
then, treading that same path, though I was just short
of five years old that summer.

    And while we were sucking up caffeine in the cafe
at the start of the day, Z and Terry appeared completely
by coincidence on the sidewalk outside and the ever
sassy Z plastered herself in an X-shape flat against the
front window and mimed flabbergastion. And when they
came in she cried: "Well, lookie there! It's M'bao!
Right here in Lahontan two thousand miles from home!"
-- Turns out the cafe is one of Terry's favorites too.

    -- Oops, and lookie here! Z's now coming in the
door of another cafe a hundred and fifty miles from
that one and here he is again, the same grossly
displaced and yet also utterly-at-home jyzerman fiercely
scratching away right in the middle of it! Her Deep!
Maybe not so evil after all! -- And for sure all
tangled up in her own deep roots....
                          *

    (A little more while she hits the head and gets
herself a cup of chai.)

    That evening a relaxed dinner with Terry and Frank
outdoors, a French restaurant near the capitol building.
Then a walk over to the lakeside center where Terry
works (designed by the same celebrated architect who
grew up here), then a long crosstown hike to the terrace
of the student union for ice-cream cones (same place I
used to get them with Mother and Nana all those decades
back). And sleeping that night in Terry and Frank's
quirkily remodeled (by Frank) home.

    Yesterday, Frank's green home-baked "message frog"
muffins for breakfast. The three-hour drive down to the
western fringe of Centropolis. Meeting Z's mother,
doing dinner with her at a Chinese place (more on all
this later because this is speed jyzing under the gun).

Afterwards Z said nobody'd ever been better with her
mother (Z's big anxieties about our meeting -- another
huge tension source -- how could I have failed to mention
those before?). "And now I owe you a million chits."
-- And up to our hotel for sleeping and loving. This
after a late shopping trip to some truly big outer-city
big boxes in search of replacement and upgrade items for
Mama E's apartment and wardrobe. And a lazy morning
today -- instead of hustling out to Gatewood and then
down to the U. of C. as originally planned -- but we've
vowed we'll visit both of these crucial roots
destinations "next trip" instead (if we're not dreaming)
and no hard feelings on either side, honest, we kid each
other not -- dang! Can you beat it?

    (And mention this. The timing of Barb and Keith's
visit to Mentoka, Jeff says, was strictly coincidental.
By the time Z and I hit Lahontan and crossed their trail
again, they'd already flown back home.)

    (Day 8)
    -- Take it straight from the top. As Z breathes
deep. Meditating in bed, she is. Except she's stopped
now and gone silent on the breathing. She's sitting
cross-legged and motionless like the Buddha himself
(except a whole lot more fetching I'll daresay) in her
gray "Mestizas Rule" nightshirt with her back propped
against the headboard.

    As I do my jyze thing on the small green couch in
the parlor area. She directly to my left about ten feet
away. This in one of the more aptly named hotels
anywhere for jyzing (and so the override clause in the
jyze rules permits my naming it, especially since we're
in the Greater Mentoka fictive zone anyway): the Authors
Hotel. Near the hotel entryway three leather-bound
volumes lie open under glass like antiquarian holy books,
all works by the master himself and inscribed by him --
the master whose museum stands across the street. A
tasteful small plaque outside our door names this suite
in which jyze is now going down: "In Our Time."
Perfect! And Z gets all the credit: she discovered the

place months ago during an internet search and picked
out the suite and made the reservations.

We're half a block north of the park at the center
of this leafy upscale burb. "The world's largest
village," it dubs itself. Across the street adjoining
the museum is a long row of old but meticulously well-
kept four-story brownstones. The likes of these
certainly can't be found in my own home burb eight or
ten burb tiers up the road to the northeast. This, in
short, is a kind of ur-burb, an early model for those
others where the form eventually became more refined,
that is, stripped of any grubby remaining urban traces.

We ride up and down on what's advertised as the
village's oldest elevator. "Be gentle with me," pleads
a sign by the "up" and "down" buttons. The elevator
itself looks a lot like the matched pair in the hideaway
building back in J. City. (Being here reminds me just
how relatively small that adopted burg of ours really
is. It's much closer in size to this "world's largest
village," population around 60K, than to the megalopolis
of Centropolis engulfing us here but centered eight or
ten miles to the east.)

Now Z pads by, brushing lightly against me --
intentionally, I believe -- and hope -- without saying
anything, and I get a slight whiff of the funkiness we
brewed up last night (in an exceptionally long and
heated session which climaxed, literally, with the jyzer
pumping in "gob after gob of steaming G-essence" -- Z's
chortling phrase trotted out later -- as he knelt
straddling her inner left thigh) and then again, but in
a more standard configuration, this morning. So yes,
we're still cookin'. Last night she took me aback by
saying afterward -- first warning I'd probably find
what she was about to say "pookie or atavistic" -- "I
kept thinking I want to have your baby." And I agreed
we should keep after it forever and never mind how poor
the odds of success at our Glennarian III stage of
(blessed) reproductive dysfunction.

*

-- Going back then. Z's mother. The main point,

303

as noted before but surely worth repeating: she and I
seem to get along quite well. For starters her life in
the old apartment building isn't a whole lot different
from mine in the subsidized B-2 of pre-Z days. She pays
$370 a month; I paid $385. She must negotiate two more
flights of stairs than I did, but her two-room unit
contains at least half again as much space and also
commands a wide western "largest village" view across
flat chimneyed rooftops (instead of, in B-2's case, a
constricted western alley view with dumpsters, an
elevated freeway, and for compensation a couple of
narrow slices of waterfront and bay). -- And the list
of comparables could go on quite a while.

She's eighty-three. White-haired, about Z's
height, still vibrant and sharp. Striking blue eyes. A
longish face you might guess is Polish (and it is). A
self-deprecating style of talking with lots of warmth
and laughs and cackles mixed in and sometimes an amusing
fade at the end of sentences. Still bears considerable
resemblance to the buxom blond "My Little Chickadee"
movie star of five or six decades back, just as in the
old photos I've seen of her, except in her younger days
the resemblance was even greater. Wears a hearing aid;
you have to speak loudly.

Her life at this stage seems to consist mostly of:
watching the soaps and game shows on TV and listening to
talk radio, reading the supermarket tabloids (her stack
of discarded papers rivaling in height the one next to
my chair at home), hanging out at a franchise burger
joint just a block up the street with a group of senior
cronies (about whom she tells lots of funny stories),
and soaking her arthritic feet and legs in the bathtub.
But she's jolly and unbowed. Doesn't like to complain
or ask for anyone's help and tries to keep everything
simple. Rather than call in the manager to replace the
broken chain on her bathroom ceiling light she's been
using a flashlight in there for months or maybe years.
(I tried to reattach the chain and failed, so Z bought
her a battery lamp and a big package of extra batteries,
along with, among other things, a nightgown, a winter

jacket, towels, sheets, a couple of jersey tops, and a
telephone with a volume enhancer -- a device which her
TV and radio, I might mention, definitely don't need.)

    Yesterday the three of us drove roughly twelve
miles northeast to the city neighborhood where Z was
born and grew up. Her parents stayed on there until her
father's death nineteen years ago. We visited his grave
in a far corner of a huge nearby cemetery -- this on a
splendid warm autumn day -- and Z reciprocated by
introducing me to his spirit as I had intro'd my
father's to her. As at Buena Vista, she broke into
sobs. And it happened again later when her mother
pulled out a small monogrammed magnifying glass her
father used for decades and gave it to her (and tried to
give her some jewelry of her own and other small items
as well, but Z wouldn't accept them). ("VRB" is the
monogram -- R for Regalado -- and he also had it
tattooed on his left arm, I learned.)

    Her father's grave is located near a number of
headstones bearing Japanese names in a mostly Asiusan
corner of the cemetery. But Mama E -- Elza on the
papers but Elsa or El to most -- said he chose that site
to be near the Eurusan family whose graves border the
same area. This is the family he'd lived with and
worked for as a handyman/cook for years before he and
Elza met (he was twenty years her senior). When this
family moved to Centropolis from the West Coast, he came
with them; and then when, as the Depression wore on, the
family could no longer afford to employ him, they
underwrote his training in linotype and helped him find
a job in a print shop. They also arranged, several
years later, for the operations on Z's feet at the
charity hospital. (So see, we're not all bad all the
time, we cracker rulers of the world. And if we hadn't
invaded and occupied Papa Z's country -- genocided it,
could truthfully say, much as with the natives here --
I'd have no daughter Z to love. Brute fact. -- And
Papa Z emigrated to the U.S. mainly out of desperation
to avoid becoming the priest his parents wanted him to
be (he was named after a colonial priest of Spanish-

Italian heritage). -- And for his first decade in this
country he lived the brutally hard life of a migrant
farmworker moving up and down the west coast.)

Then onward to "the street where little Lulu
lived." Lulu, what she was sometimes called as a kid;
Louise, her official first name because she was born on
St. Louise's feast day. (Her half-sister Camilla,
seventeen years older, was the one who called her Weezie
and sometimes Looney Tunes.) A tidy neighborhood of
brick two-story duplexes. From birth through high
school she lived with her parents and no one else in the
same second-story flat. Their building, as far as she
could tell (we decided not to try to gain entrance), is
virtually unchanged from those years, except for gray-
painted plywood bad-weather paneling added to the
rickety back staircase.

And I saw: her elementary school a few blocks away,
the homes of several friends, the spot where she first
came across her pet squirrel Squeaky (who loved to lick
her ear), the former public library where she often
studied after school (now a private music academy and
closed for the day when we arrived -- deeply
disappointing her, since it was her "favorite hangout of
all time"), various Greek establishments (that part of
the hood was primarily Greek), the Catholic church that
the B. family attended (but her father rarely did so, in
part because he and Elza as a mixed-race couple drew too
much attention and more than a little overt racist
hostility) and her high school (it's a mile or so to the
northwest and she usually got there on city buses,
transferring once en route) (and just a couple of miles
west stood the electronics factory where my own father
spent most of his working life in the legal department
and I toiled two summers on the assembly line while of
course remaining utterly oblivious to the nearby
existence of my future Deep, then still, though just
barely, in teen-angel form).

-- And now my allotted max jyzin' hole's about to
close up again before I can even take a flying pass at
describing our dinner at Mama E's favorite hangout in

the old hood. It happened to be another franchise
burger joint, same chain as the one where she hangs out
in her new hood now -- and also the same one where I buy
my vanilla cones back home. All three of us ordered one
of those cones for dessert (but Z took only a
perfunctory lick at hers -- too sugary -- so I finished
it off for her) (and last night I licked her ear and she
said Squeaky was "less slobbery").

(Day 10)
-- And at five this morning (Sunday) we arose as
Jeff and Angie slept on in the next room and we slipped
away from the town of La Chevalle in the dark and drove
a few miles northwest to the nearest crossing (where the
river was shrouded in thick white fog) and from there
headed briefly southward through hilly driftless country
to connect with the freeway and then rolled westward --
usually with no other vehicles anywhere in sight -- and
then northward on another freeway to the same airport
where we landed nine days ago.

And since we encountered no problems along the way
and allowed ourselves plenty of cushion to allay Z's
always-be-early anxieties we had almost two and a half
hours to burn upon arrival here and still have about
half that much left now.

(why anxieties? She worries a lot, that's why.
"Hyperactive amygdala." As noted before by her, she
didn't fail to bring those gnarly brain parts -- for
actually we all have two amygdalas, I now happen to know
from the unabridged dictionary conveniently on tap in
the Authors Hotel lobby, and presumably we have two
instead of one for the usual backup redundancy purposes,
much like, say, lungs or breasts or testicles -- she
didn't fail to bring both of those amygdalas along on
the trip, correct. And on the way down to La Chevalle
from the airport on that first day we ran into a couple
of lengthy detours, and at various points over the nine
days the gearshift knob came off in my hand several more
times, and the driver's side of the car sustained a
fairly nasty three-foot horizontal scratch, probably

engraved by a carelessly driven truck while the car was
parked on the street overnight outside the Authors
Hotel. So Z's abundant amygdalic worries can sometimes
be justified, true enough. And at all times had better
be respected, yes. And they are! No matter what I for
one may seem to be saying so scoffily about them during
my more Paleolithic regressions.)

     So a quick overview. Friday afternoon we again
drove deep into Centropolis, this time via a different
set of astoundingly jam-packed freeways, to a near-
north-side highrise condo building wherein reside Z's
half-sister Camilla (on the twenty-first floor) and her
son ---

                         *

     (At which point a series of minor disturbances
arose and then suddenly the flight began loading almost
seventy minutes before scheduled takeoff time. So once
again Z can crow that her ABE policy often pays off.
And now we're aboard. And Z, still wearing the new
chartreuse vest she bought in Lahontan, is back into her
flight-anxiety-suppressing lady-detective novel (set in
Centropolis in the very same neighborhood where she
used to live while attending U.C., which hood
incidentally at one point we were scheduled to visit,
before all hell broke loose on the freeway between
Coutawa and Lahontan). -- And I ought to say all
appears well with us at this point right here at the
airport. Or why not throw caution aside and say all
appears better than well. In any event we're agreed the
"DRRT" venture has been a smashing success despite, and
maybe even because of (or maybe in some sense surely
because of), those serious early and midtrip glitches.)

     -- And residing four floors beneath Camilla's
condo, I was about to say, her only child, Jacob,
thirteen years Z's junior, and his wife, Jackie, and
their nine-year-old daughter Jillian ---

                         *

     (More disturbances. We were in the wrong seats.
Then it turned out the overhead rack for our new seats
was full and competing claims for the one next to it had

to be settled by a churlish flight attendant.)

So. Where was I?

Word is I "scored big-time," according to Z, with
Camilla, Jacob, and the others. That's the key point,
the "major Deep Roots takeaway," as Z dubbed it.

Camilla, just two years younger than my mother was
at her death and easily fatigued owing to a stroke she
suffered seven years ago, couldn't leave her apartment.
We stayed there with her for an hour or so, mostly
talking about computers -- she's obsessed with them!
She's a raving digital libertarian! Very charming,
though, quick and well-spoken and also very good to look
at in a way that clearly runs in the family and seems
all but impervious to aging (those high Asian
cheekbones no doubt having something to do with it in
the half-sisters' cases). Then the rest of us, joined
by Jackie's mother Justine, went out for dinner at a
lively Italian spot (on a rainy night that inspired
lots of jokes about our own rainy city). Dishes piled
high on the table, gales of laughter, bustling servers,
big check, which Z picked up. And hanging on the wall
above the maitre'd's station the venerable poster in
which a certain famous wet-bloused Italian movie star
looks startlingly like numerous photos I've seen of Z in
her twenties and a fair amount like Z as she is right
now (and Jacob told me he agrees -- but with a wink and
a nudge) (but she really does!). Jacob a fast talker
who makes an enviable living selling novelties out of
his apartment, never went to college, witty and in-your-
face in a very likable way. His wife Jackie blond,
sweet and quiet, with a Ph.D. in music theory.

-- Speeding up again. The high-altitude
vulnerabilities of the J-stick will prevent me, just as
during the flight out, from keeping this account going
once we've taken off, assuming that actually happens.

-- On Friday, up at six at the Authors Hotel for
the long drive back to La Chevalle, where we arrived
before one, and with no altercations along the way,
perhaps because most of the time Z slept -- or on the
other hand that might've had nothing at all to do with

it. Who knows! Then we hit the Apple Affair at the
picturesque nearby town of Rushville (putative site of
"the American Garden of Eden"), having agreed to meet
Jeff and Angie there, but some unexpected last-minute
business in Lahontan detained them. After waiting two
hours we headed back to the hotel. There we found Jeff
and Angie holding down adjacent stools at the crowded
bar (though I didn't see them at first, leading to
hilarity when I finally did spot them from a distance of
about two feet as both stared straight at me). A couple
of drinks and dinner, a leisurely walk along the
riverfront, and that was all we had time for -- Z and I
badly needing to get some sleep before this morning's
early departure.
     -- And that's gotta be it. Plane's rolling.
                    *   *
     So here's the doubly wild grand finale. Back home
in J. City and now at the hideaway for a few minutes
after putting in a tough six hours at the scope office
starting only four hours after our arrival. But those
four hours -- wow. High drama! Preposterously apt
theatrics! (And once I've snatched a little sleep and
reorientated myself here at the start of what Z and I
have agreed will be the "fully settled-in" portion of
our time living together as Deeps -- which time after
all is strictly limited because it'll be ending when we
hitch up for real next year -- why, then I'll resurface
in here hoping to fill in a few of the gaps on the trip
and maybe to do some sort of jyzey coda. And then
it'll be time to close out this little travel J-book for
good and shift back to a full-size volume, a new one,
which won't cramp my hand so much -- and my style too,
somehow making it both much choppier and much more
longwinded, seems like.)
     So first the arrival. For reasons never explained
our flight wound up taking off about half an hour early
and landing here forty minutes early, only to sit on the
ground for most of those minutes for want of a "joey" to
open the plane doors. By the time we finally fished our
luggage from the carousel we were back to the original

schedule and Betty and Kat should've been arriving to pick us up, but they were nowhere to be seen. We waited almost an hour more before giving up on them. A shuttle bus was about to pull out at that moment, so Z oversaw the loading of the baggage and found us seats while I jogged down to the booth to buy tickets. Just as I was making ready to hand over my twenty-dollar bill (one of the lopsided new ones) a small black-mop-haired mutt latched onto my leg and started humping it from behind -- or no, it was Kat! She was viciously hugging my left thigh! So then we dashed to the bus, Kat in the lead as always, to get Zoelie off. The majorly unhappy driver, who had already delayed his departure for us, had to clamber back out and unlock the luggage compartment to return our suitcases. Z gave him a fin.

What happened? For some reason Kat's swimming lesson ran late (her mop was still damp). Betty looked frazzled and embarrassed. Our ride into the city was rollicking but also a little awkward. As we unloaded our luggage in the driveway at 1511 Kat was insisting we go upstairs and wrestle but Betty declared they were heading straight home so she could take a much-needed nap.

(And by the way, my J-stick is still leaking a bit at the barrel joints from air-pressure changes on the plane. Because I know from much messy experience that this brand and model of J-stick is likely to do that, I no longer carry one in my pocket when I'm flying. I sealed this one, and the backup as well, in a plastic baggie in my pack.)

And onward? Time's short again. But up in unit 203 (looking just about exactly the same, it was, all the plants appearing to have survived June's shockingly excessive watering regime -- big puddles on the dining table itself and a wet carpet!) Z took to the bed almost immediately and I joined her there for a brief "last vacation snuggle-up" after completing the minimal necessary amount of unpacking. The whirl of events over the previous two days had forced us to break our string and we hadn't gotten it on at all during that time, so

now I was horny, and I thought maybe she was too (though
she'd plunged right back into the same detective mystery
the moment she hit the sheets). On the other hand I was
worn out from the flight, the long early-morning drive
to the airport, the previous rugged day driving up to La
Chevalle from Centropolis, and a severe shortfall on
sleep over several days -- or over the whole trip,
really, and the days leading up to it as well.

However: I quickly found myself almost surreally
turned on. Stripped off my jeans and then (while
kneeling between her legs, already inside her) my black
henley. This was the highest-quality hard-on obtainable
for this old jyzer, no question, bone to the bone of the
bone, and we were engaged in some truly righteous high-
energy in-and-out when -- an eruption of god-awful high-
pitched WHEEEEEEEEE. The fire alarm! And feature this:
while still inside her, atop, I improv'd a quip seconds
after the alarm went off, almost worthy of some goofball
Hollywood comedy if I do say so: "I knew this was hot,
but I didn't realize it was that hot."

(Okay, it wasn't really all that great, the quip:
it just seemed so at the time. Perhaps because she
broke up over it, yeah, and with me still inside her.
Gave me an unusual ride right there, yes she did.
-- And now I gotta pack up and go. No slack left.)
                    *   *
And back home. Z's taking the day off tomorrow (as
a "buffer" between vacation and work, for gearing up)
and when I walked in, the bedroom door was open and she
was even a little awake. Jet lag has her sleep pattern
all bollixed up, as expected, and is doing the same to
mine but to a lesser degree (so far).

A big pile of mail awaited me on the black
armchair, almost all of it either magazines or reviews
or subscription mailers for magazines and reviews. Also
a postcard from the Z-woman herself which beat us back
-- "Greetings from 'The Largest Village in the World'"
-- and laid out across the coffee table, a bright yellow
"Troll Crossing" sign she picked up on the sly at the
Rushville fair. She's already thanked me several times

for "giving such good road trip." The not-so-good parts
of the trip seem to have been successfully suppressed on
both sides, at least so far. -- And I've wasted half an
hour looking fruitlessly for certain articles I promised
to send to Jacob and Jackie. The dining table's still
jammed with the plants, all of which we placed there so
June wouldn't miss any (better we'd hidden them). And
the refrigerator's almost bare. In short: a helluva lot
remains to be done around here before we can resume our
full normal, or not so normal but nonetheless largely
and happily familiar, lives and get on with the business
of truly settling in. We're giving ourselves one week
to accomplish this transition.

   And back to the grand finale. So there we were
caught in flagrante in our own bed by a fire alarm. We
both got up, still naked, and I draped my still-fully-
fledged hard-hard-hard-on with a red henley snatched
from the dirty clothes mound as a kind of warning flag,
as on log trucks. For once old Possum was refusing to
do a foozle! Was it all the high drama that was
responsible for this aberrant marsupial behavior?
Meanwhile something had to be done about that horrible,
almost unbearable WHEEEEEEEEE issuing from the fire
alarm on the ceiling in our interior hallway -- the same
alarm I'd repaired a few months earlier. So, still
naked and still in pretty close to maximal priapic
state, I mounted a chair and tried to dismantle the
alarm as Z cackled a couple of feet away, her eyes
taking me in from a vertical perspective entirely new to
her just above phallus level while she was standing up,
pretending to dodge the humongous member as it swung
ponderously about. "Hey, watch out with that thing!"
Eventually I succeeded in breaking down the alarm (and
the priapic state slowly subsided too), but by then we'd
realized the sound was building-wide. And just seconds
later, almost unbelievably, a fire engine roared up with
siren blaring on the street below our balcony and we
both threw on some clothes and in a totally jangled
state headed for the sidewalk in front as battle-geared
firefighters charged by going in the opposite direction

like a squadron of invading soldiers in yellow hazmat
gear. I mean these guys were serious!

Never did we smell any smoke (though one of our
neighbors claimed to). And for good reason: it turned
out the whole thing was a false alarm -- "just a joke
someone was playing on you-all," as we overheard one of
the fire dudes say to Ciro from 102.

Or was the joke specifically played on Z and me?
Several kids had been goofing around out in the hall
when we came in with our luggage. Possibly one of them,
or all of them, had heard our love-sounds, or rather
hers mostly, through the wall a short while later
(despite my "soundproof" headboard) and decided, yes,
to have some fun with us. The pull-alarm in the hall
on the third floor was the one that was activated and
the kids had been playing right next to it. But there's
no way to prove they did it and no urge to do so either,
and most likely we'll never know what really happened.

But for sure it was some kind of homecoming
excitement. I'd never been caught in the act that way
before and Z assured me she hadn't either.

And then the best part of all. When we returned to
203 we stripped right down and jumped back into bed.
For a while Z couldn't stop laughing over the whole
incident, but then suddenly she was turning on again and
lo and behold, so was I. And we fucked a last "Deep
Roots fuck," and the splendid hard-hard-hard-on came
back like a reentered dream, and then also a reentering
dream, and for my money it was once again our "best ever
so far," complete with powerful invag ejac, Z moaning
"you...you...you" dozens of times, or more likely
hundreds or even thousands, and it was fine...fine...
fine (hot...hot...hot). And now we're both thinking
many more at least somewhat like it could lie ahead if
we're lucky, and especially if we can manage to find
some way to go to bed together at the same time every
night. Though that of course will likely be impossible
"for the foreseeable future," yes.

*   *

(And forget the coda. Enough is enough.)

314

BOOK IV

[Tell It Jyze]

31

And here's the real autumn. Possibly I've
announced its arrival earlier, maybe I'll do so again
later, but I don't doubt this is the best time to make
it jyzically official. Chilly night, windblown drizzle,
just bad enough you're gonna get wet if you go outside
in anything less protective than scalp-to-toes raingear.
Nor will an umbrella help much, no matter how you deploy
it, including upside-down as a lifeboat.
    I'm referring to my Monday-night 1.93-mile downtown
circuit. First to the usual burger joint for a couple
of double-stacks, then a browse at the nearer chain
bookstore and a stop at the other usual burger joint for
a large vanilla cone (in honor of Mama E, could say now)
(and at both burger joints I usually read a few pages in
a book I've brought along -- I leave my pack at the
hideaway -- and tonight's book is another prog-neoprag
absolutist-trasher which I first took up weeks ago and
dipped into a few times during the "Deep Roots" trip and
yet I'm still not up to page 100 because I'm relishing
every word and rereading many of them, even a third and
fourth time). -- And the whole way I was moving slowly
and creakily as an aftereffect of the long WOC session
that ended about eight-thirty p.m. I missed eleven days
of workouts while we were gone and now my body's taking
at least that long to get back to where it was.
    So the signs are legion: the vacation's over.
We're back in harness. Z's finally sleeping through the
night again after a week of readjusting (several times
greeting me wide-awake at one-thirty a.m. when I arrived
home -- and one night, after a spell of restlessness,

calling out from the bedroom at three a.m., "I need some
of that G-man loving or I'll never get to sleep!") (and
the G-man obliged, though perhaps a bit hesitantly at
first -- because he'd just cracked open the night paper
and settled into his black armchair with a mug of cherry
cider after a hard night of scoping). The trip photos
are all developed (except for the half-exposed final
roll) and some are quite good and just about everyone
who's anyone in G&Z circles has seen them already. The
fridge is restocked, the sheets changed, the laundry
done, the suitcases put away, the plants dried out and
restored to their normal spots, and Z's back to cursing
out the Cawk neighbors when they rev their souped-up hot
rods in the driveway below our south-side windows. Oh
-- and we're both pretty much caught up on the
workplace backlogs that built up while we were away.

        (While cranking out the jyze I'm nibbling at a bag
of purported red-flame grapes which are turning out to
be something other than seedless. Every single grape
but one has yielded a seed, and one's yielded two. Odd.
-- But I found these grapes at one of the produce
markets I walk by every afternoon as I pass through the
Asian quarter on the way in. One day I noticed bananas
for sale in the outdoor section at a very good price and
since then, on days when I'm not in a hurry, I've been
stopping in for similar bargains on peaches, nectarines,
tomatoes, even potatoes. I like buying from our local
markets this way, especially since I'm often the only
non-Asian doing so: reminds me of Japan/Korea days.)

        -- Today's cranking is happening at the hideaway
desk. Donald, the guy who moved into No. 231 last
month, just flipped off his lights and I assume turned
in for the night, as apparently did the new guy in No.
224 on the other side a few minutes earlier. With
apartment rents shooting up all over the city, this
building here is becoming more and more a clandestine
boardinghouse. So far the building owner, Allen W.,
seems to be tolerating the change, probably because
construction in the area is making his office suites
temporarily less desirable, resulting in many more

vacancies than usual. The past couple of nights the guy
in No. 224 was playing loud hip-hop music for hours on
end and I was on the verge of going over there to ask
him to tamp it down a bit, but then Donald beat me to it
and persuaded him to do just that. Donald and I are
becoming palsy-walsy like back-fence neighbors. We
frequently run into each other on the downtown streets
in the evenings -- both of us working in other people's
offices more than in our own. Exactly what he does I'm
not sure yet, but at least at times it involves
evictions. Could be he's about to become a regular bit
player in the jyzarama.

   And I still haven't gotten to the main stories of
the week. Three of 'em, all coming neatly together
over the weekend. They even fit in well with the post-
road-trip theme (how our "Deep Roots" explorations have
changed us forever, more or less, maybe) and also with a
couple of other long-running story lines.

   First, the reversal. It's still shaky at times,
but so far my sexual revival seems to be holding up.
Suddenly I seem to be able to fuck almost at will. It
happened again last Sunday night (only eight hours after
the in-flagrante fire alarm and the astounding recovery
which followed) and then again on Monday and Tuesday.
That's four fully articulated ejacoshags in three days
-- and several fully articulated non-ejacos as well.
All of a sudden I'm Mr. Satyr!

   But this is such a switch it's causing problems
with Z. Now I'm the "insatiable" one and she's the one
who can't keep up. It might even be she's becoming
bored with serving as a jizz receptacle. Or it could be
her perception is that I'm not sexually fussing over her
as much as I did before the reversal (and it just might
be true, because back then I was frantic to show that my
foozles had nothing to do with lack of desire for her).

   That's one story. I'd love to go into it in more
depth and likely will try to do so later. But the key
point for now is that she began coming up with excuses
ahead of time for not getting amorous on a particular
occasion. She took to fending off my advances (mostly

by turning "chatty Cathy" in bed or by applying "the
clamp" when I tried to get at vulnerable parts, or
simply by turning away). I teased her about this and
didn't really worry about it too much -- the sensation
was so new for me in my relations with her it was almost
welcome. For once I could be the one who was too much
to handle! (She also said she hoped I wouldn't become
"permanently cocky." I guess I must've been crowing a
bit. Roostering. And can I blame myself after all I've
gone through over the past sixteen or seventeen months?
Hell no! I'm forgiven! She even said so herself!)
     The second story, related, had to do with the road
trip. In trying to understand how I could've
metamorphosed sexually as I did, Z focused on the fact
that we went to bed together at the same time every
night while we were away. That did have something to do
with it, I'm sure, maybe even quite a lot. But of
course now with the vacation over we can't do that
anymore. And we both miss it. And she grumps about it
a bit, and probably would do so even more if she weren't
having second thoughts about whether she'd want to be
sleeping eight hours every night with Mr. Satyr.
     And then the third story is of a more familiar
kind. Z's volatile best friend Aida is now getting it
on with Z's former lover Kirk M. Things are moving
along very quickly. Aida's even allowing him to come
over and play with son Charles. And she's calling Z and
describing what she and Kirk are doing in bed (perhaps a
little extra-gleefully as a way of rubbing it in, for
Z's not talking with Aida about her own sex life with
me, as per our longstanding agreement -- and since Z and
Aida have always included sex as part of their standard
"girl talk" topics up until my arrival on the scene,
Aida's probably been feeling this is another area where
Z's betraying her in some sense). "Kirk has such good
hands!" Aida raves. And more annoyingly still she
passes on things he's told her about Z. For instance,
he says he's the one who broke it off with Z because, as
Aida puts it to her, "You wanted to get serious and he
didn't." (Maybe it's true, Z told me at first. She has

a hard time remembering the details. She swears she can
recollect nothing of what Kirk was like in bed -- "which
probably means," she sniffs, "he wasn't much." Then she
recalled her big problem with him -- and maybe the
reason they broke up -- was that he wanted to have kids
and she didn't. But she's not at all sure this was
really it. Mostly it's all too cloudy now, too distant.
-- Which still doesn't mean it's not painful for her at
times. The Kirk M. affair came during a very bad period
in her life. Kirk was a secondary player until she and
Brian S. broke up, and then when she and Kirk started to
see more of each other, it quickly fell apart with him
too. That was also the period when her father died.)

    -- So those are the three stories that came
together this weekend. Not in a big explosion or
anything -- but intriguingly. And I'll try to say
something more about that next time. (Because now --
surprise! -- it's time to bust my last-bus move.)

*   *

    Where was I? I'm pretty sure I know well enough
not to need to glance back. Could check out just the
last paragraph or two but best not to do that either.
Better to plunge in afresh. Something in me almost
always resists the rereading. It could be part
laziness. Or it could be I don't want to be trying to
fit myself into a mold -- or maybe better to say a way
of framing things -- that already somehow feels old.

    So it's now Thursday night. -- Which reminds me:
I'm officially abandoning my old system of jyzing only
on the odd-numbered days of the J-week: first, third,
fifth, seventh. It's just not practical. From now on
I'll simply do it whenever I can, after first trying to
crank out as many as possible of a week's quota of pages
on J-day itself -- that is, the first day -- or soon
thereafter.

    -- And where was I, yes. But before that, where
am I now. The hideaway, scratching away at the desk at
exactly (more or less) 11:57 p.m. The building heat's
on. Donald appears to be all tucked in for the night.
The guy on the other side is keeping quiet at the

321

moment. (But last night he had a woman up here at this hour and she was wandering around druggily in the hall with her blouse fully unbuttoned -- revealing an overbrimming red bra -- and she even poked her head in the partly open door here and invited me to come on over and party with them, which I declined to do, no doubt for a whole lot of foolishly uptight reasons (but I'm still glad I did -- declined, that is). And then later when I passed through the cloud of happy smoke on my way out she reappeared and asked for a ride up to the Yuke, still in the same state of glassy-eyed dishabille, and I took a pass on that one too. Guess this just goes to show how deeply into Deepdom I've now rooted myself. -- But I do want to note I've never before seen anything quite this blatant going down around here. Could be the hideaway building is about to take a quantum leap up the drama scale.)

This is my heavy week. But it's turning out to be much less heavy than expected because the newly empaneled grand jury is being shown the ropes and slowly broken in, hearing only a few witnesses in relatively simple cases (routine counterfeitings, bank robberies, drug busts, including one involving a scene quite similar to ours last night in 224). Thus I've had several free hours on a day when I almost never have any, Thursday of GJ week.

And then last weekend's mini-crisis. It flared up again on Tuesday night, so maybe it's better I didn't get around to tackling it "in depth" last session. What it amounts to is this. Things are shifting -- mainly, I think, because now I'm suddenly much better able to perform conjugally, but also because we've entered our ballyhooed "truly settled-in" period (by mutual agreement) and because the experience of the road trip seems to have changed our views of each other in some subtle and not-so-subtle ways we weren't aware of before -- and we're both a little uneasy with the changes (which isn't to say we're not excited about them too).

So, to recap, now I'm wanting to fuck more. And so naturally, I suppose, Z suddenly wants to fuck less.

She's worried about repercussions. About rhythms or the
lack thereof. About what she's expected and/or
"permitted" to do (like, can she mount me anytime she
wants now? Is the reinvigorated Possum ready for
that?). -- And is this revival really for real? Will
it hold in normal workaday life or is it mainly just a
vacation phenomenon, an artifact of an out-of-normal
bodily and/or psychic state? And will she be enough for
me now that I've become such a raging bull?

　　　Except for a brief grocery-shopping expedition we
stayed home "all weekend" (which for us essentially
means one p.m. Saturday, when I get up, through seven
p.m. Sunday, when I leave for work) and passed most of
that time in bed, reading and talking. Loving only a
couple of times. She held me off and then apologized
for being "such a sex wimp right now." We discussed
various matters in detail -- sexual confidence and
whatnot. I observed she suddenly seemed nowhere near as
interested as before and asked why this was and she
didn't really have an answer. I pretended to be jealous
about Kirk and at times actually was. In the end we
came up with a new protocol under which, if she needs to
be "perky" the next day, she'll hang a "Perky Alert"
sign on the bedroom doorknob to let me know when I get
home. If that sign's not out there, it means she's open
to loving, either at my bedtime or when her alarm goes
off (or for that matter at any point in between). To me
this is much preferable to the previous arrangement
under which she specified in advance exactly when she'd
be expecting to get it on (leaving a note on my chair,
for example, saying, "I'll set the alarm for nookie at
five") -- though in truth we didn't pay much attention
to that protocol anyway.

　　　So what's happened since then? The first night she
left a note on the door specifying a time for a.m.
loving but also saying she needed to be perky at work.
"Mixed messages, Z-duck! They're driving me crazy!"
Her reply: "Unreliable, that's what I am." (To the tune
of "Unforgettable," with a clef sign and musical
notation and a partial set of lyrics, all written out on

323

the cover of a fold-open blank card, with a lovey-dovey
message inside.)
     Then on Tuesday evening, after telling me she'd
been looking forward to lovemaking all day -- and would
be needing to be perky the rest of the week, meaning
this would be the last opportunity for a while -- in bed
she sprang a brutal elbow clamp on me at my first move
(and a very tentative move it was). More earnest
discussion followed. I revealed my conclusion of the
moment: she doesn't really like these prescribed midweek
dinner-hour nookie sessions. Too often she gets that
uptight "you're a stranger" look and pushes me away.
So, I suggested, how about we try chaste Tuesday and
Thursday evenings for a while? (I also warily floated
the idea of canceling our evening meetings on these days
-- since we're now seeing each other at the WOC on most
Mondays, Wednesdays, and Fridays -- but she wouldn't
hear of that.) -- And she agreed on the chaste Tuesday
and Thursday evenings. So we're trying those.
     Meanwhile, yesterday morning, Wednesday, a
gangbusters quickie which broke all the rules we'd just
put in place. She loves to rebel against her own rules.
I do too, but apparently nowhere near as much as she
does. We agree this difference between us is likely
another reflection of our Catholic/Protestant split, and
this despite the fact that we've both long ago rebelled
against and repudiated our respective religious
trainings, such as they were, and in truth they never
were all that much for either of us, though still much
more for her than for me.
     -- What, 12:51 already? And so many pages to fill
before the end of the year? Tomorrow night another
chunk for sure. Meanwhile I'll mention that I've talked
to Mama E twice on the phone -- as part of Z's regular
Sunday calls -- and she's sent a thank-you card
addressed to both of us in which she describes me as a
"wonderful fellow" and Z's gone through an uproarious
and embarrassing series of events at work because she
allowed the in-house newsletter to print an item about
her vacation in which it's reported that her mother

thinks her "fiance Glen looks just like John Wayne"
(jyze-rules exception!). For several days Z could
scarcely set a toe into the hallway at work without
drawing hoots. And even the boss of the utility,
Roberta C., was reported to have discussed our
relationship with one of her underlings, including this
snippet of dialogue: "what's Zoelie like when she's in
love?" And the underling: "very nice. very different."

Hear hear! -- The point of course being Z hates to
have that word "nice" applied to herself. "Different"
of course is -- different, yes. Or as she put it to me:
"'Difference,' Jyze Guy, is what it's all about." And
so I say: viva la diff and joie de vivre!)

*   *

Again jumping ahead further than I'd like --
another three days. Which doesn't bode well for my
revised plan to fill up this book by the end of the
year. But onward.

It's Sunday night. Again the hideaway. Tonight
was my night out with brother Rob to celebrate his
birthday (which fell on Thursday, which is to say the
first day of this entry). We met at the digi-cafe in my
old hood, then did dinner with a bottle of merlot at the
funky burger restaurant/bar nearby (right on his usual
walking path from the old "north pole" to catch the bus
home). For me it was a little strange being back on my
former home turf, and not least because, though it was
all totally familiar, it somehow didn't feel a whole lot
like a place where I used to live. It was more like a
place I used to walk through a great deal (which of
course is exactly what it is now for Rob).

But I'm thinking I'll wait until next entry to
tackle the evening with Rob, and also last night's visit
to Betty and Kat's house. Better I should try to pick
up some loose threads from the prior week before I lose
them completely.

Thread #1, Wei applied for Z's pared-back former
job -- it's minus the newsletter -- and this week was
informed he's gotten it (little do they suspect what
they're in for; as Z herself says, "Compared to the

325

typical city worker he's even weirder than I am").

Thread #2, June stopped by one night and during another of our lengthy living-room chats let me know she disapproves of Aida's "going out with" Kirk. "So many men around -- why him?" And she did well in reminding Zoelie, when Z was moaning to her about our being unable to go to bed at the same time every night as we did on the trip, "Don't forget how you like to have free time for yourself." June was also full of news about her son Michael's photo appearing prominently in a spread on biz-school diversity in a national news mag.

Thread #3, a card came in from Justine, Jacob's mother-in-law who joined us for dinner at the Italian joint back in Centropolis. She asked us to choose which theme we'd prefer, frogs or turtles, for the wooden cigar box she'll be hand-painting for us as a wedding gift. (Or if we really, really like both, then she'll send us one of each; and we've greedily gone for both.) This is our very first wedding gift, with one exception I just recalled that's for Z alone: a gold-nugget bracelet her half-sister Camilla gave her, also during the trip. Tough-minded June has appraised it at $300; easygoing Adele thinks a thousand. (And I find myself playing the role of the antimaterialist wedding advisor, the scoffer. It seems almost built in. I'd like to lose the role but still somehow keep the formal and material aspects of the wedding to a bare minimum.)

Jacob himself e-mailed asking Z to call because he had a personal question for her. She predicted it would be about the state of my divorce from Lady S, which she'd mentioned in passing as we were saying goodbye to everyone at Jacob and Jackie's condo. It was.

And right away Z was back into her busy extracurricular life. She's putting in two or three nights a week working on the campaign against I-200, the initiative to end affirmative action. She saw Aida twice, once for dinner in the Asian quarter and once (today) to check out a museum show. She also attended a women's caucus meeting and did a "girls' night out."

And then our crazy sex life. It's still chugging

along. One morning she even took me at my word about
"permission to mount at any time." And it worked! And
this past weekend, possibly to make up for her previous
sex wimp-out, she was in one of her own "insatiable"
spells, which of course put any and all of mine to
shame. Last week she was experiencing "gushes" on and
off at work, she said, for example while riding the
elevator suddenly envisaging the jyzer as he'd looked
stretched out naked on his back in bed that morning,
"Possum long and fat but not hard -- looking sassy."
In general she's being more verbal in specifying what
she wants from me ("Let's gaze into each other's eyes
more often when we come -- I love that"). She's saying
she's realized I'm influencing her in many ways,
including boosting her "body confidence." ("Now if one
of those twenty-something golden-bod types struts by
naked in the locker room I make a point of strutting by
her the same way.")

32

Here's just to get started. It's almost half past
three in the a.m. and we're trying out a new anything-
goes sleep regime and much remains for me to do tonight
before turning in and I don't want to be sleeping late
tomorrow because tomorrow looks tight too. But neither
do I want to let J-day slide off its schedule. Never
again, I swear. If it's J-day, always at least a few
J-scratches.
     Only two days since the last session but lots is
happening. So maybe a sentence or two for each
happening and that'll have to be it until next time.
     Jess P. went through a breast-biopsy scare but

327

she's now been declared cancer-free: that's the big one.

After two straight days of rebelling against her own "Perky Alert" sign Z had a eureka moment: why not drop all attempts to schedule loving. (Well, we know why not. We've tried this several times before. But now with more experience maybe we can do better.)

Today I drove to the biggest of our local big boxes to pick up the last package of developed photos from the trip. While there I yielded to a series of impulses, buying my first new shirt in three or four years (not counting the ones Z and I bought together which she picked out and I've hardly ever worn) (this new one being a blue denim workshirt for twelve bucks). I also scored a brand-new college dictionary (splitting the ten-buck cost with Z) and stocked up on various staples in bulk (toothpaste, deodorant, applesauce). For me this is about as consumeristically crazed as it gets.

A lengthy front-page story in today's far-coast paper describes our state's battle over I-200, the outrageous anti-affirmative-action initiative which Z's been furiously campaigning against (and which the polls say is almost certain to win).

-- So okay, that's it: the start ends.

*   *

-- A few moments ago Donald knocked lightly and stuck his head in the gap left by the cracked-open door. "I finally figured it out. I put two and two together. Our friend next door is running a call-girl ring."

It does make sense. The clouds of weed smoke, the late-night hours, the half-naked women running around in the halls, the flurries of activity on weekend nights, possibly even the raucous thumping and banging we frequently hear through the walls. And just to make sure we don't miss out on something memorable, Donald and I will wait a while before ratting him out. (If the guy would just be a little more discreet we'd leave him alone. Basically he gives us no choice: he's putting us at risk too. To the rest of the building's occupants the pungent happy smoke could just as well be coming from our adjoining offices, Donald's and mine. Next

328

thing we know a DEA task force will be breaking down
our doors as well as his. Rarely does a grand-jury
session go by without at least one such case under
consideration.)

     Another oddity: I saw this same guy (his name is
Nolan and he's hard to miss: Cawk dude about six-five,
late twenties, closely cropped light brown hair, lots of
tattoos, looks like a cross between a trucker and a
punkish neo-Nazi thug who's perhaps making a token
effort to clean up his act, maybe because he needs a job
real bad) -- saw him taking an introductory tour over at
the WOC. Our eyes met and locked for a moment, as in
"Hey, I know you -- or do I?" But neither of us said
anything. (And on the glass door of his office a hokey-
looking hand-lettered sign that may even signal a sense
of humor: "Triangle Advertising.")

     -- Last Sunday and Monday nights were especially
fine and for that reason this week's chronologizing
stuff will start there. These were the nights on which
Z had declared a "Perky Alert" and then subverted it.
Sunday was the first time she's ever pulled/pushed me
inside her after coming several times herself. (We
humped a while and she got off that way a couple of
times too, then I decided to pull out -- had the
feeling I probably wouldn't be able to come -- and did
her twice more by hand, first nipples and then clit,
and to my surprise I stayed stiff the whole time and
she didn't fail to notice this and pulled me back in,
guiding by hand, and this time I did have the pop.)

     The next night was exceptional too because I was
deliciously sore and rampant to the max -- feeling
almost shockingly swollen inside her, as if an extra
little pulse could've shattered her pelvis (no
exaggeration!) -- and what's more, despite the previous
night's activity, and that on top of the weekend's lewd
doings, was able to ejac within moments. (In fact that
was the one that apparently persuaded her to drop the
"Perky Alert" procedure and grant carte blanche
permission to fuck -- and why not if the deed could be
accomplished so quickly?) (But here's Donald again.)

[Deep Jyze]

*   *

   -- Tonight just seventy minutes. It seems I'm
enjoying life too much these days -- and at the same
time trying to do too much -- to be able to come up with
even faintly realistic jyze plans. And that applies to
the long and middle terms every bit as much as the
shorter ones. (But then again when hasn't this been the
case? Not anytime recently. Probably only during those
brief periods when I was between writing projects.)
   A picturesque foggy night in the triangle. The
Victorian street lamps and turn-of-the-century brick
buildings make for striking Sherlock Holmesian London
images -- and then a horse-drawn carriage driven by a
man in a black cape and top hat clip-clops by on the
cobblestones and cinches it: you're trapped in a cliche!
It's a Friday night too, though, and one with a fair
amount of noticeably un-Victorian activity, for example
scores of young folks in skimpy outfits shivering in
line outside the live-music joints. (The evening is
apparently much milder outside the fog zone, which seems
to be limited to the low-lying parts of downtown.)
   For me it's been a typical weekday of the
nonscoping variety. Up at noon (after a fine five a.m.
boink), breakfast of cornflakes, toast, and two mugs of
coffee at home while flipping through the paper and a
couple of mags (as the stack of unread material atop my
chairside table mounts ever higher), and also talking
with Z on the phone (she in a rapturously happy mood
because the reading glasses she lost on the bus
yesterday turned up at the transit lost-and-found this
morning) and dashing off a note for her before leaving
(this one with a talking-pumpkin theme for Halloween),
cleaning up the kitchen, making the bed, watering the
plants. And today I also conducted a failed search in
our basement storage closet for Z's "floor chair" which
she'll be needing for the two full days of meditation
slated for her Sufi retreat this weekend. (At one point
I was supposed to attend the second day so that a
visiting Sufi dignitary might bless Z and me as a
couple. But it turns out that this eminence blesses

330

only legally married couples. Deeps don't qualify,
whether same-sex or otherwise. -- And this despite the
man's celebrated liberality and tolerance and also the
widely known fact, Z tells me, that he has a batch of
"illegitimate" kids of his own scattered on several
continents.)
     And so, trotting at times because I was running a
few minutes late, the downhill trek and the bridge
crossing, the view today spectacular with thick white
fog cloaking the A.Q. valley and the lower but not the
upper stories of downtown highrises clustered on the
hillside opposite -- a phenomenon I've never seen before
in this city (but common in my earlier city 2/7).
     A quick stop at the hideaway to pick up my WOC
gear, then the two-block walk to the WOC itself. I beat
Z onto the floor by about two minutes. We stretch and
then tromp adjacent treadmills up on the balcony. We
dish. She's looking exceptionally fine in a red "Talk
Trash with Me" T-shirt and blue headband and clingy blue
running pants. Says my ponytail is off-center, which
she allows doesn't have the same lubricious effect on
her that the off-center ass-seam of my jeans supposedly
does. -- And then after twenty minutes of parallel
iron-pumping, off she goes (stopping by after her shower
as always to say goodbye, except that today she didn't
have time to shower) and I hang around for two more
hours, including another round of treadmilling (but
jogging this time). I don't get out of there until
after nine. And then, after backtracking here to drop
off my WOC bag, I hike the mile uptown and make the
usual circuit there (burgers, chain books, cone) and
then head back (via the old "edge road" this time) and
sit right down at the desk and crack open the J-book and
look up at the clock and it's ten minutes to midnight.
     Well, it's okay for now. I'm still shaping up.
But by the end of the year I'm hoping I'll be where I
want to be on that score and ready for other things.
(This jyzer after all is in his first full year of
Glennarian Stage III. He's seasoned. Can scarcely be
more ready to take on a truly major project. All's to

do now is to figure out exactly which one it'll be.)
     -- The fine loving this morning, it was doubly or
triply so because I turned in an hour late (devoting way
too much time to working up altered cards for Jacob's
mother-in-law Justine and Serafina's daughter Tala on
her fifth birthday -- the one who calls me "Mr. Bean")
and was already tired after sleeping too little the
night before. But the alarm went off shortly after I
hit the bed -- and I took Z's usual side of the futon at
her insistence "So we won't be in the rut" (with "when
we rut" implicit to be sure) -- and she rolled into my
arms and, unusual for her if she wants to rut, just
snuggled with no sign of sexual interest showing for
quite some time. And meanwhile I was slowly turning on,
meaning erecting. And finally a little whimper from her
and we took off into that fine fuck, which ended with an
invag ejac for me and Z breaking into tears of joy after
murmuring "I'm home, I'm home" numerous times. (And
later she said of the slow start: "It was...interesting."
Slowness is not usually her style, though, and wasn't
before we met either, she's assured me, and especially
it's not now because in our first year together she
developed the habit of moving quickly so that whatever
was going to happen would happen before I foozled. So
this is another instance of the ongoing "reversal" fine-
tuning process.)
     Four minutes left. Not enough time to go into the
evenings with Betty and Rob. Best just to hit the men's
room here and then gird up for tonight's visit to the
grittiest bus stop in town.
                    *   *
     This going down in the only hour of the year that
exists twice -- the intercalary "fall back" sixty
minutes when Daylight Savings reverts to Standard Time.
And it's special in this way even for those of us who go
by Nightscoper Upside-down Time, also known as (though
repetitiously not to say slanderously) NUT Time.
     A slow jazzy ballad playing. A car sizzling by
below. The wall clock ticking. I'm curled up on the
new couch (as I'll probably still be thinking of it ten

years from now), the far left side by the reading lamp,
looking out into the living/dining area and beyond that
the kitchen behind its waist-high L-shaped bar-like
wooden counter and to its right the start of the zigzag
hallway leading to the bedroom where Z at this moment is
sleeping. Presumably. Tomorrow for her is another day
of all-out meditating. Ironically meditation can be
very tiring for her. And it calls for full alertness or
otherwise she wastes too much energy warding off
sleepiness and can't focus on the crucial matter of not
focusing on her thoughts, that is, on "letting go" and
"watching them float by" (if I'm following her on this).

  She says she recalls previous Sufi conferences of
bygone eras where she looked around wistfully for
potential "companions," meaning, not to be too coy about
it (and she rarely is), sexual partners. "That's what's
really different about this one." On the other hand
she's been seeing lots of the same old faces. Olwen,
the only person there she really knows (excluding a
certain Amanda I know nothing about myself), told Z she
thinks the mindset produced by meditation is great for
lovemaking after the "sit" is over. (Olwen, by the way,
seriously sprained an ankle the other day and is now
hobbling about on crutches.)

  Tonight we tested Olwen's notion. This came as a
surprise, at least to me, as I was tucking Z into bed at
nine-thirty or so. And Olwen's notion proved correct.
A full-service copulation, ejac included (and at no
extra cost, I'll say, challenging the "semen-retention"
doctrine of the Taoists and the Tantrists and maybe even
certain Sufis). Z said she felt "more relaxed" and
wondered if I could tell the difference. Honestly I
couldn't; her ways of loving on this night didn't seem
to fall outside her usual spectrum, which even in its
most subdued state is still spectacular. What does
stand out for me is how dependable it's becoming that
I'll be able to get it up and in and then to come with
the standard spurt-spurt-spurt (seven or eight of them
usually, I'd estimate, maybe nine once in a while, or in
other words about the same as always, including peak

333

teen years). Interestingly, today's round happened
during what I'd presumed would be a recharge period,
since Z had said beforehand that she'd be going
abstinent for the entire Sufi retreat period.

Also with her away most of the weekend I'm trying
to use the free time to put in extra hours working out
and thus to power myself over the hump on shaping up
(gauged by weights and reps and scale I'm still not back
to where I was before the road trip). It would be the
perfect time to fast, I thought, since I needn't worry
that the resulting enervation might leave me unable to
perform sexually up to the demanding new standard. So
today I ate little and walked much -- about nine miles
in all, hiking clear across town to drop off a set of
our vacation photos for Rob at his bookstore. And then
ironically I was called upon to perform anyway. And
remarkably, I could. So yes, I think the "reversal"
must be for real. I'm indeed "Lazarusing," as Z once
put it (chortling). And isn't "Lazarusing" at least one
step more valiant than Possuming?

Midway during the hike I stopped in for coffee at
an old public-market hangout of mine. I was no longer
recognized there, sad to say, and so had to pay the
regular tourist rate for coffee (an outrageous $1.65 a
cup). In fact I saw no one I recognized myself, staff
or customers. But I wasn't fooled; I hadn't forgotten
the torturous loneliness and banality of my life during
the time I was hanging out there, sometimes as often as
several days a week for a couple of hours or more.

-- And so (as the clock moves within ten minutes of
where it was an hour ago) a few quick recalls regarding
last week.

First, visiting Betty last Saturday night. What
had been intended as a chance for her to get away from
the daily round of single-mom chores and duties -- we
were planning to take her out to dinner and a movie --
somehow wound up with her fixing us dinner (meatloaf)
at home followed by the three of us watching a video
there. I'm quite fond of Betty -- more so than ever
-- but without Kat present (she was staying overnight

at a friend's) the evening dragged rather painfully at
times. The video was special: dredged up by Betty
because our Mentoka tales reminded her of it. It's
about a woman of Turkish descent living in Germany and
forced to prostitute herself. To escape from a gang
of nasty pimps she takes up with an oddball musician
recently released from prison and they head for the
States to start a new life, winding up in a part of
the rural heartland that's never specified but looks a
whole lot like western Mentoka, in a town that might
almost be Turtle Rapids. Small-town American life is
depicted as being shockingly primitive by German
standards. But this only made the movie more fun to
watch, although Z had to leave the room during a
couple of violent incidents (on screen, this is) and
wound up reading a "nonviolent mystery" in Betty and
Manny's miracle Swedish bed (and this caused no
problems; Betty's just as accustomed to Z's
idiosyncrasies as I am, if not more so).

     And also the evening with Rob -- back to that. At
the restaurant we were lucky to find an empty window
table where he could smoke his pipe. He wanted to hear
all about the trip and pressed for more and more detail
(if anyone's a real detail person in our family it's
Rob). We ordered a bottle of wine, spread the trip
photos on every available flat space, and traced the
journey almost mile by mile from beginning to end. Then
I unloaded a bag of birthday presents for him, including
a couple of poetry books (one by Riley U. of Mezzu
days), a used hardback copy of a protojyze favorite of
mine (a randy young Scottish J-slinger hits the big city
two centuries ago), a wooden model (partly hand-painted
by me) of the Fritsch Building in Wachute, and a fifth
of the same kind of scotch he'd accidentally given me
for my birthday. (It was good to be able to lavish some
extra stuff on him after my several lean years.) -- And
in a touching moment he told me he's now thinking he'd
like to be buried in the Sandefjord section of the
graveyard in Turtle Rapids when the time comes -- as a
way of ensuring upkeep of the family graves -- and

wondered if I might want the same. I was startled by
this, but not because I hadn't thought of something like
it for myself in the past. And I'm still thinking about
it. But now, of course, I have Z's wishes to consider,
and I seriously doubt she'll want to be laid out for all
eternity in the very Turtle Rapids boneyard she was so
eager to get out of a few weeks ago. Which is to say her
view on this would be pretty much the same as ol' Mom's
-- and also that of the Turkish woman in the movie.

Rob also gave me a more detailed description than
ever before (and by the way, we've long since moved out
of the pleat in Gregorian time) -- gave me a description
of the brief first round of his relationship with Gail a
quarter century ago. They met in the spring and "dated"
a few times; then Rob went home to Gatewood for the
summer while Gail stayed on in Lahontan. When he
returned in the fall she'd converted "from a guitar-
strumming longhaired hippie chick into a Jesus Freak."
They didn't last long after that. On what ironically
turned out to be their last date for about fifteen years
they joined Mother and Dad, who'd come up for the
weekend, at a U.M. football game and then they all went
out to dinner -- Gail's introduction to the family
turning out to be almost a duplicate of Lady S's (as
Rob knew because he was there in Mentoka Falls as a
twelve-year-old for the Lady S intro). Most touching
about Rob's telling of this story was his sudden pained
comment, "I'm just thinking Gail wouldn't like me to be
talking about that period. It's really embarrassing to
her now." I assured him I'd never mention it in her
presence and certainly wouldn't chaff her about it. (I
knew about the Jesus Freak part before; I just hadn't
heard the story in detail from Rob himself. Mother had
filled me in on most of it years ago.)

-- Wow, I'm still jyzing away. Could even toss in
a few more odd tidbits about the week.

For one, I had a wild sexy dream about Lady V, the
first I can recall since my early days with Z. But
sorry to say the details have all vanished.

Another, a photo of Nathan L. appeared in the

reunion notes for Z's college class in the U.C. alum
mag. He's one of the Cawk guys who traumatized her
youth by chasing her home from grade school yelling
racial epithets -- "Jap," "Chink," etc., including the
nonracial but equally ugly "crip" -- and later, after
moving away from the hood, he reappeared as a fellow
student at U.C. and at one point tried to hit on her at
a party when both were drunk, and she finally got some
"cosmic revenge" by vomiting on his shoes.

     And: Z's boss, Dale, said it's not the right-wing
icon Duke I resemble, it's that French guy, Gerald...
Gerard...you know. The same thing Z said last year!
(Rob hears this about himself quite often. And of him
I'd still say it's a whole lot closer to being true.)

     And: one night when I arrived home from work I
found my bedside radio sitting on the floor in the hall.
An electrical outage had caused the time to reset and
the alarm went off at midnight and Z couldn't figure out
how to shut it off and wound up yanking the cord from
the socket, accidentally bringing down at the same time
a shelfload of papers and books. She was not happy
about this. And so I was forced to remind her that her
alarm wakes me up almost every morning and when it does
(because she wears earplugs and frequently can't hear
it) I have to wake her up to shut it off (because it's
way too complicated for me to figure out on the spot,
just like mine for her), and sometimes this takes what
seem like endless minutes as the high-pitched beeper
keeps yelping. So who's suffered more from the other's
complex alarm mechanisms, I suggested she ask herself.
Ooh yeah, she said; she hadn't thought of that. So rack
one up for the "lawyer-like" jyzerman.

     Lots more of these little tales I could come up
with. Every time! All of them tiny things, obviously,
but not necessarily so tiny at the moment they happen
nor in the way they cumulatively make up a couple of
conjoined lives. -- And we talk about them, write notes
about them. They become the basis of everyday motifs,
woven together, one braiding into the next....

[Deep Jyze]

33

    We roll into November. Jyze is showing up in these
pages the requisite eight days after the previous entry
but a full twelve days after the previous official J-day
(and the first number there, eight, I'm not even sure
about). The next scheduled J-day is Thursday and I hope
to be back on track by then. This means I'll need to do
a whole lot of jyzing tomorrow and maybe squeeze some in
Tuesday too. Because in the twenty-five minutes left to
me here at the hideaway tonight I won't be cranking out
very much at all.
    What's going on? Day after tomorrow is election
day. Our next-door neighbors at 1511 (in 202, the ones
who were robbed) are moving out, or by now, since it's
past midnight, probably already have (and it follows
that election day, strictly speaking, is tomorrow, yes).
All the trees in our hilltop hood that can turn yellow
or red or some shade in between have done so and many
have already lost most of their leaves. Here and there
a carved pumpkin still sits on a porch, its facial
features, if any, or even if none, sagging
surrealistically. And then Z and I have gone through a
number of small crises -- but in any life with Z small
crises are strictly par for the course (and to be sure
are part of what makes the course such a kick).
    Meanwhile our sex life is in what I hope is a
merely temporary downswing. Why this is happening now I
have no idea. In the past week I've come only once and
that was from a Z handjob. Another three or four times,
including tonight, I've been inside her but haven't been
able to push it to money (jizz!) and gave up -- stopped

on my own, by choice in a couple of cases and because I
was deflating in the others -- after she'd come a time
or two or three. Yesterday, owing to what was probably
a mutual misreading of wants/needs, we didn't get it on
at all (and this in turn became the main source of
today's small crisis).

Last come for me was Friday afternoon. So I'm way
overdue. It could be I was unusually inhibited earlier
tonight by the seemingly high probability she was about
to burst into major meltdown mode. Hopefully the crisis
has eased now.

Ooh, such scuzzy, spunky and yet also sometimes
spunkless stuff here. But this is how it must be if I'm
to describe what seems most important right now in this
old jyzer's life.

So I'll shut down operations for tonight and resume
them tomorrow with an update.

*   *

-- And now, even though technically it's still the
same day (for twenty more minutes), the update.

Last night when I went to bed at five or so I was
feeling fresh, from having slept almost nine hours the
previous night, and randy. In line with our recently
launched "All's Fair" policy (either of us may initiate
lovemaking at any time; quarantine "Perky Alert" nights
are no more) I initiated. And she turned on right away
and so did I. But for some reason my most indispensable
sexual instrument never became more than semi-involved
tumescence-wise, and when I stuffed it home anyway in
hopes it would crank up the rest of the way once inside,
it gave a few sputters and then foozled completely. "I
think we need another road trip," Z joked, but kindly,
consolingly -- seeing I needed this. (But then again,
we'd just read in one of the Sunday papers that the
average USAn couple does the deed once a week, and even
at our least boffish we're far exceeding that -- and in
our state of relatively advanced decrepitude -- so
what's to whine about? Let's be grateful here! And I
am! And I mean it! -- But of course this doesn't mean
I, or I'll even dare to say we, shouldn't be trying to

339

do better. Of course we should! Being able to do
better would mean a great deal to both of us! -- What's
more it's because we're already doing much better than
we were doing earlier in our time together that we can
be fairly sure of the truth of this. And I think we
both believe, despite the occasional setback, that the
general trend is still upward. Or to put it
differently: if the "reversal" is itself reversing, it's
not necessarily reversing completely or permanently.)

   Meanwhile life goes on. Whooee, does it ever!
(Last night, I should mention, one reason Z was so
interested in sexing the cherry -- and did get off
several times despite my e-funk -- was that an erotic
scene in the movie "Beloved," which she'd seen with "the
girls," had aroused her. "Something in the way this guy
in the movie moved reminded me of you." -- Also she
said my "gen set" had looked very sexy in the morning
when she bestowed a farewell kiss upon it -- "your
rollers looked so shapely and rosy!" -- and the image
had stuck with her all day, and if I hadn't "initiated"
right away when I slipped into bed she would've done so
herself.)

   And what else. Tomorrow's election day and Z will
be getting up early so she can rush down to the main
intersection on the far side of the high bridge by seven
a.m. to hold aloft a "No on 200" banner. ("After you
retire will you register to vote again?" she asked
plaintively. Well, maybe I will and maybe I won't. I'm
just grateful that this year I haven't been called upon
to deliver my spiel on voting and nightscoping and how
and why the twain can never meet. -- It does help,
though, that Z's pal Manny was an avid nonvoter. "He
thought it just supported the system." And of course it
does do that. But then what doesn't? More to the
point, what will change the system for the better, yet
without making life even harder for people in other
lands depending on, say, other systems? A very, very
tough question! Would a reformed, more efficient, more
productive, more prosperous, more economically dominant
U.S. be better for the world as a whole? For the planet

as a whole?   -- But...maybe this question is a tiny bit
less vexing, whether realistically so or not, for those
of us -- however small our numbers -- who believe in the
long-term transformative powers of jyze.)

      -- Then there was Halloween. This year we did
virtually nothing to observe it. I bought a few cheapo
buttons and earrings for Z and Kat (and a card for Betty
so she wouldn't feel left out) but I never got to see
Kat wearing the earrings and I never got to wear the
button I bought for myself, a carved copper pumpkin face
smoking a cigar that lights up. We had hoped to drop in
on the Halloween party thrown at the digi-cafe by our
favorite radical fortnightly -- if only for an hour or
so because the crowd would no doubt be too young for us
-- but it turned out I had a big job that night and
couldn't do it. My celebration was limited to feasting
on leftovers from the scope office's Halloween blowout,
and I'm still disgusted with myself for overindulging on
those. (Couldn't help myself, I was once again that
hungry kid with the unappeasable sweet tooth -- and the
fact that I was doing all this feasting on the sly,
unknown to the scope firm, only made it more exciting,
just as ferreting out the secret hiding places for
sweets did when I was a kid. Thrill of the forbidden!)

      We went out Saturday night instead -- hiked down to
the Asian quarter to see a production of "Flipzoids." I
didn't bring up the fact to Z -- I had mentioned it once
before to her, long ago, and I don't know if she
remembered -- but Lady U had performed several times in
that same space and I couldn't help but be conscious of
this. -- Neither Z nor I liked "Flipzoids" very much, I
should note. It revisited the familiar issues around
immigration from the Philippines in mostly hackneyed
ways and the acting was barely passable at best.
(Interestingly, Aida had been asked to play one of the
parts -- the most poorly acted one when we saw it -- and
turned it down.)

      And what else is doing with Aida? She's becoming
fonder of Z's former lover Kirk. And surprisingly,
considering that declared fact, she and Z appear to be

getting along better now. For a while it seemed a major
crisis had arisen -- Aida's ex, Tom, wanted her to take
Charles, their son, full time, instead of the fifty/
fifty deal they've been holding to for several years --
but then he changed his mind. Nonetheless Aida's view
on this crisis scraped fingernails up and down my spine:
she was ready to boot Tom out of Charles's life for good
if he persisted on the "full time" idea, even if it
would only be temporary. For hours after hearing this I
was stuck in queasy replays of the Lady S era.

     -- And speaking of crises, we had our weekly
portion of same in apartment 203. I can think of at
least three. One had to do with a slight Z received at
work from the high honcho herself, the utility boss, who
before the assembled utility execs and exec assistants
-- of whom Z is now officially one -- called one of Z's
proposals "stupid." The moment I got home that night I
was called into the bedroom to do some major soothing
(and did manage to persuade her -- I think -- to scuttle
the revenge mission she was cooking up). And she
thanked me later for playing the therapist role and
heading her off from "going postal."

     The second crisis, which is still with us, was
ignited by a note from the holder of Z's school loan
saying her loan payments will be increasing now that her
salary's gone up. This laid poor Z low and got her to
worrying about her credit-card debt, and that in turn
gave rise to some glooming about her longstanding "three
addictions" (sex, work, money) and especially the last-
named of those. She's now laid bare to me her credit
records and she's talking about seeing a financial
counselor and wants me to accompany her when she does,
and I've said I will. (And we've talked plenty about
this. And I'm trying to cajole her into taking it all a
little less seriously. Today I altered an old noirish
movie postcard for "Condemned Women" to say "Condemned
Tri-Addiction Women" and added scarlet triple-A's to the
brows of the furious women shown locked behind bars.
"They got HOOKED -- BEWARE -- now they're COOKED." (In
recent weeks I've been leaving her an altered postcard

when I go out in the afternoon. This was today's.)
    And the third crisis had to do with our mixed
signals about sexplay Saturday night. No time to go
into this now, though, and perhaps that's just as well.
    -- One a.m. already. And since I'm at the hideaway
(maybe I should call it the staging room, I was thinking
today) I've got to be hiking up the hill right now.
    (Yes, Nolan next door is running an escort service.
And Donald, sweet guy that he is -- as Z thinks too --
it turns out he did three years in the pen for tax
evasion and that's where he picked up his paralegal
skills.)

34

    Couldn't do it Tuesday or Wednesday night. Jyze,
I'm saying. A couple of big rush scoping jobs came up
(one I'm still working on) and no gaps opened in other
realms. True, I could've given up some basic reading
time, but it seems I just don't want to do that anymore.
So now we've come to a new J-day and I have no choice
but to abandon the previous entry in an incomplete
state.
    However. Before starting up this entry I put in a
full hour working on the chart for next year's jyze
"special edition." And I'm pumped. It'll be more than
twice the normal number of pages -- and at the same low,
low price! So to heck with all that other stuff.
    This at the hideaway. And what's truly bizarre,
it's only half past seven in the evening. But still I
have no choice but to tender the usual apology: can't
hang around long. Rush job to finish up.
    So first a word on the election results. When I

arrived home Tuesday night at the usual time an unusual
scene greeted me: the TV was turned on in the bedroom,
its garish flickering light revealing Z stretched out
sideways asleep beneath just the white comforter
(usually the bedroom door's open these days but it's
dark in there and the air cleaners are roaring away).
The strange, almost tortured posture she was twisted
into -- looking as if she'd been strangled -- suggested
Initiative 200 had won, and that turned out to be the
case. It won big. Affirmative action in our state is
done for, at least in the form we've known it. And Z is
devastated. (Yesterday at the WOC we schemed about
political buttons she might make to vent her anger.
"Colorblind? No -- Color Proud!") Not too surprisingly,
for the moment she's seeing me more than usual as one of
"them," the privileged Eurusan colonial-settler majority
(over ninety percent of state voters this year were
Cawk). She admitted as much herself. "It'll take me at
least a week to get over this."

Yet the overall election results were much better
than most people, myself included, had predicted, and
this was true both locally and nationally. In general
the further right of the two major right-wing parties
(and of course there are no other major parties) took it
on the chin for pushing their reactionary agenda so
hard. In this state the initiatives proposing to boost
the minimum wage and legalize medical use of marijuana
passed; the one proposing to outlaw certain types of
abortion failed. The slightly more moderate of those
same two major right-wing parties regained control of
both houses of the state legislature. This means that
for at least the next two years the political atmosphere
statewide should be somewhat less hostile than it has
been to the left-leaning views favored by the vast
majority of the residents of Jyze City (though Z's not
seeing this just yet).

Her remark yesterday: "I felt like the people at
work would chase me home yelling racist epithets" (that
is, as did those Cawk schoolmates of hers when she was a
kid).

Meanwhile she and I are still in a down period sexually. She's complaining about it too. "A month or two ago we were so much hotter!" she moaned on the phone yesterday. (An hour later she called back just to be sure it was clear she wasn't saying she thought I was the only one responsible for this setback.) -- Right now we seem to be engaged in a bit of a withholding contest. She's announced this is "Let G Sleep" month and therefore she won't "initiate" in the morning when she awakens. But last month she was insisting I should let her sleep a solid eight hours, meaning I shouldn't "initiate" at my bedtime, and she's not taking that back. So it would seem we're stymied. And therefore she's now proposing we talk it over again. And of course I agree we should do that and I stand ready to do my part whenever she can free up the time. Meanwhile the demand for erotic action on both sides seems substantially reduced.

The other night she pouted, "I don't think Possum likes me anymore." She seemed serious, and right away I was fearing a slippery-slope slide into meltdown mode. Although it's true her natural way of dealing with any perceived problem is to try to shine a spotlight on it, for this particular problem (and this particular person, meaning me) this kind of approach often makes matters worse. It did last year and it probably will now if she persists with it. So far she seems to be easing off and pulling back, but I'm still wary. We're writing notes back and forth about it. They're teasing and playful but clearly show more edge than usual.

We're also on the brink of a serious talk about her "three addictions" (the "dreaded scarlet triad"), with the main focus on the financial one. She's provided me with all the papers regarding her various loans and credit-card debt. The amount totals roughly 70K. Revealing this fact to me, she said, "was even worse than telling you about my herpes." She's made me promise not to spill a word about it to anyone (not that I'd ever dream of doing such a thing). And I'm toying with the idea of using my deep reserves as collateral

for a loan to pay off her credit-card debt, a good
portion of which is or soon will be charging usurious
interest rates of almost twenty percent (with bank loans
available now, if I'm right, at under eight percent).

That's a quick overview of the large issues of the
moment. (I also want to say I'm thinking of using the
deep reserves not just as collateral to pay off her
debts but to pay them off directly. Why not? After
all, when I retire -- so to speak -- my income will
actually go up, since Social Security will pay me about
ten percent more per month than I'm averaging from Jyzer
Ink now. If she'd agree to pay our full apartment rent
in perpetuity -- thus compensating for the quarterly
investment income I'd be losing -- I just might do it.
In effect everything would be the same except she'd be
paying me a much lower interest rate on her debt than
she's currently paying the bank and, especially, the
credit-card companies.)

-- Next the hike uptown to the scope office. And
no dinner tonight either. I'm still determined to get
over the (maddeningly resistant) hump on shaping up.
I'm working hard at the WOC, even jogging three miles
per visit on the treadmills, yet the pounds aren't
melting away as hoped. So now I'm sucking on dried
fruit as my sole permissible between-meals snack (and
discovering I like doing so and thinking I'll continue
with it indefinitely). Also I'm substituting a protein
bar for one of my three daily meals. Tonight's dinner
is such a one. I need a breakthrough.

*   *

Because I'd finished most of my scoping work last
night, I thought I'd be able to launch into the jyze
tonight around eleven. But I messed up and it's now
12:17. And the whole building's rocking out as usual
on Friday nights, and I don't mean just metaphorically.
I mean you almost need an aluminum-frame walker to make
it down the hall to the men's room. At times the
windows vibrate so loudly they seem about to shatter.

And on to page two. The news.

Which above all else is this: we finally got it on

again.

Last night when I tiptoed in after work I found a card from Z on my chair saying "Nookie Tension Building." This was written on the back side of a postcard showing a painting of the hideaway building. Later she explained why she chose this card: not because, as I thought at first, the painting looked vaguely vulvar or to razz me about the "sex workers" partying here on weekend nights (though I haven't seen any lately), but because she associates this building with tense nookie-related moments in our early days.

And this time, happily, the jyzer's temperamental flesh-based "detensifier" worked. Not fully, and not immediately when I went to bed (though I can't be sure about this since Z didn't respond then anyway), but well enough to keep a "yes-fuck fuck" going for a respectable period. And that's just a whole lot better than having to settle for a "fuckless fuck."

At first I thought the night might turn out to be a repeat of the previous one, with both parties more or less resentfully holding back. But when the alarm went off she snuggled up and then when I started turning on -- wanger creaking upward and outward in that delightful aching/glowing/ratcheting way, internal blood spurt by internal blood spurt, sort of like breaths blown into a weiner balloon -- she responded, meanwhile whispering "Stay asleep now," and she went down on me for a while, and then I "sleepily" spun her around sixty degrees or so and slowly and deliciously pushed on in while she lay on her back and I on my side, and then was able to get her off four or five times while thus conjoined (simultaneously working on her nipples and clit for two or three of them) and then rose up into basic missionary for a fifth or sixth before I faded (and she kept playfully whispering "Stay asleep" the whole time).

Later today she told me she liked that one a lot. "I want more sex! We must have more sex! Enough of not having enough sex!" Flashing memories of that morning session had kept her horny all day, she said; she even confessed to finding men on the street and at work more

"visually interesting" while she was in such a state.
And she had a new proposal: that I make a practice of
hitting the bed right after arrival home at one-thirty
a.m. (but after chowing down) and then getting up again
later if I can't sleep. I said this probably wouldn't
work for me -- I need time to unwind, just as she does
when she gets home -- but I proposed instead that I go
to bed an hour earlier than I've been doing, since that
way I'd at least be a bit more rested when her alarm
went off. In the end we decided to try that. And we
agreed to drop the "Let G Sleep" campaign, declaring it
an ignominious and yet somehow still honorable failure.

*   *

-- Yup, two nights later, same station and almost
same time, quarter past twelve. I tear myself away from
list-making (trying to come up with tentative venues for
next year's jyze, in advance!) to see if I can very
quickly go deep. Or anyway as deep as quickness allows.
But first the chronology news. Last night Z and I
did dinner with Jess and Gwen (winding up at the same
Japanese restaurant in Z's old hood where she and I had
one of our early dates a year and a half ago) and then
the four of us saw "Pleasantville" at the theater across
the street. Today Z and I met Betty up at the bargain
theater farther north and saw "Next Stop Wonderland" and
then, while looking for a place to get coffee, happened
upon an exciting new bookstore/cafe. The only problem
is it's about fifteen miles off our usual beaten track.
And next the latest sexual/romantic developments.
In a nutshell, we're suddenly back into a hot phase.
Yesterday morning she got me off with a humdinger of a
handjob (so explosive was it, she marveled afterwards,
that she saw a gob of come fly by her nose as she
nibbled on my chest while looking up toward my face and
pumping away down below). Then last night when we did
our usual Saturday-night thing of reading in bed we got
it on right at the start, and then early this morning
went at it again when she woke up. And this latter
session was a special kind: she intentionally slowed
herself down and tried it "your way," as she said, slow

348

and sensual, and even climbed aboard as I lay on my back
(erect to the max too) and she got herself off a couple
of times that way, and then later when I finally started
to fade while atop her I slid down and licked her off
just as a bit of lagniappe. ("And it was good!")

When I got up I found she'd written me a short poem
about realizing she could be "more open and relaxed"
with me now. One of the lines rubbed me a bit wrong and
when I said so, in an unobjectionable way, as I thought,
she burst into tears and I had to scramble like crazy to
keep the matter from blowing up into something major.
As she explained (not at all for the first time, though
it almost seemed she thought this would be news to me),
most of the men in her life have been "wham-bam-thank-
you-ma'am types" and that's the kind of sex she's always
been drawn to: fast, hard, overpowering, impersonal
almost. "Story of O" type, she likes to say. Now she's
trying to adjust to my vastly different ways. (I felt I
had little choice but to reply to her line about all the
wham-bam men with the true statement that most of the
women I've known have also found my slow/stretch-it-out/
"mutuality" way of loving very different from that of
the men they've known, and this pleased her about as
much as her wham-bam statement pleased me. Nor did she
fail to mention that all these men of hers had been
plenty happy with her way of getting it on, nor did I
fail to reply that my way with those women of mine
usually seemed to go over pretty well too.) -- But we
worked it out. Basically all I had to do was
acknowledge for the umpteenth time the simple truth that
she's sexually gifted to a degree far beyond anything
I've ever come across or even heard about. (Sounds
hokey, I suppose, or at least diplomatically hyperbolic.
But it's not. It's the straight goods.)

And there it is, the quick depth such as it is.
Now if I manage things well maybe I can add some
shadings next time. That'll be tomorrow night --
because it's a Monday and I won't be working -- and I
think I'll commit myself right now to two full hours of
jyzing. See if I can catch up to where I'm spoze to be.

Then the next entry will be tough timewise because
J-day falls on Friday and this is a heavy workweek for
me and we have tickets for the Polish film festival
that night and then early Saturday we'll be leaving for
a reprise of last year's first out-of-state road trip
-- same destination, right down to the funky old grand
hotel -- but this time with Wei and Alison accompanying
us, or rather we'll be accompanying them in their van.

*   *

    A day later and I didn't make it -- but almost
did. It's twenty past eleven instead of eleven. A
hundred minutes to go at it instead of the full one-
twenty.

    Resting near the top of my deskpad are six dried
apricots and two dried pears ready for gobbling like
bonbons. This dried fruit is pretty much a new thing
for me -- I've tried it before but found it wanting
and don't even remember why -- but now I'm moving into
it in a big way. I suppose this too is something I
ought to credit Z for. Thanks to her I'm becoming --
well, not exactly more health-conscious, no, but more
health-committed. If not in all ways, at least in
some. (In the old days my worktime snacks tended to
be cookies or potato chips from mom-and-pop stores.)
    So today's been fine. Mondays almost always are.
As usual I dawdled too long at home -- mainly because I
was putting together a card for Z, combining picture
postcards featuring the Eurusan Duke (for whom I'm now
infamously, even if wholly inaccurately, a near double)
and the female Italian superstar (who's undeniably Z-
like) -- and I had to rush to meet Z at the WOC at five.
On the phone she told me she loved the way I called out
as she was leaving the bedroom after kissing me goodbye,
"Didn't you forget something?" It was a plea for the
ritual Possum kiss. "You'll say it's just the lark in
me talking," she said on the phone, "but I can't stop
thinking you're always so cute in the morning." And
I'm still reaping the returns on Jess's remark Saturday
night that I'm "looking so trim." Now Z suddenly thinks
I'm looking trim too. "I just love to gaze at your

350

body" (saying this while leaning toward me so no one
else could hear as we strode adjoining treadmills
tonight). "You know what? I think we should have more
open-robe days -- when we walk around the apartment in
robes and we're required to leave the belts untied." My
wholly sincere reply: "Okay by me!"

    -- I've also taken to socializing at the WOC. Over
the months I've gotten to know a number of people there
and I enjoy bantering with them. Z never ceases to
profess amazement that I'm turning out to have this
casual sociable side. Among my favorites are Jay the
Scandi juggler, Clio the fresh-faced Asiusan realtor
(who grew up in greater Kaskieki just blocks from where
Popeye lived), Malcolm the gay Eurusan diversity
facilitator who looks like a skinnier, more affable very
first premier of the Soviet Union, Marcus the bearded
Afrusan former football star who has an airhole with a
plastic plug in his throat to help him breathe during
sleep-apnea episodes (in three years he's sliced off 120
pounds to get down to 320 and is massively muscled), and
Corey the police detective of Samoan ancestry who worked
as a weightroom instructor for years and struts around
with something like an invisible spotlight shining on
his remarkable oiled-up buffness. And then there are
Jess and Leola from Z's office, and once in a while I
see Leola's husband Gerry too, and I often talk with
Estella the Eurasian (Portugal and Hong Kong) marathoner
when we jog on adjoining treadmills (she does anywhere
from six to twelve miles on the things every day except
Saturday, when she puts in fifteen at the park).

    Next a little follow-up on what I was jyzing about
yesterday (for once I'm actually doing this!). First,
going back to the way Z and I worked it out after the
brief "wham-bam" mini-meltdown, I neglected to mention
we immediately tumbled onto the couch and got it on
there, but not going beyond nipple comes for her (zilch
of any kind for me) because we were due to leave for the
bargain theater in a few minutes. And I can even
produce a verbatim copy of the short "instant poem"
(hers) which led to the incident. Here it is:

[Deep Jyze]

11/8
   I don't get what I'm
               used to.
   My body questions
               the difference.
   I am a lab rat
               pressing old
               buttons
   while pellets roll in
               from other directions.
   My cells mull the
               possibilities.

I shouldn't say another word about this. But I will. I
don't want her cells to be mulling, I want them to be
celebrating! And my saying something to this effect to
her (and lovingly) is what led to her writing the poem.
(Obviously I shouldn't've said anything to her. I
should've gone directly to finding new ways to get her
cells to celebrating.)
    Next the evening with Jess and Gwen. It had been a
long time since we'd seen "the doggies," Cy and Kiba,
but they still remembered us. The newly refurbed garden
with its rock sculptures and flagstone pathways and
layered exotic flower clusters was looking spectacular
(and all this in a yard of ordinary size). The house
has been repainted again, covering up the bad paint job
Jess's father had done (and what's more he applied
colors outside the range J&G had requested). Jess's
mother had just left for home after a weeklong visit
and had sworn to keep silent on the fate of Pop's paint
job. Otherwise Mom's visit was an "unmitigated
disaster" and Jess grumbled about it for much of the
evening, humorously I thought, but to the point where
Gwen later upbraided her for going on and on like that
(as we learned from Jess herself today at the WOC).
    That very day Gwen had bought a new black leather
jacket identical to the one she'd given Jess for her
birthday. Now the two of them were dressed almost
exactly alike -- black dance oxfords, tight powder-blue

352

jeans, black tops, the black jackets -- and they were a
bit embarrassed by the "twinsy effect" they were
presenting, but neither one could bear not to wear her
new jacket. (While out shopping they'd "paid a visit to
the rings" -- the wedding rings they have on layaway at
a jeweler's. Gwen says she does this at least once a
week on her own just to make sure the rings are okay.
-- Like Z and me, J&G are planning to "get married" next
year, although of course strictly speaking they can't do
so legally. One reason Jess was bad-mouthing her mother
was her mother's lack of enthusiasm for the wedding
plans. "She didn't ask me a single question about
them." J&G also offered to hold a wedding reception for
us in their new garden and I'm pushing for that as the
site over Aida's backyard, but so far Z is unwilling to
commit. I've also said that if Z insists on having Aida
at the wedding itself -- which will be limited to a very
small group -- then I want Jess and Gwen to be there
too, and she's agreed to this. Probably the only other
attendees will be Rob and Gail and Wei and Alison. I
have no other candidates at all. (If I had to come up
with a body or two to provide some groom-side balance
I'd probably have to fall back on my exercise buddies at
the WOC. Or maybe Kar and Kerani, I suppose. -- But
why am I going on and on about this? This is a topic
for next year's annal!)

*   *

Talk about rushed. This round I've left myself all
of twenty-two minutes. Then no more free time until day
after tomorrow, Friday, which is also the next scheduled
official J-day. And precious little free time then.

This going down at the scope office, in one of
several upholstered chairs clustered in the entrance
waiting area, right beneath the clock (which is set to
run seven minutes fast, I'm remembering now, so I'm a
little better off than I'd been thinking -- just about
enough better off to cover these first two paragraphs
plus maybe a couple of lines in the one coming up).

It's Veterans Day. For Z it's a holiday. Yeesh,
was she ever hot for some loving last night! And again

353

this morning! And again this afternoon! -- except this
afternoon I had to be the naysayer because for me
today's not a holiday. And poor Z lying there literally
writhing on the couch -- but having fun playing the role
to be sure. (And also whimpering about feeling too
languorous to do the vacuuming -- one of her chores --
she'd been talking for weeks about doing today.)

   Some luscious moments. And also, just as good if
not better, some close tender ones. The mushiest of
these latter came last night as we pillow-talked in the
silvery dawn light on a number of topics, including the
latest twists in her ongoing struggle with Aida.
"You're my best friend now," she told me. It wasn't the
first time she'd said it but this time she herself
seemed moved by the words, as if she meant them in a way
she hadn't before. (Something similar: at the WOC she
asked me to help her come up with some new exercises and
even to design her next workout program. It was an open
show of trust of a kind I hadn't seen from her before.
-- And we've been talking about trust a fair amount
lately because of an article she came across that
explores the concept from a cultural-anthropology
standpoint. And this takes me back about twenty years
to the time when the impasse with Lady S on Elgie had me
agonizing over similar issues -- and that experience in
turn enables me to talk about these issues today in a
way I'm sure I wouldn't otherwise be able to do and so
makes having gone through the agonies back then seem to
be producing something like a long-delayed payoff.)

   The latest twist with Aida is that now she's saying
she misses seeing me and even hopes I'll pitch in with
baby-sitting for Charles. Personally I think it's a
ploy -- she may be fearing I'll veto her bid to do our
wedding reception, especially if Z's told her I'm
leaning that way (though she says she can't recall doing
so) -- and also I feel she's again trying to exploit me
concerning Charles. Z swears Aida has no conception
anything's wrong between me and her, but after all
that's gone down over the past year and a half I just
can't believe this. Z also thinks Aida still resents me

"unconsciously" for having supposedly queered their
friendship. Yet Z herself says their friendship was
already falling apart a year before she and I met.

Hot loving moments -- better to go back to those.
Two comes for me, one a hard-driving quickie which was
about as lusty a fuck as I've ever thrown (but not my
normal style, admittedly, which isn't to say I disliked
it -- not hardly).

And I'm again rethinking next year's jyze. The
latest idea is to start it up in July and stay with it
for twelve months, with six-month breaks before and
after. In both cases the break would go for making a
dent or two in my long list of neglected projects.
-- But more on that another time. I'm outta here.

                    *   *

Kwikjyze. Next afternoon, three p.m., and I should
be leaving any moment for downtown. (Up at one, reading
the papers and Sunday's far-coast book review since
then.) And propped on the table in front of me, the
large window sign that once said "No! on 200" but now
reads, after Z's alteration of it, "No rest for the
rutting!!" But last night we did rest. First time in a
while. What, a week or so. We do go in spurts in our
current era.

I couldn't let this eighter pass without noting a
major political episode. The temptation's just too
great. This past weekend the supremely abrasive holier-
(and far-righter-) than-thou speaker of the house in
D.C. resigned. His party's wide-ranging failures in
last week's elections basically forced him out.

I see these election results (as do many others) as
a repudiation of the so-called New Puritanism which the
far right has been trying to foist on the country (as
epitomized by the campaign to impeach the president for
"lying about" being involved in a trivial affair).
"Down with liberal morality once and for all," the bad
guys were saying. Now the public has spoken and said:
"No, instead it's down with you."   -- And for sure,
even though I don't consider myself a liberal, I'm happy
about this and newly hopeful in certain realms.

[Deep Jyze]

     Still to do before I leave: make the bed, spiff up
the kitchen, water the plants, write Z a note, get
dressed. Eep! Wrapping a set of the road-trip photos
for mailing to Jeff and Angie and writing a note to
accompany them will again have to wait.

35

     -- Except it's not J-day. That fell on Friday the
13th and I don't know if it can be written off as a
matter of bad luck or not, but I'm arriving in these
pages two days late. A dark and stormy Sunday night --
typically nasty in the way of November storms around
here -- and it also happens to be Dad's birthday. He
would've turned eighty-one today.
     Despite the storm I hiked a mile up the old middle
road to score a vanilla-yogurt cone. Luckily this trek
came during a relatively untempestuous period. Earlier,
walking down from the hilltop at eight p.m. (shortly
after Wei and Alison dropped us off at the end of our
three-hour drive home, with my stay in the apartment
limited to a change of clothes, a makeshift meal of two
tomato sandwiches, and a quick tumble in the sack with
the fabulous Zoelie B.) -- after all this, I say, I had
to negotiate an obstacle course of fallen signs and tree
branches, large wavy puddles, even a couple of cars
abandoned in the middle of a side street for no obvious
reason, and meanwhile dodge all manner of blowing debris
-- newspapers, garbage, cardboard boxes, a plastic
recycling bin. Truly it was an adventure, especially up
in the desolate warehouse district at the eastern end of
the Asian quarter. (And for the first time in years I
tied the drawstrings of the hood on my green jacket --

very tightly -- because the wind was so fierce and cold
that the rain was blowing upwards at times like ice
needles jabbing my cheeks and chin and lips.)

Earlier we'd passed through the main body of the
storm while rocking along the freeway in Wei and
Alison's perilously high-riding van. But we were
talking up such a storm of our own we didn't really take
much notice of what was going on outside.

Before leaving town Saturday morning a couple of
notable moments. One, Z wrote out a kind of pledge --
did this completely on her own -- which pretty much laid
to rest the trust issue (and it's only right she did
this, since she'd brought it up and made so much of it
in the first place). Essentially it declared her
"trust" that we would be together the rest of our lives
-- as a kind of "living trust," as it were, she
explained. As a statement of commitment it struck me as
being on the same level as the "troth" pledge I made to
her on Valentine's Day nine months ago, and so I propped
it atop the green plastic stackers in the bedroom right
next to the big "troth" card. True, it's been a while
since I felt she might be less than fully committed to
me. But I'm still glad she's put it in writing so I can
gaze up at it or remind myself (or her) of it during my
shaky spells, just as she does (all of those) with the
"troth" card during hers.

And the other notable moment, I flip-flopped on
Aida and decided to make a big new effort to get along
with her. And if this means doing some baby-sitting for
Charles or even double-dating with Aida and Z's old
boyfriend Kirk, so be it. It's not that I'm any happier
than before with Aida's treatment of me, or that I
believe she really does "miss" seeing me and will suffer
terribly if I'm not part of her life, but rather that I
just don't want to be responsible for causing further
tensions between her and Z. Which is to say: I don't
want Z to be hurting because their friendship is falling
apart when I might be able to do something to help keep
it going. It's no big deal for me to swallow a little
pride and try to get along with Aida. I should just do

it, and so I will, and that's bloody that. (But I also
should note in advance Aida seems to know instinctively
how to press my hot buttons and I might not be able to
pull this off despite all the noble intentions.)

   And I told Z about my new jyze "special edition"
plan. I even hinted ever so gingerly it might entail
postponing the marriage a few months strictly for jyze
charting purposes. She laughed off this latter part; I
don't think she thought I was serious. And maybe I
wasn't. If it seems likely to upset her too much, I
wasn't. In which case: back to the charting.

   So then the trip. This time we stayed in a smaller
room on the third floor of the same vintage hotel (Wei
and Alison by sheer luck drew a larger room on the
seventh floor). After getting little sleep Friday night
-- about three hours -- I managed to stay passably alert
for the drive down but only by gobbling caffeine pills.
That same afternoon shortly after arrival we visited the
Saturday market, a kind of ongoing indoor/outdoor crafts
fair, where Z spoke with one of her favorite eco-
conscious Afrusan jewelers about making wedding rings
for us from glass shards found on beaches. (Z decided
months ago this was the way she wanted to go for her own
ring and I said I'd be happy to wear the same kind of
ring if she'd like, but as of now she seems to be
rethinking the whole idea and has placed no orders.)

   Then to the major bookstore in town (and one of the
finest anywhere). We staked out a table in the cafe and
for the next couple of hours, taking turns, one of us
held the fort there while the other three prowled the
store (though I nodded out during my café watch, my head
resting on my arms on the table). Then to a nearby
warehouse-district "Gulf Coast style" restaurant for a
late dinner -- good too, and not too expensive, and my
first taste of lamb shishkebab in a very long time.
Then back to the hotel, where we, the two couples,
immediately retired to our separate rooms.

   Z had let me know a day earlier she was sensing a
herpes outbreak coming on (those mysterious "prodomo"
rumblings) and by now she was pretty sure it had arrived

-- or if it wasn't that, it was a hemorrhoid -- and so we restricted our loving in the usual "H rag" way and it turned out to be very hot and long-lasting, as it often is when even an attempt at invag is out of the question. We both were recalling our earlier visit to the same hotel just about exactly a year ago and how torrid that was. I especially liked, this time, the confident way she got me off by hand after coming a number of times herself (she wouldn't have been able to do it like that to me a year ago, and neither would I have been able to ejac so easily). -- I'm lying on my back with my head propped up, her head's cradled against my shoulder and we're both gazing down at her lefty action, awaiting the eruption. -- And after that (yup, there was one), well before ten, we both conked out. And slept through until our eight a.m. wake-up call.

At eight-twenty, shortly before we were due to meet W&A for breakfast in the hotel dining room, Wei called to say they'd decided to stay in their room and read the papers. Were they fighting, we wondered, or fucking, or what? Never did find out, nor did it matter a great deal that we didn't. If they want privacy, by gum, they're gonna have privacy! -- The hotel dining room being fancy enough and old-fashioned enough that it reminded me of places Mother and Dad took me and the sibs during family trips. It was quite odd to realize that many of the other guests, despite the extremely casual way Z and I were dressed, likely saw us as older folks, the same way I used to see my parents' generation when we traveled (and of course this is an inescapably renewable realization in all areas of life these days). -- And as a tribute to the special occasion I indulged in a pure cholesterol breakfast: chopped sirloin steak and three eggs over hard with hash browns and toast. Z had never before seen me tear into anything like that -- but managed to put up with it all right as she worked on her blueberry waffles with a side of bacon.

-- And that's where I have to stop for today. Next time for the rest of the trip -- the art museum and more, more, more.

[Deep Jyze]

36

    Ah, a fine day. Doesn't even matter that the last
entry fell far short on pages and now this one's
starting late. -- On a day when the stock market hit a
new all-time high and my weight hit a new Glennarian
Third Stage low. A day when Marcus G. and I argued
politics and something we were both idiotically pleased
to call philosophy for well over an hour at the WOC. A
day when I told Lynn, manager of the deep reserves, I'll
be needing to withdraw another chunk; and therefore,
even though I won't be making the request official for
another week, a day on which I was and still am feeling
flush, at least for the short run.
    And a day which started out lusciously with predawn
no-fuck fucking which Z in particular relished (and said
so!), first because I did a lot of heavy breathing in
her ear and then because her fine handwork engendered a
fountainlike ejac which squirted swarms of white-clad G-
man homunculi all over her naked torso (as I lay on my
back with the rampant Possum aimed in that direction).
(No doubt it's absurd to be noting this sort of thing
every time it happens, but then I must be noting it and
she must be marveling over it precisely because -- or
maybe not all that precisely -- but because it still
feels like such a triumph for ejacs to be happening at
all. And perhaps as we get ever older and creakier it
will seem, if indeed it does keep happening, even more
triumphant and so I'll never be able to stop noting it
or she to stop marveling over it -- or at least so I can
hope, especially regarding the latter part, and of
course so I do.)

    (And I'll say this morning's fountain with the
hard-breathing sound effects came only nine or ten hours
after an even more triumphant roll in the sheets
complete with invag come, for me, and the usual
spectacular array of comes for her. And this starting
just moments after we'd seen off Kat and Betty after
answering an emergency call Friday night -- extreme Mom
fatigue -- and tending to Kat the rest of the weekend.
And what made this earlier coital triumph truly unusual
-- inspiring one of the two treadmill "aha"s Z laid on
me this afternoon at the WOC -- was her open
impassionedness right from the start -- being hot for it
and being uninhibited about showing it -- and the
electrifying effect it had on me. This caused her to
realize maybe I'm not the assertedly typical guy (as she
sees things) and I really do find a woman much more of a
turn-on if she's openly interested from the start rather
than playing hard to get, as Z certainly does love to
do. -- And to me it's a surprise that she can still be
surprised by this. -- And I'm also aware of some likely
dangers: for instance, she'll expect me to be similarly
electrified every single time and she'll be stung on
those occasions when I'm not, or she'll see this as
another of those class things and suspect condescension
("You think you know more about sex than I do!" "You
think I've been benighted all my life and you're the
enlightened one!"). -- But on the whole I'm delighted
and hope we can keep expanding this beachhead of new
"mutuality" awareness.)
    -- And a day when fresh peach slices and thawed
frozen cherries and raspberries joined the sliced banana
in my wake-up bowl of cornflakes: mmm, very fine indeed.
And a day when, after another staff snafu at the scope
office over a back order from reporter Verna left me
with no work to do there, I staggered back to the
hideaway through roaring gale-force winds which were
threatening to strip the newly strung Christmas lights
off the street trees up around the city center. All the
way I was hugging the sides of buildings and dashing
across streets with body canted at about forty-five

degrees -- recalling a traveler of a much earlier era
scurrying across a bridge while chasing his hat in the
postcard ukiyo-e print tacked onto my bookcase here --
that bridge still existing in a city where I was living
twenty-two years ago, or at least it was when I was
there -- and meanwhile, as I hugged and dashed, sucking
on a green apple caramel sucker pilfered from the scope
office -- and then had to outmuscle the gale to tear
open the side-entrance door to the hideaway building.

   -- It's Thanksgiving week, incidentally, but only
the start of it, Monday, and I still have a heavy load
of scoping to grapple with before and maybe even partly
during the holiday. A series of lengthy depositions
popped up last week, all involving the wife and kids of
a local tavern owner killed by a convicted murderer
released from prison at the FBI's behest to act as an
informant against an alleged drug-running motorcycle
gang. Fascinating, wrenching stuff. Now I've got to
get the finals out by Wednesday -- and new jobs may come
up in the meantime -- and also I've been "tasked"
(standard utility jargon) with producing a monster fruit
salad for the annual Wei/Alison Turkey Day blowout.

   And time's running short. To be sure! And yet
it's no biggie. Because at this point I've conceded I
have no chance at all of filling this J-book by the end
of the year. And yet one way or another I'll be back
soon regardless to keep on giving it my best shot. Yes!
And jyze will keep right on striving to go as deep as it
can during this final splurge before withdrawing into
its six-month hibernation.

   -- And before signing off tonight, a couple of
serendipitous personal news items. First, Verna's told
me she was mistaken and it'll likely be six to eight
months before she can funnel any court-related work to
Jyzer Ink. This means, in effect, I'll be able to
devote more time to the spree rewrite after the first of
the year. It feels as though I'm being offered a second
chance to make last year's jyze something worthy of the
sequel which this year's jyze is turning out to be.
Yup, I'm gonna run with it. Fast and furious as I can.

    Second, and for the second year in a row, I found
an excellent Christmas present for Z lying free for the
grabbing on a downtown sidewalk. A pristine yellow
utility hard hat this time, the authentic thing. And
it's terrific. And it'll be even more so after I do
some decorating to make it "The Fabulous Zoelie B.'s
Mokstraumen Hard Hat."
                    *   *
(Next night.)
    Well, just a quick scan of the previous entry
reveals a lot that needs to be clarified or elaborated
upon or explained. And if I'm lucky I just might be
able to do some of that at some point this week --
though certainly not now. Not in the thirty-five
minutes remaining before bus time.
    So the last of the murder-case deps is a wrap. And
as it turned out I didn't have to do the back order for
Verna; she cranked it out herself today because it was
short and the attorney needed it right away. But she
did confess she, not the day staff, was responsible for
the screwup on the unreadable diskette she sent over
yesterday. We had a useful little talk about the matter
on the phone this afternoon. True, I wound up doing a
lot of hustling for no return at all on the aborted back
order (even getting up at seven-thirty a.m. to make a
couple of calls) but strangely enough I'm not really
bothered by the fact. It's all part of the baggage that
comes with the job. And I like the job! I always
figure I've got it easy as hell and therefore I ought to
be -- no, I am, purely am, grateful as hell. So I pay
some unexpected dues every now and then, I swear it's no
big deal. (No one, Z included, can understand my
attitude here. But this doesn't really matter either.
What counts is she gets the big picture of how much the
job matters to me, and on that I have no doubt at all.)
    Another interesting (no SQUAWK!) day. A couple of
minidramas with Z, par for the course. I left her a
"Lost Chord" postcard yesterday and she replied to it
with a somewhat harsh note asking if I really see her as
an "ethereal angel." Ha! So I concocted a goofy reply

363

which seemed to successfully smooth any truly ruffled
feathers. And she in turn replied with a card showing
a fetching Italian waif (female) blowing a trumpet,
confiding that she, Z, felt this presented an image of
the inner Zoelie closer to her own (recalling that this
same waif played a hooker in "Nights of Cabiria" which
we saw last year -- and also in real life became the
wife of that film's celebrated director).

The other minidrama, Z got a bit upset when I again
mentioned the possibility of postponing our wedding nine
months or so -- not just "a few months," as I'd said
before -- for purposes of enhancing the jyze (by setting
up the wedding as the climax of the "special edition").
"I trust you, I trust you," she pouted, with tears
streaming down her cheeks. Oh god. Backtrack, scramble.
But maybe she'll be thinking it over now, who knows.
She's surprised me plenty of times before.

And then the sex news. Some "unpressured
snuggling" (her term) when she came home from work today
that led to a yes-fuck fuck in which she declared over
and over "Oh god, oh god, it feels so good" -- but then
I faded and we had to leave the ejac for next time.

And that's it for tonight. Not much, I know. Of
"depth," very little, and of "Deepness" not much more.
Maybe I can do better tomorrow night. It's turning into
a fairly light workweek after all and with the holiday
coming up I might be able to focus here for the first
time in a while.

*   *

Thanksgiving eve and again it's nasty out there.
For the past two weeks it's been nonstop nastiness. Or
so it seems. This time of year you just assume that's
what it'll be. You get in a nastiness frame of mind and
you can't get out of it and you don't even want to
because it just feels so right and so timely. ---

*

(A break there while Donald leaned in the door and
we yammered awhile. And earlier tonight I chatted for a
few minutes on the lobby staircase with the odd, short,
stocky, shifty-eyed Cawk dude I've been glimpsing around

364

here and often getting hostile vibes from ever since I
moved in. Turns out he's not all that bad. Roger, a
few years my junior, occupation astrologer. I've always
assumed the yuppie-looking "clients" I've seen him
meeting in the lobby at strange hours were picking up
some sort of contraband, but apparently it's not so.
Roger says he knows the owner of the building, Allen W.,
quite well and serves as a kind of watchdog for him.
Mr. W., he says, is a retired philosophy professor (as I
knew) who owns property all over the country and is
worth about $20 million but wears thrift-store clothes
and loves to bargain down flea-market merchants. He's
also a "ditherer" who'll talk your ear off about German
Idealists and the categorical imperative. -- Oh, and
Roger says he knows of "twelve people for sure and two
maybes" living illegally in the building and Mr. W.
turns a blind eye to them as long as they remain
discreet about it. The same's not true, however, for
tenants engaged in illegal businesses and vice, drug
sales, etc. -- for example, my next-door neighbor Nolan
running the call-girl operation under the cover of
"Triangle Advertising." He'll be booted out pronto if
Mr. W. gets wind of it. Roger himself learned of it
just this week; that's why he was snooping around on our
floor tonight when I ran into him.)

   A long WOC workout, a long midtown walk to pick up
a check, a vanilla-yogurt cone, a couple of double-
stacks (these stuffed with double tomatoes by the impish
short-order cook Anna who speaks only a few words of
English -- she's of Guatemalan origins, like Kat -- but
always flashes me a big smile from behind the grill and
says, "Double-stack man, double-stack man, you want
two?" -- and holds up two fingers in what looks like a
classic peace sign, and I flash the sign right back at
her and nod vigorously).

   As I arrived at the scope building a big Christmas
tree, maybe twenty feet tall, was just going up in the
lobby. When I came back down from the office the place
stank and the tree looked so strangely dark I sniffed it
up close. Whew! One of the building guards told me he

couldn't stand near it for more than a minute without
becoming nauseated. He was sure the tree was artificial
and had been sprayed with some sort of oily pine-scented
toxins to make it seem real. I didn't doubt about the
spray but I wasn't so sure the tree itself was unreal; a
tiny twig I broke off for inspection appeared sort of
woody beneath all the gunk. I concluded that the
building owners wanted the tree to look and smell
supernaturally piney -- sort of like, say, those
supernaturally wild wildflowers fed by automatic
sprinklers up at this past August's mountain resort.

   Nasty weather again. Back before Donald popped in
I was about to note that my bag's gone through three
separate drenchings in the past ten days, causing water
damage to a couple of books and several magazines and
even a little to this very J-book, along the bottom
edge, and this despite my efforts to protect the
important stuff with a makeshift plastic inner lining
for the bag. So now I've added a new item to my
shopping list awaiting arrival of the big $3500 chunk
from the deep reserves (hopefully sometime next week):
a couple of truly waterproof lightweight three-ring-
binder-size baggies. (No. 1 on the list, and not for
the first time, is "fail-safe divorce.")

   -- And this brings me to the big story of the day.
The note Z left on my chair last night asked point-
blank: would I please agree to marry her sometime next
year? In return I dashed off a note saying this: "Okay.
Why not. Good deal. It's settled. Love you. -- G."
This morning she left a stickie attached to my note
saying "And with such unbridled passion!" (Maybe she
meant "ungroomled"?) -- But I'll admit it wasn't easy
for me to cave on this. Before I could do it I had to
devise a new plan for next year's jyze. And what I hit
on is this: a yearlong J-book that would start in late
spring, with our wedding serving as the first highlight
about a third of the way through, so in August or
September. The second highlight, at roughly the two-
thirds mark, would be the Christian millennium (I've
been trying all along not to mention that this is coming

up, but now it's punched through and it probably won't
be going away). The third highlight, close to the end,
would be the true Christian millennium the following
March, which will take some explaining -- but later for
that. Maybe even next year later.)
     Today I brought all this up with Z. I also asked:
since she was getting to set the year of our marriage,
could I pick the date? She said yes.

*   *

     -- Two days on. And once again a big chunk of
pages it won't be. A small one. It's twenty past
midnight already. The usual Friday-night scene down
here at the hideaway building. (Wish I felt inspired to
check it out up close, or rather down close, the dance-
bar goings-on more or less directly below me at two
different clubs, the music and sometimes the crowd
sounds from both of which I can hear so clearly -- and
confusedly, and dissonantly -- up here. But I don't.
Guess I've crossed that bar, so to speak, for good.)
     Our Thanksgiving holiday is turning out to be an
uninspired one. We're not getting it on the way we'd
been doing or the way Z was figuring we would -- she'd
proclaimed it to be "eatsleepfuckplay" days -- and we're
both puzzling over why this is, although I'm doing it
silently and she openly. She's back to wondering if
she's simply "less horny now" and if this is the way the
future will be. I can't tell to what extent she's
trying to provoke me with talk like this. As it is I
think I show plenty of interest -- maybe even too much.
The trouble is she may still be right in that it's a
little less than it was before, when it was near total.
Or really, by any previous conception of mine regarding
such interest, far beyond total. (And that includes my
time with Lady S, yes. And the raunchy Kristi K. too.)
     Or then again it could be mostly a reaction on her
part to a screwup of mine last night at Wei and Alison's
Thanksgiving banquet. Alison invited a youngish
coworker of hers at the county jail who's fairly new in
town and currently partnerless, Carol T., to join the
festivities, and told her in advance about my newspaper

367

days and the jyze projects of the past few years because
she knew Carol took an interest in those sorts of
writerly things. My mistake was to let Carol corner me
several times during the evening and ply me with
questions for fairly long periods. What's more, she's
nice to look at, charming, smart, and well spoken, a New
Zealander of mostly Maori ancestry with cascading black
hair and a fine crooked smile. And Z's reaction? At
the time it appeared she wasn't noticing anything, but
she also withdrew a little bit and I worried she might
be getting upset. Yet it also seemed wiser not to try
to take her aside and talk it over while we were still
at the party.

Conversation during dinner itself turned into a
lengthy argument between me and a fellow who lived in
Japan for several years and now has nothing but bad
things (mostly, to my mind, mistaken or grossly
exaggerated) to say about the Japanese. The others at
the table (ten in all) joined in at times on one side or
the other and Carol plied the two of us with provocative
questions. (Wei, oddly enough, couldn't be coaxed to
contribute, even though -- or maybe because, yes -- his
mother is of Japanese ancestry.) -- And the feast, I
ought to say, was superb, including even my hand-sliced
"old-fashioned" fruit salad. (And then because another
attendee had also brought fruit salad -- unbidden -- and
hers was more popular, I got to take most of mine home
and it just might last until Christmas.)

Immediately when we left the party Z let me know
she hadn't failed to notice the goings-on with Carol.
She said I'd handled things just fine and she had no
criticism but she was jealous anyway, feeling insecure,
in part because I'd also alluded to Lady U (though
without mentioning names) at dinner during the Japan
dispute. And that insecurity basically was the
underlying theme for the rest of the night and today.
She was wanting me to show she had no cause for alarm
but at the same time driving me half crazy with
questions and statements that made it hard for me to
show anything. "Why do you love me?" "Do you sometimes

wish you were with a younger woman?" Scores of zingers
like that, and many repeated again and again. A very
tricky and frustrating situation.
     -- Well, but I don't want to be working myself up
over this. All I want to say is no matter what (and I'm
not suggesting real temptation will never come along
either, for her or for me, nope, nope, of course not) --
but no matter what, I won't be letting the Z-woman down.
Not now and not ever. It's a done deal: "trust and
troth." And I hope she feels the same and is just as
determined to hang in there as I am (and I believe she
does and she is, yes).

37

     Final hours of Thanksgiving weekend. Up at the
scope building that new Christmas tree in the lobby was
fully decorated (not to say foully, as well as slickly,
pompously, ostentatiously, and yet somehow still quite
attractively, I have to admit, at least as seen from
certain angles and, most important, a considerable
distance) -- and it wasn't really all that foul-
smelling anymore. Down here the hideaway's as quiet as
it ever gets. The rains have finally stopped,
presumably because this is already the wettest November
in local recorded history and so why should they
continue? If they did, it would just make the record
all that harder to top next November.
     A couple of headline-grabbing news events over the
weekend. In one a double-length city bus, its driver
shot by a passenger, plunged off the high bridge just a
few blocks from Z's old place; it landed near the huge
concrete Norski troll that squats under the northern end

of the bridge. It's one of the bus routes that Z used
to take to and from work. The racket made by news
helicopters hovering almost directly overhead drove Jess
and Gwen out of their home for several hours Saturday.
The gun-wielding passenger, it turns out, was a psycho,
a lonely deluded Cawk crazy who hung out at the downtown
missions, and therefore the incident is not drawing as
much attention as it should to the issue of endemic
violence on the buses. (Lord knows I see enough of it
on my bus rides home -- an incident or two virtually
every night, though so far they've all been minor.)
      The other big news event was the death of the
charismatic ex-army general who became the city's
superintendent of schools a few years ago. The leukemia
that he was vowing with military bravado to beat offed
him in just eight months despite the efforts of "the
best doctors in the world." The man was widely loved
and respected, and not just in the Afrusan community (he
was Afrusan), and he'll be missed even by folks like me
who didn't think much of his policies and deplored his
martial approach to the job. And I'll acknowledge he
never did call the tanks and paratroopers down on the
schools as I several times jokingly predicted he would.
      June is another who'll miss him. Last night she
was feeling depressed and came over to stay with us. Z
had already gone to bed and so I wound up talking with
her for a couple of hours in the living room (until Z
lowered the boom). Always I'm struck by the many ways
June resembles Lady S. Her easy tears. Her struggles
with English. Her pride and ambition. Her tendency,
despite her declared liberalism, to favor authoritarian
and hierarchical solutions in traditional Confucian or
better to say neo-Confucian fashion. She's starting to
feel more confident about law school now and this showed
even in her posture as she stretched out with a cup of
tea in Zoelie's Filipino rattan chair, insouciantly
crooking one leg over a chair arm (definitely not a
Confucian move, neo or otherwise). I asked for her help
and advice in my campaign to establish better relations
with Aida and she promised to do what she could. Her

main piece of advice on this score was that I should
shrug off any lingering resentment over past incidents.
Confidentially she tells me that Aida -- this after
prefacing that she, June, feels very close to her --
"has some loose stones in her foundation."

June says she understands Z much better. Z's
biggest weaknesses in June's eyes are her "romanticism
and idealism" and also her loose ways with money, and
the first two of these June sees, just as I do, as the
flip side of her social compassion and political
activism. June can't understand at all why Aida and Z
attended the leadership institute; to her mind the
"New Agey" aspect of its training is all but worthless
and the extreme assertive individualism even worse.

The most touching moment of the talk came when June
said she thinks romantic love is the one thing, other
than "helping people," that can be inspiring in life and
then confessed she thinks it's unlikely she'll ever find
another man she can get serious about because her
standards are too high (and she's certainly not about to
expend a lot of energy looking) -- and the whole time
tears were rolling down her cheeks and she was
maniacally/manically grinning through them, just as Lady
S used to do.

Also this news item: Paz and Tobey have bought a
house. It's just a couple of miles northeast of us in a
run-down area near the high school; but the hood, like
ours only more so, is rapidly gentrifying. Yesterday Z
and I dropped by to look the place over, taking along a
couple of housewarming gifts: a doormat made from
recycled rubber (on which I inscribed some fractured
homilies with permanent markers) and a winsomely
scraggly little evergreen we picked out at a nursery
down in the valley. Just a few months ago, of course,
Paz and Tobey were going through a big crisis in which
it appeared they'd be breaking up for good. Nobody has
a very definite idea, Z tells me, on just how they
managed to emerge from this showdown confident enough
about their future together to buy a house so soon.

(Aida, by the way, isn't seeing much of Kirk these

days because his father, who's in his nineties and still
lives here in J. City, is in very bad health and
probably near death. In June's view this shows that
Kirk doesn't really care all that much for Aida; if he
did he'd want to be talking with her at such an
emotionally wrenching time. Then there's also the fact
that Kirk's former wife -- from whom he's been separated
for a few years, in a situation Z suspects is like mine
with Lady U (but can't possibly be all that much like
it) -- Kirk's former wife is now making noises about
their getting back together. Supposedly he's not
interested, but kids are involved, Z thinks, and so in
the end he might be swayed regardless. Looks to me like
Aida might be in for some tough times if she's let
herself become seriously attached to Kirk.)

    And today, finally, a very good ejacohump. Wheee!
(Z and me this is, yes.) After two less good non-
ejacos, one at eight a.m., one shortly after noon, in
both of which ol' Possum pulled a classic foozle (though
after staying up and in for at least a decent period),
this evening I crept into her room around seven, finding
her at work on her finances while sitting cross-legged
on the bed (which folds out from her convertible couch).
Plenty of red meat and sleep, not too much debilitating
exercise, no ejac over the past sixty hours or so -- I
was ready. And of course the two nonconsummatory rounds
earlier in the day had put an even stronger charge on
me. So in a flash I was gratifyingly rampant and felt
confident enough of being able to stay that way to pull
her atop me for a change. She quickly got herself off
several times in that posture, while crying out "I can't
stop, I can't stop," and then when she asked what about
me I rolled her onto her side and twisted her hips
around so I could push in from behind and quickly got
off that way. Afterwards she kept moaning, "Oh, I liked
that, I liked that."

    And: she proposed we stop calling Possum by that
name (but didn't want to return to Mercutio or any of
the others and dismissed my tongue-in-cheek proposal of
Thumper but had nothing new to offer herself -- said

she'll think about it, because she does like having a proper name for it as opposed to something impersonal like "your thang" or "your gnarly whatzis").

What else? I hung two more rows of "cubes" for her bedroom shelves. We came up with thank-you cards for Jacob, Justine, and Wei and Alison (and I made a special cartoon refrigerator magnet for W&A using a psychedelic-yarn turkey we bought during the Mentoka trip).

And time's up. More tomorrow, I swear.

*   *

-- Well, technically tomorrow, yes, since I was jyzing then very early in the morning of the 30th and it's now very late in the evening of the 1st. Three minutes before midnight, to be exact. We're almost a full day into December.

The weather, sorry to say, is still stuck back in November. It's rainy and squally just as pretty much that whole month was. Yet it also has some December-like aspects. Steam pours out of the grates at downtown intersections. At the midtown plaza a mawkishly beautiful sight, the Christmas carousel spinning slowly at nine p.m., a single rider aboard, the seasonal reds and greens reflecting off rain-glistening brick walkways and the sides of surrounding buildings like glinty shards from a mirror ball (and "The First Noel" barely audible, somewhat like dancehall music heard across a sloshy lake). -- And windblown flights of yellow leaves come swirling up the center of the trafficless very high road, right past the carousel. And the carcasses of two sprung umbrellas are snagged pathetically on a grate in a nearby gutter. And a double-length bus plows through a huge puddle up at the corner, splashing a tsunamic wave onto and over the top of a row of newsracks. (Earlier at the ORB -- still the only real bookstore -- I was momentarily disoriented upon entry by the "ruppa-pup-pum" of "Drummer Boy.") -- And at the scope building I gawked yet again, despite myself, at the preposterous lobby evergreen with its opulent decorations (including sparkly blue and silver silk scarves in place of tinsel). It smelled good now, I

373

must say: just like natural freshly cut pine. (Could it
be all the fake stuff wore off? Or did it simply take
this long to get up to sniff?)

    -- Not much scoping awaited me. Again. I read a
bit, hit the usual burger joint for a cone, hied on down
to the triangle. -- And so it's a good thing the
thirty-five-hundred-dollar chunk from the deep reserves
will be arriving in a few days. Looks like it'll be
slim pickings for J. Ink the rest of December as far as
paid work goes. Though it's true, I never really know.

    As it happens, Lynn of the deep reserves is in town
to visit her sister for the holidays and today she and I
had our annual meeting at the digi-cafe. (I stepped in
the door just as she and Rob were finishing up at a
window table.) She confirmed I'm her smallest account,
Rob is the second smallest, Barb the third smallest
(Jeff cashed his in shortly after they opened it). But
her brokerage is still glad to have us, she assured me.
In truth I suspect we're mainly comic relief and
conscience salve. "How do you think it is," she asked,
"one family produced four kids who have such unusual
lives?" Well, heh-heh, however it happened, I'm quite
sure it wasn't something our parents were aiming for.
(Barb, like me, I learned, is working half-time so
she'll have more freedom to write; Rob of course is
essentially doing the same thing except his "day job" is
full-time because he hasn't lucked out as Barb and I
have in finding relatively remunerative part-time work;
and Jeff, he's doing an odd mix of construction jobs and
just barely scraping by as always, or almost always,
except when he's recently hit the jackpot by selling a
house he's built.)

    On the way back from the digi-cafe I was on cloud
nine -- singin' in the rain. "I'm flush, I'm flush --
and without a single dime in my pocket!" Stopped by the
newsstand at the public market to pick up a batch of
free calendars for next year and realized yet again how
much the details of my daily routines have changed from
a year ago even though in broad outline my life is very
similar. Last year it was a rare day when I didn't cozy

up with the market newsstand for thirty or forty minutes
at least once; since then I've done that only a few
times and not at all in the past several months.

    The daily routines. Little details of the diurnal
life. -- Well, first, I'm about to make what could turn
out to be an important modification in bedtime ritual.
I've installed a second reading lamp on our headboard
and I'm planning to hit the rack an hour earlier
hereafter and do more reading in bed. I expect this
will lead to a more active sex life as well, maybe
something like the nights we were sleeping together in
Mentoka. Z's okayed the plan on a trial basis. For me
the main advantage is I'll have something else to do if
she's not in the mood and I'll have a way to get in the
mood myself if I'm not in it initially. -- And I'm also
hoping I'll be able to move my wake-up time earlier, as,
again, I've been wanting to do for months. Even under
the best of circumstances I won't be making it to bed an
hour earlier every night, but I'll consider this plan a
success if (A) it happens half the time and (B) we get
it on more often than in the recent era on weeknights.

    So then some even smaller details. For one, June
inadvertently left her contact lenses sitting in a spoon
on Z's bathroom basin and Z, not knowing about the
lenses, put the spoon in a bowl of water in the sink;
when she and June called about them from work I found
the lenses still afloat in the bowl, looking like tiny
curved ice chips. (Before today I didn't even know June
wears contacts. But this probably explains why she
seems to squint quite often as we're talking late at
night when she's presumably not wearing them.)

    And more:

** Those rowdy Cawk hot-rodders in the house next
door have put up a huge Christmas display on their roof
and second-floor front porch, frustrating Z "because it
becomes harder to see them as pure evil."

** I've informed Z I'll be keeping my deep
reserves with Lynn's investment outfit for at least
another year and not using them to pay off her debt,
since she specifically told me she didn't want me to do

that. Her reply to my decision: "You mean you're not
going to rescue me?" No question about it, she was
hurt. Later, though, she apologized, admitting that one
of the first things you learn in those twelve-step
addiction groups is not to expect someone to rescue you.
(And besides, the penalties -- which I didn't learn
about until recently -- for early payoff of her loans
would wipe out any financial benefit of the change. And
would we really gain anything from having me be the one
she was cursing out every month at bill-paying time
rather than the banks and credit-card companies?)
     ** Last weekend Min, the landlord, changed the
locks on the lobby and garage doors, the main reason
being that poor Ciro (in 102) has twice in the past
few weeks had his fancy late-model car cannibalized
for parts. The final straw came last week when the
thief jimmied the lobby-door lock and stole Ciro's
trunk lid. Before this Min hadn't known the lobby door
could be jimmied; now he's mounted a metal guard which
is supposedly jimmyproof. (Z's comment: "Aren't you
glad our car is so old no one wants to cannibalize it?"
My reply: "And aren't you glad I dress so shabby when
I walk downtown at night nobody wants to cannibalize
me?" -- And it's true, that's one reason I dress as I
do. But of course another one, equally important, is
that I couldn't afford to live as I do if I didn't.)
                    *   *
     Yup, two days on. (Still can't decide. Should it
always be two days on? Should that be the default
restart? Maybe it wouldn't have to be an ironclad rule
for all jyze everywhere and at all times but maybe just
for Jyzer G in the current era?)
     It's been a laundry-and-groceries kind of day. And
last night the read-in-bed experiment did not get off to
a rousing start. No loving, no pillow talk, scarcely
even any affection. Z was wearing her old "Zoelicious"
T-shirt and a sleep mask (earplugs too) and lying with
her back turned to me and I learned later she was irked
by the way I kept putting my hand on her back and then
taking it off to turn a page and then putting it back

on. She swears she could feel this even in her sleep.

But it seems we no longer wrangle too much over such things. The small stuff gets fairly quickly sorted out or smoothed over or simply swept away by other small stuff, whether irksome or not. And this is how it oughta be! -- Or usually anyway. Not necessarily always. But as for truly hardcore battles, I hope they continue to be rare. (I'll admit it seems unlikely they will. As Z declared several months ago in her "Theory #7": "I'm 'used to' having 'regular' fights for drama, adrenal exercise, hormonal fulfillment, acorn pinching, distance adjustment.... So maybe hicketiness is my evolving approach to Buddhist calm.")

But yes, we'll give the reading-in-bed experiment another try tonight. And I'll take care not to be tapping her back with my hand between page turns. But I'm also thinking maybe this time I should launch a serious coitus attempt. Except for a couple of wake-up nipple comes for her we haven't really done the deed since Sunday. In part this is because she's been unusually busy at the office, in part because I've been exhausted from working out extra-hard at the WOC. But regardless: such long sexless intervals just won't do.

-- And meanwhile the regular old day-to-day quotidia -- to be tautologous about it, and maybe even aptly so -- keep on rolling out. Or go for succinct and call them diurnalia. (I'll say first, though, that in seeing Lynn earlier this week I had my second near close encounter of the fall with sister Barb, because Lynn had seen her just days earlier at an anniversary bash thrown by the investment group. It featured a historian in "Sage of Monticello" costume reading bits of the great man's prose -- perhaps with a chorus of his slaves providing amens? According to Lynn, Barb loved it. I find this just about impossible to believe and therefore I'll concede it's probably, yes, true.)

Elsewise, the daily rollout:

Z says she's about to plunge into hilltop politics in a big way. Her goal is to become the "air-quality person" for our local neighborhood group. Lots of

infighting there recently as factions square off over
the impact of a big dot-com's long-term lease of the old
marine hospital that sits picturesquely at the northern
prow of the hill about a block and a half from our
place. (I needle Z at times over the way she gets so
worked up about this environmental-health stuff -- and
rightfully so -- but tends to overlook the fallout from
the gentrification which we ourselves are helping to
bring on. Once in a while I go too far and she wonders
whether I'm for her or agin her. But no doubt about it:
I'm for her! And that includes her political causes!
-- Last night she was bothered when I said I tend to see
advocacy of home air cleaners as one more of the
numerous ways the rich avoid their social
responsibilities. Not for the first time she said she
dislikes my lumping her in with the privileged, which I
really wasn't trying to do. But even so I couldn't
resist pointing out that such lumping makes at least as
much sense as her lumping me in with suburban/colonial-
settler Cawkazoids. -- And eventually, as usual, we
managed to smooth all that over -- the lumpings, that
is.)
     Other items:
     ** Z's mother sent Z and me separate Thanksgiving
cards and always at the end of phone calls tells Z to
give me her, Mama E's, love.
     ** Dale, Z's boss, wrote Z another note thanking
her for being so helpful. Next week he's unexpectedly
taking her along to a major management conference out in
the foothills somewhere. To me it's surprising she
isn't making more noise about all this. She seems
quietly pleased. I'd expect either embarrassment or
delight or a raucous mash-up of the two.
     ** The Z-mobile's six-month checkup resulted in a
whopper of a bill: almost five hundred bucks, mostly for
a new brake master cylinder (or some such thing). These
big upkeep bills make me uneasy because I contribute
very little toward paying them: fifty bucks a month and
that's for everything, gas and insurance included. But
Z long ago insisted on covering all car expenses beyond

my fifty a month by herself and she's never reneged or
even groused about this. (And in my own defense I'll
say I rarely use the car on my own.)

*   *

-- A quiet Sunday night, fairly early: only half
past seven.

Z and I seem to be doing just fine. She's been
disappointed, it's true, at being unable to "drive you
crazy the way you do me" -- this is what she says -- but
as of now it's not bugging her enough to bring on a
meltdown. For the time being it suffices to remind her
she had me breathing plenty hard last week (and also how
vastly improved our sex life is over, say, a year ago --
speaking in terms of hard-ons and ejacs, not to mention
yes-fuck fucking and ejacohumps). If I can't get back
up to snuff soon, though, meaning the new, improved
snuff, her grumblings will doubtless intensify and I'll
have to search for other ways to reassure her -- verbal
or symbolic ones, I mean -- and doing this is always
dispiriting for me, maybe almost as much as it probably
is for her.

But I still insist we're getting along extremely
well. So well, in fact, it's (again) a bit unnerving to
her, and she says so out loud and frequently. We're
simply not fighting. And how could this be? At times
she even seems to be trying to pick fights just to have
something to do. She also accuses me of being
"noodgie," but the truth is I'm usually not; more
likely the accusation itself is another of her fight-
picking tactics, unconscious or otherwise. And in any
case, we always seem to be able to ease almost
instantaneously any tensions that do arise. And the
question is, again: why is this?

Maybe it's a matter of the growing "trust and
troth" we've been talking about for the past month or
two. Or maybe (as she's suggested) it's a matter of
growing fear of the dire consequences of "m_skstraumen-
level battles." Or maybe it's our vastly improved
conjugal sex life even if it does still fall somewhat
short of perfection (as if sexual perfection were

possible). But whatever it is, it's working. And if
I'm surprised by this (and I am), she's a lot more
surprised. In her entire life she's never had a
relationship anywhere near so harmonious. Or at least
she tells me this. And I absolutely believe her.

Some of the "little tensions" during the past few
days arose around, for example, her suspicion that I was
secretly angry over her failure to wash her dishes for a
couple of weeks, or that I found her to be "incompetent"
because she'd neglected to pick up a copy of a certain
periodical when she stopped by Rob's bookstore yesterday
(yet I said nothing to suggest this and even insisted
right away it was my own fault for not writing a note to
remind her about it as she'd asked me to do when I first
mentioned it). "You're just such a nice guy," she says
quizzically or poutingly or even ruefully. "You're so
easy to get along with. You put up with all my
pookienesses and they hardly seem to bother you at all.
It's very disorienting! I'm not used to this!"

(Why am I able to be this way with her?
-- Assuming I actually am and she's not making it up to
flatter me. -- But I know she's not; flattering's not
her game. (Provocation is.) -- So okay, why? Well,
I'd say it's mainly because she's so quick to suspect
I'll be upset by this or that and therefore she's almost
always able to disarm me immediately. And the fact that
her touchiness on many matters is so manifestly an
outgrowth of what she herself calls her "chronic
insecurity" has much the same effect of undercutting any
sense of grievance I might feel. These two combined
seem to drive the main underlying dynamic at work in
producing the relative harmony. -- Or maybe all this
is just another way of saying I'm too crazy about her
and feel for her too much for any sense of grievance to
ever get a chance to start building in the first place.)

-- So this weekend we were together relatively
little. She had a women's-caucus meeting yesterday
afternoon and an appointment with Olwen this afternoon
just past -- to look into a Sufi ceremony new to both of
them -- and I consequently came down to the WOC both

afternoons. Last night we dropped by a hilltop council "validation event" concerning the city's latest plans for the neighborhood and then went out to a Christmas party thrown by the Filipino city employees group at a community center in the Scandi quarter. A pickup six-piece Filipino band was playing in front of a twinkling Christmas tree and we even danced a few times (despite the shatteringly bad music) and Z seemed to be getting a big kick out of showing off not only her dynamite new black velvet dress but also her new Cawkazoid Deep (and just about everyone in the room seemed to have already heard about Z's mother likening him to the Duke).

Meanwhile yesterday was June's birthday and she was feeling lonely and rocky in the wake of yet another tragedy involving a close friend (she learned of this friend's inoperable stomach cancer while writing a eulogy for another friend she had just lost to breast cancer, and a few months ago a third friend died from colon cancer). She called to ask if we'd mind her sleeping over at our place. Of course we urged her to come, and when we arrived home stuck some candles in a peach pie we'd bought for her and marched into the bedroom singing "Happy Birthday." Poor June wept with gratitude, a resolutely bright smile once again shining through the tears. After the three of us demolished most of the pie at the dining table Z went off to bed and June and I schmoozed on in the living room. At one a.m. Z called for me to come join her but June was so wound up I couldn't get away for another hour. (At the rate things are going I'll soon know more about June than about any other woman in my life who hasn't been a lover, and maybe even most who have.)

*   *

-- So what's new this week is this. The main thing, a tentative schedule for next year's jyze is finally set. In fact that's why I didn't make it into these pages Friday night: I was poring over calendars, trying to minimize drawbacks and maximize advantages of various overall schemes. Oh, and we also have a tentative wedding date: September 25th. Peak day of the

381

Chinese Moon Festival. Nine months on from Christmas
Day. About a third of the way into Jyze Annal 6, the
title of which will probably be "The Jyze Millennium."
     And other things? Not many. I've got lots of big
plans but will remain all but paralyzed until the
booster from the deep reserves kicks in. That is, I'm
broke. For the first time in many months -- is it
almost a year now? -- my bank account is down to a
single digit (7) and change. I can't buy the trimmings
for my Christmas cards, the makings for my gifts. My
one non-grocery purchase of the week was a six-dollar
pair of running shorts from a bargain rack to replace my
last usable pair, which are aging badly, and it turns
out these new ones are so revealingly thin and flimsy I
can't wear them in public ("positively obscene!" cried
Z, encouraging me to don them at home but only if no one
else, and specifically not Kat or June, is present). I
have to admit I found this quite flattering.
     Anything more? Well, our Christmas plans are
pretty well set, including five days of house-sitting
for Jess and Gwen, Christmas Eve with Betty and Kat,
Christmas Day dinner at Rob and Gail's, and an all-day
Saturday-before-Christmas outing with Kat alone
(featuring a children's-theater production). Z and I
have agreed to set aside a single day -- the Sunday two
days after Christmas -- for making our presents for each
other, and otherwise to buy nothing. She's working on a
special Christmas card which announces she won't be
"buying stuff" anymore at Christmastime; instead this
year she'll be taking everyone on her list (mostly kids)
on outings. (This campaign is also linked with her vow
to cut back spending and reduce credit-card debt, though
I expect it to have the reverse effect in both realms.)
     What I liked. Hmm. The trays of delicious
homemade Christmas cookies, both at the "validation
event" and the Filipino dance. How gorgeous Z looked in
that sexy short black velvet dress while stepping out to
"Jingle Bell Rock." How luscious she looks by the soft
white indirect light of the new bedside lamp as she
sprawls asleep, almost always prone and with half her

face pushed into the pillow and those supremely kissable
full lips slightly parted (and a light whispery ZZZZZZ
sometimes issuing). And: the unexpected late flowering
of the yellow daisies on the outdoor balcony. The daily
hits of cornflakes with frozen fruit of various kinds
mixed in along with the usual sliced banana (the bowl is
so overfull and unwieldy I no longer dare to take it to
my armchair and instead attack it at the dining table
while propping reading matter against our tabletop
message chalkboard).

And mention this. A day or two after Z said she
wanted to drop the name Possum I jokingly offered a new
replacement: Oblomov, or Ob for short. (I also thought
of Pushkin.) To my surprise she said she liked it --
and had read the book and seen the Russian film version,
and loved both -- and then she used it for a few days.
"Ol' Ob." Recently, however, it's faded. Maybe we're
reaching the point where special monikers are no longer
needed now that the equipment's functioning normally, at
least at times. (Have I ever mentioned it before? She
took two years of Russian in college.)

*

And looking at the big picture, national and
international. Things are bumping along strangely, I'd
say, and still ominously though apparently somewhat less
so. The stock market has zoomed back after last
summer's crash -- it hit an all-time high last week
before falling back a bit this week. Everyone's at a
loss to explain why this recovery is happening in the
face of the continuing Asian economic crisis. Is it
mainly a matter of the money having nowhere else to go
-- everything overseas seeming highly risky right now --
and therefore it's all being invested at home, with lots
more coming in from the troubled lands overseas, thus
bidding stock prices "artificially" higher? Apparently
no one really knows. Since a large chunk of my deep
reserves was invested in Asian stocks at the time the
bottom fell out (or more accurate to say was pushed out,
mostly by USAn financiers) I've come nowhere near
recouping the losses of last summer and fall. Lynn's

latest report showed my account to be about halfway
back, putting it at almost exactly its value when it
came into existence after Mother's death three years ago
(though this doesn't consider the money I've taken out
over those years; and that, including quarterly income,
amounts to probably close to twelve thousand dollars, or
roughly a sixth of the account's current value).

Is so-called neoliberal capitalism failing? A few
months ago it appeared to be. Now people are starting
to say it's saved itself by stanching the bleeding at
home and thereby causing people of other lands (with
weaker militaries) to suffer. It's a sad thing to have
to hope for the catastrophic failure of the present
system before you can expect to see significant change
for the better. But realistically now, given the coming
many-faceted ecocalamity, what other hope is there?

38

Yayhoo -- my check came in! I'm flush again!
Ready to get out there and spend uncontrollably!
-- Well no. But I'll be stocking up on running
shoes (chucks, of course, three pairs, one black, one
black-and-white, and one khaki or tan, if available),
waterproof bags (two) for protecting items inside my
backpack, new non-obscene gym shorts, and a big batch of
books.

With those exceptions I'll be setting the money
aside for anticipated major future expenses, including
subscriptions soon to expire (totaling over $250),
annual renewal of my Jyzer Ink business license ($75)
and district taxes ($25), coverage as a Deep on the city
medical plan ($200 or more), the precautionary divorce

from Lady S ($500), materials for birthday presents for
Z which I'll make myself ($100), and some marryin' rags
($100). The remainder, roughly $2,000, will serve as a
cushion against the income vagaries of the nightscoping
trade and if I'm lucky will carry me through to the end
of the upcoming year and thus to the new millennium. Or
at least that's the plan. No doubt it falls well short
of gritty realism. And in fact it's not even complete
in the realm of predictable major expenses. Because
I've just thought of another one in that category, and
it may be the most major of them all: the honeymoon. If
I'm not extremely careful, that one could wipe out the
whole cushion all by itself.

So that's it, the big news. An hour ago, after
bidding my workout friend Marcus goodbye at the
triangle bus stop (with a big bear hug -- our standard
culture-wars political disputes suspended for the
holidays -- standard, that is, except he's a right-wing
urban black dude and I'm a left-wing burban pink dude)
(burban by early enculturation, that is) -- after that,
I say, I hiked up to the bank machine near the scope
building -- it's just about the only one I ever use,
the exceptions coming mostly when it's shut down for
some reason -- and deposited the check. How sweet it
was to tap in that big number, larger than my usual
fortnightly J. Ink paycheck deposit by a stupendous
decimal order of magnitude. Now all I have to do is
wait for the check to clear, a process that, if form
holds, should take about a week.

But this isn't to suggest I can't write checks
myself right now. I can and I will, starting tomorrow.
Whooeeee! Gangway swarms of Christmas shoppers!

(Okay, okay, all this excitement is a little hokey.
Call it holiday hyperbole. Seize any chance to lighten
the heavy quiver of exclamation points one must carry
around for the season.)

-- Meanwhile it's that hour again. The bus. And
just so I don't forget, in the next installment I'll
want to be looking into Z's new "aha"s about her own
formative racial incident and her family's antiromantic

atmosphere (and my counter-"aha") as well as an annoying little episode at the scope office which still has my nostrils flaming. -- Oh, and also a word about the new sexual accolade Z has bestowed upon me (which I'm sorry to say isn't the one I'd most like to receive from her) and our new venture into "piggybacking" (which I should note has nothing to do with sex).

*   *

"How time flies!" (How? Dunno. But it's now six days later.)

It's been an unexpectedly heavy grand-jury week and also a week of frenzied I'm-flush-again shopping, including some of the Christmas variety, and also a week of maximal effort expended at the WOC. Of free time, just about none. -- And today, while Z went out with Aida and Adele, I helped Nurse Betty with some electrical and moving work at her house and also did dinner with her and Kat at the slightly more upscale of the two funky fifties nostalgia joints we all love so much (where Kat was as splendid a picture of childhood delight as can be imagined as once again -- and again and again -- she rode the loudly galumphing Batmobile). I also assisted in setting up B&K's Christmas village atop their stereo cabinet and stringing lights on their outdoor trees and all in all had quite the family-style early-holiday blast with them.

How sweet my life is right now. This thought has been popping up again and again all week long. How lucky I am to have caught a ride on this carousel. I'm blessed with a hot and tender and inspiring love, a batch of absorbing book projects, a fine place to live, an almost ideal "day" job (a big part of its allure of course being that it's at night), a terrific little girl who loves me and is depending on me to act as a kind of stand-in papa to her, a number of admirable friends (none of whom are too intrusive!), a financial cushion large enough to ease my worries about unemployment (just the other day I realized I could give up J. Ink entirely and the deep reserves would still carry me -- if I watched every penny -- to the point where early-start

386

Social Security kicks in) -- and on top of all this I'm
in good health (at least as far as I know) and also
closing in on my goal of being in good shape, and I mean
just about my best shape ever (at least in some
respects).

So -- wow. Savor it while you can. Make the most
of it. Don't let it go to your head. Be prepared for
the inevitable setbacks and down cycles and sucker
punches, intended or otherwise.

(And my reinvigorated conjugal sex life -- how
could I leave that off the list? And geez, what about
jyze? If Zoelie didn't save me, jyze did. But no, both
did, first jyze and then the Z-woman; and only at that
point was I ready to stumble upon all the other
aforementioned joys.)

Meanwhile the times are also becoming engrossing.
The year of the millennial rollover is almost upon us.
This very week our congress in the far-off USAn capital
is considering impeachment of the president (and what a
deliciously disgusting spectacle it is as the rabid
right smells blood). Even the weather is becoming
downright riveting as global broiling ratchets up and
extreme storms, droughts, temperatures grow ever more
common and dangerous changes in climatic patterns begin
to cause massive social and ecological disruptions with
tragic consequences, including eventual possible
extinction of a great many mammalian, including human,
and other kinds of species. -- And even for those who'd
avoid exposure to any of this by escaping into, say,
sports (and of course the WOC is crawling with this
type, my sparring partner Marcus leading the pack) --
even for those, I say, the times are still unusual: the
pro hoops season has yet to begin owing to a lockout by
team owners and the entire season might be canceled.
Horrors! (Personally I hope it is canceled, since I'd
then find it much easier to break my own foolish habit
of following pro hoops by checking out the box scores.
This is the only remaining trace of the spectator-sports
addiction of my youth -- the football and baseball
aspects of it went overboard decades ago, except for

brief fair-weather-fan lapses -- and at several points
over the years I've very nearly succeeded in driving
this last one off the gangplank too, but each time it's
somehow managed to come creeping back from the brink.)
        -- And I can squeeze out no more tonight. Tomorrow
night maybe a little. And then the next day will be a
new official J-day and I'll also have to get moving on
Christmas cards and gifts in order to meet the demands
of my new socially connected life. (Yeah!) -- And yet
I think I can still tear off a slab of jyze, oh yes I
do: in this J-book right here and also with respect to
the larger projects arising out of earlier J-books and
the protojyze and even the urjyze (a/k/a chronbooks) of
deepest yore. So I'm pumped. I'm juiced. I'm
testo'd. (I guess I am. Or do I want to be saying
that? Can I legitimately say it and then do I want to.
Got to think about this. And a zillion other things,
sure. This is how it oughta be!)

-------.

39

-------.

        Just like the old high school and college class
periods: exactly fifty minutes until the bell rings.
Here at the hideaway. On the ides of December, and it's
blessedly rainless out there and also not too cold.
        I've finally jacked myself up into high Christmas
card production mode. Little calligraphy brushstrokes
of red and green brighten up the back of my left hand.
All evening I've been trying to come up with ways to
salvage the stack of leftover cards I made at Wei and
Alison's a year ago. A collage maybe, cutting them up
into puzzle pieces, sticking them on a blank card more
or less randomly with seasonally appropriate colored

glitter glue. Oh yeah, outstanding idea! -- But that's
for later at home.

     When done with the cards I've got a second batch of
ideas regarding possible presents for Z (in addition to
the hard hat). But compared with last year the pressure
seems minor. We're still planning to limit our gifts
for each other to what we can make by hand on the Sunday
two days after Christmas (that is, the third day of
Christmas). Today I learned Z had the impression this
giftmaking would be entirely spontaneous; we shouldn't
be giving it any advance thought at all. Now she's
starting to stress out on it, she says, because she
knows I've got stuff in the works and she doesn't.
-- But I'm sure it'll all turn out just fine. How could
it not? It's Christmas! We're in lo-o-o-ve!

     Quick now, a few details about the past week, not
even trying to tie them together.

     ** Z's been hit by another herpes outbreak. She
wept in frustration over this.

     ** Jess and Gwen's cat died. Rooney. The morbid
joke is that he'd been doing all right until he heard Z
and I would be coming over to house-sit again next week.

     ** Kat, when I brought her up here (hideaway) for
her first visit, was eager to see pictures of my former
girlfriends. As soon as one came up in the album pages
I showed her -- it was Lady S -- she lost interest and
started working on a notecard containing my address and
the combination for the side-entrance door. Was it that
she was hoping to see a parade of the blond blue-eyed
princess types she admires so much? (Or was it that her
mother, when she arrived to pick her up after doing some
shopping, was disappointingly -- to me -- in such a
hurry to get back home to watch a TV program?)

     ** Z tells me Aida is now careful to say nearly
every time they meet, "And how's my friend Glen?"
Plainly June had a talk with her (or maybe Z herself
did, or maybe they both did).

     ** Aida also proposed that the three of us see a
movie together Saturday night, and I readily agreed, but
then without consulting me Z and Aida changed the time

to Sunday afternoon and decided on a movie I didn't want
to see ("Elizabeth") which was playing out in the
eastern burbs where I didn't want to go, and they
invited Adele along too (she lives near the theater),
meaning nothing significant could be said among Z, Aida,
and me, subverting the intimate nature of the get-
together which to me was the main attraction in the
first place. And so I tentatively dropped out. To my
surprise Z put up very little squawk, so I took the
"tentatively" out of it, and she was fine with that too.
     (Z can't tell for sure how interested Aida is in
Kirk. Kirk's father died, though, with several long
obits in the papers mainly quoting Kirk and not his
politician brother Ed, and now Aida and Kirk will
presumably be finding out just where they, A&K, stand
with each other. -- Oh, and when Aida's parents, "the
D's," recently returned from a one-week tropical
cruise, they had the usual pages of advice carefully
written out for all five of their offspring on how to
improve their lives along with those of their families.
This is why they go on vacation each year, Z says: so
they can plot out their kids' and grandkids' futures in
peace. And they also asked how honorary family member
Zoelie was doing with her new boyfriend Glen and
whether we were still planning to marry. When Aida
told them the wedding had been put off until September
of next year their reply floored her: "Oh, that's good,
so they'll have time to get to know each other a little
better." (The senior D's being notoriously rigid in
their old-school Catholic morality. When Aida and Tom
lived together for a while before marriage they had to
keep it secret from her parents. And in recent years
Aida herself has become ever more the churched good
Catholic of the "relapsed" variety, or so Z tells me.))
                  *   *
     Christmas closing in, yeah. Hearing carols over
P.A. systems is no longer a pleasant change from the
usual muzak; it's long since become the usual muzak
itself, only worse because so repetitious. And in the
elevators at the scope building it's also sounding

tackily frayed and staticky. Possibly they're saving
the good stuff for the day workers and running a banged-
up backup tape for the night crew: we've known them to
do such things in the past. Meanwhile I'm falling
further behind on my cards.

Tonight Z's book group is again meeting at our
place. I helped her clean up for a couple of hours and
then took off just as the first members were arriving.
Midway through the cleanup Mama E called to thank us for
our Christmas cards and packages. As it happened, her
cards for us also arrived today. I hadn't had a chance
to open mine yet and did so while Z chatted with her on
the phone. Inside was a sweet little message and a
money order for twenty bucks. This amazed Z. Her
mother had never done anything like it for any of the
previous men in her daughter's life. "You're in with
her for sure, Mr. Duke!" Her own gift -- Z's from her
mother -- was a money order for fifty bucks. Seventy
altogether -- that's a lot of money for Mama E (just as
it would be for me).

Z's still "under quarantine" for her latest herpes
outbreak, wearing her intentionally unsexy "unners" to
bed at night to ward off accidental contact and "as a
reminder." In the early days we wouldn't let one of
these outbreaks slow down our sex life in the slightest
-- if anything we'd gear that life up a little, in part
because we hadn't yet gotten to the "yes-fuck fucking"
stage (and so the stress from trying to do just that --
to get there -- was relieved by the H outbreaks) but
also to show each other we were undaunted. But matters
are much different now. We're both more relaxed, taking
things as they come, not as worried we'll miff or hurt
the other by pulling back at these awkward times. Also
we're both more conscious of the need to get adequate
rest and resigned to the loss of some canoodling time in
order to do so. And I suppose we might simply be
growing more accustomed to each other and sexual desire
might be cooling off somewhat as notoriously happens
with most couples after their first year or two
together. And we're now approaching the one and three-

quarters mark.

However. Despite all this, the old lust is still there. In some ways it seems stronger than ever, and not just mine for her. I'm still learning my own strength under the new "yes-fuck fuck" regime, after all, and she's still responding to it whenever I'm able to show it. It's true I haven't been able to live up to the full promise of the first couple of months of breakthrough -- which is to say that even under the most arousing of circumstances ol' Ob, nee Possum/Mercutio/ N'dow/Slacker, et al., is still not always "bone to the bone of the bone" -- but there are a number of possible proximate causes for this and they're the same ones I've been struggling with all along: too little sleep, tiring workouts, unsynchronized schedules, and Z's H outbreaks, among others. -- But I'm still chalking it up as a triumph that I've come back this far and hoping even more comeback might lie ahead. I'm not yet convinced the overall upward spiraling has leveled off, to say nothing of starting back down again.

(The other day in talking with her nephew Jacob on the phone Z offered an explanation for what she likes about our life together: "It's so vivid!" And just yesterday a card came in from Jacob addressed to Z "and the Vivid Guy." -- This term of course working equally well for my own perception of life with Z, as has been true right from the start. But I'll admit I'm tickled an incandescent pink that she's seeing it this way too.)

-- So tonight again no J. Ink work. Three days in a row Naomi's job has canceled or failed to order. Since I'm flush anyway I'm delighted with all the unexpected free time. And then last night I found a bonus check for a hundred bucks clipped to the fortnightly J. Ink check. Naomi's note called me "the best collaborator a court reporter could ever hope for." This is the first bonus she's given me in many years if not ever (that's not including the traditional batch of Christmas cookies or brownies, which stopped a couple of years ago when her husband started, as I perhaps had a bit myself, porking up from her frequent baking).

[Tell It Jyze]

*   *

    So now Sunday night. Bitterly cold out there and a
little chilly in here as well (at the hideaway).
Moments ago I watched a brightly lit-up Christmas ferry
glide in. Amid all the steamy/foggy glitter it almost
seemed to be sliding on snowdrifts like a giant white
sleigh -- albeit one with three decks and a pilothouse
topped with a fully trimmed Christmas tree.
    So much is happening on the grand political stage
I'd scarcely know where to begin should I try to jyze
it up. Of course I have no intention of doing that.
Nonetheless I'll mention it involves a president being
impeached, a speaker of the house resigning (another
one!), and bombs falling on Iraq (our bombs I suppose I
should say for anyone wondering about whose).
    Meanwhile it's snowed in our city. Kat happened to
be staying with us when the huge first flakes started
feathering down. She and I bundled up in whatever we
could find (looking so ludicrous Z brought out her
camera) and rushed over to the hilltop park for some
cheek-stinging merry-go-rounding and tire-swinging and
eventually some snowball fighting and snow-monster
making. (Then later at home we rassled in the bedroom
while Betty and Z napped elsewhere. I'll confess I get
a big charge -- of course it's entirely innocent, except
maybe not totally entirely (but certainly enough
entirely) -- when Kat "accidentally" tries to feel me up
as we rassle. I'm her main specimen of adult malehood
to be studied up close and I selflessly sacrifice my
dignity to the task. I'll also say she can run me
ragged with her eight-year-old's energy and my recovery
can take a whole lot longer than it takes her to run me
that way.)
    -- And after she left yesterday Z and I
unexpectedly found ourselves with a free evening on our
hands (we'd thought Kat would be staying with us all
night but a last-minute pajama-party invite for her
arrived by phone and we got preempted). This being a
Saturday it was highly unusual for us to be free. It
was also copacetic because I needed the time to grind

out the rest of my Christmas cards. A marathon session
ensued for me, from six p.m. to five a.m. with scarcely
a break -- to produce a dozen cards! But I can't
refrain from reporting that the earlier batch has
already started drawing oohs and ahs all over town.
These are more or less mandatory kudos, true, since for
some odd reason Z always tells people I'm expecting
them. But I do believe they're sincere anyway. (I know
mine are. These are fabulous cards! My best ever!)

Yesterday Betty and Kat opened theirs. "It's
another framer!" cried Betty (boy, does she know how to
butter me up). Tonight Jess, Gwen, Paz, and Tobey did
much the same at Gwen's birthday party in Z's old hood
(we start five days of house-sitting for J&G tomorrow
night while they hit the mountains for snowboarding).
Five lesbians and us (maybe six lesbians and me if Z is
partly one, as she certainly at times would like to be,
except women turn her on only in theory and fantasy
whereas men do so in practice and fantasy -- well, and
maybe theory too, I suppose, if her "Story of O" musings
can be called theory as well as fantasy, as I'd say they
can) (and all evening we were bantering about a former
beauty queen, several years our senior, who a few days
ago was busted for running a high-level call-girl ring,
including a fully accoutered "S/M love den," as the
papers called it, sheltered in an ordinary-looking
frame house half a block down the hill from J&G's place
and only a few steps farther from Z's former apartment).

And one other thing. Today I finally met Z's
overall boss and bete noire, Roberta C., the utility
director, at a sumptuous Christmas party in a fancy
neighborhood up north. This as an authentic string
quartet (wearing immaculate tuxes) sawed away live in
the next room. I quickly saw exactly what it is Z
dislikes so much about Roberta: a quintessential
northern-far-coast Waspy frostiness and condescension.
Other than the way her fingers were quivering behind her
back, presumably wanting to go for Roberta's throat, Z
handled the encounter quite well, I thought. (Or maybe
she was just nervous. That's what she said afterward.

[Tell It Jyze]

But if she was, I saw no other sign of it.)
                    *   *
     Three days on and I'm hoping to finish up entry No.
39 right here. Probably I could've done it earlier
except I'm not feeling so good tonight. I'm not sure
why. A cold coming on maybe? Just the usual seasonal
shortage of sleep?
     Maybe I could try again at Jess and Gwen's house
later tonight. But then if I'm barely able to function
when it's still fairly early in the evening by NUT time
(it's eleven minutes past midnight) how likely is it
I'll do better when it's truly late for me? And in a
house that'll be more than a little chilly because one
of the circuit breakers (for the wall heaters in the
basement, among other uses) is malfunctioning. And Z
might be feeling spooked a bit by being in a relatively
strange bed, as she was last night, and call me upstairs
to keep her company for a while, and then it might be
very hard -- maybe even impossible -- to leave.
     Could it be jyze might just want to let the string
run out from here until year's end? Well, I hope not.
     Some very sexy loving in the dark last night. Long
and languorous. It didn't get going until I'd been up
there quite a while. I couldn't drift off to sleep, in
part because I was nearly hanging off the edge of J&G's
notoriously soft-mattressed bed to accommodate the
presence of the two dogs on Z's far side, in part
because I was trying to sleep roughly an hour earlier
than usual in that -- for me too -- relatively strange
bed. I was naked and holding Z close, buried under the
covers, squirming to escape the cold draft coming up
from the edge of the bed behind me. And what happened?
Yup, ol' Ob started cranking up. Very slowly, yes, but
inexorably, puff by puff, eventually turning into one of
those rare hundred-and-ten-percenters. "Full bone plus!
Petrified-forest night wood!" And I certainly couldn't
let that go to waste. Z was still wearing her "herp
rag" unners, but this was the night the quarantine was
supposed to lift. She was asleep too, but I slowly
awakened her with light touches until she "jolted" a

couple of times, and then I pulled off the unners and
maneuvered into lazy-man fucking position while lying on
my side, with Z on her back with one leg crooked over my
hip and the covers still atop both of us and the dogs
somehow remaining more or less undisturbed. At first I
pushed in only a little and then pulled out for slow
vulvar tantalizing with Ob's sensitive bald dome until
she came for the first time and then back in for good, a
long, slow, deep churn with Ob turned ninety degrees
counterclockwise from straight-up missionary, several
more comes for her, until finally we were both exhausted
and she actually dozed off with Ob still inside her and
maybe three-quarters bony ("Ob-long"?) and twitching,
both voluntarily and involuntarily, excitement growing
again and then waning, several delicious cycles of this.

Lovely it was, yes. But I never did come. And so
was relieved that she'd drifted off, and I did the same
while still intussuscepted (ooh, that fine word, even if
I'm probably misusing it just as always) and was still
buried there maybe half an hour later in a semi-tumefied
state when her travel alarm pip-pip-pipped.

Today I left the house early and caught a bus for
downtown (after gobbling a hunk of Gwen's leftover
chocolate birthday cake in lieu of breakfast), then did
some shopping at various craft stores for items to use
in decorating the utility hard hat for Z. Didn't arrive
at the hideaway until after five and by then I was
feeling so loggy I crashed in the armchair for an hour
with a towel folded over my eyes. Caffeine deprivation
may have undone me; I didn't get my first cup of coffee
of the day until after seven p.m. at the ORB cafe. (How
odd it felt -- and uncomfortable too -- to be drinking
coffee and reading the house copy of the far-coast paper
in that cafe in the evening just as I often used to do
back when I was a single guy taking a short break from
the writing wars and trying hard not to go on the prowl
upstairs, for books or maybe even for a woman. Shudders
tonight as I looked over the other similar loners
scattered around the room -- a couple of them appearing
vaguely familiar -- and wondered if I could've kept

myself functionally together for this long to still be
one of those guys if Z hadn't come along.)

A card from Jeff and Angie arrived yesterday. Or I
should say a card from Angie, since she filled most of
the two inner pages and the back with a lengthy
handwritten note and Jeff didn't even sign his own name.
Typical Jeff -- certainly not one of his most winning
traits. Angie's message almost makes up for it, though:
it's warm and loving and takes careful note of items we
sent them and matters of importance we talked about
during our visit and what's happened concerning them in
the intervening three months (Angie's back troubles, for
instance, and how they've eased since she installed the
rubber floor mats Z recommended for her basement work
area).

Cousin Kar and wife Kerani also sent a card, but it
contained only Kar's usual mass-produced "What We've
Been Up To This Year" travelogue and this read almost
like a puff piece written by a promotion department, and
what's more a subversive one slipping in whole
paragraphs of hilarious self-parody.

-- Here's Travis.

40

The eve of the Eve finds me at the scope office
again. The conference table. And I'm pouting because
the feast of leftovers I was expecting is not here. The
firm held its Christmas party today at noon and it was
announced as a "potluck" this year and I was counting on
finding the remains of a high-quality spread. Instead
the pickings are so slim -- mostly candy -- I have to
shift into pilferage-disguise mode. From the contents

of the overflowing trash bins I can see some good stuff
was available earlier -- meat plate, fruit salad, cake
and cookies and ice cream -- but with one exception it's
all long gone, including most of the crumbs (the cake
plate on the counter appears to have been licked clean,
complete with probable tongue prints). -- The one
exception being a single strawberry so prominently
displayed I suspect they left it there to mock me. So
I'm gobbling it right now.

Take that, strawberry! Take that, scope-firm
punks!

A very good thing I brought along my own veggie
juice and dried fruit. -- And I didn't need more
chocolate anyway. I've already consumed so much that a
big juicy pimple has popped up on my right cheek maybe
an inch out from the nostril. And I left my trusty
pimple cover-up ointment back in the apartment! Imagine
the spectacle I'll make for Betty and Kat tomorrow!

On the chair to my left stands my old blue Japan
"Remember" bag with the fraying rope handles. It's
stuffed with the makings of Christmas gifts for Z,
including more gewgaws to adorn the yellow utility hard
hat. I have to admit I'm still nervous about how our
gift plan will work out in practice. That bag also
contains about two dozen lesser gifts, most of them so
lame I've rejected the idea of giving them to her
several times in the past. Will she nonetheless see
their existence as perfidious because we agreed not to
buy each other gifts this year? Best, perhaps, to focus
exclusively on the hard hat. But will that be enough?
And after the big mutual cascade of gifts last year?

Because of the unusual setup at Jess and Gwen's, Z
and I are seeing much less than usual of each other
during these house-sitting days. We don't even talk on
the phone since I leave the house in pursuit of coffee
soon after getting up. She dinged her baby toe on a
bureau footing in the dark in the unfamiliar garret-like
upstairs terrain and so hasn't worked out at the WOC,
and with Dale on vacation this week she's acting boss at
the office and so is too busy for me to call her there.

And as a result of all this, or at least I'm
guessing cause and effect are at work here, she's been a
little more hyper than usual. And this in turn might be
contributing to a bout of insomnia she's been going
through. Last night she eventually hopped out of bed at
J&G's and toasted herself a couple of frozen waffles (I
had hunkered down with some periodicals on the heated
floor in the bathroom to avoid disturbing her). When I
came up to bed shortly after that, we both read awhile
and then she suddenly almost assaulted me sexually. It
was strange, as if she'd been silently wrestling with
herself over whether to do it and abruptly given in to
the urge. HUZZAH! (I loved it. But she was so hot it
was over almost before I had a chance to turn on. Three
rounds for her, BANG BANG BANG. She's still the same
phenom she's always been. -- But we knew that.)
     A glance at the clock tells me if I wanted to hit
the nearer of the chain bookstores I'd still have
fifteen minutes to get there before it closes. (Only
during Christmas week does it stay open so late -- until
midnight! My daily routine might be far different if it
did this year-round.)
     The big surprise of the day came when Donald, my
next-door neighbor at the hideaway, presented me with a
grossly sentimental Christmas card containing a ten-
dollar bill. The sealing flap of the envelope was still
wet when I opened it. I was so touched I went right out
and used the tenner to buy him a blank coffee mug,
kicking in seventy-eight cents of my own to cover the
tax. Then I hand-decorated it with a big "D" and in
antic smaller letters "Donald's Mug" and then lots of
hokey Christmas symbols (all this done with my handy
ultra-markers). I also dashed off a "Dreamsicles"-style
card (like last year's) for him using the calligraphy
brushes. I'm not at all sure either of these items will
be his cup of tea, or cup of whatever he might put or
imagine in there, but at least he should get the message
that I appreciate his kindness. (I sometimes wonder if
he might be gay. Once in a while he seems to be hinting
he is. If so, it hasn't caused any awkwardness with us

so far, and I doubt it will in the future.)

So now what. Trying to think of any other seasonal bits I could mention. The cold has moderated somewhat, I'll note, but out on the street I'm still wearing gloves and the black wool stocking cap with the "G" sewn on it which I gave Z last Christmas to use as a nightcap (but she's worn it only once in bed because it messes up her hair). The sidewalks are still icy in many areas from last week's storm and the continuing cold snap and for these reasons the crowds are much reduced in outdoor gathering spots (you've got to be hardy indeed to ride the city-center carousel in this weather). The inner city's remained snow-free the past couple of days but the northern burbs have been heavily hit and today numerous cars from up there could be seen bearing thick snow blankets as they crept along downtown streets, their chains clanking.

The most moving decorations I've seen anywhere so far this year are the strings of hauntingly mournful red lights attached to the pergola in the triangle and visible from the lobby of the hideaway building. The most spectacular tree is the one with the colorful silk scarves for decorations right here in the huge glass cube of the scope-building lobby. And I like the single white star perched atop the old marine hospital on our hilltop (conspicuously visible for miles in all directions except due south, where we live almost in its shadow -- except its actual sun/moon shadow falls in the opposite direction).

What's ahead? No big news. Our Christmas plans remain about the same, but we've decided to stay home New Year's Eve and work on our gifts for each other that night instead of this coming Sunday. Then on New Year's Day we'll be facing a conflict, having received invites to parties at both Adele's and Leola's. Most likely we'll try to hit both. It's almost a sure thing I'll finally be meeting Kirk M., Z's former lover and Aida's current one, either at Adele's party (Aida has hinted she'll be bringing him) or, if not there, at Aida's open house the next day. Too bad both of those events will

take place after jyze has gone on sabbatical. (Yes,
jyze will be out of action until midspring. It won't
reappear until the last week in April. After almost
five full years of scarcely ever missing a jyzeday --
only two or three at most before this year -- it
deserves a rest. And even more than before it needs the
time to prepare for the big millennial edition.)

*   *

        -- Five days later, the hideaway, my first chance
to get back to it.
        It's been an odd Christmas, full of bright and
merry Christmasy stuff and yet a little hollow at the
core. This is presumably because Z and I postponed our
own gift-giving ceremony. And yet something else just
as good, maybe even better, arose as a result. That was
the sense we had of being joined in a strong bond --
"both unorthodox and loving." (All right, those words
are unforgivably inadequate. Even in my present
schmaltz-ridden state at the height of the season of
maximum schmaltz I can recognize this. Worse yet, being
mired in this very same seasonal state encourages me to
follow the jyze rules and leave such lame words in.)
        The heat never did go back on at J&G's. (As Jess
informed me today, an element in the thermostat had worn
out, which was a relief to hear: this meant it wasn't
something we'd done that had fritzed the system.) Z was
mostly a good sport about putting up with the general
discomfort and inconvenience of being away from home,
especially considering how iffy she'd been from the
start about doing house-sitting during the holidays and
I was the one who encouraged it. But she did lose it a
couple of times. (One of these was when we were out
walking Cy and Kiba on their leashes and encountered a
woman with a pair of huge, mean-looking, unleashed dogs.
Z loudly cursed her out -- openly called her a bitch!
-- while I skedaddled across the street to safety with
Cy and Kiba, both of whom were itching to launch
kamikaze attacks on the monsters. It was Z's theory
that this woman was the "S/M Madam," currently reported
to be out on bail. I didn't get a good look at her,

401

but we were just half a block down the hill from the
madam's house of forbidden pleasure.)
     Upon our return to south hill Z vowed never again
to do house-sitting in December after the 15th of the
month. She also decided she wanted to cancel our
planned appearances at the round of New Year's parties
over the weekend so we could just kick back at home and
maybe put in more work on those "spontaneous" Christmas
gifts (we'd already agreed to expand the time allotted
for those from a single day to the entire ten-day
holiday period beginning with Christmas Eve and ending
the Sunday after New Year's -- and a good thing too,
since we got absolutely nothing done on them Christmas
Eve or Christmas Day or for that matter any of the
succeeding three days, right up to the present).
     I had no problem accepting this plan to cancel the
New Year's partygoing, but I couldn't help wondering if
(A) she'd be able to hold out against the pressure of
her friends pleading that we come, and (B) if her main
aim wasn't to avoid the likely run-in (maybe even two
run-ins) with Kirk and Aida. But on Saturday concern B
became moot when Aida called and revealed she and Kirk
had just decided to go their separate ways -- and for
the very reason I had predicted to Z: the death of his
father had apparently caused Kirk to seek to shore up
relations with his estranged wife who had already been
trying to get back with him. (Not "for the kids' sake,"
though, as I had also prophesied; it turns out they
don't have kids.) (And he's the one who broke up with Z
because, at least as she shakily remembers it, he wanted
to have kids and she didn't.) (Z was asleep when Aida
called and so I was the first to hear the news.
Surprisingly she told me the whole story, although
leaving out the X-rated parts, if any. But the talk
with her quickly turned extremely awkward and reminded
me again how unlikely it is Aida and I, even if we're
both trying hard, will ever get along well.)
     And then today at the WOC -- Z limping pathetically
because of her dinged toe, wearing one running shoe and
one open-toed sandal -- I learned her resistance is

already starting to melt to Leola's pleas that we show up at their party. (And Gerry was just so impressed with my card, she teased me, as if to suggest this fact was making her task of resistance even harder.)

And now we're scheduled to go over to Aida's tomorrow night to have dinner with Mark, Cawk widower husband of the deceased Chiusan close friend of Z and Aida, Julie K., and their eight-year-old biracial kid, Ben, in town together for a short visit. (Aida informed me on the phone, by the way, her own main problem with Kirk was that, for whatever reason -- and she really didn't specify -- he had failed to offer the one quality she wants most in a man: "emotional availability.")

As for our Christmas doings, on the Eve we went out to dinner at a fish house in the Scandi quarter with Kat and Betty and Betty's friend Wanda (the same one who joined us at the coastal resort last spring as a potential match for Nick). This was Betty's Christmas present for us, chosen mainly because she thought we all (and I especially) would go for their celebrated mountain blackberry cobbler. And we all did go for it (and I especially!). -- As small wooden fishing boats tied up at the dock just outside bobbed gently in floodlit splendor (probably their main use these days -- stage props -- with the fishing industry in such doldrums).

Afterward we all went up to "Manny Lake" and attempted to launch small lit floating candles in his, Manny's (Betty's husband's, Kat's adoptive father's, Z's good friend's), memory. He died of complications from a liver transplant on Christmas Eve four years ago and used to love that lake so much we all agreed it was only right to rename it in his honor; and Z promised to do what she could to see that the city makes it official. -- But though we trudged through a muddy semigrassy area out to the shoreline and fought like fiends to light the candles, the wet, windy conditions foiled us. (Once a sailboat Manny was operating by remote control on that lake capsized and a photo of the event made the front page of the local section of one of the Jyze City

dailies -- another reason Betty chose the site for her
attempt to inaugurate a Christmas Eve tradition honoring
his memory -- and especially for Kat's sake.)
*   *

Now the eve of another Eve, this capped Eve itself
being the last day of jyze year five (and in fact we're
already thirty minutes into it), and I've left myself
just thirty minutes to wrap up this entry No. 40, and
Travis the janitor's likely to appear in the middle of
it. -- Or I could continue at home later tonight,
breaking out of the usual winding-down ritual. But I
don't know if I'll have enough steam left to do that.

First to say, quick items. I watch the cops arrest
a very young-looking pair of female Cawk "sex workers"
(satin hot pants, no less, on both of them, one pair
silver and one black, under ankle-length open coats) --
this just half a block up the street from our house.

I'm wearing the mod-looking red enamel-art pin Rob
gave me as a Christmas gift, saying he knew immediately
when he spotted it (in a thrift shop) that it was meant
for me. No question at all he was right.

And it appears Z is now leaning in the other
direction again, toward a New Year's weekend of
isolation. She's refusing to tell anyone else why she's
canceling all engagements, so naturally everyone's
guessing. Leola's guess, according to Z, is that we're
planning to elope and get married.

Another cancellation, the dinner with Mark and Ben
at Aida's. Their flight up from the megastate
scratched because of bad weather down there and after
waiting futilely several hours for another flight they
gave up and decided to deep-six the whole trip. This
means it'll likely be another year before I meet them.

And the loving's been good. A quickie this morning
and it was hot and ol' Ob (still the preferred sobriquet,
though Z did once jokily conjoin it with "noxious" in
our pillow talk) -- ol' Ob erupted invag, I say, and mmm
mmm mmm it felt so fine! And later she was teasing me
about how sexy I've supposedly been lately. Sunday
morning and Saturday night, see, were also hot. (Last

404

night she confided that her vagina twitched a couple of
times during her mentoring conference with the sexy and
seductive Filipina Gloria at work. She associates this
sort of responsiveness with the clitoral touchings her
mother bestowed upon her as a kid. "That's when
excitement and fear got all mixed up for me, I think."
And is that perhaps a contributing factor to her being
so extremely sexually responsive now even with the
utterly unfearsome likes of me? A year ago I was
thinking it might be. And now? No change.)
     We're still working on turkey leftovers. Sunday Z
cooked a full meal for us in 203 for the very first time
-- she'd been planning it for weeks -- and it's just a
shame it came so soon after the Christmas Day turkey
dinner at Rob and Gail's place. As a kid Z was always
the one being cooked for and it was her father who did
almost all of it, and every now and then I sense an ache
in her for that same kind of special culinary treatment
from me. But by and large I'm just not up to it --
especially when it comes to competing with her highly
skilled father. (Which is to say: I have to spoil her
in my own way. And I do! -- Or anyway try like hell.)
     -- Here's Travis now. No longer ho-ho-hoing or
wearing his Santa hat, I see. Like last week I mean.
And it's a minute after one anyway.

-------·

41

-------·

     On the far coast and in much of the rest of the
country, and for that matter the world, it's already
next year. Here the crossing's still a couple of hours
away. In "the nation's midsection" (an hour ago we
talked with Mama E there) it'll be happening in just

minutes. Or less than a minute, I see now. -- Well no,
it's right this moment. Cheers and "Auld Lang Syne" on
the radio and a car honking crazily right here, meaning
outside on the street. Have some other former nation's-
midsection types maybe fetched up on our hilltop? On
our very block no less? Or of course it could just be
another car-prowl -- and if so, a cannily timed one.

I'm holding down the couch, Z's sprawled on her
chair. A huge poinsettia dominates the low wooden table
between us, this being her late concession to my deeply
ingrained annual Christmas craving for the plant --
those sensational bright red leaves! -- even though she
herself doesn't like poinsettias all that much. (She
surprised me with it on Christmas Eve.) An hour ago we
tried to watch the far-coast ball-drop celebration on
her ancient thirteen-inch black-and-white TV in the
bedroom but discovered the event wasn't being shown live
on any of the channels we can get (and they're a very
small portion of the total available -- just the
networks, and a couple of those fluctuate between
extremely fuzzy and pure interference).

-- And I'm buzzing along somewhere in that same
range myself. Earlier at the artiest bar in town (still
the same one) we had a few drinks (she two, I three) and
we drink so seldom that these five taken together were
enough to knock us both for a (proverbial!) loop. Even
after a long wait for a bus, the ride home, heating up
more turkey leftovers for dinner, reading the papers,
the call to Mama E -- yes, the fuzzy and staticky
effects still linger.

A few days ago I bought a small flask of my
favorite bourbon at the state liquor store (they'd sold
out on all the larger sizes) but now I doubt I'll be
wanting to imbibe yet more of that particular potion
(surely don't wanna say poison) tonight.

Will Z manage to stay awake until midnight? Not
likely. She told me so herself. For the moment,
though, she's immersed in a whodunit. And she's wearing
her gray Hotel La Chevalle sweatshirt. My authentic --
real life, not merely fictive -- but that too! --

Mentoka honey. First time we've put on this degree of alcohol buzz together. And the occasion is right for it: as of midnight we'll have lived together as Deeps for exactly one year. And it's also true we're coming to the end of our first full January-through-December year as lovers (since we didn't meet until March of the previous year) and my own first full Gregorian year as a Glennarian Third Stager (and her second such year).

And a great year it's been. We're in full, deliriously happy agreement on this. (She was the first to use the term "deliriously happy" earlier today, with a smiling little seductive ironic twist to it -- I suppose maybe to show she was well aware it might sound just a bit sappy and therefore might compromise her tough-city-girl image.) (My own cornball reply was, "That's because this was the year we nailed it, Zoelie B. -- yup, yup." Or -- like that.)

I met her at work at four and we walked uptown in the rain, recalling our crosstown treks a year ago from her office as well as my treks by myself to good old B-2. Our mission today was to buy a new set of dinner plates for everyday use since we've broken two of the full-size glass plates (hers) we've been using all year and several of the others are chipped around the edges almost like Stone Age hatchets, only sharper. She'd seen some good replacement candidates in ads for the annual post-Christmas sales at the big downtown department stores. As it turned out, though, we hit on something we both liked better that hadn't been advertised, a full four-place setting in an Indonesian pattern. I carried the box with the plates inside on my shoulder the rest of the evening. Z was afraid I'd drop it, especially after downing those drinks and then even more so after a lurch by me into the gutter as we left the bar (intended as a goof but then I almost lost control, just as with Kat during our spin into the park bushes last summer, except that one I really did lose control). -- Then I nearly left the box behind at the bus stop when our double-length trolley rolled up, catching me unawares because the kind of bus I'd been expecting was one of the standard-length, gasoline-powered, fume-belching rattletraps which run on that same route much later in the evening when I usually ride it.

This mission to buy the plates had a very marriagey feeling to it, no question about it. I couldn't stop thinking of a similar quest with Lady C at the mall near Gatewood way, way, way back in my near-juvie days (and daze, yeah). (But no hauling of a box containing fragile dinnerware was involved there or on any similar occasion with Lady C or anyone else later on. For me this was a virginal premarital experience and thus likely to be the real reason, as I told Z, I was staggering so weirdly under the load.)

(Z's just put aside her book and stretched out next to me on the couch. "I'm not saying anything at all," she announces, reminding me of similar "jyze-widow-type" pronouncements during our Mentoka trip except her tone is much less confrontational this time, I'm pleased to say. It's even close to encouraging. Meanwhile I feel an almost irresistible urge to reciprocate by stretching out next to her or maybe on top of her. Heroically I'm resisting it so far -- and even though it's true my eyelids are feeling quite heavy. -- And now she's pulled the white comforter over her sweet shapely curled-up Deep self. She had to slide down a bit first because the top of her head was in a place where the elbow of my jyzing arm was beating out a tattoo on it, sort of like a typewriter carriage kicking back at the end of each line -- and I remember writing pretty much the identical thing during our naked tandem jyze session on my birthday sixteen months ago yesterday.)

And so -- scene setting. "Great room" of our apartment No. 203 with half a dozen lamps on, sizzle of cars rolling by on the street down below. Lots of clutter and lived-in-ness on view up here. I'd be plenty happy to be settling into this place forevermore deeply and I'm in no way abashed to say so. -- And doing just this, settling in of the lifetime variety, may even be a real possibility of sorts. Doug and Thuy upstairs have been feeling out landlord Min about the possibility of buying the building from him and converting it into condos, and they've asked us to go in on it with them. Already in just the past couple of weeks (presumably because of massive local job cutbacks in the aircraft industry that threaten to undermine the local real estate market) Min's asking price has come down from 900K to 800K. At slightly less than 90K per unit this would be a very good price for a condo building in the current city market. But there are problems. Who, for starters, would get the more desirable third-floor units? (D&T want two of them and there are only three in all, and the one they don't want is the one on the back side lacking a view.) And how sound is the structure of this building? (From the evidence I've seen, not very.) And is it possible we might someday want to live somewhere else -- for example, with Jess and Gwen in the western part of the city? (They've inquired about this and we've already told them we might be interested.) And finally, if we don't act quickly the price on this building could be going up again, rapidly, as the big dot-com outfit begins moving its hundreds of workers into the neighborhood in the next few months and demand for nearby living quarters skyrockets. (Already we're noticing changes up here -- including what appears to be a serious crackdown on street prostitution.)

The sale of the marine hospital is the big local news of the past year. Since it's far and away the largest structure on this end of the hill, it can dictate the quality of life for all of us. Is there any point in trying to resist this? We'll be looking into that question in more depth starting in the next week or two, when Z will be joining the hilltop residential council.

(The mountain states just welcomed in the new year and the broadcast is switching to our coast, to a jazz club on the outskirts of the longest-run hometown of my adult life before this one (and it's sister Barb's current one and the scattering place for Mother's ashes,

so yes, we're talking my lifetime city No. 2/7, as
defined back in Annal 2). -- And Z appears to have
dozed off. -- And now I'm hearing that the featured
artist for this hour is a jive-talking pianist, live,
sure to be distracting, so I'm turning it down.)

*

   -- The big news these days, the U.S. Senate is
about to start the trial of the impeached president.
I'm sorry, I just can't get very interested. What it's
really all about is a spasm of moralistic, not to say
appallingly hypocritical, overreaction. It's one more
battle in the same old culture war, except that for most
people out here in the real world the war is long over
(it ended in a surly live-and-let-live truce). -- Acch,
I refuse to try to say anything more about it.
   Quickly then (more quickness!) the rest of the
Christmas stuff.
   First, some touching moments with Kat during our
Christmas Eve get-together. For one, she declared I'd
make a good busboy (this was at the fish house where
she'd been looking over the servers and kitchen staff)
because I'm "tall, thin, and attractive." I loved that
-- Kat talking like someone three or four times her
age. Better, I loved the content, even though maybe
it's not all that accurate. But better still, I loved
it that apparently she doesn't yet see me as a total
fossil. And then as she and Betty were about to drive
off afterwards, Kat suddenly vowed, completely on her
own, to write me the moment they arrived at the farm.
They'll be back from there in just a couple of days now
and nothing's come in from her so far, but of course
that's not really the point. I'm just very pleased
that, even if only for a moment, she could feel she'd
miss me that much. And since it appears I can get to
her emotionally a little more than I realized, I'm
encouraged to think I might be able to play a little
bigger role in her life than the very minor one I'd been
trying to resign myself to before now. (But for me to
actually play that kind of major role she and I would
need to be together a lot more than we have been in

410

recent months, and that's probably not in the cards.)
    Next item, Christmas dinner with Rob and Gail. Bad
weather kept Rob's kids from crossing the mountains and
so it was just the four of us, and it was warm and
intimate, casual, relaxed. For thirty minutes or so
Gail and Zoelie did the bonding thing down in the
kitchen while Rob and I retreated to his cozy little
garret study (where he had the window wide open so he
could smoke his pipe). I suggested the possibility of
his writing a kind of parallel account to my "special
millennial edition" next year -- in the spirit of, say,
those notorious nineteenth-century French protojyzing
brothers -- and he seemed intrigued by the idea. (The
context was his regretting the lack of exciting new
subject matter for his own protojyzing in the past few
years.) Otherwise we covered pretty much the usual
topics: similarities in our lives, our long-running
reluctance to clamber aboard the cyber bandwagon any
more than society forces us to (though he's not entirely
a technophobe: he's now voluntarily buying his first
CDs), concerns about brother Jeff's financial troubles
and his failure to stay in touch, dismay about sister
Barb's bizarre behavior in a number of realms. Also
talk about books we've been reading and the latest
wrinkles in our efforts to make the journals and diaries
we've both been keeping (under whatever nomenclature)
for most of our lives more presentable to others beyond
just ourselves and family and friends. -- And this jyze
right here is of course one of those efforts.
    A fine evening. At dinner, alas, Z knocked over a
glass of wine while making an emphatic point about the
lame new edition of the utility newsletter (the first
one not under her editorship), putting a big stain in
Mother's old red-and-white-checked tablecloth. A
golden-brown turkey, Rob carving masterfully. Two pies,
blueberry and sweet potato, for dessert, both bought by
Z at the co-op and both fruit-juice sweetened, as is now
pretty much de rigueur for her.
    The next day Z and I baby-sat for Tala and Dalisay,
Serafina's kids, ages five and six, taking them to the

new far north bookstore/arcade for a used-book-buying
binge -- this was their Christmas present from us -- and
then back to their house for game-playing and endless
horsie rides. (Later Sera complained that Z had told
the girls to "go ahead and be as bad as you want" --
and she had in fact done just that, but of course only
kiddingly and as part of her campaign to shuck the rep
of being "the tough-love bad cop" always demanding good
behavior -- sometimes with a "Filipino pinch" as an
extra tool of persuasion -- from the kids of her
godmotherly realm, in which these two happily reside.)

     -- So my couple of hours are just about up. And I
haven't even touched on the usual sort of year-end
summing-up topics. Could try real fast, I suppose. (As
tension builds at twenty minutes before midnight. Z
still snoozing, yes, but fitfully, and the crowd at the
jazz club in my city No. 2/7 down in the megastate is
already fired up, whooping in anticipation.)

     My best year ever? Surely one of 'em. Can't think
of any better, though admittedly the one just before it
came pretty close (except for the first couple of
months, before Z popped up). And all the elements seem
in place, I'd say, for another doozer this coming year,
even better maybe. Going for the trifecta! Getting
hitched! Come the millennium! And you, Zoelie B. --
extra-gentle tap on her shoulder here as she snoozes on
-- you're the one. The chief source. You. You hear?
(Still snoozing on. But I suspect she hears anyway.
And beyond that, what really matters: she knows.)

     Acccch, okay, enough. Sixty-five pages still to
fill in this J-book, notes at the end not included:
eleven more minutes wouldn't make much of a dent. So
let this jyze thing rest for a few months starting right
here. Then do it as it oughta be done, all out, a full
year, twice the number of pages allotted to any previous
annal. What I've been waiting for: the big millennial
blowout!

END

www.ingramcontent.com/pod-product-compliance
Lightning Source LLC
Chambersburg PA
CBHW070742120726
47910CB00001B/140